Outstanding pra
a

HEAD GAMES

"A chilling chase to find the killer before he strikes again."

—*Publishers Weekly*

"A sizzler . . . a tensely plotted thriller that compels the reader to the last shocking page . . . Dreyer deftly displays her droll sense of humor while spinning a tale of tense, taut terror . . . she leads the reader on a ride comparable to a death-defying roller-coaster ride . . . the pace starts intensely and events twist, turn, and collide . . . the characters . . . are complex, riveting, funny, and compelling. Not many authors create a thoroughly terrifying villain who performs heinous acts and yet manage to make him a sympathetic creature . . . Dreyer has done an amazing job of creating a riveting and mesmerizing story."

—*The Denver Post*

"A superb writer who manages to keep surprising the reader with one unexpected revelation after another . . . fans of Patricia Cornwell and Robin Cook will love *Head Games*."

—*Midwest Book Review*

MORE . . .

"Ever have one of those mysteries that you just have to carry from room to room and in your car just to see what happens next? *Head Games* was just that and more . . . a novel for all . . . with full force psychological tension and characters seared in your memory."

—Mysterylovers.com

"A fast ride through a few head cases . . . tautly written . . . *Head Games* is unputdownable, scary, and funny, all at the same time. It's another of those books you should not start late at night and expect to sleep well."

—reviewingtheevidence.com

WITH A VENGEANCE

"Fast plotting, thorough research, and a swaggering cop . . . a complex, conflicted heroine, defiantly macho and yet so scarred by family violence that she refuses to use a gun even when doing so could save the lives of those she loves."

—*Publishers Weekly* (starred review)

"Retribution, fear, and betrayal are at the heart of this intriguing novel. The hospital emergency room is drawn with frightening reality, and the ease with which a staff member can move unseen through trauma rooms to deliver fatal doses to chosen victims may instill fear in readers. Brightly written and with a smart but vulnerable heroine . . . this first appearance of Maggie O'Brien is surely not the last."

—*Dallas Morning News*

Also by Eileen Dreyer

Head
GAMES

Eileen Dreyer

St. Martin's Paperbacks

HEAD GAMES

Copyright © 2004 by Eileen Dreyer.
Excerpt from *Sinners and Saints* copyright © 2005 by Eileen Dreyer.

Library of Congress Catalog Card Number: 2003058632

ISBN: 0-312-99677-2
EAN: 9780312-99677-2

Printed in the United States of America

St. Martin's Press hardcover edition / March 2004
St. Martin's Paperbacks edition / September 2005

St. Martin's Paperbacks are published by St. Martin's Press, 175 Fifth Avenue, New York, NY 10010.

10 9 8 7 6 5 4 3 2 1

To Rick, who believed through four long years of college tuition without help. There's nothing big enough I can ever give you back.

ACKNOWLEDGMENTS

My thanks to the usual suspects. Dr. Mary Case and Mary Fran Ernst, St. Louis County Medical Examiner's Office; Michelle Podolak and Lieutenant John Podolak, St. Louis Police. Also for this book, for their specific information, Forensic Anthropologist Gwen Haugen, Armed Forces Bureau of Identification; Retired Special Agent Dave Cunningham, FBI. And the lovely Thea Devine, who performed a mitzvah for her friend the shiksa. All mistakes are mine.

To the Divas for sane heads, especially Karyn Witmer-Gow, who always saw. To Jen Enderlin of St. Martin's Press for editing extraordinaire, and Andrea Cirillo for support and sense. To the real Marianne Senkosky Fournie and her staff at St. Mary's Medical Center ED for their hospitality and sense of humor. (Her staff voted on what would happen to Marianne. She let them.) And to my sister Peg, who really liked Kenny all along.

No man becomes depraved in a single day.

—JUVENAL

PROLOGUE

There is comfort in ritual.

There is order.

There is the security of knowing that our most precious needs can be protected by enclosing them within the high, strong walls of familiarity and precision.

Kenny understood this. He recognized the need for ritual, the joy of it. He cherished the keen anticipation of each deliberate act. Kenny practiced his rituals as carefully as a priest performs high mass.

One of the keystones of Kenny's ritual was the ten o'clock news. Kenny watched the news the way other people read obituaries. Once he knew his name wasn't going to be mentioned, he could get on with planning the next day's work.

But not just the ten o'clock news. The ten o'clock news on Channel 7. Kenny preferred to get his news from Channel 7, because it tended to carry the most lurid stories. Kenny liked to hear the breathless outrage in anchorwoman Donna Kirkland's soft voice when she said words like *startling* and *gruesome*, almost as if she derived sexual pleasure from them. He liked the way her plump little lips wrapped around the vowels and her eyes widened at the words. But that wasn't something he figured he should dwell on when he had his new friend with him, as he did tonight.

Flower. Her name was Flower. It was such a wonderful name, Kenny thought, turning to her. She was such a wonderful person, comforting and quiet.

"Ten o'clock is the only time to watch news," he told her as he settled himself back down on the nubby brown-plaid couch and wrapped his arm around her shoulder. "By now, anything that's going to happen has happened. No big surprises, ya know?"

Flower agreed with him. She always did.

"Today," Donna Kirkland intoned with barely suppressed delight on TV, "a grisly discovery in Forest Park . . ."

Grisly. Another word she seemed to get off on. Kenny found himself getting hard. Reaching over to retrieve his beer from the end table, he took a long swig. Beer went well with the news. Beer went well with everything, but Kenny especially liked it with the news.

So he smiled. He had his beer, Flower was here with him, and there was murder on television. And to make it all perfect, Donnatheanchor—Kenny always thought of her as that: Donnatheanchor, as if it were her entire name—was excited by it.

". . . two park rangers found the partially clothed body of a woman in the woods while clearing brush."

On the TV the camera panned over the obligatory stand of dead trees silhouetted against a gray sky. Caught clustered in a fold of land like cattle sheltering against the wind stood about a half dozen uniformed officers bent almost double, an ambulance cart, and a couple of fat guys in down vests and baseball caps.

"Now they'll get the official report from the homicide officer," Kenny said with some disgust. "You'd think they'd change the format just a little."

"Jamie?" Donnatheanchor called out to the reporter. "Have there been any official statements?"

A slick twenty-something guy showed up, standing in front of the downtown police station. "Well, Donna," he said, frowning, "identification has not been made. We spoke with a representative of the Medical Examiner's office a few minutes ago."

"*Not* homicide?" Kenny objected.

The TV now showed the inside of some generic government office. A woman stood quietly listening to a question being asked off camera. Kenny saw her and forgot all about the homicide officer he'd expected. He forgot the story entirely.

His heart suddenly raced. He felt the surprise right there in his throat. Squinting, he leaned closer. He opened his mouth to say something and then didn't remember to say it. He thought maybe he'd stopped breathing.

"My God," he whispered, stunned.

She was petite, small-boned, and trim. Short, neat auburn hair. Bright brown eyes with laugh lines and lots of experience stamped on almost pretty features, small hands tucked in the pockets of a serviceable gray suit jacket.

Older, much older, it seemed to Kenny. But then, so was he.

"My God," he breathed again, shaking his head. "It's *her*. Why didn't I know?"

"The Medical Examiner believes the victim to have been at the site for about four days," she was saying with appropriate solemnity. "We won't know the cause of death until the autopsy has been performed in the morning."

Kenny always remembered her smiling. But he remembered this look even better. Her sad look. Kenny remembered her looking at him this way, like she wanted to say something or do something that could make it all different.

Maybe that was why he suddenly recognized her. He'd finally seen her sad look. The look he'd always thought was all his.

Forgetting his beer, forgetting his friend Flower, he focused on the TV, so excited he could hardly think.

"Molly Burke is a death investigator for the city of St. Louis," Jamie the reporter said as he appeared again on the screen.

"Molly . . ." Kenny's laugh was sudden. "Oh my god, Molly. Yes, of course!"

He turned to Flower, truly thrilled. "You don't understand," he said. "I knew her. I *know* her. I wondered for so
long what's become of her, and now to realize that she's been
right here, that I've *seen* her! I wasn't sure . . . I mean, you
hope, ya know . . . but . . . well, I've just got to let her know
I'm back."

Kenny turned to the TV, but he was too late. Donnatheanchor had moved on to recap the top news story, which
charted the various government agencies that were temporar-
ily shut down in the wake of the latest congressional budget
deadlock. Molly was gone and wouldn't come back. But
Kenny knew where she was, and he knew just what to do
about it.

For a few moments, he just sat there alongside Flower and
considered his good luck. Kenny had never been the kind of
person who had good luck. And even on the rare occasions he
did get it, usually he didn't know what to do with it.

Well, he knew this time. He knew because for more than
twenty years he'd been anticipating what he'd do if this very
moment ever came. He'd been practicing hard in his head so
that it would be perfect.

Twenty long years. And now he would finally get to act out
his most precious dreams. Tilting the long-neck Busch up to
finish it, he set the bottle down and stood up.

"Time for lights out," he said to Flower. "I'm going to
have a busy day tomorrow."

His friend Flower smiled back. But then, she always
smiled. So Kenny smiled as well, because tonight he was
happy, too. Then, with the exquisite care he showed all his
friends, he lifted her head off her shoulders and put it back in
the refrigerator where it belonged. Then, turning off the
lights, he went to bed.

i am nobody

nuthing

she says so

ONE

Molly Burke was going to die because of a clown.

And not just any clown. An alien clown. With AIDS.

She really had to quit. It was all she could think as she lay splayed out on the floor of trauma room one with a screaming, two-hundred-pound psychotic sitting on her chest.

"Clowns!" the woman howled from above her, spittle flying across Molly's face like a lawn sprinkler. She was leaning so close Molly couldn't possibly miss the glitter of fresh blood on the butcher knife her new patient wielded in her face. "Big clowns!"

If it hadn't been her own blood Molly was looking at on that monstrous knife, this whole thing would have been really funny. It would be later, she decided, when she told it over drinks at the local watering hole. She'd make sure it sounded funny.

Then she'd come back into work and quit.

If she lasted that long.

She was just getting too old for trauma. Her reflexes had failed her. And without her reflexes, a trauma center was the last place Molly should be working. Especially when she couldn't spot a perfect ten on the crazy meter until it was too late.

"Big clowns with red noses."

Triage had announced a new patient to room six. Short-
ness of breath and chest pain. Twenty-nine-year-old female.
Well, the twenty-nine-year-old female had been short of
breath, all right. She'd been short of breath because she'd
been holding it. Against contamination from those AIDS-
infected clowns—to whom Molly evidently bore a striking
resemblance. By the time Molly had caught on to the urgency
of the problem, she'd been flat on her back on the floor being
held down by a betrayed paranoid schizophrenic in full cry.

With a knife.

"They want the Water Child," the woman intoned in a
high, eerie voice as she rocked back and forth on Molly's
much-abused sternum. "They want to kidnap him and give
him AIDS. They told me."

"The Water Child?" Molly managed on a gasp and a wrig-
gle. Maybe if she could just dislodge that massive knee from
her neck . . .

"Yes-s-s-s," the woman hissed, sounding distressingly
like Gollum. "Didn't you see them? They're waiting for him."

"I didn't . . . see anybody. Maybe if I could look."

She was beginning to lose brain cells here. She had to get
to the panic button on the wall so she could sound the alarm
for the cavalry. She had to figure out what the Water Child
was so she could climb inside the delusion and herd this
crazy woman into a safety net.

She had to get her butt off this terrazzo floor before her
pelvis shattered like an eggshell.

"Please," she begged. "Let me help you."

The patient stared at her. "All right."

And then, as precisely as a debutante, she simply rose to
her feet. Molly sucked in her first breath in about ten minutes
and scrambled up after her.

"Thank you," she rasped. "Now I can help you look."

That was when she saw the blood on the floor. Clots of it.
Right beneath the patient, who Molly now realized was wearing a grimy, full-length oversize raincoat and galoshes, the
kind of schizophrenic uniform that made Molly really nervous. Even without the knife.

And then Molly heard the mewling, like a kitten. From one of the big, saggy pockets.

Great, she thought. Knives and animals. All they needed was a few candles and they'd have a scene from *Rosemary's Baby*.

"Now then," Molly said in a calm, supportive voice. "Clowns, right? We're looking for clowns? How 'bout if I check the hallway?"

"No. Help me offer up the Water Child. He's the protection . . . his gift will end the AIDS. . . ."

His gift. His gift.

And Molly, shaky and sweaty with adrenaline, couldn't think straight enough to decipher the code.

"What's your name?" she asked gently, taking another small step toward the wall and that big red panic button.

The woman stiffened. "Why, Water Mother, of course."

"Of course . . ."

Water Mother.

Molly stumbled to a halt. She looked down at the blood. She heard that curious mewling sound again. She finally put the pieces together.

"Holy shit . . ."

The clowns might have been a delusion. The Water Child wasn't. The Water Child that crazy bitch was about to sacrifice with her big, bloody knife. And she was already reaching into the pocket of that raincoat.

Maggie never hesitated. She slammed into the Water Mother like a Green Bay Packer at the line of scrimmage.

Both of them crashed into the wall. The Water Mother screamed. Molly smashed the knife hand against the wall. She got kicked and just about bitten, but the knife clattered to the floor, splattering more blood. Molly threw a shoulder against the woman's chest. The Water Mother spun backward, and Molly caught the newborn infant just as he fell from his startled mother's hand.

Then, finally, she hit the big red button on the wall.

Molly had worked in trauma for thirty years. She was not given to panic. The last time she'd fallen apart on a work line had been the first day she'd laced up her combat boots and walked into the evac hospital at Pleiku thirty some years ago.

But there was one thing that brought her close. And she held it in her hands as she ran out the treatment room door, the Water Mother screeching behind her and security pounding up the hall.

Babies in trouble made her panic. And the Water Child, all two pounds of him, was in serious trouble.

"She's got a knife!" Molly yelled to security, who skidded almost to a stop at the sight of Molly carrying a handful of dusky infant past them. "And she's pissed!"

At least Molly wasn't alone in hating the idea of caring for a tiny life. Most trauma staff hated kids. Hated trying to deal with their tiny bodies, their tiny hearts, their huge emotional payload. Kiddie codes were almost always an exercise in distress and disaster unless they were handled at a real kiddie hospital. And Grace Hospital, no matter its level-one status as the primary gun and knife club in St. Louis, was not a real kiddie hospital.

But nobody, nobody at that hospital hated critical babies the way Molly did. Nobody saw what she saw when she held them, when she fought for them and lost them.

Fortunately for Molly, there was one staff member on tonight who was impervious to the more terrifying elements of a kiddie code. As she scuttled into the pediatric code room, Molly screamed out for the desk to call a code. Then, she went for the big guns.

"Sasha!!!"

Molly threw open the door to find the room already occupied by (believe it or not) a guy taking the temperature on a sniffling toddler. Not tough to throw out, especially when the mother caught sight of what Molly was carrying and jumped straight in the air.

"Sweet Je-sus!" she shrieked, backing away.

"I'm sorry . . ." Molly nodded to both the skinny, young African American woman and the forgettable white male tech Molly didn't recognize. "This baby is in distress. Could you . . ."

God bless the mother. She grabbed her kid right out of the tech's hands and hit the back door at warp speed. The tech, nervous and dingy as the Water Mother's coat, jumped back a couple of steps when Molly laid the tiny, flaccid body on the cart.

"You new here?" she demanded, yanking open the drawers of the crash cart.

Flushing a dirty red, he gulped. "They, uh, pulled me from the floor. I'm cross-trained from, uh, housekeeping . . ."

No wonder she didn't know him. He was one of the interchangeable mass of undertrained serfs that medicine now used to staff their hospitals. He wouldn't even have imprinted on her at all, except for the red rope of keloid scarring at his collarbone. Like seeing a bloated worm crawl up a guy's neck.

Forcing a smile, Molly motioned the tech toward the door. "You might want to catch that mother and find another room for her baby."

He fled, which left Molly with one near-dead preemie, a personal heart rate of close to two hundred, and a thousand decisions to make.

"Code Blue One, Emergency Department room three," the pager announced overhead. "Code Blue One, Emergency Department room three."

Code Blue One. Dead Baby Alert. People would run fast, breathe faster, and pray somebody else would take the responsibility. And Molly, still alone in the room, knew better than to do anything to this fragile, barely formed package without help. So, with sweating, shaking hands, she gathered equipment.

The baby lay in a growing pool of water and blood. The umbilical cord still dangled to the cart, the end of it looking gnawed and raw. Otherwise, the Water Child was perfectly formed: tiny hands and tiny feet and a beautiful little head. And a purple, still body.

Molly could barely look at it.

"You bellowed?" a cool voice greeted her from the door.

Busy yanking out suction catheters and ET tubes and O_2

setups, Molly damn near fainted in relief. "It's a submariner, Sash."

A "submariner" being a baby who'd been born right into the toilet. A "Water Child." Sasha Petrovich took a second to evaluate the lifeless form on her bed and nodded. "Okay."

That was all the reaction they were going to get. Sasha, with her classic blond looks and spotless attire and dust-dry wit, was the perfect pediatric critical nurse. She never saw fit to be flustered by the fragile lives in her care. She never wasted that much energy.

"How long?" she asked, slipping on a gown and gloves.

Molly's hands were shaking so badly she could barely attach the EKG leads to the patches. If she'd tried to put the patches on the baby's chest before connecting the leads, the simple act of pushing in the connectors would crush those gossamer ribs. "I don't know how old. I heard it making noise till about a minute ago."

Sasha nodded again. "Then let's tube him. Give me a two-point-five, okay? And give me an umbilical cath. Good thing it's warm out today. Fidget might just have a chance . . . geez, who cut this cord? Lassie? Get me some Betadine. Lots of Betadine."

Sasha had just gotten the endotracheal tube down when the rest of the team tumbled in the door. Respiratory took over bagging so that Molly could do one-fingered CPR, and a supervisor stood in paralytic shock over by the crash cart.

"Take a breath," Sasha advised Molly dryly as she drew blood from the umbilical vein before hooking up the IV line.

"I will," Molly assured her, her own focus on imagining a viable rhythm on the monitor. "Later."

This wasn't the time she should be doing this. Not this. She could barely keep her feet in the room. Fortunately, the pediatric resident finally sailed in, coat flapping like a kite in a high breeze, lunch still clutched in one hand. Molly relaxed in minute increments. Bill was almost as sanguine as Sasha about these little crises.

"Who was fishing under the limit in here?" he brayed. "Throw this little carp back till it's bigger."

"That particular pond is dry, Bill," Sasha informed him, drawing up meds in tuberculin syringes.

"Where is she, this nurturing body of water that spat out our little fish?"

"With any luck," Molly answered, "being introduced to the joys of four-point restraint by security. She was in the process of sacrificing the Water Child here before the clowns got it."

"The clowns did get it," the resident assured them with a rattling laugh. "Jesus, Molly, what'd you do, wrestle a Wookie to the ground to bring this kid in?"

"As a matter of fact, Bill," she said with a shaky grin, "yes I did. You don't behave, you're next."

Bill waved his sandwich at her. "Don't toy with me, Molly. I have a weaker heart than our little fish here."

Their little fish had a stronger heart than Molly had thought. After only another hour and a half of sweat, swearing, and a judicious application of the Pediatric Advanced Life Support treatment algorithms, the team bought the baby a viable rhythm, a quivering attempt at breathing, and a transfer to the real pediatric hospital down the street.

It also left Molly as spent as her bank balance and fully horizontal in the nurses' lounge.

"Ya know," Sasha said from where she leaned against the doorway, "you've been a nurse since Nixon was a crook. You'd think you'd be used to this shit by now."

"It was the surprise," Molly said without opening her eyes on the couch, where she lay like a slug. "If the Water Mother had just said right off, 'Hey, I have a one-kilo preemie in my pocket,' I probably wouldn't have hyperventilated. But she was too busy trying to redesign my face with a flensing knife."

"A face which is going to need some attention," Sasha said.

Molly waved her off. "Right after I start breathing again."

Sasha just watched her for a moment. "You're not going to save them all, ya know. You're probably not even going to save most of them. Which most of them might just thank you for."

A sentiment Molly would do well to cross-stitch and hang

over her locker. But not one she needed to hear right now, especially when she was trying so hard to keep herself together all by herself. To cram the old memories safely away where they belonged, but where they refused to stay during Christmastime.

"You really are much more fun to live with in October," Sasha admitted, as if she could hear Molly's thoughts.

"I told you," Molly admitted wearily. "My regression festivals are scheduled every Christmas and summer. I wet the bed and throw tantrums." She sighed. "And I have a little more trouble dealing with kids."

She had a little more trouble dealing with everything. She had ever since her halcyon days in Vietnam half a lifetime ago, but she'd been managing pretty well until the last eighteen months or so. In that time, she'd forfeited her savings and the job she'd held at one of the more posh St. Louis County hospitals to a malpractice suit, and she'd lost her psychiatrist to suicide. Now she had two jobs, no money, and a once-again precarious hold on her peace of mind.

But then, she also had the friends she'd found when she'd been relegated to the battered old halls of the Grace Hospital ED in downtown St. Louis, and a new sense of purpose in her second job as part-time death investigator for the city Medical Examiner. For the moment, though, stability was still something that she'd relegated to "mirage in the distance" status.

But heck, she'd survived before. She could do it again. She just didn't feel like doing it at Christmas.

Or summer.

Or around two-pound preemies.

"I think I should retire, Sash."

Sasha even had an elegant snort. "And do what? Play death investigator full time? Even with all those buff young police to dally with, you'd be bored in a minute."

"At least it would be easier," she retorted.

As death investigator, her job was to filter the notifications of death throughout the city. Report the naturals and show up at the unnaturals to examine and take control of the body before seeing it safely back to the morgue, where the Medical Examiner would take over. Help organize the information if the case had to move toward trial.

Time consuming, yes. Detail-intensive, sometimes emotionally exhausting, since the death investigator usually notified families in the bad cases. But not dangerous. Not overwhelming. Not ever out of control, which trauma always was.

Molly sighed again, her attention on the Olsen Twins poster somebody had tacked to the ceiling and then redesigned with glued-on feathers, sequins, and G-strings.

"I'm tired," she said. "I'm old. I'm too cranky to be empathetic anymore."

Sasha lifted an eyebrow. "And the problem is?"

Molly had to grin.

"Please don't expect me to be your cheerleader," Sasha all but begged. "You know I find it distasteful."

"You're charge nurse. It's your job."

"Balancing the staff like a circus juggler and not massacring the doctors is my job. Yours is to come to work so I have someone worth talking to."

Molly didn't bother to look over, even for such a compliment. Sasha was fifteen years younger and a hundred years more world weary than Molly on her best days.

"Would you consider accepting a bribe?" Sasha asked.

"Is that part of your job, too?"

"Whatever it takes."

Molly heard Sasha reach into her pocket. She heard the rustle of cellophane. She almost came straight off the couch.

"You're fighting dirty and you know it," she accused, already salivating.

"It's a present from James," Sasha said. "He heard of your act of heroism and tubed me something special for you."

Molly's eyes closed in ecstasy. James was the evening pharmacy supervisor and supplier of the drug of choice for most of the nurses in the hospital. "Well, why didn't you tell me right away?" she demanded, her body reacting without her consent. "What is it?"

Sasha smiled like a pimp with a virgin in the closet. "What is it you want?" she asked.

Sighing, Molly briefly let her eyes go closed again as she battled a sharp flood of saliva. "Ding Dongs."

Sasha swept her hand from behind her back with a flourish and dropped the cellophane-wrapped package on Molly's stomach. "Have we ever disappointed?"

Anyone who saw Molly rip through the cellophane would have thought she'd been starving on the desert. She took one bite of saturated fat, sugar, and preservatives and felt her life force returning.

"I might just make it," she said with a profound sigh.

"Security, Emergency Department, stat! Security, Emergency Department, stat!"

"Oh, shit!" somebody yelled outside the lounge door. "She got away!"

Feet pounded down the hall. Molly sank back into the couch, her treat all but forgotten. She should have known.

"Uh . . . Ms. Burke?" came a hesitant voice from the doorway. The voice of that security guard she'd warned not two hours earlier.

"You let the Water Mother get away," Molly accused without opening her eyes. "Didn't you?"

"Well, ma'am, she seemed . . . well, quite calm . . . uh, after you left."

"Tell me you at least took the knife away."

"Uh . . ."

Molly took a few long moments to battle a sudden, flashing rage. She really was too old for this. And the rages never got easier, untidy bequests she'd inherited from the post-traumatic stress disorder she'd brought home with her from Nam. She came within an inch of giving this guy a broken nose just because he was incompetent.

"Ms. Burke?" the security guard ventured.

"Give her a minute," Sasha advised dryly. "At least until her eyes stop glowing."

Molly wanted to laugh. She couldn't. Hell, she could barely breathe.

"Call the police. It won't take long before she accuses some other clown of stealing her sacrifice."

The security guard got out of there so fast his big shoes flapped.

"See what I mean?" Molly asked a wryly amused Sasha, who still stood quietly by. "I used to be able to just laugh off stupid shit like that."

Sasha motioned for Molly to finish her Ding Dong. "Babies always set you off."

Molly did. "And, more and more, idiots," she admitted around a mouthful of mood elevator. "And more and more idiots are working in hospitals."

"Your security friend there's been with us all of three months," Sasha admitted. "I hear he worked at a Safeway market before that."

"Protecting frozen foods from potentially violent condiments, most likely." Finally giving into the inevitable, Molly tossed the remaining cellophane in the trash and climbed to her feet to finish her shift. "And who the hell was that new tech I threw out of three?"

Sasha's laugh was as dry as insurance forms. "Another cross-trainee in the brave new world of Kmart management. He's one of those housekeeping guys who's also doing patient care now."

Molly glared at her friend and charge nurse. "And you let them send him down here?"

Sasha shrugged. "He's mostly been emptying linen and cleaning crash carts. Don't worry. He'll be back up on the floor before you know it."

"By which time I'll be retired, puttering in my garden, and thinking fondly of the good old days."

Sasha didn't bother with empathy as she led Molly back up the work lane. "No you won't. You'll get in a good gunshot wound and be fine again. Just stay away from the kids."

Just stay away from the kids. Yeah, Molly thought as she pulled up in front of her home three hours later. Sasha was right. It was the kids who mostly set her off. In the hot, humid

summers they transported her back to the red mud of the
Vietnamese highlands. In the winter, they made her dread
Christmas, when happy families forced her to remember that
she had none of her own. If she could stay away from the
kids, she'd be all right. If she could stuff the memories back
where they belonged.

Shutting off the engine in her faded red Celica, Molly
gathered her purse and nursing bag and climbed out of the
car. The air was soft and damp tonight, the temperature hov-
ering in the fifties. Typical St. Louis December. Fifties one
nanosecond, minus twenties the next. Like Sasha had said, it
was a good thing the Water Baby had decided to make his appearance on a warm day. If the temperature had been down
another twenty degrees, he never would have survived the
ride in.

He was still surviving. Barely. Surrounded by enough
high-tech equipment to launch a space shuttle, wrapped in
cellophane and foil to preserve his body temperature, so that
the NICU nurses would call him "Spuds," isolated and alone
and dependent on strangers to remember to stroke him so he
could recognize himself as human. And all that so he could
end up being discharged from the hospital just about the time
his mother got custody back.

No wonder babies made her crazy.

Molly deliberately stopped a moment to consider her
lawn. Even in the dead of winter, it pleased her. The flowers
wouldn't be back for months, the trees were skeletal and
scratchy in the wind, and the grass was brown and dormant.
But there was order here. There was a predictability and pattern she could affect with her hands. There was beauty and
structure and life. Considering what she usually had to deal
with from either one of her jobs, not a bad thing to come
home to.

It would have been nice if that feeling had only extended
to her house. Sighing, Molly trudged on up the concrete
steps to the small square porch that fronted the Federalist
house her grandparents had passed down. A classic, black-
shuttered, red-brick box chockful of expensive artifacts her

parents had collected and cherished, it reeked of security and elegance.

Most of her friends saw it as a privilege to live there. Maggie saw it as a prison, the place she finally came back to when she couldn't run anymore. A trap of family pretension she'd never quite escaped and certainly didn't own.

Molly slid the key in the front door and wondered again what her life might have been like in a different house. A crowded, messy, noisy house. Instead, she'd grown up smothered in social snobbery. She'd had two parents who spent all their energy on achievement and their diplomacy on strangers. She had memories of housekeepers serving up Christmas and infrequent visits from a brother who devoted himself to carrying on the family tradition.

Molly never had. She'd fought every restraint and grown contempt like cancer. She'd become a nurse because they'd wanted her to become a diplomat, like a good Burke. She'd slogged through the mud of Vietnam instead of embassy hallways and come home disinherited.

It was her brother Martin who owned the house she lived in, his two sons the ones the valuables were held in trust for. Maggie, the failure, would be allowed to live there on sufferance as long as she kept the Burke Shrine intact. She could touch nothing, change nothing, expect nothing.

Molly had run to the ends of the earth to escape the trap they'd set for her. After two failed marriages and thirty years of flight, here she was.

She'd sure shown them.

Well, at least the house wasn't the ED. There were no babies here to panic her, no trauma to survive. Only silence, expensive trinkets she hated, and a shower of bills scattered across the glossy hardwood floor where they'd fallen from the mail slot. After the shift she'd had, she couldn't say she minded so much.

The minute she stepped onto that hardwood floor, a monster the size of a small truck let loose with a spate of barking that should have awakened the dead.

Molly smiled. Okay, expensive trinkets she hated and a big, sloppy dog she loved.

"Hey, Magnum, it's me!" she called, shutting the door behind her and setting the alarm.

Magnum didn't seem impressed. A massive red-and-brown head popped briefly out the kitchen door, slid back in to safety, and continued barking. Maggie bent to pick up her mail and chuckled.

"Knock it off," she crooned, just as she did to the babies at work. "Burglars aren't impressed unless you actually come out of hiding to bark at them, honey."

But she was grinning anyway. She'd wanted children. Somehow she'd ended up with a puppy the size of a Clydesdale. A puppy who was now whining as if she'd personally insulted him. Maggie was chuckling at his noise as she leafed through the most predictable of her bills.

She stopped, one envelope caught in her suddenly shaky hands.

Magnum whined. Maggie didn't notice. Her heart stuttered. Her chest hurt. Her gut clenched.

It was just a plain white envelope. Nothing more. Her name and address in black ink.

She couldn't bear to open it.

Holding it tight in her hand, she looked up into the shadows, struggling for breath.

Not now. Oh, not now. I can't deal with any more tonight.

It was such a stupid reaction. So embarrassing. She was standing alone in the most secure house in the city of St. Louis, and she was suddenly afraid. She was checking shadows and startling at noises because of a plain white envelope.

But she'd gotten four others, and they'd frightened her, too.

She wanted to just stand there. She wanted to hide. She wanted to feed the damn thing to her dog. She opened it instead.

DIE BITCH

Not even original. Not particularly poetic or flowery. Not something that should cause palpitations.

But it wasn't the words that upset her. Heck, she'd been called worse by Sasha. It was finding them tucked away in her mail like spiders in a basket. It was the subterfuge of a plain white envelope and careful printing. It was the black, slashing letters inside that tore right through the paper, as if words alone couldn't possibly express the rage.

It was not knowing who sent them. Or why.

She'd called the police. They'd said to save the notes, and let them know if anything escalated.

She guessed she'd have to call them again.

Molly was just turning toward the kitchen to do that, to feed Magnum and let him out to maul her sleeping bulbs in the backyard, when she realized that she wasn't out of surprises for the night.

For a moment, she just stared into the darkened living room. Dared the precise shadows of her house to reassemble themselves into their correct pattern. The pattern she'd seen no more than twelve hours earlier.

"Magnum," she muttered, suddenly really afraid. "Just who did you let in here tonight?"

The late Catherine Louise and Martin Francis Burke, Sr., had spent their lives traveling in the service of the government and collecting tasteful collectibles with what was left of the family inheritance. As far back as Molly could remember, the Burke house had held the finest that Waterford, Chippendale, and Sèvres had to offer, not to mention the odd Feininger oil or Hopper watercolor. Molly knew each one like an adversary and checked on its health more frequently than her remaining family's. Which was why she would realize so quickly that there was an empty square of wall space over the Steinway. A square where the Rembrandt sketch had always resided.

Molly's spirits, already dangerously low, sank straight to her toes. She looked at the wall. Around the room. Back over her shoulder as she tried to remember whether she'd set the alarm properly that morning. She walked on into the room and checked behind the furniture and potted plants, as if she really could have taken the damn thing down and then forgotten where she'd put it.

"Please let this just be an episode of *Twilight Zone*, where I'm in an alternate universe that doesn't include Rembrandt," she begged.

Almost in response, Magnum started barking again. Molly jumped a foot. Her night had been bad enough. But this was seriously teetering toward chaos. She held on to that note, as if it were her only proof of sanity, and turned to the kitchen.

Magnum was delirious to see her. Molly almost ended up on her butt beneath eighty pounds of sloppy enthusiasm, but she managed to get him out the back door, and then she turned for the phone.

Molly had managed to punch no more than the nine when Magnum started barking again. A second later her doorbell rang.

"With my luck," Molly groused to herself, trying hard to ignore the sudden reacceleration of her heart, "it's the Water Mother coming back for her sacrifice."

Even so, she grabbed her portable phone and headed for the front door. And noticed on the way what was missing from the Queen Anne cabinet in the corner.

Molly took one look through her peephole and laughed. "I'd heard response times were getting better," she said when she got the door open, "but this is ridiculous."

The cop on her doorstep reminded her a lot of Magnum. Huge, a little sloppy, kind of clumsy, and smiling. Dee, or Delight Jackson Smith, was one of the local uniforms who walked a beat in the Central West End. Because a certain amount of Molly's calls for the Medical Examiner's office also happened to be from the same general neighborhood, she saw a lot of Dee.

Tonight she was particularly glad to find him on her porch.

"You lookin' for me?" he asked in his deceptively slow voice.

"I was. I've been robbed."

Dee scratched his bald head. "No kiddin'. Wanna hear a coincidence? No more'n half hour ago, I sees this kid hoppin' fences with a picture under his arm. One of your pictures, I'm thinkin'. Admired it when I was over 'bout those notes you been getting. Tried to call you at work but you already gone."

Molly was astounded. "You found my Rembrandt *before* I reported it stolen? You deserve a raise, Dee."

His grin was huge and shambling. "From your mouth, girl. Thing is, I got a kid here says how can he steal somethin's his anyway? Well, I figure, 'fore I smack his head for bein' a smartass, I should aks you. Be sure. This your painting?"

He held up his burden. Ten-by-twelve inches of faded yellow paper that held a red-charcoal-sketched girl in peasant dress, all wrapped in enough carved gilt to deck out a ship's figurehead. Molly sighed in relief. Well, at least one of her problems was solved. "It is."

"Well, then, who's this?"

At which point he reached out to his right and yanked over Molly's third or fourth surprise for the night.

She gaped. "Oh hell."

Magnum had started up again. It was after one in the morning, and her dog was throwing himself against the back door and howling. Molly had to take care of it.

In a minute.

"He lyin' to me, Molly?" Dee demanded, shaking the teenager like a rat in his meaty grasp. "'Cause I already told him what'd happen, he was. And bein' you be gettin' those threatening notes and all, I thought I might jus' be sure."

As achy and tired and overwhelmed as she already was, Molly damn near sat right down on the floor and cried.

He was sixteen. Beanpole tall, waiting to fill out. Blessed with the face of a poet and the grace of an angel. Molly took in thick, curling strawberry blond hair, a soft auburn goatee on a young, fey, triangular face, huge, lash-heavy hazel eyes that were now leaking tears of frustration. She saw the five-hundred-dollar leather-and-khaki duster, work pants, plaid flannel shirt, and, ruining the gangsta image, Bruno Maglis.

He was the very last thing Molly needed tonight. She almost told Dee she'd never seen him before and shut the door.

"Well?"

Molly shook her head. "He isn't lying, Dee. He does own it. Kind of. Stand up straight, Patrick. You have some explaining to do."

"I'm sorry, Aunt Molly," he all but whispered in a marginally masculine voice.

Molly sighed, stood aside, and wished hard for something stronger than aspirin. "Might as well come in. This is going to take some time."

"I bet," Dee agreed, pushing the boy in the door ahead of him.

"I didn't mean it," Patrick insisted in aggrieved tones.

"Of course you didn't mean it, Patrick," Molly assured him drily. "It was an accident that you got a thousand miles from your house in Virginia, to walk off with the Rembrandt"— he'd just about been ready to step past her when she grabbed a corner of duster—"and the jade hung-ma."

"The hung what?" Patrick echoed innocently.

"The *jade* what?" Dee echoed much more darkly one step behind.

Molly didn't take her eyes off her nephew. "Believe it or not, I do notice those things, Patrick. The small carving on the third shelf of the Queen Anne cabinet in the dining room—the deep blue one that looks like it's part horse, part dragon? It's missing. It was also a good choice. It's quite rare."

Tears welled all over again and he gulped. "I needed to get away. I didn't think you'd care."

She didn't. That was the worst part. No, the worst part was having her only brother's older son on her doorstep four weeks before Christmas when the only thing she possessed less of than yule cheer was Christian charity. Especially toward her family.

"You've been getting threats, Aunt Molly?" the boy asked as she closed the door behind them. "Maybe I could stay and help . . . uh, protect you, okay?"

"You get in the kitchen and sit down," she commanded. "As soon as you hand over the hung-ma."

Magnum was going to wake up the baby at the end of the

block. Pointing to her nephew, Molly addressed her friend the cop. "Don't let him out of your sight. I'll be right back."

"But Aunt Molly—"

But Aunt Molly was already stalking through the kitchen, where she could just make out Magnum's massive head outside the door.

He had something. Something he dropped every time he started barking, and then picked up again, like a furry bellboy with room service.

Something white.

That shouldn't have given Molly the creeps. Tonight, it did. It looked like a flower box, the kind long-stemmed roses come in.

Probably something that had been tossed over the fence from the neighboring streets. Molly's yard sided along Euclid, where an eclectic crowd frequented the trendy shops and restaurants tucked all along the Central West End. Since she'd moved home, Molly had found everything from condoms to a full-sized mannequin dressed as Fidel Castro in her backyard.

But the way Magnum played with that box made her think she had more than Castro on her hands.

Pushing the door open, Molly reached out, and Magnum obliged, dropping his prize in her hand. Slick with dog drool and ragged with careful gnaw marks, it was, indeed, a flower box. And it wasn't empty.

"Uh, Dee?" she called, suddenly even more worried about those notes she'd been getting than she had been. "Can you come in here?"

He did, which set Magnum off all over again. Molly shushed the dog and motioned the policeman over as she laid the box on her kitchen table and opened it.

She saw the glint of gold first. Nestled in layers of white tissue. Heavy and solid. But not all gold. Decorated in gold. Painted with gold hearts. Gold hearts and red crosses.

And letters. Words.

"What the hell—" Dee muttered, leaning in for a closer look as Molly pulled the last layer of tissue apart to fully reveal what lay within.

"It's a fake," Molly insisted, even though she knew better.

She didn't touch it, even though she wanted to. She didn't pick it up or tilt it over just to make sure she was right.

She didn't have to, really. After all the time she'd spent in EDs and Medical Examiners' offices, it was virtually impossible for her not to recognize a human thighbone.

A thighbone painted with the salutation "This is for Molly Burke."

sHe tuched me
she tyed me up and
sHE hurt me
    there

I cant pee now it hurts
   so Bad
I deserve it she says so

i'm so scared
I am five .
   'it's my birthday

TWO

This is for Molly Burke.

Painted on that bone in gold. Painted in careful, precise gold letters right down the shaft.

Like an invitation.

Or an accusation.

"You wouldn't know anything about this, would you?" Dee demanded of Molly's nephew.

Patrick couldn't seem to do much more than stare at Molly's find. "What the hell is it?" he demanded, tentatively reaching out to touch it.

Molly grabbed his hand and closed the box. "Probably something somebody tossed over my fence by mistake," she said. "Happens all the time."

"It's a *bone*," Patrick insisted, as engrossed as he was appalled.

He probably thought she spent all her evenings like this, Molly thought wearily. If she weren't so nauseous, she would have laughed.

Dee scowled. "I'm calling the detectives."

"I didn't do it!" Patrick immediately protested.

"He didn't say you did," Molly assured him quietly. "He just said that you haven't given back the jade figurine yet."

For just a second, Patrick challenged her. "It *is* going to be mine."

Molly damn near smiled. "Going to be, Patrick. Future tense. For the present, the figurine is part of a trust that nobody can touch. And your dad and I are in charge of the trust. Not you. Not for a long time. So hand over the figurine till it's your turn."

"But what about that bone?" he demanded, his hand dramatically thrown out toward the box. "The bone that's addressed to *you*?"

Molly deliberately looked away. "That is probably going to keep me up all night while we poke and probe and find out it's just a gag from some medical supply shop."

"I'm calling anyway," Dee insisted.

Molly simply nodded and let him use her kitchen phone while she dosed herself with ibuprofen. She hurt like a kickboxing victim, her stomach was doing cartwheels over the surprise on her table, and the night was looking to get a lot longer.

Beside the gleaming steel stove, Magnum grumbled in his throat, his great head swiveling back and forth between Dee and Patrick. Molly gave him a good scratch behind the ears and pointed to the floor where he settled with an indignant huff.

"And now," she said to her nephew as Dee hung up. "To you."

She'd already seen the bulge of the carving in Patrick's duster pocket, but she wasn't in the mood to just take it. For a brief, petty moment, she wanted to make him give it up. Patrick, who had everything. Looks, intelligence, money, stability. A life of privilege in an upscale community with parents who indulged him and his brother shamefully.

As opposed to his aunt, who had no inheritance, no living parents with deep pockets, and a hole in her pocketbook big enough to require two jobs to fill it.

And yet, here was Patrick lifting family heirlooms in the middle of the night four weeks away from Christmas. Molly guessed that she was going to get to talk to her brother Martin during the holidays whether she wanted to or not.

In the meantime, she crowded Patrick a little so he was caught between her and the wall of police Dee represented. No matter what else was going on here tonight, she needed to immediately impress on Patrick that the road he'd chosen was now closed.

"I'm not going to press charges this time," she said and saw Patrick go white all over again. "As long as I get the carving."

"You wouldn't press charges," he insisted, the bravado a little thin in that young voice. "I'm family."

Molly scowled. "I don't care if you're my mother. You don't steal things without suffering consequences. Don't your parents take you to church? They're Catholic, for God's sake. They should have dosed you up with enough guilt and responsibility for you to be in therapy. God knows *they* were."

Her answer was a stiffening of the spine. A darting of the eyes toward the policeman, who wasn't family. Well, Molly thought disparagingly, he's certainly learned that all-important Burke lesson. Hold firm to the family facade.

"You said *this* time," Dee prodded, so he could get back to what really interested him.

Molly nodded. "Take a good look at this face, Dee. 'Cause if you catch him again, he's all yours."

"But Aunt Molly—!"

She lifted a finger and fleetingly thought how fond her mother had been of that gesture. "You and I will discuss it after this nice gentleman gets back on his beat."

Molly got silence, a flash of rage, a hint of disdain and tears. But Patrick kept quiet, and in the end, reached into his coat pocket.

Even Dee sucked in a breath when he saw what Patrick pulled out. Molly didn't blame him. Most people didn't really notice the workmanship on the jade figurines her father had collected, because he'd bunched them all on five shelves of glass like a display at a discount store. But one by one, they did, indeed, take the breath away.

This figurine was a deep lapis blue, alive with the light rippling along the lines of the tiny creature like water. Exquisite. And at least six hundred years old. Molly accepted it with good grace and walked it in to replace it carefully along with its companions on the backlit shelves.

"One final thing," she said to her now-impatient nephew as they rejoined Dee. "Do your parents know where you are?"

His laugh was way too old for that beautiful face. "You kiddin'? They're on a fact-finding mission to China. They won't know I'm gone for two solid weeks. And by then . . ." Molly saw the flicker in his eyes, the reshuffling of thought. The halfhearted shrug. "I could be dead."

He was right, of course. His parents were true Burkes, born to serve and succeed. His father was the new Undersecretary of Foreign Affairs or Fiscal Responsibility or something, and his mother was the perfect Washington wife, delivered up of the heir and spare, and semiemployed in a job that wouldn't interfere with or outshine her husband, after whom she tagged like a patient, well-groomed dog.

Which meant that Molly would have to call Patrick's nanny or boarding school, or whoever was caretaking the boys these days, but she didn't have to worry that his parents were out pacing the streets of Virginia searching for their oldest son.

It didn't take Molly much to transfer her anger from her hapless nephew to the real culprits of the piece.

"We set to get on with this bone business?" Dee asked, his police pad open, his posture almost as impatient as Patrick's.

Molly fought the urge to clean the red-tile counters, rearrange the African violets that slept on her windowsill. Knit an afghan. Instead she nodded and sat down at her kitchen table.

"Might as well."

"You think this has anything to do with the notes you gettin'?" Dee asked as he seated himself across from her. Patrick, left uncertainly on his feet, claimed the third chair.

Molly gave an elaborate shrug. "Your very own department considered those notes harmless, Dee. Who am I to argue?"

Dee cocked his head. "Bones change things, don't ya think?"

Molly wanted to walk again. She was a trauma nurse. She did her best thinking walking. It was also the best way to run far and fast. But Dee wasn't going to let her, and she wasn't ready to let anybody else know how unnerved those damn notes were making her.

Not to mention a bone with her name on it.

So she threw Dee another shrug. "I don't know. To be perfectly frank, I haven't really paid much attention to the notes."

He obviously didn't see her nose growing. "You called us."

"Only because I'm a public official. It's kind of office policy, ya know?"

Dee didn't bother to comment. "You still have 'em?"

"Of course I do."

"Four notes, right?"

She sighed, resettled herself, fought against a fresh surge of nausea. "Five. I got another one today."

Dee perked right up. "Same as the others?" he asked, scribbling on a crumpled, coffee-stained page.

"Same as the others. 'Die, bitch,' or variations thereof. Delivered to the house, mailed in St. Louis."

"Wow," Patrick breathed. "Don't they scare you?"

Molly managed another shrug. "Occupational hazard."

Dee focused on his notebook. "And now that bone."

That bone, which was still sitting not two feet from Molly's elbow. She fought the urge to open the box again, just to check and see if it was still there. Make it somehow less weird. Maybe magically turn it into real flowers from a secret admirer.

That just gave her the shivers all over again.

"I'm telling you," Molly protested, rubbing at the area directly under her sternum that churned from chronic abuse, "it's going to be a mistake. Somebody's idea of a joke. The wrong yard. Something."

Dee looked at the box, too. He nodded without noticeable conviction. "Uh-huh."

"*I'd* be scared," Patrick said to himself.

"Can you get me the notes?" Dee asked.

Molly creaked to her feet. "Sure."

The latest note she just handed over. The rest were in her room, tucked into her bottom drawer in evidence envelopes into which long training and habit had compelled her to stash them. Four notes, the first showing up in her mail not four weeks before. Addressed with a heavy hand on plain white bond paper in plain white envelopes, the real messages saved for inside. On the surface unimpressive, each and every one. *Just die. Fuck you. You'll scream.* And for a little poetic license, *Bitch witch.* All now residing beneath her carefully folded sweaters like old love letters.

The notes bore no identification, no indication of why or where or when. Molly had just assumed they were from either a dissatisfied customer, or a customer's dissatisfied family. It only made sense, since she happened to practice two professions that produced the highest incidence of stressed-out clients in the city.

Molly often gave bad news in the ED, and always gave it in the Medical Examiner's office. It could take no more than one slip of the tongue for somebody to hate her forever.

If it hadn't been for that handwriting, those little rends in the sturdy paper, she wouldn't have been that concerned. The notes didn't contain flights of ideas or escalating threats of violence. She hadn't been told she belonged to the writer or needed to be sacrificed for him to assure his immortality. She'd just been getting expressions of rage, and Molly understood rage.

But for some reason, these particular expressions of rage made her wake up in the middle of the night to watch her dresser drawer, as if she expected them to crawl out and claim her. She was more than happy to get them out of the house, and with them that silent, strident voice.

Not to mention that bone. Molly might have understood rage. She did *not* understand bones.

Giving her old iron bed a brief, longing glance, she sighed and headed back down to the kitchen, where Magnum still kept a weather eye on her guests from his place by the stove.

"Can I get you something to drink?" Molly asked, dropping the envelopes in front of Dee on the empty teak kitchen table.

"Beer?" Patrick asked with a half-brash smile.

Molly just smiled back at him.

Another problem. Another stressor with hopeful, half-pleading eyes. It seemed lately that it hadn't so much been rage populating her life, but people with half-pleading eyes. The population of her winter.

Rubbing hard at her own gritty eyes, she turned to the fridge for some carbonated chemicals when Magnum lifted his head and huffed a small warning. Molly braced herself for a full broadside of barks, but they never came. He just tilted his head and perked his ears. Then the doorbell rang.

"I hope you're just quiet because I'm here," she threatened him. He happily wagged his tail, as if she'd praised him.

A bagged letter in each hand, Dee started to shuffle to his feet. Molly held him off on her way by. "Probably the detectives. I'll get it. You keep an eye on my silver."

At any other time she would have checked the spyhole. As tired as she was, she just neutralized the alarm and threw open the door, ready to greet one of the Fifth District detectives. When she saw what was standing on her porch instead, she remembered just how dangerous it was to assume.

"What are you doing here?"

He smiled like an evangelist with a fresh soul in sight. "It's good to see you, too, St. Molly. How am I? I'm fine. Although it is a little wet out here."

Molly took in the classic black Irish good looks decked out in about a thousand dollars' worth of slate-gray Armani and sighed. She knew she'd reached her nadir twenty minutes ago. And yet, she kept sliding.

Frank Patterson was one of the most handsome men she'd ever seen. Tyrone Power with better cheekbones. Mel Gibson, only taller. She'd met him eighteen months earlier over a deposition, and had been tormented by him ever since. And even before he told her why he'd shown up on her porch at two in the morning, he made her want to laugh and swear at the same time. Just like always.

"Go home, Frank," she admonished. "It's late, and I'm not in the mood."

Frank just smiled that crooked pirate smile that made Molly so mad and other women so weak at the knees. "Come on, Mol. I know you're working. There are police in your driveway. Besides, it's never too late for you. You don't sleep. I just figured that you might be interested in some . . . whoa, mother! How'd he know I was about to make an objectionable offer?"

Molly turned to see Dee looming in the doorway behind her. "You okay?" he asked.

She laughed. "Oh, sure. This is just another thorn in my side."

"He like to write notes?"

"He's still learning how to spell."

Dee just nodded and turned away. Out on her porch, Frank hadn't moved. "Notes?" he asked. "You get another one?"

Molly found herself still wanting to smile. "Something like that. Are you really here for some reason, or is it just to annoy me, Frank?"

Frank flashed another totally unrepentant grin. "I wowed the Midwest Bar Association conference with my talk on maintaining a client base in the age of the Internet, and was going to share my triumph with you . . . along with a chocolate shake?"

Damn him. He more than anyone knew how to hit her where she lived. Molly took one look at the Steak n Shake bag he lifted and groaned. Real milk, real ice cream. Real decadence.

"Oh, for God's sake, get in here. Dee'll probably want to grill you, anyway."

Frank stepped in, holding the bag out in front of him like a bribe. Molly made an ungracious grab for it and turned back for the kitchen.

"What happened to you?" he asked behind her.

That almost brought Molly to a halt. Leave it to Frank to be the first one tonight to notice the line of staples over her left ear and the limp from her very tender hip. Still turned where he couldn't see her reaction, she allowed a half grin.

"Workmen's comp."

He brightened considerably. "Wanna sue?"

Frank wasn't just a normal thorn in Molly's side. Frank was a lawyer. Frank was, in fact, the lawyer who had successfully brought suit against not only Molly's former employer and one of its physicians for malpractice, but Molly as well. A classic case of medical cluster fuck in which Molly had been caught between an incompetent physician and a suddenly dead patient. She'd be paying the rest of her life for the privilege of knowing Frank Patterson.

Which made Molly wonder each time she'd allowed Frank in her door in the last six months, why she hadn't dropkicked him across the street yet.

But right now the notes, the bone, and most of all, the Steak n Shake bag, were distracting her. Which was probably why she kept letting him past her guard. Or it could have been the fact that like her, Frank had survived Nam, although he'd done it on JAG duty. Or maybe it was the three kids he was raising alone. She liked them even better than her dog. She certainly liked them better than Frank.

"There aren't a whole lot of hospitals left in town who'll hire me, Frank," she said, leading him through the house. "And I'm not about to reduce the pool even more by suing one of them for letting a crazy woman into the ED."

"Come on, Mol. You know they were at fault. Surely there should have been a warning notice somewhere. Something like 'Patients may be hazardous to your health.' In Spanish, maybe."

"There is," she said, grinning. "It's called Abnormal Psych, and you take it junior year of training."

"Just trying to help, Molly."

"Thanks anyway, Frank."

"Well, thank heavens you let me in," he mused, catching sight of the group in the kitchen. "Otherwise you might have been overcome by all the levity."

Dee was just settling himself back down alongside
Patrick, who was trying to take surreptitious peeks inside the
white box. Magnum took one look at Frank and wagged like
Lassie.

Molly scowled at her eighty-pound puppy. "Traitor."

Frank laughed and bent down in his good Armani to nuggie the dog.

"Who's he?" Patrick demanded.

Frank looked up. "Who's *he*?" he echoed.

"Molly's my aunt," Patrick offered with some disdain.

That brought Frank all the way upright. "Why, St. Molly.
You have a family. And here I thought you'd sprung full-
armored from the skull of Florence Nightingale."

Molly barely stopped slurping. "Shut up, Frank."

Frank gave Patrick one of his patented "between boys"
smiles. "She adores me. I saved her life, you know."

Patrick straightened, his interest caught. "No. I didn't."

"Wrong verb, Frank," Molly interrupted. "The one you
want is 'ruined.' You *ruined* my life."

"Oh, you love me and you know it, St. Molly."

Dee raised a hand. "If you don't mind. . . ."

Molly decided that she didn't want to try sitting again. It
was too achy getting up and down. So she leaned against the
counter, sipping at her shake and almost forgiving Frank for
being Frank. Which happened every time he brought her
junk food.

"Did I hear you say you knew about the notes?" Dee asked
Frank.

He nodded congenially. "Yeah. Obviously somebody not
as enchanted by Molly's gracious nature as the rest of us."

Damn it. That made her grin again. "I'm not gracious,
Frank. I'm stupid. If I weren't, I wouldn't keep letting you in
the door."

"Wouldn't know anything about bones, would you?" Dee
asked.

"Bones?" Frank leaned against the sink and shrugged.
"Beyond the 'thighbone connected to the knee bone'? Not
much."

"You had to mention thighbone," Molly muttered.

"You like to paint things?" Dee asked.

Frank actually looked appalled. "Paint? Me?"

"Hearts and crosses and things? Gold paint?"

Frank lifted an elegant eyebrow. "You looking for some-body to decorate for the prom, or is there a question in all this?"

"He wants to know if you've been painting bones and flinging them over my fence, Frank," Molly told him. "Please say yes. That would get everybody out the door and put you someplace where they can actually control you."

Frank, being Frank, was delighted by the insult. "Deco-rated bones? Hot damn. I knew if I hung around long enough you'd dig up some more excitement for me."

"More excitement?" Patrick demanded. "What do you mean?"

"St. Molly here just loves a controversy. Don't you, Molly?"

"I do, Frank. Especially if it can put me at opposite ends of an argument with you."

"She's famous in St. Louis," Frank continued. "Probably the most notorious death investigator in the country. Good Golly Miss Molly, they call her."

"Death investigator?" Patrick swiveled his attention to-ward Molly. "You're a death investigator? Like a coroner or something? How come we didn't know that?"

"Well, that's the secret to your aunt Molly," Frank con-fided. "She only gives bits and pieces of herself to everybody she knows. Then I guess she expects us all to get together at some kind of friend and family reunion in the park and con-struct the whole picture ourselves."

"Is that right?" Dee asked.

Molly groaned. Not only was this getting way too compli-cated for two in the morning, she'd run out of shake. "Don't listen to him, Dee. Don't even make eye contact. You don't know how dangerous he is to your sanity . . . not to mention your wallet."

"Which is why I wouldn't threaten Molly," Frank informed Dee equably. "It would be anticlimactic. I've already sued her."

Dee stared.

Patrick whistled. "You *sued* my aunt Molly?"

Molly was sure she didn't like the avid look in Patrick's eyes, or the answering triumph in Frank's. Two peas in a pod. Just what she needed. She was about to ask Dee to arrest them both just to give her some peace when his radio crackled to life. Molly was an old enough hand that she could interpret the mumbles.

"Go on," she said, waving him away. "You have another call. Unless the detectives are Jekyll and Hyde, you don't need to be here when I talk to them. And they're going to be the ones to take the bone and the notes."

Dee scowled at both Frank and Patrick. "You sure?"

Molly grinned. "Honey, I can handle those two in my sleep. And you know I'm not going to compromise possible evidence. Go on."

After admonishing Frank to leave the evidence untouched, Molly showed the shambling cop out her front door. And then for a minute or two, she just stood there watching him amble off her porch.

The clouds had settled low outside, so that they swept by in ragged file. A breeze lifted the rain into a mist that haloed the streetlamps and glistened in the grass. Traffic was sporadic out on the through streets, and off in the distance, a dog barked.

It was quiet. Soothing. Molly damn near walked out the door right behind Dee and kept on going. Responsibility waited back inside her kitchen. Trouble. Danger. And she hadn't even really considered yet what that damn bone could mean.

This just wasn't the time of year to be surprised with a full-grown child. Not one so perilously poised on the brink of adulthood. Certainly not one with all that distress tucked away behind those great hazel eyes of his.

Molly was a sucker for kids. But even more, Molly was terrified of kids.

And she'd been tossed one just like a bone over the back-yard fence.

It took ten minutes to wake up the Burke housekeeper in Alexandria, Virginia. It took another torturous twenty minutes of Molly's fractured Spanish and Juanita's noisy tears to ascertain that Patrick was safely found with his aunt Molly, that his parents hadn't been apprised of his disappearance, and that his younger brother Sean was safely home in bed where he belonged.

By the time Molly hung up, her head was pounding as badly as her butt. Patrick didn't so much as lift his head from where it was cradled in his arms. Million-dollar suit coat unbuttoned and thousand-dollar tie pulled, Frank sat on a chair that was tilted against the wall, a beer in hand and Magnum's head in his lap.

The single Fifth District detective who ended up arriving, a short, squat woman Molly didn't know or particularly like, had already come and gone with bone, notes, and disinterest firmly in hand. It was only left to see what to do with Molly's surprise guest before she could collapse upstairs.

Molly considered her nephew and battled twin instincts to comfort and chastise. "You could have said something, Patrick."

"About what?" he demanded, head lifting. "My being kicked out of school? You were a little preoccupied, Aunt Molly. I couldn't tell you that without telling you why, and once you get the words 'I was expelled from school' out, people tend to stop listening."

She didn't relax her posture, as if that could protect her from further surprise. "So, try me."

Patrick was picking at his sleeves, throwing off little shrugs as if they were accusations. "It wasn't my fault."

"Not exactly original, Patrick."

He threw off a couple more halfhearted shrugs. "They blamed it on me because I was in the library right before it happened. But it was two other guys, and nobody'd believe me when I told them. I swear, Aunt Molly. I didn't do it!"

"And that would be?"

His eyes dipped again, like signal flags. "Set the fire."

"Ah."

He faced her again with a glare of outrage. "See what I mean? You don't believe me either."

"I don't know you well enough to believe you, Patrick. Especially considering the fact that the first time I saw you in six years you had a purloined Rembrandt sketch in one hand and a priceless jade carving in the other."

"You picked the best stuff right away, I see," Frank acknowledged. "Good instincts."

Molly ignored him.

"I figured . . ." Down went Patrick's head. Up went the shoulders. "I don't know . . . nobody gives a damn what I do at home. Why should you?"

"Juanita was beside herself," Molly said. "She was just about to get in touch with your parents."

"I told you. They're in China."

"You know, it's amazing. China is getting to be a very modern country. It even has phone service now. Which means you don't have an excuse for not calling them with the news."

He just shrugged. "Like they really give a rat's ass what happens to me."

With any other kid, Molly would have argued the point. *Of course your parents care what happens to you. It may not seem like it . . .*

But Molly knew Patrick's parents. At least she used to know them. And truth be told? She didn't have a clue whether Marty would even notice Patrick had disappeared if he were still in that fancy house in Virginia with him.

"What about Sean?" she asked of Patrick's younger brother.

His sneer said it all. "Ah, the shining light. The real heir apparent. Obvious to everyone from the day of his blessed birth."

Molly could have been a lot tougher on Patrick if she

hadn't understood that sentiment all too well herself. It was tough getting noticed when you had to be seen past perfection.

"Juanita also seems to be missing some cash . . ."

That brought Patrick right to his feet. "I didn't take it! I've been using my credit card. God, what do you think I am?"

Molly carefully shrugged. "I don't know. But whatever's going on, you're going to have to go home and face it."

For a second he closed his eyes, as if struggling with her betrayal. When he finally opened them and faced her, Molly saw the kid who didn't relate to anything but abandonment.

"Why?" he demanded. "They don't care where I am. I can go to school anywhere. What if I just stayed here for a while?"

"I work two jobs, Patrick. And no matter what you'd like to believe, you're still not an adult. And to be perfectly frank, I'm not sure I'd leave you alone all day with the booty in this house."

"Give me a chance," he pleaded. "Nobody else has."

No, she thought. Yes.

A child. A child who was the age hers might have been. Back in the days when she'd wanted children so badly she'd tried anything to have them.

It was a stupid impulse, one her therapist would have identified and quashed in a minute. If she still had a therapist. Number three on her list of things to do tomorrow. Get in touch with Patrick's parents. Make sure the bone was a stupid mistake. Find a new therapist.

Tomorrow was going to be a very busy day.

"We'll talk after I get in touch with your father," she decided, straightening. "Which, blessings to the gods of communications, I can do tomorrow. Which also, thankfully, is two full days before I have to go back to work, so that I can keep an eye on you. Till then, you can do some manual labor around here to make up for my having to spend my evening with the police."

"I didn't do anything," he protested yet again.

"You can have the room you and Sean share when you

come into town." When they'd come into town the three times in their lives. "Don't try and sneak anywhere, because Magnum will let me know. He's not used to you yet, and he might hurt you."

"He's sure used to *him*," Patrick challenged, motioning to Frank, who still sat on his tilted chair enjoying the drama.

Molly scowled. "I have no explanation for that."

"Dog has taste," Frank said with a lazy smile.

"Dog's been bribed," Molly retorted, and stretched with meaning. "Now then, gentlemen, before anyone has a chance to do something stupid like dump the rest of that skeleton or my other nephew over the backyard fence, I'm going to bed. I suggest you do the same."

Frank grinned like a sailor on leave. "Happy to."

Molly glared. "At your house, Frank," she said. "Where your children live, who probably miss you, even in their sleep."

Even so, Frank waited until Patrick was safely upstairs before letting Molly usher him out the door. As he stood there on her porch, the mist glistening in his hair and his shoulders hunched a little against the breeze, Frank took a considered look upstairs.

"Far be it from me to give you advice, St. Molly—"

"Considering I'd never take it."

He grinned. "Considering that." He motioned up toward the light that had just gone on in the right front window. "Be careful, St. Molly. I'm not sure that's your battlefield."

Molly didn't know whether to laugh or cry. "I know it isn't, Frank. But sometimes we don't exactly get to choose."

Frank contemplated her a minute and shook his head, his eyes wry. "No wonder you're the Martyr of the Midwest."

She scowled. "You can call me names the day you desert those three kids of yours and Joey, your homeless friend."

"I didn't have a choice," he challenged. "My wife died and Joey was my catcher when I pitched Khoury League."

Joey, who went to Vietnam with Frank and never really came home. But that was a problem for another day. Frank was still staring at her, waiting for an answer.

"I'll be fine, Frank."

His grin was the stuff of sexual harassment suits. "I know how to make you better."

Molly laughed so loud her voice echoed off the house across the street. "Dream on, tort boy."

Frank laughed, too, but Molly knew damn well he wasn't retreating. He smiled and dipped his head in a formal kind of salute.

"Just remember what I said," he said. "Never trust a teenage boy. Especially *that* teenage boy."

Then, with an elegant flick of his wrist, he pressed the instant start button on his keychain, and his Mercedes purred to life in the driveway.

"Now, this teenager is going home," he told her. "Unfulfilled. Unloved."

"Unrepentant."

He grinned, just as she knew he would, and dropped a kiss on her forehead before swinging down the steps.

Maggie watched him go, and then locked up the house.

She went to bed that night and dreamed of other battlefields where she'd cared for other young boys. She dreamed of hot jungles and cold indifference and fear.

And the worst part was that when she woke up the next morning, it was the fear that followed her into the light.

nobody sees what she does
even my daddy
nobody sees me in the
dark place

I HATE her

THREE

Molly's wake-up call the next morning sounded distressingly like an accusation.

"You obviously think I've been bored."

Rubbing hard at sleep-encrusted eyes, Molly turned to check the bedside alarm clock. Nine A.M. Way too early to be fielding outraged phone calls from her second boss.

"Morning, Winnie," she grated, closing her eyes again and settling back into bed to ease the pounding in her head. "How are you?"

"I'm seriously considering hiring a new death investigator," the St. Louis City Chief Medical Examiner informed her with little patience. "One who doesn't go out drumming up new business for this department. I have real work to do here. I do not have time to play with painted Tinker Toys."

Which meant that Winnie had gotten hold of the bone before Molly'd had a chance to explain.

Molly sighed. "I agree with you."

That didn't mollify her boss a bit. "Get down here," Winnie growled. "Today."

And hung up.

Molly groaned. She did not want to go in to see Winnie. The Chief Medical Examiner, when in a less than charitable mood, was a terrifying spectacle to behold. And Molly just

wasn't up to terrifying spectacles today. Every joint and muscle protested at shattering pitch, she was exhausted, and she
had to figure a way to get Patrick back home before she made
the inexcusable mistake of trying to save him from himself.

Ah, Patrick. A bigger problem than any she faced at either
of her real jobs. A bigger potential disaster wrapped in hormones, self-righteous indignation, and bravado.

But, God, she thought, closing her eyes, she felt sorry for
him. She'd grown up in a house much like his, with parents
always off to more important obligations than their children.
She'd spent way too much of her life trying to be good
enough to merit their notice.

Martin and Catherine Louise Burke's real children had
been framed on their walls and tucked onto glass shelves in
the sitting room, their real accomplishments listed in obscure
State Department dispatches from unexceptional countries.
When they died, they were mourned by no one, least of all
the daughter who had disappointed them from the day she'd
been born.

One Christmas about eight years ago after sufficiently for-
tifying herself on egg nog and scotch, Molly had tried to
warn her brother Martin that he was perilously close to
matching his parents' behavior. He'd been so grateful that he
hadn't said another word to her for five years.

Until today, Molly really hadn't cared.

Oh well. Nothing for it but to get her next confrontation
with her little brother over with. Wincing her way out of bed,
she spent a long few minutes soaking away morning-after
agony in a hot shower and then gingerly made her way downstairs to let her dog out and ingest vitamins, Paxil, and coffee,
in that order.

Patrick was there ahead of her.

Molly would have sworn that teenagers never rose before
noon of their own volition. But there was Patrick, now in
white T-shirt and the same rumpled, oversize khaki work
pants, standing before the Picasso in the family room as if
sizing it up for market.

"You can't have that one either," Molly greeted him from the doorway.

The family room was the only room in the house that was truly Molly's. While the rest of the house reeked of pervasive museumism, this room was lived in. A brace of overstuffed chintz couches sat at ninety-degree angles beneath windows that exposed her own museum-quality yard. End tables spilled over with magazines, books, and tchotchkes her neighbor Sam had given her. A utilitarian TV sat in one corner, and an underused sound system took up another. At center stage reigned the Picasso, a sharp, savage painting from his postdivorce period, all angles and great misplaced eyes with tears that pierced like weapons.

Old Picasso and Molly had become good friends. Besides the Winslow Homer watercolor she'd absconded with for her bedroom, it was the only indigenous part of this house she truly enjoyed.

"Ya know," Patrick mused, head tilted to consider the jagged passion of the piece. "I remember the first time I saw this house. I mean, I'd heard Mom and Dad talk about it, but I guess I really didn't believe them. It seemed . . . too much. Like a story kids would tell to impress their friends."

Molly thought of the priceless artifacts she mostly ignored these days and nodded. "Yeah. I know."

"I didn't want to live in our house. I wanted to live here. Our house is . . . seriously unexceptional. Carefully tasteless, like a chain hotel with money."

Molly had seen his mother's decorating, and she had to agree. Bland extraordinaire, with abortive attempts at *House Beautiful*. Everything in precise place and clean enough to do open-heart surgery on. But without any real taste. Molly's parents might have had many faults, but they had never lacked style.

"It's not all it's cracked up to be," she said anyway.

But then, Patrick couldn't hear the whispers of disdain that crept along the floors or smell the old, stale secrets that were forever hidden away beneath exquisite carpets.

He turned on her, stiff with resentment. "You don't even like it here."

Molly smiled. "Nope. But that doesn't mean I'm leaving." And then she walked out to get that coffee.

It took the entire morning to track down Patrick's parents in Beijing, where it was even later the next morning. Molly felt absolutely no remorse at interrupting an official luncheon.

"Patrick?" her brother Martin said in bemused tones. "He's fine. Why are you calling me in China to ask me about Patrick?"

"Because he's here with me, Martin. He evidently decided to make use of his inheritance a little earlier than expected, and came a thousand miles to collect it."

What followed was a silence punctuated by bursts of muffled mumbles. Conferencing with the missus, evidently. What Molly noticed was that her announcement hadn't been met by any outraged disbelief. *What? Our Patrick? Impossible. I just talked to him* kind of thing.

What she finally did get was a disconcerted clearing of the throat, and then a sigh. "It's nothing," Martin insisted. "Probably a misunderstanding."

Molly laughed out loud. "Martin," she assured him, "this is not a misunderstanding. This is a sixteen-year-old boy in my kitchen instead of his own house half a continent away, who was caught red-handed committing a Class A felony."

"Yeah . . . yeah, I know. But we're awfully committed here, Molly. We're *in* the middle of something important. And we wouldn't be able to straighten it out till we got home anyway."

"In time for Christmas, I assume."

"If all goes well, of course."

"And in the meantime?"

"Just send him back. Juanita will take care of it."

Molly saw red. "Juanita is a semiliterate Nicaraguan housemaid," she accused, "which would make her less than ideal to talk to the Jesuits about Patrick's expulsion from school, don't you think?"

"He . . ."

"The reason he thought he might need a little ready cash, evidently. He'll explain it to you when you get home."

Another sigh. A bitten curse. "We'll take care of it," he assured her. "And trust me. He'll be punished. He shouldn't be bothering you like this."

Bothering her. What a charming term for attempted burglary.

"Sean wasn't with him, was he?" Martin demanded suddenly, concern finally edging his voice. "He didn't talk Sean into this stupid stunt?"

"No. Evidently Sean is still safe in the arms of the Jesuits."

Molly was sure she heard a relieved sigh. "Well, we'll take care of it. As long as everything is intact at the house."

"What about Patrick?" she asked. "Who *is* at my house. What do we do about him?"

"He'll be back in school when the new term starts. I can promise you that."

Molly wasn't concerned about the new term. She was concerned about the next three or four weeks. She was terrified she was going to end up with this kid in her house for Christmas.

"Martin. What do I do with him now?"

"Just . . . oh, I don't know. Send him back to Juanita."

Molly said it before she even thought about it. She said it because she knew that if she sent Patrick back right now, he'd just think of something even worse to get his parents' attention. And in this day and age, at sixteen, worse covered a lot of ground.

"Tell you what," she said. "Stop by St. Louis on your way home and you can pick him up here. I'll put him to work to pay for the trouble."

She got another telling pause, and then her brother's hesitant voice. "You sure? Between you and me, he can be a real handful."

"I gathered that. All I ask is that you keep in touch. You want to talk to him?"

"Oh . . . well, I'm sure his mother would like to, of course."

Molly fought a surge of renewed anger and remembered just why she only had these family chats when they had to update the trust.

"Patrick, your father's on the phone," she said, handing it over. "You're going to stay with me till they get back."

Patrick didn't react. He just took the phone and walked to the other end of the kitchen.

The conversation lasted only a few minutes. All Molly could gather from Patrick's end was that he'd mastered the art of the sulky grunt and bitten monosyllable. She found herself wondering by the end of it if his parents even knew he could speak English.

"My mother says to say thank you for taking me off their hands," he said finally, holding the phone out to her as if she'd used it to betray him.

Hand out, Molly snorted. "She did not."

Patrick just lifted an eyebrow, those soft hazel eyes briefly and intensely disdainful. "Thank you."

Well, at least his mother had said something. The punishment when Molly had been a child had been cold, exquisite silence. She could still see it on her mother, pursed lips and frosty eyes and a deliberate turning of the back. Molly would have sobbed with relief if her mother had given way to just one snarky shot.

"Did you bring clothes?" she asked, hanging up the phone.

"Some. Juanita will send me more."

"Okay," she said. "Next item of business is a job. They need bussers at a couple of the restaurants on Euclid, which is a block over, so you won't have to worry about driving."

Patrick glowered. "I drive."

"Not in my only form of transportation, you don't. I don't have any money to replace it. In fact, I don't have any money at all, so you're going to have to figure out how to enjoy yourself on a third of your paycheck, since the rest is going to go into room and board. But I'm happy to have you, Patrick. As long as you abide by my rules—which, I might as well tell you, are strict. Not only that, but my best friends all look just like Officer Smith. Do you get my point?"

He also seemed to have perfected the sneer. "You don't have any money? Have you seen what you have in your living room?"

"Not *my* living room, Patrick. I can't touch a thing in this house. I can't so much as move anything farther than two rooms in any direction. I only get the privilege of living here rent-free till I die, so it's intact for you and Sean and your children to be able not to touch. Next time you decide to take advantage of the trust, you might read its stipulations first. Now, I repeat. Are we agreed?"

"Without even knowing what the rules are?"

Molly's smile was dry. "This isn't a business deal. I will give you rule number one for free, which is an oldie but goodie. Thou shalt not steal. Not a Picasso, not a paperweight. The rest are just as easy to comprehend."

"Just your basic prison without so much as a VCR or Nintendo."

"I get enough death and violence at work. I don't need to rent it from Blockbuster, too."

"I bet you don't even have Internet."

Molly's smile was cheerful. "Sure. At work, where I actually might need it."

"Then how do I get hold of my friends?"

"Ya know," she said, really tired of this already. "I hear there's a great new invention by this guy named Franklin. It's called a post office. And it costs under fifty cents to use. You might want to try it."

For just a flash of a second, Patrick betrayed rage. Hot, teen frustration. Then he seemed to reconsider. He took one long look around and shrugged, determined to be surly. "Well, it'll probably be the only chance I'll have to live here until I'm fifty."

Molly smiled. "You're welcome. Now go on upstairs and make your bed. I'll have the rules printed up and taped to your door in an hour." Patrick was set to turn around, when a thought occurred to Molly. "By the way. What were you going to do with the Rembrandt? You don't know anybody in St. Louis to sell it to."

He didn't bother to face her. "I don't know . . . I guess I wasn't thinking."

Molly didn't believe him for a minute. But she figured she was going to have plenty of time to get the real story. In the meantime, she took a step closer and spread her arms, intent on sealing her welcome with a hug.

Patrick startled like a horse faced with fire.

Molly had never felt so ineffectual. She'd hugged families she'd never met, patients and parents and paramedics. Other nurses, children by the dozen. For some reason, though, she couldn't manage that elementary act with her very skittish nephew.

A simple hug. A pat on the back. And standing three feet away from one of a handful of blood relatives she had on earth, Molly knew he wouldn't accept it. So she threw off a casual little wave and left it at that.

Patrick turned and headed toward the stairs, and Molly sighed. Too bad it was too early in the day for a drink.

"And just what are we supposed to do with this?"

Perched on one foot in front of the mahogany desk of the St. Louis Medical Examiner, Molly looked from the bagged femur to the rigidly furious woman holding it like an unhappily discovered rat.

"I don't know," she said. "Wait for the left one to show up and make book ends?"

Dr. Jemimah Winnifred Sweet Harrison did not smile. Seated before a wall decorated in ferocious African war masks, she was the most ferocious presence in the room. Tall, elegant, with smooth mocha skin and almond-shaped eyes, she had the posture of a model and the temper of a longshoreman. Winnie was the best. Which meant that she had no time for anything or anyone who wasn't.

"I suppose you're going to want this tested," she challenged, her voice as sharp as a gunshot.

Molly sighed. "Not me. I voted to ignore the whole thing.

I'm telling you it's a harmless prank that ended up in my possession by mistake."

"There's another Molly Burke in your neighborhood who might consider this amusing?"

Molly couldn't take her eyes off her own name, painted in gold poster paint, swinging slowly before her eyes.

"If necessary, I'll find one."

Winnie went very still. A bad sign. "And?"

And.

Molly shrugged, disconcerted at how quickly her cavalier disregard for her own safety should come back to haunt her. She'd kind of forgotten to share some now-relevant bits of news with Winnie. "I've, uh, been getting notes."

The handsome face tightened into a scowl of epic proportions. "I know. I found that out, too. Not from you, of course. From some jumped-up meter maid named Plante from the Fifth, who, by the way, thinks you're doing this to yourself for the attention. Seems she's read a book on Munchausen by proxy."

Molly lifted an eyebrow. "The detective can read?"

Both of them wasted a second on half grins, and Molly had to admit that sometimes she was as impatient with the rest of the world as Winnie.

Winnie dropped the bone with a clunk that let everybody in earshot know that this wasn't a cheap plastic imitation. "I want a list of people who might want to threaten you. Plante might be right. You may be doing this because you're bored. But I won't be made a fool of if you show up dead and this was serious all along."

Molly barely controlled a laugh. "I don't think anybody's mad at me," she protested. "Well, except for a few people still waiting trial from the summer. But this doesn't strike me as that kind of thing. I thought the notes were more the 'You let my mother die'–type thing."

She'd *hoped* the notes were more the "You let my mother die"–type thing.

"It doesn't matter. I want the whole list. And I want that adolescent out of the Medical Examiner's offices."

Molly turned around to see Patrick perched on the edge of Winnie's secretary's desk smiling down at the woman as if she were a centerfold on the verge of unstapling.

"No problem."

Molly was creaking her way to her feet when Winnie finally noticed the obvious. "You get hit on the head with that bone, or is this some other little indiscretion you failed to notify this office about?"

It actually took Molly a second to figure out what Winnie was referring to. "Nothing for you," she finally said, "unless you suddenly get a surfeit of clowns in for autopsy. We had a clown-kicking commando in last night, and I happened to be the first clown she kicked."

Winnie nodded briskly. "Well, get it taken care of."

And here Molly thought stitches and pain medicine *were* taking care of it. "You bet."

"One more thing before you go."

Molly sat down. She knew that tone of voice.

"You get all the evidence in on the Wilson case yet?" Winnie demanded.

Molly took a second to regroup.

The Wilson case.

She didn't want to talk about the Wilson case. She didn't even want to think about the Wilson case.

Latesha Wilson was a twelve-year-old girl who had gone missing. A task force had searched for her for eight days. Posters, ribbons, pictures, rewards, the works. And all along the little girl had been lying alone in a wet, cold basement two blocks from home, nylons tied around her throat and her clothes in a pile in the corner.

Molly had been unlucky enough to catch that call. It had been her responsibility to take control of the body at the homicide scene, assessing it just as a homicide cop would, but with a medical as well as a forensic eye. She'd taken pictures and body temperature and documented rigor mortis, liver mortis, decomposition, insect activity, and every injury, great and small. She'd wrapped that thin, small child in a white sheet to protect microscopic hair and fiber evidence while the mother had screamed nonstop on the stoop outside, and she'd transported little Latesha back to the city morgue.

Now Molly was in charge of coordinating the information about the forensic findings from the Medical Examiner with the police and DA's office until they could get a perpetrator to trial.

And Molly wasn't the only one involved in the case who knew without being able yet to prove it that that screaming mother had known all along that her own boyfriend had killed her baby and stuffed her in a basement.

A terrible, lonely way to die. But standing down in that horrible basement, Molly had also thought of what Latesha Wilson would have had to look forward to had she lived.

No wonder she wasn't anticipating Christmas. Especially with another cast-off child on her hands.

"I'm still waiting for the lab to finish microscopics and DNA," she told her boss. "Everything else is there for you."

Winnie was nodding briskly, making a note to herself. "Just make sure this office doesn't screw up. I intend to have all the evidence the police need for a conviction."

"Me, too. Anything else?"

With her sharp gaze, Winnie kept considering the bone Molly had brought her, until Molly could almost believe that she could discern its secrets without a microscope.

"Tell me why this thing makes me nervous," Winnie suggested.

This time Molly did laugh. "Probably because whatever your idiosyncracies may be, femur tossing just isn't one of them."

"Or femur decorating." Winnie shook her head. "Is this something I should expect from you on a regular basis? If it is, let me know now. I hate surprises."

"Don't be silly," Molly scoffed. "If you hated surprises, you would have worked in a hospital lab. Not a city morgue."

Winnie didn't react past lifting the bone. "Here. Give this to one of the techs to sign in. We'll pass it along to the forensic anthropologists and see if it's a problem."

Molly accepted the bone and headed out of the office for

the morgue downstairs. She hadn't made it four steps before
Patrick popped off the secretary's desk and followed her.

"This is *such* a cool place," he said. "Why didn't you tell
us you worked here? There are, like, bodies back there, aren't
there, Aunt Molly?"

Molly stopped dead at the bottom of the stairs and faced
her too-excited nephew. "Whom you are not invited to visit.
Stay here. I'll be right back."

"You could get me a job here," he suggested to her back.

"No jobs open."

She could almost hear his cold displeasure, but he remained on good behavior by visiting with the receptionist
whose desk was the only thing in the echoing foyer of the
old white granite block building. Molly continued on back to
the morgue area where she could pass the bone off to one of
the intake techs who logged in bodies and protected personal
effects.

The tech was even more excited than Patrick.

"It'sch real pretty, ischn't it?" Lewis asked with a decided
lisp when he saw the bone. Lewis was shorter than Molly,
roly-poly and disheveled. And, unfortunately, he had a lisp. It
seemed to Molly, suddenly, that everybody was hissing at her.

She found herself staring at him. "What do you decorate
your house with, Lewis?"

He grinned to show a gap or two in his teeth. "Wouldn't
you like to know, Misch Burke? Wouldn't you juscht like to
know?"

Miss Burke was sure she just didn't. She hadn't worked
with Lewis long, but she figured they should be past the Miss
Burke stage by now. But then, Lewis was unfailingly polite
and devoted to the details that would have driven Molly in-
sane. And, to be frank, Lewis wasn't exactly waiting for that
big astrophysics grant, which made him content with the odd
hours and odder clients.

"Winnie would like it logged in," she said, motioning to
the bone in its bag. "It's going to need to be tested."

"One bone full of red and gold paint," he said, taking hold
with short, square hands. "What'sch to tescht?"

Whether or not the bone was from a medical supply house. Whether it was an old bone, the kind that kept popping up in the St. Louis area every time the mass transit needs crossed old, untended cemetery land. Whether it really was enough to give Molly fresh nightmares.

Oh no, she thought with a mental shake of her head. That was a path she did not plan to follow. Her nightmare schedule was already booked up, thanks very much.

"Winnie has a call in to an anthropologist," Molly said and thanked him. And got out before she let Lewis creep her out, too.

"Now," she said, picking up her nephew from where he was making the receptionist smile. "Let's go find you a job."

They found him a job. Even better, they found him a job with hours that almost matched Molly's. So they bought him black pants and white shirts—on his credit card—for his bussing position and got him keys for the house. And for the next three days Molly redesigned her life to accommodate another person.

"It's not really that bad," she told Sasha on the fourth day as the two of them drew up meds side by side in the medicine alcove.

Sasha snorted. "Wearing pantyhose is not that bad," she retorted. "Inheriting a teenager is a disaster."

"Yeah, well, I guess this is God's way of letting me know once and for all if I could have made a good mother."

Sasha stopped cold. "You are not being a mother," she informed Molly. "You're being a baby-sitter. You are keeping the little monster out of prison until his parents come back from wherever the hell it is they are to lock him up in his own city."

Molly grinned. "That's what I love about you, Sasha. Your almost maudlin sentimentality. Trust me. I have no intention of making this a permanent situation. I'm too old and poor for that. Patrick is a kid who needs deep pockets . . . and deaf parents. You should hear what he listens to. I am really not used to that."

"My point exactly."

"Besides, what with the notes and all, it's kind of nice to have somebody else in the house."

"As long as he isn't the one writing the notes."

"They were mailed in St. Louis, Sash. Besides, he hasn't even seen me in six years. How could I make him that mad?"

Patrick had also really seemed surprised by the sight of that femur. The femur Molly hadn't told Sasha about. But then, there was just so much disapprobation she could handle in one eight-hour shift. Especially one as busy as this.

"Hey, you guys," one of the brand-new nurses greeted them on the run, her eyes wide like a bunny. "What do you know about giving thrombolytic treatment for MIs?"

"I know you want to make sure the patient's upstairs before they try it. It's a one-on-one nursing situation."

"He wants me to give it now."

"He who?" Sasha demanded.

"Spizer."

"Does the guy fit the criteria?"

The nurse, a young Korean girl named Nancy, shrugged. "I don't know. What's the criteria?"

"See, that's what I love about working here," Molly philosophized, capping the syringe that held her patient's Ativan. "It's so challenging that for a few hours I can forget all about silly things like the rest of my life."

"You were going to quit three days ago," Sasha reminded her.

"Three days ago I didn't have a family to support. You want to do the tPA or shall I?"

"I'll do it. You pick up my other ten patients." They were already walking as they talked. "Room five is waiting for films, room six is old Mr. Peabody, and Wilma's in five for her regular pelvic."

"We have any new staff I should know about?"

"You mean housekeeping cross-trainees? Not tonight. Tonight we're lucky."

"Yeah. Tonight we have a ten-year-old nurse and Spizer, who wants us to treat everything right here, just like he sees on *ER*."

Sasha shrugged as she bent for IV equipment to start treatment on the cardiac patient. "It could be worse."

Molly smacked her on the ass. "Bite your tongue."

Because, of course, it would almost certainly get worse. Especially when called like that, like an incantation.

And it did. At least it did for Molly.

She was in trying to talk Spizer out of doing a lumbar puncture on a lady with a bladder infection a couple of hours later when she was paged to the desk. Molly only had to step out into the hall to realize that whatever the secretary wanted her for, it was definitely not business as usual.

"This came for you," Marianne said, just pointing, her eyes wide with disbelief.

So were Molly's, but for a completely different reason. After working with Molly for less than a year, Marianne Senkosky, a snotty blonde with a sincere aversion to effort, simply couldn't imagine that anybody in his right mind would send Molly long-stemmed roses. Molly took one look at the box that rested at the secretary's station and knew that the question was far more complicated.

"Don't touch it," she warned, her hands suddenly sweaty.

Marianne lifted a penciled-on eyebrow. "Afraid I'm going to contaminate it?"

Yes, Molly thought, her head whirling. Behind her Sasha and Spizer showed up for the surprise. Molly didn't even turn to acknowledge them.

"Who brought this in?" she asked Marianne, trying her best to see something identifiable on the box.

It was just plain. White. Long. Full.

"A florist, I assume. But heck, I could just be jumping to conclusions here."

"You want to explain this sudden paralysis over horticulture?" Sasha asked quietly.

Molly sucked in a breath. "Can you do me a favor?" she asked just as carefully. "Get me a pair of forceps."

There was silence all around the desk now. But leave it to Sasha. She just reached into her lab coat pocket and lifted out what, in lay terms, would have been called big tweezers. Then she handed them off to Molly as if assisting in surgery.

"Is this about the notes?" Sasha asked.

"Kind of," Molly responded, sliding one side of the forceps up under the lid to make sure there weren't any barriers. "I, uh, got a kind of weird thing landed in my yard the other night . . . in a box like this."

"What?"

By now, several more people had shown up, all facing the box that lay on the high secretary's counter like a sacrifice on an altar. Molly was busy trying to get a good grip on the lid without contaminating it.

"Oh, something just a little twisted."

Considering the fact that anyone who worked in an urban trauma center was perfectly acquainted with twisted, each person there leaned a little closer. If Molly thought this deserved special merit, it must be memorable.

Molly barely noticed. Her attention was on the effort it took to lift the lid off the box, which was only happening in fits and starts. She could hear paper rustle inside. She could feel the sudden thunder of her heart. Her stomach was churning, and sweat trickled down her temples. After all, one bone could be a joke. Two was definitely a problem.

The lid lifted clear, and Molly smelled it. Faint, fresh, familiar enough to send her into a rage.

"Aw . . . *shit!*"

It was Marianne, of course, who offered the first comment. "Well, I'm glad I'm not the only one who'd think it's weird that somebody'd send you flowers."

Roses. A dozen of them. Garnet red, exotic and lush, their perfume tickling Molly's nose and inciting even greater frenzy. Because there, tucked in the folds of the tissue, was the note.

Thought this time you'd like something more fun than hearts and crosses.

> love
> Frank

"That son of a bitch," Molly breathed, shaking with the effort it took to control the urge to take that box and heave it out into the street. To heave something at Frank's head.

"You're right," Marianne sniped. "I'd think a guy was a total jerk if he sent me flowers."

"Frank the lawyer sent you those?" Sasha asked.

Most of the rest of the staff was laughing and walking away. Molly couldn't quite put the lid back in place. "Yes," she snapped.

"And you think that's . . . what?"

Molly finally turned on her friend. "Pretty goddamn typical. He's not being sweet, Sasha. He's being a jerk. Because he was there when I got the last box."

"The last box. That being?"

Molly sucked in a breath. "A human femur decorated in paint."

Even Sasha reacted to that. "Really."

"Addressed to me. In paint. On the bone."

Unfortunately, Sasha couldn't seem to help smiling as she shook her head. "He is something, isn't he?"

Molly wasn't in the least amused. "He's going to be one of Winnie's clients pretty damn soon."

Sasha wasn't particularly impressed. Pulling one of the roses from the box, she expertly broke it close to the bud and slid the bud into her lab coat like a boutonniere. "So let me get this straight. You're mad because you *didn't* get a bone instead of flowers?"

"I'm mad because he isn't taking this seriously."

Molly hadn't, either, of course. Well, she'd been trying not to. Not until she'd seen this second box, anyway. But Sasha didn't need to know that.

Sasha shrugged. "In that case, don't give him the satisfaction. Enjoy the flowers. We'll talk about this bone business later."

And Sasha walked off. Molly took a couple of minutes to dump the other eleven roses in the trash and then headed the other way.

By the end of the evening, everybody sported roses in

their lab coats courtesy of Frank Patterson. And Molly, still furious, had to at least admit that Frank had served a purpose. Not only was the staff looking pretty darned dapper, but Molly found herself resettled into her "It's all a mistake" frame of mind.

Unfortunately, that only lasted another twenty-four hours, until she opened her back door to find her dog licking something in the backyard.

Something that glittered.

he dosn't believe me
i told him i told him i told him
she ment it
she Held my hand rite there
rite there
in the door
and then she slammed
she sed its because Im slow
and stupid
my fingers are broke
and he dusnt beleeve me

FOUR

Molly had put in another long evening shift, this time in the Medical Examiner's office, where she cleared nine natural deaths and investigated a suicide and a double homicide. It was always this way so close to Christmas. The quotas for the Heavenly Immigration Bureau had to be met by New Year's, and, as usual, St. Peter was playing catch-up.

So, by the time she pulled into her driveway at about one in the morning, Molly was ready for some tea, some quiet, and a good stab at sleep. What she got instead was company.

There on her front porch, in the cold, waiting for her.

Molly really wasn't surprised to see her neighbor Sam standing there. Eighty years old and alone, he didn't sleep much more than Molly, and knew this was his best time to bring her any little problems that needed solving.

He was perched right under her porchlight; small, square, hunched, and panting with the exertion of crossing her lawn, a cigarette in his wide mouth and his eyebrows bushy enough to take flight. But he wasn't watching for Molly. He was in the midst of a discussion with Sasha.

Sasha, who rarely saw fit to cross another threshold—especially bearing gifts of alcohol and cheese.

Molly's first thought was that she wasn't sure she enjoyed all her sudden company. Her second was, of course, that it was better than putting up with a still-sulking Patrick. So she stepped out of her Celica and slammed the door shut.

"Why didn't I get an invitation to this party?" she demanded.

Sam beamed like a kid and let go a racking, emphysema-fueled cough. "Molly, *bubbe*. Such lovely company you give me for waiting."

Molly headed up the walk. "And what's Myra going to say when she finds out you're ogling blondes behind her back?"

Sam laughed. "I'm not meshugge, sweetheart. Myra never needs to know."

Sasha was watching them both as if they were mimes. Sam patted her like a five-year-old.

"And such a shiksa," he said. "Being lucky enough to spend time with both of you, I could die happy, *nu*?"

Molly had lived in her house for five years. In that time, she'd seen Sam go from Lee Iacocca to Georgie Jessel. Of course, she'd also seen his wife, Myra, disintegrate into the morass of Alzheimer's in a nursing home, and both of his children move away with his grandchildren.

But heck, who really minded being cosseted by the grandfather of the year? Besides, it was huge fun to see that great white business shark peek out from those apple-doll eyes every so often.

Gaining the small porch, she bussed him on the cheek. "You can lighten up on the Sholom Aleichem roadshow a little, Sam. Sasha makes it a point never to be impressed by local color."

He wagged a finger at her. "There's an old Jewish saying, you know."

Molly laughed. "I know. Respect your elders. Especially when they bring you tea."

Sasha lifted an eyebrow. "This is getting much too Catskills for this Episcopalian."

"You should get out of West County more, Sash," Molly said, then shook her head with an amazed little grin. "But then, it seems that you have. Hello, Sasha. What are you doing here? Natural disaster? Impending scandal? Or did you finally kill Spizer and just wanted to help me with the paperwork?"

Sasha didn't so much as smile. "Illegal blood alcohol level. I was at a Christmas party and decided it wasn't prudent to try and make the wilds of Eureka right now. This seemed a likely way station."

Molly pulled out her keys to open the door. "Sure. What the hell? You want me to adopt you till Christmas, too?"

"God, no. A cup of coffee and a Breathalyzer will do."

As she attacked the front door lock, Molly cadged a quick look at her surprise guest. The wine in Sasha's hand was a rather vintage Châteaux Margaux, and the cheese something even Molly didn't recognize. She wished she got invited to that kind of party. She wished she looked quite as well put together as Sasha with an illegal amount of alcohol in her system. Sasha was in a sleek black silk pantsuit and tailored cashmere coat. Molly, coming off duty in her moss green death investigator business suit, looked for all the world like Tootsie after a hard day under the television lights. But then, it didn't take Sasha to impress Molly with the fact that life was unfair.

"Come on in," she invited them both.

Sam patted Sasha again, which was threatening Molly's composure. "You're a good girl. I'll make tea for you, *nu*?"

Molly punched the alarm code and ushered the way in. "Not if she wants to drive home sober, Sam."

Sam waved her off. "*Feh!* It's just a little added warmth on a cold night."

"There's an old Irish saying, you know," Molly retorted as she ushered everyone in.

Sam just chuckled and headed for the kitchen, where Magnum greeted him with joyous barks. Magnum loved Sam. Sam fed him the leftovers Molly wouldn't.

"Good God," Sasha drawled when she got a look at the dog. "Is there any small wildlife left in your neighborhood?"

Molly set things down and turned on the bright kitchen lights to uncover dirty dishes in her usually spotless sink, a milk carton on her kitchen table, and her African violets on the windowsill pushed aside to make room for a CD player. She sighed. This other person in the house business was beginning to wear.

Blithely ignoring the mess, Sam creaked and clattered his way over to fill Molly's teapot. Sasha sank into a kitchen chair and laid down her booty. Magnum took one step her way. Sasha stopped him in his tracks with a single glacial look.

Molly shook her head in wonder. "How do you do that?"

"I practice on residents and nursing students."

Molly gave her dog a consolation rub and let him out.

"Myra sends her love, by the way," Sam wheezed, his attention on stove settings. "If you don't mind, I have a few forms for her I need help filling out."

"No problem."

"And a few questions about her new medicines. You know so much about medicine. I just know the *momzer* insurance companies are screwing me."

"Then you know more than most people, Sam. I'd be happy to. Is Myra doing well?"

"Beautifully, *kine-ahora*. She loves the new television."

Myra wouldn't recognize a television if somebody implanted the definition straight into her cerebral cortex. Molly smiled anyway. "Good, Sam. That's wonderful."

"Oh, another thing," he said. "When you were over before, did you see my milk money?"

His milk money. The money he kept squirreled away for the delivery boy who brought all his groceries. In this day and age of superchains and discount stores, one chain in St. Louis, Straub's, still held by tradition and cosseted their special customers by delivering groceries without resorting to the Internet. And Sam was a special customer.

"It was in your cookie jar," she said. The one shaped like Winnie the Pooh for the grandkids who rarely got to see it anymore.

Setting out mugs, Sam nodded. "Ah. I thought I'd put it out for Little Allen. Such a good boy."

Little Allen being thirty and taller than Sam. But then, if a guy was still delivering groceries at thirty, maybe he did deserve the appellation "Little Allen."

"Speaking of good boys," Sasha said. "How is the great experiment coming along?"

Molly was busy cleaning dishes out of her sink. "I'll let you know in a week."

"*Gottenyu*, such a sad thing," Sam mourned. In front of him the teapot whistled, adding tenor counterpoint. "A beautiful child like that left on a doorstep."

Molly grimaced. "He wasn't exactly left on the doorstep."

Out in the back, Magnum suddenly began to bark. Excited, defensive, anxious. Molly peered out the window to see a shadow drop down over the grille fence that separated her yard from Euclid. Ah, the great experiment itself.

Both Sasha and Sam looked up as the back door opened.

"Wow," Patrick greeted them. "You sure keep odd hours, Aunt Molly."

"Patrick," Sam beamed. "How was work?"

Patrick shucked off his duster and smiled back. "Fine, Mr. Spiegel. How's Mrs. Spiegel?"

"Fine. She sends her love."

"You're coming in kind of late from the restaurant," Molly said.

Never making eye contact, Patrick tossed his coat onto a chair and opened the cabinet above the sink. "We had some deliveries we had to put away. Did you know Magnum's outside gnawing on something? He didn't even come to the fence when I showed up."

Molly took a superstitious look out the back window. "Gnawing on something?"

He nodded, his eyes just a little too avid as he pulled out a mug to set in line with the others. "Uh-huh. I thought it was one of those bones Mr. Spiegel throws him, but he was acting weird. It was from you, Mr. Spiegel, wasn't it?"

Molly looked over at Sam, but Sam shook his head. "Not since that unfortunate accident on your aunt's new shoes."

Molly took a careful peek outside. It was stupid. It was

childish. But she was suddenly very nervous. "You didn't see it."

Patrick shook his head, breathing a little fast, eyes really wide now. "He wouldn't let me close. You don't think . . ."

Molly sucked in a breath and pulled open the door. "Magnum!" she yelled. "Come here!"

She got nothing more than a single bark. Magnum never disobeyed. Except when Sam threw him one of his soup bones.

"Oh, I hate this," Molly moaned to herself.

"You really did get a human bone?" Sasha asked.

"No, Sasha," Molly snapped. "I made it up because I wasn't getting enough attention at work."

And then, because there was nothing else she could do, she stalked out into her yard.

And found out that this time she hadn't gotten a bone.

She'd gotten something far worse.

Molly didn't call the police. She knew she should. She sat in her kitchen for five hours staring at the flower box she'd been able to get away from Magnum, and she still couldn't force herself to take the next step.

Eyes.

Someone had left her eyes.

Tucked into cotton this time. Cotton that had been drawn on, in glitter like eye shadow and Magic Marker for a nose. And eyes, real eyes, nested in a soft, cotton face. Part of a face. A slice of a face, as if seen through a fence.

Eyes.

Eye.

By the time Molly had gotten outside, Magnum had been stained with marker and glitter, and only one eye lay in the box.

A blue eye.

A blue eye surrounded by a child's art project face and addressed with the kind of gold letters teachers tacked to blackboards.

This is for Molly Burke.

Molly wanted to vomit. She wanted to cry.

Sam had begged her to call the police. Sasha suggested the *Enquirer*, so Molly could pay off her lawsuit. Patrick asked if he could call a couple of his friends in D.C. And Molly, wishing with all her heart she'd get a call from Frank saying it was somehow another joke, just sat there.

She simply couldn't face what was in that box. She couldn't face the fact that somebody was angry enough to send it to her along with those nasty notes.

No, though. That couldn't be it. Anybody might send nasty notes. They wouldn't go to the trouble of finding a femur.

And eyes.

Blue eyes.

Did medical supply houses have eyes? They supplied cow eyes. Molly had dissected them in training. Would ophthalmologists need human eyes to practice on?

Would somebody be angry or crazy enough that they would seek out someplace like that? To lay in a supply of body parts for the purpose of terrorizing a forensic nurse?

Molly simply couldn't wrap her brain around it. She couldn't face what would happen the minute she shared the news. So she put off the call. Instead she sat there at her kitchen table long after Sam walked home and Sasha drove out to West County. Long after even Patrick gave up and headed upstairs. She broke open a bottle of Stoly and gave herself a real cup of Sam's tea and still didn't feel better. But she didn't call.

She waited until she walked out into her foyer to get her mail the next morning and discovered her sixth note.

"You're threatening to become more trouble than you're worth," Winnie warned.

Molly had called the police. Winnie had called her back. Now Molly sat with Winnie and Kevin McNally, the city's senior death investigator, in the conference room at the ME's office, where she was supposed to come up with some idea of what was behind her little gifts.

Tough to think straight enough to do when she was still shaking. She had spent another bad few minutes on the floor of her foyer. She had spent even longer in her bathroom. Patrick had pounded on the door for five minutes to get her to answer Winnie's call.

Above her shoulder now the winter sun poured through the dusty window like watered milk. The conference room was uninspiring. Off-white walls, dim gold carpeting somebody must have stolen from an old convent, and one dingy window that looked out over the equally uninspiring granite police station next door. It was the room that had once held the coroner's inquests. The perfect place for a little light grilling.

"Do you have my list?" Winnie demanded.

Another answer Winnie wouldn't like. Molly had sat at her kitchen table with that damn pad of paper in front of her all morning long. She'd pulled out a pencil. Broken the point. Pulled out two ballpoints and another cup of tea—this one unadulterated—and tried her damnedest to put one name on that page.

She simply hadn't known where to start.

Eyes. He'd sent her eyes.

"I tried," she said without enormous enthusiasm, her attention on the fine tremor in her hands where she'd splayed them over the scarred tabletop. "I just can't imagine anybody who'd be . . . uh, creative enough to do this."

"Doctors," Kevin McNally offered from across the table.

Kevin was Molly's immediate boss. Kevin had hired Molly one week into her malpractice trial, and had quietly supported her through some fairly tough times. Kevin was the exception to the rule that redheads had fiery tempers. He might look like the poster child for St. Patrick's Day, but even caught in an archaic political system like St. Louis and working with someone as mercurial as Winnie, he'd never been caught raising his voice. But then, Kevin, who was skinny and slow-moving in the office, was also a triathlete. Probably took out all his frustrations on his feet.

Molly shook her head at him. "Doctors don't need to go to this much trouble. They can just cost me my job." She grinned wryly. "It's sure been done before."

"Someone involved in that lawsuit of yours," Winnie suggested.

Molly had considered the lawsuit. It had certainly made *her* mad enough to send nasty notes.

It hadn't been that complicated a disaster. A chronic patient had come into Molly's last ED complaining of abdominal pain and died of a stroke. Everyone had been sued for misdiagnosis and neglect. Molly had been sued because she hadn't tried hard enough to pry the ED doctor out of the bathroom where he'd hidden so he didn't have to see another patient. Just another stellar chapter in the life of Molly Burke.

Again Molly shook her head. "The only person frustrated enough to send hate mail from that is me. The family got a fortune, the hospital passed enough blame around to not get stiffed for the whole amount, and the patient's lawyer could finance his way to Congress on what he made."

"The lawyer you're now dating."

Molly bristled. "I am not dating him." When Winnie glared, Molly retreated to a shrug. "He just keeps coming over."

Even Kevin didn't know quite how to react.

"He wouldn't go to the trouble," Molly assured them both. "Trust me."

He would, of course, send roses just to make Molly mad. But she'd already made the phone call to clear up that little prank. Molly was convinced that Frank had just been . . . Frank. He wasn't mad. He wasn't crazy. He was just . . . Frank.

"What about the doctor? Didn't you testify against him?"

Molly shrugged. "His insurance covered it. He now has a lucrative practice in Alton."

"Somebody else, then," Winnie snapped, tapping the desk with manicured fingers. "Another patient. A lover. A neighbor."

A lover, Molly thought with a wry grin. Definitely a lover. She'd had so many of those she'd lost track. No, come to think of it, it wasn't the lovers she'd lost track of, it was the sex. She couldn't remember the last time she'd had sex. In fact, if she maintained her current condition, in just a few more months, she could consider herself rehymenated. Maybe she should have taken Frank up on his offer after all.

"Nobody's said anything," she said.

"And nobody saw or heard anything either time," Kevin said.

Molly shook her head. "I asked everybody I could think of. My neighbors said the only time they heard anything before we found the box was when my dog barked around eight o'clock last night, but Magnum has been known to bark at boom cars and trash cans. Sam looked out the window, but he didn't see anything."

Bupkeus was actually how he'd put it. Then he'd patted Molly's hand and passed the bottle of Stoly.

"And your nephew? What about him?"

Molly shook her head. "Nothing. You can ask him yourself. He's downstairs."

Winnie was not mollified. Straightening, she managed to give the effect of looking straight down at Molly without standing or dipping her head. "It had just better not be the family of one of the patients who went through here."

"Sending eyes on decorated cotton?" Molly retorted. "I just don't think so, Winnie."

"Eye," Winnie retorted. "I only have *one* eye in my possession."

Winnie knew perfectly well what had happened to the other eye. In fact, she'd suggested retrieving it without benefit of anesthesia.

"You have to admit," Kevin said with a quiet smile, "it does beat all hell out of 'my dog ate my homework.'"

Winnie glared. "We're sure that neither of these . . . artifacts could have come from our morgue."

Kevin nodded. "Checked and double-checked. Where would you like to go from here?"

"Home to put my head under the covers," Molly suggested.

Winnie huffed. "Hard to pretend it's a mistake anymore."

Especially with the newest note sitting alongside the

bagged flower box, like an exclamation point at the end of a statement.

YOU DESERVE WORSE

Delightful. Even Patrick had been impressed.

"I've talked to Detective Butler," Winnie said.

Molly literally blanched. "Rhett?" she retorted. "Why? He's in homicide."

Winnie glared. "Because I don't trust that incompetent clock-puncher from the Fifth who didn't even think this merited her attendance. At least I know Rhett will follow something up."

Even tense as a time bomb, Molly damn near laughed. Rhett would faint when he heard Winnie's left-handed compliment. Rhett—John Jason Butler, who had, naturally, become Rhett to the force—lived in terror of the Medical Examiner. But then, Rhett had a strong sense of self-preservation.

"What did he say?" Kevin asked.

Winnie made gathering-up motions to alert her staff that the meeting was over. "He'll do some checking. He wants to talk to Molly, of course. And we'll be getting the report back from the anthropologist soon on the femur."

Kevin stood on cue as Winnie glided to her feet. She took both their measures, her amber eyes as cold as yellow could get. "It has to stop."

Again, Molly fought the urge to laugh. "Sure, Winnie. Anything you say."

Winnie swept from the room, and Kevin walked across to lay a hand on Molly's shoulder.

"Whoever it is, they're an idiot," he said.

"Not the description I would have used," Molly said.

Kevin, bless him, laughed. "You're in a better position than just about anybody in the city to figure out who's behind this. You're the first person I'd put on the team anyway, Mol."

Molly smiled then, grateful at least for Kevin's support. Giving his hand a quick pat, she lurched to her own feet. "Then let's get a game plan together, boss."

• • •

Downstairs, the first floor of the Medical Examiner's office
echoed with age and memories. Built in the early part of the
century of granite, high white walls, and dark wood, it said *institution* in big letters. It even smelled of institution. Radia-
tors, old building, and bathroom air freshener. And, closer to
the back where the terrazzo floor metamorphosed to tile,
musk, more disinfectant, and the heavy tang of formaldehyde.

Stepping down from the stairs that swept quite regally up
to the office floor, Molly couldn't help but think that no matter what else happened from this mess, she hoped like hell it
wouldn't get her tossed out.

She really did like it here. She liked the people who
worked here. She liked solving the puzzles brought here. She
even liked being able to gentle the impact of the business
done here on the families who clustered in untidy clumps in
the viewing room.

On her better days, Molly thought she was good at her job.
That if she could bring nothing else to these echoing, solemn
rooms, she could make sure no one died unnoticed.

But that was on her good days. Today she just knew she
felt oddly at home here. And that she needed the added income, especially with a new and ravenous mouth to feed. A
ravenous mouth that was supposed to be waiting for her here
in the front foyer.

That, in point of fact, wasn't.

"Damn him," she muttered, stalking straight through toward the business end of the building.

"What are you doing back here?"

Patrick startled like a straying husband caught on videocam. Molly was not amused. She'd only allowed him to come
down with her because he'd promised to remain on good behavior. And, of course, she found him leaning against the
tiled wall of the morgue laughing with Lewis, the intake tech.
Not five feet away, autopsy tables gleamed beneath tucked-
up surgical lights, and bagged bodies lay along the wall on
morgue carts.

Three bodies lined up for autopsy. Three souls who definitely did not need a morbidly curious teenager peeking down their zippers.

Patrick shrugged and smiled, as if he'd been caught cadging a smoke behind the garage. "I was just saying hi to Lewis."

Molly glared. "Well, say good-bye. You know you're not supposed to be here."

Patrick took one more look around the room. "I just wanted to see."

Standing alongside the grinning, badly shaven Lewis, Patrick looked completely out of place in his Dockers and polo shirt and Hilfiger jacket. Too clean, too neat, too eager. Molly sighed and wondered if all teenage boys were this gruesome.

"Well, you've seen. Now, come on."

She got a quick glare of fury, and then cold complaisance. Hands shoved in pants pockets, head down, half smile reserved for his new friend Lewis, who shuffled back to his cubbyhole, where the bodies were signed in. Molly rubbed at the fresh acid gnawing at her chest and led the way back to the civilian side of the building.

"Now that you've seen your dead bodies," she said, "you can stay home next time I come down."

Patrick swung on her, a hundred-eighty pounds of high dudgeon. "You're acting like I'm six years old!"

"No," she said as evenly as she could. "*You're* acting like you're six years old. I told you my rules were strict, Patrick. That's because I'm not a florist or a cake decorator. Those were people back there. People who deserve a little more respect than a kid trying to cadge a sneaky peek to see what they look like dead."

She saw too many emotions skitter too quickly over those beautiful hazel eyes before they shuttered hard and tight. She wished she hadn't lost her temper. He probably needed to talk.

Molly had seen more dead guys than most people should in their entire lives. She forgot sometimes that other people, trying to come to grips with life and death, thought they could see something in the left-behind husks.

Molly could have told Patrick that there wasn't anything to see. She'd found that out by her eighteenth birthday. But Patrick, sheltered, privileged, protected, hadn't had the chance.

"We'll talk about it when we get home," she said as if he'd actually asked the question.

He watched her for a moment, his eyes almost half closed to show his disinterest. Then he turned to the door. "What did your boss say about your new present?"

Molly sighed, but she followed. "She is not pleased. Are you sure you never noticed anything in the backyard before you left for work?"

Patrick stopped so fast Molly all but ran into him. "You *still* don't believe me. I swear I don't know anything. I didn't see anything. I didn't hear anything. I didn't *do* anything!"

Molly wanted to yell and apologize at the same time. "I was just hoping . . . I mean, the first time you were at the house was the only time that night Magnum barked until the police came. You might not have been the only one around."

Another too-quick change to earnest sincerity. "I swear, Aunt Molly. If I knew anything, I'd tell you." He shuddered, hands shoved in pockets. "I mean, Jesus, it's just creepy."

Molly couldn't have agreed more. Sighing, she resettled her purse on her shoulder and turned for the door. "Oh, what the hell, Patrick. Let's you and I go get some hamburgers."

He grimaced. "Do we have to?"

And that was the worst of it. Somehow God had burdened her with the only teenage boy in North America who did not appreciate the spiritual value of junk food.

Some days she just couldn't win.

A cold front had swung through sometime during the evening. An Alberta Clipper, they called it. All Molly knew was that she was freezing her ass off as she gingerly stepped through the frozen grass of Forest Park at seven in the morning in her moss green pantsuit and battered boots to assess a freshly found body.

What was it, suddenly, about people coming to the park to

die? she wondered. Couldn't they die in their bathrooms, like they were supposed to?

But the poor parks crew had stumbled over another one, and it was up to Molly to climb down and deal with it.

"That's it," one of the guys cried in real distress when Molly showed up. "I'm gonna get me a job in a sewer. No bodies in sewers. Just alligators. I can *deal* with alligators."

At least this body was routine. A homeless guy just trying to get some warmth in the woods. Curled in on himself like a hedgehog, he'd died in his fatigues and the five coats he'd cadged from Sal Army.

"I don' know," the homicide detective offered as Molly approached. "I heard about that stuff you been gettin'. Could be, this guy donated somethin' for ya."

For just a second, Molly's heart caught in her chest.

"What do you mean?" she demanded, only able to see the jumble of coats that lay frozen against the long grass in the ravine.

The cop, a grizzled veteran with three stripes and a giant handlebar mustache he waxed like a surfboard, grinned and bent over.

"Well, look. He's missing a part or two. Any of them yours?"

She didn't want to, but Molly bent over.

Then she smacked the cop so hard his homicide fedora went flying. "If anybody's comin' across this guy's spare parts," she retorted, assessing the single lower leg and foot that peeked out from beneath that nest of coats, "they're doing it on the Korean peninsula. That leg hasn't been attached since Truman was president. Besides, Wilson, before you get excited, make sure it's the right part. He's still got the bone we're looking for."

"He got eyes?"

Even though Molly shouldn't have been creeped out by one cop's lousy humor, she checked anyway. First thing.

"He's got eyes."

"Well, hell," Wilson groused. "And here I thought I'd caught me a big red ball."

"You caught you a poor son of a bitch who couldn't get into a shelter last night," Molly retorted.

Molly checked the body, saw he was frozen as solid as the pond behind him, and estimated his time of death to be some ten to twelve hours earlier. No obvious injuries, no sign of struggle, no reason to think that John Doe number fifty-eight had done anything but crawl into the woods to die. The good news was that he'd tattooed his rank and serial number on his left forearm. They'd know within a day who he was.

Not like the last body they'd found here. It had taken a week to identify poor Sharon Peters. Another two days for her distant family to claim her. It had been up to Molly to tell that taciturn farm couple that their little girl had been raped, strangled, and left half naked in a public park. There sure as hell hadn't been anybody laughing that night.

"You finished?" Wilson asked forty minutes later as he clapped his gloved hands together for warmth.

"Yeah," she said, closing the case that held her equipment. The transport team was already zipping the bag over their John Doe. "We'll take him back and ID him. But I think he just died of homelessness, like you thought."

"Well, then, if you're finished, you have a gentleman caller up by the road."

Molly turned to look and scowled. "Oh hell. And here I thought I was going to spend my day with adults."

Instead, it seemed she'd gotten Doogie Howser, homicide detective.

Standing there by her Celica with his homicide fedora in his hand, as if he really was a potential suitor, was Rhett Butler himself.

Tall and gangly as a half-developed teenager, Rhett had bought the homicide persona whole cloth with his appointment to the squad. Homicide suit, skinny tie, and snap-brim hat that were so traditional in the older homicide coppers in St. Louis. He even had the homicide mustache, trimmed with military precision to the corners of his mouth. All it did was make him look as if he were collecting candy on Halloween.

The mopes he investigated seemed to think the same thing, which was why they tended to tell him things they never told anybody else. After only eight months in homicide, Rhett was setting confession records to rival the local archdiocese.

And he was here to look into Molly's little correspondence.

She wished Winnie had talked to someone older than Molly. Maybe as old as Molly. Molly just couldn't feel comfortable confiding in a Junior Explorer, no matter how good he was.

"You got a minute to talk?" he asked as she slogged up the hill.

Molly accepted his hand to help her the last few steep feet, and punched the trunk on her Celica. "Please tell me you just needed some fresh air, Rhett, and that you didn't come out into this deep freeze because you found something significant."

"No, Molly. I was just in the neighborhood and heard you were here. Thought I'd catch you before you had to go into work."

She lifted an eyebrow at him, now. "I *am* at work."

He blushed. He actually blushed. "Your other work. The one with all the bodily fluids. I'm, uh, not good with bodily fluids."

"You're a homicide officer, Rhett. Bodily fluids are a big part of that job description."

"Yeah, but usually they've finished . . . uh, being fluid."

"Uh-huh. Well, you got a car?"

"I got dropped off. I figured you could . . . you know . . ."

Molly sighed and slammed her trunk shut. "Get in."

So they sat there, on a side street in a frozen park, and talked murder while her windshield defrosted.

"First of all," Rhett said. "I checked to make sure that all the bodies that have come through our shops went out intact. Well, as intact as . . ."

"I understand."

He nodded, ironing his hat brim with his hand. "Dr. Harrison thought that maybe this guy was getting his . . . uh, stuff from medical supply houses. Is that really possible?"

"Sure. At least with bones. Heck, there's a place called Bones on the Internet that sells complete skeletons. I'm not sure about the eyes."

Blue eyes.

One blue eye, which still seemed to stare at her when she tried to sleep.

Rhett shook his head. "Go figure. Well, have you had any more ideas about who could want to do this to you?"

Keeping her gaze fixed on the pristine winter landscape outside her window, Molly shook her head. "No. I've had the normal number of crazies and cranks from work, but nobody I'd finger for that kind of problem."

"Any crazies in particular?"

Molly shrugged. "Oh, you know. Bob from Atlantis, Milly who thinks the microwaves at Wal-Mart are talking to her, manic depressive twins with an enema fetish. The regular assortment of hookers with clap and johns with the drip and all our lonely little people who just come in for some lunch and a shower."

"Nobody seriously mad at you."

"You tell me how to tell the serious ones from the just stressed ones, Rhett. I had three people punch holes in the quiet room wall this month, but then, each one of them had just lost a kid. I'd punch walls, too."

"No gang problems?"

She grinned. "The yos around here don't do notes and body parts. They just show up with their equalizers."

"What about this job?"

"The death investigations?" She shrugged again, leaned against the seat, and closed her eyes. Suddenly she just felt tired. "I don't know. I don't think so. I'd have to go over my records. Unless it's Wilmetta Wilson trying to spook us into not finding Latesha's real killer."

Rhett perked up a little. "Wilson. That little girl they found in the basement."

"The very one."

"I'll do a little checking."

Molly smiled. "I'm sorry I can't be more help. I'm afraid nobody's vocalized anything more particular than 'You slow, stupid bitch' lately. And ya know, on a busy Friday night I only answer to 'You slow, stupid bitch.' "

Rhett closed his notebook and pocketed it before grabbing his hat. "Well, let me take a peek into it."

"Better you than me."

"I still need that list Dr. Harrison asked you for."

Molly put the car in gear. "Where can I drop you off, Rhett?"

Rhett settled his hat back on his head. "The station. You'll let me know?"

"I'll let you know."

"Until we can get anything more solid, Dr. Harrison asked me to keep this fairly confidential. You have a problem with that?"

"You mean more confidential than the entire homicide department?"

"She means, like, no talk shows or anything."

"Oh, yeah, Rhett. I've just been dying to get myself on a talk show."

He smiled, a little boy smile that was supposed to make her feel better. "Well, with any luck, this guy'll give himself away, and we can wrap this long before Christmas."

"And he'll just be a med student with delusions of Warhol."

"A performance artist you took care of in the ER."

"A hospital pathologist who can't figure out how to write a real love letter."

Rhett patted her hand. "Exactly." Then he climbed out of the car, and Molly was left with a still-cold car and a case of the shivers.

Because she knew they weren't dealing with anybody funny.

They weren't even dealing with anybody nice.

Molly was very afraid that who they were dealing with was going to be very, very bad. He was already very scary.

And he had her name.

. . .

It was ten-fifteen. Kenny held his beer in his hand as Donna-theanchor extolled the virtues of mammography by showing just enough of a young woman's breast to get a guy hard. It was raining outside, and out beyond his house an ambulance was screaming up some highway. But Kenny didn't really notice.

He was so confused. He didn't know what to do.

Nothing.

Not a word. Not a hint. And if anybody was going to find out about it, it would have been Donnatheanchor. He'd taken such care tonight, because he'd known he would finally see what he'd done on the television. He'd prepared himself just as meticulously as he did everything else in his life. Just as carefully as the last five nights he'd waited.

He'd cleaned himself up, combed his hair and put on a good shirt. He'd straightened out his living room and placed his grandmother's doily right in the center of the coffee table to hold his beer so there wouldn't be rings on the old cherry-wood. He'd even invited his friend Flower, because she was so much a part of his triumph. And then, as the montage of St. Louis flashed on the screen at nine fifty-eight, he'd popped the top on his beer and set it in the perfect center of the doily, the chalice on his altar of fame.

And he'd waited, almost not breathing, for the moment Donnatheanchor would look wide-eyed into the camera and say, "Today, a grisly story unfolding in the city . . ."

But there hadn't been a word.

After all the work he'd gone through, the timing, the symbolism, the detail. After all that wasted anticipation, there had not been a whisper in the news about what St. Louis city death investigator Molly Burke was getting in her backyard.

He'd designed it so well. He'd worked it out a thousand times in his head. A million times. Securely tucked away in his room in the basement where nobody could find him and he'd be safe with the pictures he'd carried with him since he'd been a boy.

He'd even made the effort to wait outside for her so he could make sure she got it. Tucked back in the shadows of a silent street, standing in the cold, holding his breath, holding his silence. Holding all those dreams in his head so they didn't tumble out into sound at the very moment she stepped outside.

And she'd given him such pictures. Oh, how she had, with her wide-eyed reaction, her words. Her disbelief and wonder. He'd seen it on her, just for the moments before she'd taken his gifts inside again, and he held those pictures to him now like a treasure. The fresh technicolor image of all his old, old dreams.

But there had to be more. He saw right there in his head what she was supposed to look like when she called Donna-theanchor to share her terrible surprises. He knew exactly how the perspiration would shine on her upper lip, how wide her eyes would be, how her voice would tremble when she shared the news about the gifts he'd finally, finally given her.

But she hadn't.

She'd ignored them.

Maybe she hadn't realized just what she'd been given. Maybe she didn't appreciate it.

Kenny didn't believe that.

So he finished his beer and put his friend to bed, all the while trying so very hard to stay calm and focused, when he wanted to destroy something. When he wanted to run right over and wring from Miss Burke what she was too stupid and slow to figure out.

But Kenny wasn't still alive because he lost control. He'd dreamed about this for too long to let it be less than he'd hoped.

So he'd have to plan harder.

He'd have to make sure it went just the way he wanted.

Flipping off the lights in the living room, he made his way to the basement where his dreams lived, and he prepared to make Molly Burke pay attention to him.

stop it stop it stop it stop it stop it stop it stop it
stop it stop it stop it stop it stop it stop it stop it
it stop it stop it stop it stop it stop it stop
it stop. stop stop stop stop STOP

FIVE

Two days later Molly realized that she had a list after all. She wasn't sure how valid it was, but suddenly it seemed that everybody in her known universe was mad at her.

First there was Latesha Wilson's mother.

Molly had been in the basement repotting African violets under her grow lights when Patrick yelled down to tell her she was on the news. Molly grumbled. She really wanted to ignore it. But she hadn't done any of those "cause-of-death" interviews lately, so something else must be going on. She climbed the steep basement stairs and joined Patrick before her TV.

To see Mrs. Wilson, a small, skinny woman with smoker-pocked, grayish-brown skin and rheumy eyes. Clad in her best threadbare coat and finest mother's outrage, she was busy wailing at one of the Action News reporters that the city didn't care enough to find the stranger who'd murdered the daughter she'd looked for six days.

The daughter she'd certainly known was down in that empty basement every hour of those six days.

"They'n't nothin' I wouldn't do for my baby," she protested, teary and clutching her coat closed as if standing out in the snow instead of the foyer of the downtown police station. "You knows, she a white girl, them people be fallin' over theyselves tryin' to find out who did her. But that bitch didn't even listen to me."

That bitch. Ah, now Molly understood. All the homicide guys in town right now were men. The only bitch on the scene that night had been Molly.

"Who she think she is?" Wilmetta Wilson demanded. "It's her baby, she'd do somethin'. She get the monster killed my Latesha."

I tried, Molly thought. We all did. Which was probably why Wilmetta was showing off for the press. Since she was making her outraged statement from the police station, it probably meant that the homicide guys had had her in again trying to get her to turn in her boyfriend Bobby. But it wouldn't do to betray the boyfriend. Too few of those around. And if she did drop a dime on Bobby, who'd she come home to? Much easier to rationalize the blame away onto some convenient Stranger Danger.

"Turn it off," Molly said, wiping her hands on a dish towel.

Tossed over the couch like a pile of dirty laundry, Patrick paid no attention. "What'd you do to her?" he demanded, his gaze fixed on the screen.

Molly turned for the kitchen. "My job."

That got him to his feet. "So, you, like, do this all the time? Murders and stuff? What's it like?"

Molly didn't bother to stop moving. "I asked you to clean your mess in the kitchen, Patrick. Please do it."

Patrick skidded to a halt as if he'd hit an invisible wall. "What'd I do?" he demanded. "All I did was ask about your job!"

Just like he'd been asking since he'd first set foot in the morgue. Questions, comments, assumptions. Mostly wrong, mostly inappropriate, most of which Molly could have handled with far greater equanimity if he hadn't been asking them this close to Christmas. Most she could at least have ignored if he hadn't been so persistent. So hungry.

"My job is mostly paperwork and phone calls," she said,

heading back for the stairs and her secret garden in a ninety-year-old basement. "It's not that romantic."

Flowers were romantic, plants that never seemed to notice the winter if you just bathed them in purple light. Seeds were satisfying, growing where you planted them as long as you remembered their basic needs. They didn't ask questions, they didn't demand tolerance, they didn't need things from you that you couldn't give.

Like forgiveness. Or secrets. Or shame.

"It's sure a hell of a lot more interesting to talk about than trade negotiations!" Patrick insisted, his voice even sharper as he followed hot on her heels. "And that's all I get at home. I've been thinking that I might want to do it. Law enforcement, maybe. Like what you're doing. And, ya know, I'd think if you're doing it, you'd think it was interesting enough to talk about."

Molly stopped three steps down and stared into the soft lilac light that washed her basement walls. She could see the forest of miniature plants spread out over her workbenches, their leaves still fetal and fragile, their beauty in the anticipation.

Why couldn't Patrick want to talk about flowers? Molly could talk about flowers. She could wax rhapsodic about the English garden she was plotting for the backyard beyond the koi pond. She could expound on twenty different kinds of azaleas and fifty kinds of irises. She could instruct him on the breathtaking patience it took to grow a really perfect rose.

She just couldn't talk to him right now about dead people. How could Molly tell Patrick that in other basements, young girls' terror still leaked from the cement and wept from the walls?

"Tell you what," she said, wiping again at the dirt on her hands and struggling to keep her voice light. "We'll talk about it later. Okay?"

That earned her the kind of laugh sixteen-year-olds reserved for stupid adults. "Well, I guess you're not all that different from the parents," he said, hands shoved in pockets. "Any time I want to talk about something, they tell me to fuck off, too."

Molly spun on him. "If I'd wanted to tell you to fuck off, I would have done it the first night you showed up. I'm just not in the mood for morbid fascination today, Patrick."

"It's not morbid fascination," he protested, posture suddenly rigid, as if conviction had a stance. "I'm serious! I really want to be a cop. And you can imagine what the parents said about that, can't you? I might as well have said I wanted to be a pimp."

Molly did know, of course. She knew all too well. She'd had much the same reaction the first time she'd mentioned the word *nurse* to her parents.

Funny. The best and worst thing she'd done, she'd done to appease them. She'd gone to Vietnam to serve, even if it wasn't the way Burkes usually served. And in the end, it still hadn't been right. She'd been in her second VA hospital screaming at the walls when she'd finally figured it out and told them to fuck off, too.

Of course, not one Burke had ever shown up to hear her.

Molly took another look down the steps. The ceiling was so low down there that few people taller than Molly could stand up straight. Patrick had asked her if she was growing marijuana under her purple lights. This time, she'd been able to give him an honest no. But she was growing. And she needed that.

"I can't explain this to you in fifteen words or less," she said, suddenly wondering what she'd thought she could give children of her own if she couldn't afford this kid one or two truths in the dead of winter. "And this just isn't the time to do it. If you're serious, I'll let you talk to some of the cops I know. And I'll talk to you about it right after Christmas. Just not now."

"Why right after Christmas?" he demanded. "I'll be back with the parents by then, and they'll have me clamped back into the system so hard I won't have a chance to get out!"

Molly turned back up to see him silhouetted near the top of the stairs. Tall, intense, all but thrumming with frustration. Why couldn't teenagers figure out that the next twenty seconds weren't the only ones that mattered in their lives?

"You can do anything if you want to."

"Oh yeah, like you did," he all but sneered. "You ended up living right back under their roof."

And then he just stalked off. Molly was sure there was more she'd meant to say to him. Explanations, rationalizations. All that baggage a person stores up in her lifetime for the sole purpose of dumping on some unsuspecting child. Instead, she sucked in a calming breath and turned back to her plants.

She was down there sometime later humming to her violets when she realized that Magnum was barking. Pausing a second, she also made out the faint, persistent jabs of the doorbell.

"Patrick!"

Nothing.

Molly sighed. Setting the tray of African violet babies back down, she wiped off her hands on muddy jeans and headed upstairs.

Molly peeked through her spyhole and groaned. No wonder Magnum was barking. Little Allen was standing on her porch, and he was loaded down with groceries.

"I didn't order anything," Molly said, throwing open the door.

Allen was another of the unremarkable masses. Forgettable features, even when they were red and chapped from the sharp north wind that rattled the windows.

Right now, he was glowering, which still didn't make much of an impression. "I've been out here for twenty minutes!" he protested. "Where've you been?"

"Considering the fact that I wasn't expecting you," Molly answered as kindly as possible, "I bet I wasn't waiting to hear you ring my doorbell. What can I do for you, Allen?"

"Where's that old man?" he demanded, as if Molly was in charge of Sam. Which, she supposed, she was. But not for the pleasure of petulant delivery boys. She wanted temper tantrums, she'd just go upstairs and roust Patrick out of bed.

"Wasn't my day to watch him."

Come to think of it, though, she had seen Sam driving off

down the block when she'd gone out to get her mail. Tough to miss Sam. He drove the biggest old Cadillac on the block, his head barely clearing the steering wheel. All you saw was that cute flat yellow golf cap he wore, a waving, gnarled hand, and curls of smoke from his cigarette. For years Molly had wanted to get him a car seat so he could actually see over the steering wheel.

"I think he went to visit Myra," she said. "You want to drop his groceries here instead?"

Little Allen glared as if Molly had insulted his intelligence. "Why do you think I'm at your door?"

Molly tried another one of those long, calming breaths. Maybe it was the weather, but she was having a little trouble with all the surly males today. "I know you don't want me to complain about you to Straub's, Allen. I bet you'd rather just put the groceries in my refrigerator and head on to your next drop-off. Okay?"

His face got even redder. He dipped his head and huffed a couple of times. "I'm . . . uh, sorry. It's just cold. And I always seem to end up waiting at that old guy's house for half an hour before he shows up."

Molly would have suggested he call to make sure Sam would be home next time before heading over with his groceries, but he probably had. Sam was notoriously bad about remembering Little Allen's visits. But then, Sam was eighty. He had a right to forget once in a while. Pushing open the door, Molly leaned back as Allen brushed by a little too closely on his way in.

Seven hours later Molly was convinced that it was the weather. She'd survived both Allen and Patrick, only to arrive at the ED to find all hell breaking loose. The sharp wind had disintegrated into rain and then sleet and then auto accidents. Old people bumped down front porches, gangbangers got revenge for fender benders, and children were burned by candles used when power lines fell. And everybody involved seemed to hold Molly personally responsible.

It probably didn't help that she was charge and triage

nurse that evening. Sasha, being Sasha, had decided that she simply was not in the mood to risk her Grand Prix coming in from the far county, which left them shorthanded. It also left them with three inexperienced nurses, including Nancy, and Dr. Spizer, who still hadn't figured out that medicine wasn't as easy as it was on TV. And, of course, Molly's favorite secretary, Marianne, who came in just to let everybody know how put-upon she was.

"Have we heard from the trauma surgeon on call yet?" Molly asked her as she updated the flowboard nearby.

Marianne glared from beneath her teased Clairol number 7 yellow bangs. "You want him so bad, you call him," she snapped.

Molly's head was throbbing. Her hip was aching again, and she hadn't eaten in twelve hours. Not a good path toward patience.

"I'll make you a deal, Marianne," she said through gritted teeth. "You put in the call to the trauma surgeon, and I promise I'll leave my stun gun in my purse."

Marianne tossed her hair and turned back toward the phone banks. Beyond her to the right, the radio crackled and beeped.

"Grace Hospital ED, this is City four-five-one calling to advise."

Molly sighed and walked around the edge of the desk to where the radio crouched in the corner beneath a shelf stacked with research books, one stuffed frog in fireman's gear, and a snakebite poster on which all the snakes bore physicians' names, the latest addition being the RattleSpizer.

"City four-five-one, this is Grace," she intoned, pulling a pen from behind her ear and noting time and rig on the call log. "Go ahead."

"Trauma surgeon is at mass," Marianne announced behind her as if she hadn't heard the radio. "What do you want to do?"

"Grace, be advised we are answering a house fire with possible multiple injuries," a male voice announced over the radio in bored tones. "Our ETA to scene is seven minutes."

"Beep the trauma surgeon at mass," Molly said to Marianne, "and page the supervisor stat and let her know we're probably getting multiple burn victims in, please." Then she clicked the mike. "Thanks, four-five-one. We'll be standing by for further information."

"His wife said he forgot it," Marianne told her with relish.

Molly spun on her, furious. "Deal with it or learn the phrase, 'Would you like fries with that?' " she snapped.

Marianne's heavy-lidded green eyes flashed with petulance. "When they fire you from this job, I'll be the one laughing."

Molly just finished the call and ran for a dose of antacid. Which was where the young nurse Nancy and Dr. Wilmington, the pediatric resident on that evening, found her three minutes later.

"She won't let me call," Nancy protested.

Molly took a second to chug about a quart of Mylanta. The twenty-two-year-old nurse was in high dudgeon, her round, soft face taut and anxious. Behind her, the pediatric resident, a doughy, impatient woman with bad posture and coarse black hair, came to a quick halt.

"I keep telling her it doesn't make any difference," she said, plump hands in rumpled, stained white lab coat pockets, her pasty face bored. "We've called before. Nobody does anything. I don't want to have to do all that goddamn paperwork for nothing."

Molly capped the antacid and tucked the mini-bottle in the pocket of her own pressed maroon lab coat. "And you're talking about?"

"The little boy in room twelve," Nancy said. "The one whose mother said he fell off the bed."

Uh-oh, Molly thought, her stomach sliding south. Just the presenting complaint was becoming a classic symptom.

"Injuries don't match the story?" she asked.

Nancy was all but quivering, hands on tiny hips, black eyes flashing. "He has a lot of bruises," she accused.

"He's an eight-year-old who plays soccer," the resident retorted. "Show me a kid like that without a bruise and I'll show you a miracle."

"He's pale."

"He's blond."

"The mother says the boyfriend was baby-sitting—"

Another bell-ringer. Boyfriends were more deadly than cancer, AIDS, and un-seat-belted autos combined.

"—the boyfriend said he didn't see what happened. *I* think—"

Molly walked far enough to see through the window into room twelve, where a washed-out blond mother stood alongside the cart that held her son. Her quiet, watchful, too-still son. A good charge nurse would simply dispense advice without actually getting involved. Molly had thirty-eight patients she was responsible for right now, with another twenty waiting to be seen and at least one on the way in. Without waiting for Nancy or the resident, she pushed the door open and walked into the room.

The little boy was small for his age, all bones and big eyes. He watched Molly's approach with disinterest as the mother rocked from foot to foot.

"Who have we here?" Molly asked the little boy, all smiles.

He ducked a little. "Nobody."

"Don't be smart, David," his mother chastised in high anxious tones, her eyes on Molly. "You taking him to X Ray now?" she asked. "We need to get home. I need to get to work."

Molly pulled up a chair right next to the bed so she was eye level with the boy. "No," she said in easy, casual tones. "Nancy's still kind of in training, so I double-check her cases. Is that okay, David? Do you mind?"

David didn't so much as blink. His eyes were soft green and nearly as colorless as his hair. His skin was sallow, his arms and legs too thin, with old scabs on his elbows and a Band-Aid over his left eye. But a lot of kids were too thin. A lot sallow-looking. And David was in perfectly clean, new-looking clothes, with his hair brushed and his face scrubbed.

"You fell out of a bed, huh?" Molly asked, a hand tentatively to his knee, her voice still soft and easy. "What'd you hurt?"

"His head," the mother quickly said. "His ribs. It was a bunkbed. He was playing, weren't you, David?"

David just watched Molly as if she were an alien. Molly saw the purpling that was beginning to rise beneath his left eye, the faint mottling on his cheek no camera would pick up. She saw the emptiness at the back of that little boy's eyes that betrayed more than every bruise she might catalog.

It was time to play The Game.

Molly wished Sasha were here. Sasha had experience. She'd seen the worst of it, like Molly. Sasha could help Molly play The Game and come up with a reasonable outcome. But Nancy wasn't seasoned enough, so Molly played The Game all by herself. She asked the single question that mattered.

Can we save him?

Not, can we save him physically? In a battered child, that almost didn't matter.

Can we save his soul? Can we catch him before whatever it is that makes him human is beaten and starved out of him?

There wasn't any question in her mind that this little boy was abused. There was nothing overt. No fingerprints, bristle marks, cigarette burns. It was instinct, honed over thirty years of nursing. This kid was just too careful, too quiet, and his mother too anxious to please. A little boy who couldn't even bother to be afraid of an ED had been at this for a while.

Molly knew that if she had the time she could probably pull up records from visits to half a dozen hospitals. All for falls, sports injuries, undiagnosable pains. Each and every one of them explained away. Because somebody was hurting this little boy, and somebody else was covering it up.

But that wasn't what The Game was about. The Game was about looking past bruises and suspicions and faulty stories. It was about predicting a child's future.

"Okay, Sash," Molly asked in her head, as if her friend were actually standing there observing David. "The Game has begun. Up or down?"

If she'd been there, Sasha would have looked. Not at the careful behavior, the nervous mother, the obvious history. Sasha would look instead at nothing but David's eyes, because that was where the verdict lay. The predictors, the betrayers, the reflectors. The gateways to a terrifying future.

Long years ago The Game had been a desperate question, one Molly had answered much more like Nancy. Not "could" we save him, but "couldn't" we save him? If we pulled him out right now, ran far and fast with him, handed him to helpful, faithful people who could nurture him, couldn't we bring him back from the brink?

But Molly, now looking into David's flat, emotionless eyes, knew what Sasha's answer would be.

Already by the age of eight, David was a statistic waiting to happen. A spousal abuser, a felon, a serial killer. Whatever made David a human being was so lost to rage and defense and fear that the chances of digging it out were virtually nonexistent. And Molly and Nancy were too late even now to stop it. That indefinable light that illuminated a human's eyes had already winked out of David's and left nothing behind but emptiness.

"Thumbs down," Sasha would say in her deceptively cool voice and walk away.

And Molly standing with her hand on young David's knee, agreed.

David was eight, and they were probably already too late.

So Molly checked him over with gentle hands and did her best to make him smile, at least once.

"Soccer, huh?" she asked. "I used to play soccer when I was a kid. You pretty good?"

"No." Such a passive voice. Too colorless, as if reaction could spark retribution. Trying to be invisible so he'd be safe.

"What position do you play?"

"Forward. Sometimes."

"Well, I'll tell you a secret. I really liked soccer. For about twenty minutes, until I realized that I had to run all the time. I hate running."

He was sore in fifteen places and breathing fast beneath

that careful blank facade. Molly wondered what he felt. Fear? Fury? Futility? Eight years old, and he probably already knew far better than Nancy how pointless all this was. Even so, Molly tweaked his nose and smiled for him.

"If you're a soccer player, you've been X-rayed before, I bet. Same thing tonight, okay?"

A nod. The tiniest flicker of reaction. For the briefest moment Molly desperately wished she could do more. But the way the social service system was these days, more usually wasn't available to children like David.

"Will it take long?" his mother asked, almost beneath her breath.

Molly smiled for her, too, because she knew how very wary a mother like this was. "I hope not. It is busy tonight, though."

Where David wouldn't allow emotion, the mother did. A hot flash of impatience. Resentment. "Ya know, we've been waiting here a long time," she protested. "We need to get going. You gonna drop us in somebody else's lap now?"

Angry at Molly, because Molly was safe. "Nope," Molly answered equably, because it didn't cost her anything. "Just X rays. See you when you get back, David."

And then she fled the field of battle.

"Call DFS," she told Nancy when she walked back out of the room. "I got him to wince when I palpated his legs and arms, so you might want to order limb films to check for old fractures, Dr. Wilmington. His ribs were sore, too, weren't they?"

"Jesus," the resident bristled. "Are you kidding? That's going to keep me here another three hours, and it won't end up doing a fucking bit of good."

Now would probably not be the time to ask the resident just why she'd chosen pediatrics if that was the way she felt. Instead, Molly shrugged. "Oh, what the hell? The streets are probably too bad to drive home right now anyway."

The resident glared. "It's not going to make a goddamn bit of difference."

"It probably won't," Molly admitted, her attention now

back on that little boy who didn't turn his mother's way, even though she was three feet away. "But it's not going to hurt to try."

"It *will* make a difference," Nancy informed Molly in arch tones. "I'll make it make a difference."

Molly didn't say a word. She did think of all those times when she'd been Nancy's age and thought the same thing. She remembered hiding kids in the back rooms where parents couldn't get to them before she had a chance to save them. She remembered making call after call, hounding social workers and police and physicians, knowing perfectly well that if just one person listened to her, if just one of them saw that small, broken, frightened child she was protecting, he'd see the light and get that baby to safety.

That had been before she'd begun playing The Game. Before she'd realized that it was harder to save one child than an entire nation with oil reserves.

And here she'd been promising Sasha she'd stay away from the kids.

Nancy spent a second staring at Molly with disillusioned eyes. Then she walked on into room twelve to fight the good fight. Left behind, Molly did her best to scrounge up enough enthusiasm to finish the shift.

"Charge nurse to the radio," Marianne paged over the intercom. "Multiple victims en route."

Molly trotted for the station. "Did I page the supervisor for more help yet?" she asked nobody in particular.

"You must have," Nancy said. "Because we have three people from housekeeping here to help tech."

A gaggle of misshapen humans huddled along the supply cart. Molly recognized one, the guy with the scar on his neck. When he flashed her the kind of hesitant smile that made her think of beaten puppies, she groaned. "This just isn't my day."

Molly picked up the microphone to find that they were getting four victims from the house fire. She called to advise the burn unit, paged the burn docs stat, and begged for even more help. She juggled patients and soothed tempers and did

her time in with one of the gangbangers she knew from previous visits and tried to supervise the housekeeping cross-
trainees who were much more comfortable emptying laundry
bins than doing blood pressures. And just when she thought
she might just have things in hand, she walked out of a room
to find Winnie Harrison standing at the X-ray view box.

Molly shuddered to a complete halt. She noticed that a
goodly percent of the staff had stopped to stare, too. Everybody knew of the legendary Dr. Harrison. Few, though, had
actually seen the Medical Examiner cross the sliding ED
doors.

Clad in a winter white suit and heels, her hair swept back
and up, her ears dangling exotic wood and brass, Winnie was
a vision.

"Winnie?" Molly greeted her, hands full of charts and
chest suddenly tight.

Winnie simply looked in the direction of the nurses'
lounge. Dropping the charts on Marianne's desk, Molly followed her back.

One of the night nurses was sprawled on the couch snacking
on a TV dinner before her shift. She took one look at the Medical Examiner and found a reason to be across the hall instead.

"What's the matter?" Molly asked. "Who's this about?"

Please, she thought in sudden terror. Don't let it be
Patrick. Don't let it be Frank or Sam or Sasha.

Winnie didn't sit, and she didn't relax. She just stood in
the middle of the room watching Molly as if waiting. Molly
was beginning to sweat.

"You get any farther on that list I wanted?" her boss asked
in deceptively lazy tones.

Molly blinked. She stared. She sat down so abruptly the
couch let out a little puff of dust. Then she laughed.

"Oh, God, I thought you had bad news."

"I didn't come out in this weather for trivialities."

Molly waved off her objection. "I mean personal bad
news. I'm a trauma nurse, Winnie. I always think in worst-
case scenario."

Amazingly, that made Winnie smile. But not the kind of

smile that was benign. "If you insist on a worst-case scenario, I might just be able to comply."

Molly blinked again. She'd just begun to feel better, and Winnie was ruining it.

"Who might be mad at you?" Winnie asked again.

Considering the day she'd had, Molly laughed again. "You want to know who's mad at me, point a fire hose down the hall. Whoever gets wet is probably calling me names. Why?"

"Mad at you how long?"

Molly was feeling unnerved all over again. "I don't know, Winnie. I haven't had time to think about it. It's been a shitty shift. What do you want to tell me?"

Winnie's shrug was minimal, but even that frightened Molly. Winnie did not shrug.

"We have the report back on your bone," she said.

"Molly? Molly, what did you tell them?"

They both turned to see Nancy skidding to a halt in the doorway, tears on her cheeks. Molly wanted to scream at her. "What is it, Nancy?"

"They're gone!" she accused, all but pointing an angry finger at Molly's chest. "Somehow you tipped them off, and now that baby's going back to that . . ."

"David's gone?"

"They just never came back from X Ray! What do I do?"

Molly fought the old clutch of futility and faced her nurse with as much composure as she could. "Advise DFS. Find out what's on the films. Follow it up."

The young nurse's eyes were hot. "We should have done something *here*."

"Yes," Molly said. "We should have. This is the next best we can do."

Nancy fled and Molly was left with nothing more than Winnie's news. It took her a second to get back to it.

"You got the report back," she said, wondering why the hell she was forcing this.

Winnie faced her head on. "Neither the bone nor the eyes were from any medical supply house. Not a medical school, not the Internet. Not anything traceable."

Molly just stared, her brain suddenly frozen. "What do you mean?"

"The bone was from a human. It was a new bone from a young woman. The eye was also from a woman. Probably a young woman."

"But not from a medical supply house."

"No."

"Not from a medical school."

Winnie just lifted an eyebrow. For a second, all Molly could do was stare at her boss. And wait for the inevitable.

"You're not just getting threats from somebody who's mad at you, Molly," Winnie admitted. "You have a monster on your hands."

she doesn't know what i
think.   nobody   does.
nobody sees. but i know.
i know deep in my quiet
place. and when she hurts
me i go there and hurt
her back. i hurt them all
back until they flop and
flop, just like a bird i
saw in the road

SIX

Molly's instinctive reaction probably wasn't wise. "You're lying."

Winnie froze.

Molly should have apologized. Hell, she should have thrown herself on the floor and groveled. It seemed, though, that all she could manage was a frozen stare and a sudden, overwhelming bout of nausea.

"How do you know?" Molly asked.

Winnie just looked to the open door, which made Molly feel even worse. Sucking in a steadying breath, she climbed to her feet and closed off the rest of the lane. Then she faced Winnie again.

"How do you know for sure?"

Winnie sat down. "The anthropologist was bored. Your bone was the most interesting artifact she's had to deal with in a while. Probably the decoupaging, don't you think?"

Molly kept her temper by a thread. "The point, Winnie."

"You want chapter and verse? It's pretty dry."

"Humor me. This is a big logic leap, and I've already had a bad day."

Then Molly sat down, too, if only to drive home her point.

Winnie nodded and slipped into testimony mode. "After photographing and measuring the specimen, Dr. DeVries cleaned off an area of paint to determine age. The femur is fresh. It hasn't been discolored enough to be aged at all. It certainly hadn't been in the ground for any length of time, which would have left it stained and showing root patterns. It's also too heavy to be old. Bone mass lessens over time. The femur is straight, which means it is Caucasian. The diaphysis is curved, which you find in females. You want me to go on?"

No. Molly wanted Winnie to smile and say it was all a joke, like Frank. "Yeah."

"From the size and length of the specimen, we're probably talking about a female in the range of five-foot-seven to five-foot-nine-inches tall, and well nourished. From the histomorphometric analysis and epiphyseal closure, Dr. DeVries believes the owner to have been about seventeen years of age. And something else . . ." Winnie damn near winced on this one. "Something I missed."

If she hadn't still been trying to ingest the impact of the rest of Winnie's statement, Molly would have been more impressed by the virtually unheard of admission of guilt. As it was, she was still caught in the seventeen-year-old white female portion of things.

"Well, we did establish that neither specimen could have come from a path lab or medical school. No formalin present. But Dr. DeVries did catch a faint aroma we seemed to have overlooked. She did some tests. The bone showed fresh traces of hydrochloric acid," Winnie said, then paused for impact. "And Soilex."

Soilex. Soilex. Why did that ring a bell? Molly sat there in dead silence as the hallway beyond the lounge door echoed and shrilled with a full load of injured and ill, and Winnie waited with the patience of a cat for her part-time death investigator to make the connection.

It came with an almost audible click.

"Oh, God," Molly breathed, eyes widening, stomach clutching up like a faulty bellows. "Tell me you're joking."

One raised eyebrow was enough answer.

Molly wanted to stand up. She wanted to walk off the implication of Winnie's final bit of news. She couldn't seem to make it to her feet.

Molly had first heard about it at a Masters Class in Death Investigation she had attended at St. Louis University. Each course offered updates, experts in the field, topical information on current issues. Molly vividly remembered the day they'd discussed the pros and cons of Soilex, because of the "tastes just like chicken" jokes.

She all but glared at Winnie. "You mean the same hydrochloric acid and Soilex that Jeffrey Dahmer used to soak his victims in to clean the meat off the bones? *That* hydrochloric acid and Soilex?"

"Similar enough to do the job."

That finally got Molly to her feet. "Oh, *God.*"

Winnie didn't move. "Medical supply houses don't find a need to use Soilex. At least, not on human bones. They also clean their specimens better before shipping. Besides that, most of their specimens are from third world countries, which pretty much excludes fresh five-foot-seven-inch, well-nourished white females."

Molly found herself pacing fast, cornering the little ten-by-eight-foot room like a go-cart on a short track. "Oh . . . God . . ."

"As I said," Winnie mused almost to herself. "We have a monster on our hands."

Molly walked faster, cornered harder, until she almost wiped out by the sink on water that had dripped from the coffeemaker.

"Triage nurse to the front," the PA announced overhead.

Molly tried very hard to switch gears back to the hallway. She couldn't. She kept tripping over the rest of Winnie's implied message.

They had a monster on their hands.

And he was sending his trophies to Molly.

Molly didn't sleep that night, either. She kept waiting for Magnum to bark. For him to show up at the back door with a red-and-gold mouth. She kept expecting to suddenly realize who might be angry enough with her to do something this grisly.

Outside the sleet stopped and the temperatures rose. The wind gusted and whined and then, toward morning, dropped, as if losing interest in harassing the city. Inside Molly's house, nothing stirred. Patrick had come home from work and gone straight to bed, and nobody else came to visit. So Molly sat at her kitchen table with her dog curled up at her feet and her pad of paper on the table, and she still couldn't come up with one viable name to put on her list.

She didn't know that many people. Not many she chose to remain in contact with, anyway. Molly was a compartmentalizer, carefully tucking the different bits and pieces of her life into separate boxes with the intent of only keeping one or two open at a time, because it was the only way she could deal with them.

It didn't always work, of course. PTSD lurked beneath the faultiest lid, so that she sometimes had trouble shoving it fully closed. But as she'd moved from city to city and back again and again to St. Louis, she'd ended up packing her life away and leaving it behind each time. And, for one reason or another, she'd never gone back to pick it up.

The box that was currently open contained the people at Grace ED, her co-workers at the Medical Examiner's office. Sam. Frank, when he behaved, and his three children, who had come to see her as a kind of eccentric aunt. Joey, Frank's homeless friend who lived in a cave down by the river.

But no one with huge emotional bonds, no violent upheavals, no melodramas. Her own upheavals were far behind her, her emotional bonds not even strong enough to have withstood her latest move. There was no one and nothing she could easily blame this on.

She'd helped send some people to prison last summer. She supposed she could do another check on them. Make sure once and for all none of them were so bitter they'd do something like this.

She couldn't imagine how, though. They'd been small minds. Big greed, short sight. Their crimes hadn't extended to pure evil. And whatever was going on, Winnie was right. This was the stuff of monsters.

Bones.

A human bone.

The human bone of a young girl.

And, oh, God, her eyes.

Her eyes. Could the eyes have gone with that femur? Could she be getting a corpse one piece at a time?

Or was somebody storing up gifts in his basement just to make her frantic?

Eyes.

Bones a person could almost discount. Not eyes. Not when they looked at you in your sleep, as if expecting an answer.

Eyes were an organ, just like a liver or a spleen. But an organ that carried the weight of a soul.

And Molly had been gifted a pair, like marbles, to play with.

Sitting alone in a silent kitchen that still lay in early morning shadow, Molly thought of little Latesha Wilson, who had died an unexpected death, her killer probably as surprised as she. She thought of Sharon Peters, left like trash beneath the trees of Forest Park for the joggers to find. Stunned to unconsciousness, raped and battered. A sudden crime, overwhelming, startling.

Molly wondered what it would take to have the exquisite patience to produce a bone so clean of tissue that it could hold paint.

A bone from a woman who had once been alive.

A young woman.

A girl.

Molly looked at that empty tablet of paper in front of her and knew she wouldn't find any answer that would satisfy her. Because the mind that would be able to kill like that was so malevolent Molly would surely have recognized it right away. She would have seen that kind of evil at a glance.

Wouldn't she?

God, she thought, staring at those empty lines. Who could do something like this? And what does it have to do with me?

She knew the answer to the first question, of course. She'd

taken the classes, seen the slides. Hell, she'd heard the tapes the FBI had gathered of suspect interviews.

It was tradition in the ED, though, where superstition reigned right above science in imperatives, that you simply didn't name something that scared you this badly. It was like calling down the devil. You didn't say what a quiet shift you had or all hell would break loose; you didn't say out loud just how bad a patient was or he'd die before the words were out. So Molly didn't call this person by name. But she sure as hell knew what he was.

What she had to do was figure out who and why. Because whoever the hell this was, he sure had a personal message to give to her.

Molly wanted to laugh, because she didn't know what else to do. It was too goddamn quiet in this house. Too empty and tidy and still. Molly needed movement. Leaving the empty paper behind, she headed for her answers.

Watery sunlight had begun to creep through the southern windows. The crows in her trees had begun to cackle. The family room still lay in shadow, though, the woman in Picasso's painting resting from her rage.

Molly didn't notice. Instead she focused on the penances she'd tucked into the bookshelves in the corner. The answers to questions she still really wasn't ready to ask.

For in those mahogany shelves rested the sum of her professional knowledge. Not just the *Taber's Medical Dictionary*, *Trauma Medicine*, *DSM-IV*, *Merck Manual of Medicine*, but her *Practical Homicide Investigation*. Her *Death Investigator's Manual* and *St. Louis City Criminal Investigation Procedurals*. Even more important, her collection of works from Ressler, Douglas, and Burgess, the masters of their subject. *The Crime Classification Manual*, *Sexual Homicide*, the syllabuses from every lecture she'd ever taken from those authorities.

Her answers lay on these shelves. Tucked within the statistics droll instructors had dispensed like stock options because it was the only way they could impart them with any composure. Laid out in graphic photos and even more graphic interviews that still didn't convey the horror of the subject.

Molly knew she was going to have to open those books and confirm what she already knew. She would.

In a minute.

Molly wasn't sure how long she stood there trying to work up the courage to move. She just knew that the light strengthened around her until she could actually read the titles she knew so well. Until she could see that books she cared for with the reverence of someone who respected her work, were suddenly untidy.

Jumbled a bit, as if quickly shoved back into place.

Oh, damn.

Shoving her hands into her rumpled scrub pockets, she sighed. Like she really needed even more complications right now. She was still standing there wondering what to do about it when she heard footsteps skid to a sudden halt behind her.

"Jesus, Aunt Molly! You scared the hell out of me. I didn't think you'd be up yet."

Molly didn't bother to turn to where Patrick was standing behind her in the hallway. "You either, Patrick," she said softly.

"You're still in your work clothes," he noticed. "Do you have to go back already?"

Molly rolled her shoulders to loosen them and scratched at unwashed hair. "I couldn't get to sleep last night."

She heard his bare feet pad across the hardwood floor. "Is something wrong? You get another note or something?"

Or something.

"No. Just a bad shift."

She and Winnie had decided to keep it under wraps until Winnie could assemble help. The two of them, heads together in the nurses' lounge like two friends planning a wedding shower.

"You really look beat," Patrick said, stepping alongside Molly. "Why don't you go on up to bed?"

"I have to go back down to the Medical Examiner's office later. Special meeting with the boss."

Her boss, who had driven out to the ED on a sleety Saturday night so Molly wouldn't have to find out what was going on from somebody else. Who had never once named what they faced, either, as if the longer they could keep from saying it the better they could be protected from it.

Molly caught Patrick's nod out of the corner of her eye. He was looking well put together this morning. Tall and bright and handsome.

"Tell you what," he said suddenly. "How 'bout some breakfast?"

Molly turned his way with an apologetic smile. "I'm not in the mood to go out right now."

His grin was impish. "This may be hard for you to comprehend," he said. "But I wasn't talking about junk food. I thought I'd make pancakes."

Molly blinked up at him. "You cook?"

Patrick shrugged. "Sure. Juanita can't cook a thing without chilies in it, and the parents are never home. Sean and I have gotten pretty good."

Molly nodded. "Yeah. Our housekeeper was Swedish. Miss Bartels. You hate chilies, try getting excited about lutefisk."

"No lutefisk. Just flour and water and eggs."

Which made Molly smile. "What a novel idea," she agreed. "Breakfast in my own kitchen."

He laughed. "If it'll make you feel better, I'll let you eat it in the car, just like a drive-through place."

Molly scowled. "Snot."

She took a shower and changed into khakis and sweater, returning to the kitchen in time to find the table set and the griddle working. Patrick was humming, Magnum was crouched alongside, his tail going like a metronome, and the sun had really come out. Just like a family in a television show. Molly didn't know quite how to handle it.

"Probably wouldn't be a bad idea to call home today," she said, heading for the coffeemaker.

Patrick never reacted. "Why?"

"To see what's going on with your parents. Talk to Sean. Things like that."

Never turning away from the stove, he shrugged. "Whatever."

"You don't want to talk to Sean?"

"Sean probably doesn't want to talk to me. The evil big brother? Besides, Sean's probably studying his nuclear physics or something."

Molly pulled the coffee from the freezer and filters from the cabinet. "He's smart, huh?"

"The perfect Burke."

Molly almost laughed. "How 'bout your mom? Don't you want to check in with her?"

She thought Patrick might have stiffened. "Oh, Mom'll call when she's ready."

It was all Molly could do not to stare. "She's really that mad at you, huh?"

A pause. He seemed to curl just a little over his work, as if physically shutting the questions away. "Tough to tell with Mom."

Molly tried again. "How's her job? She still designing offices?"

"No. Not anymore."

"That's too bad. I thought she was pretty good."

A shrug, striving to be noncommittal. "I don't know. She hasn't worked for a while."

Molly recognized every symptom. The stiff back, the careful words, the practiced disinterest. It was a lesson the Burkes had perfected generations ago. Denial and defense. Projecting the perfect front. Suddenly she wanted to know why, when she never had before. She wanted to understand what had put that board in Patrick's spine, that chilled disinterest in his voice.

"What about your dad?" she asked.

This time his answer was quick and true. "Oh, the undersecretary makes sure he puts in an appearance at least once a week to inspect the troops. Other than that, he's too busy fighting the trade wars."

Which meant Martin hadn't changed at all. Molly wondered if Mary Ellen had. Molly had always thought of her as one of those high-strung women. A pale, thin redhead with a breathy voice and fluttering hands, who'd always seemed to be struggling hard to maintain her balance. Martin had referred on occasion to Mary Ellen's "nerves," especially the times he'd been forced to journey alone to St. Louis. Molly had simply assumed Mary Ellen had been a lush.

Was that enough to produce this kind of discomfort and distance in a son? Had it been enough for Molly when she'd dealt with her own mother? And, come to think of it, would her own mother have forgotten to ask the most pertinent question of all when told her son had run almost a thousand miles from home?

Is he all right?

Well, Molly had had just about all she could take of that kind of parent for the day. For the month, come to think of it. Christmas and high summer. You'd think once in a while these little crises would take place in April.

"Why law enforcement?" she asked.

Patrick flipped the last of a pile of golden brown pancakes onto a plate and switched off the stove. "I don't know," he said easily, as if anticipating the question. "It's not politics."

Molly grabbed mugs and waited for coffee while Patrick got the pancakes situated on the table.

"That's all?" she asked.

He looked up, flushing. "I want to *do* something," he said. "I want to make something of myself. I've thought about it. I could start in the military. That might please the old man. MPs or something. And then, if he really wanted, I could go federal. DEA, maybe the FBI."

"Tough to do with a felony complaint on your record."

"Don't worry," he said, settling himself down to eat. "The school won't press charges. It's not the way it's done."

"Especially since you're innocent."

"Yes, ma'am."

Molly poured the coffee and wondered if she knew what the hell she was doing. "And Juanita's money?"

That bought her a sneer. "Check with the saintly Sean. I'll bet he's a little more sticky-fingered than the parents think."

"You think he stole it?"

The shrug was easy and disinterested. "Why not? Easy to lay the blame at big brother's feet when he's already deemed responsible for everything but global warming."

Setting a cup in front of Patrick, Molly sat down to consider the pile of pancakes in the middle of the table. They were damn near perfectly round and golden. They smelled like heaven, even to her questionable stomach. Molly suddenly realized how long it had been since she'd eaten, and knew Patrick had scored big points. Not big enough to keep her from addressing her new problem, however.

"What do you have planned for today, Patrick?" she asked, spearing a couple of pancakes and shifting them to her plate.

He shrugged. "I don't know. Go see a movie or something. Maybe the cyber café. I don't go into work until five or so."

She nodded. "I have to head down to the office for a quick meeting this afternoon. While I'm there, would you check in on Sam?"

"Sure."

"And one more thing."

He looked up, but she didn't smile. "I'd prefer you didn't do your early course work in law enforcement in my family room."

For a second it seemed he was going to tough it out. But after a brief show of bravado he dipped his head, that beautiful strawberry hair falling over one eye. "You knew?"

"I don't keep those books to look at the dirty pictures," she said quietly. "I use them."

"I just wanted to see."

Molly thought of the cases described in some of her homicide texts. She thought of all the deviant, frightening behavior laid out in four-color photos and realized that she should have childproofed her house before letting one in.

"Patrick," she said. "Those aren't the kind of books you can ogle and then pass around to your friends. When I get home from my meeting this afternoon we'll figure a way to introduce you to law enforcement. But I don't want you sitting alone in the family room looking at pictures of dead people. That's not what it's about."

He watched her, still not ready to believe her. "You mean it? You're not just trying to get me off your back?"

Molly did her best to smile, because, of course, she *was* just trying to get him off her back. "Hey, I have a great respect for anybody who feels the need to buck Burke tradition. I'll be happy to talk to you all about it. But I'm serious about the books."

He nodded eagerly. "Okay. I promise."

She nodded back. "Okay. Let's eat before all this work goes to waste. Although I have to tell you, you might have set a dangerous precedent. I may make you cook all the time."

"Small price to pay for the vacation."

Molly saw the carefully offhand shrug that accompanied the statement and suddenly thought of David, that pale little soccer player the night before. All that pain rigidly folded away beneath a shell of indifference. Were there any children left out there who hadn't been traumatized or abandoned?

Maybe she should get a job in a McDonald's. A circus. Someplace kids came when they were healthy. She needed, suddenly, to see happy kids, if only to believe that there were any left in the world.

"By the way," Patrick said around a mouthful of breakfast. "When I took Sam his groceries yesterday, he invited us over to Hanukkah. Is that legal?"

Molly laughed. "Sure. Hanukkah's a family holiday, and Sam's family can't be here. It's a small enough thing to do for him."

"I guess. Poor old guy. He's not the sharpest knife in the drawer, is he?"

Again, Molly laughed, and thought how much she had missed it. "Never fall for that quaint Old World grandfather crap, Patrick. Last year that poor old guy pulled off a stock market coup that netted him almost a million dollars in forty-eight hours."

Patrick goggled. "That old guy? No way."

"Let me put it to you this way. The only money I have left

after Frank Patterson got through with me is my small and cherished retirement account. I have left it all in Sam's hands. And I'm perfectly confident."

Patrick kept shaking his head. "I guess I should have tried to pawn something from *his* house."

Molly laughed even harder and thought that maybe this teenager business wasn't so bad. Even angry and unfocused, Patrick had the capacity to entertain her. Laughter and food. Not a bad combination for early on a Sunday morning. Something to shore up her nerves for what she was going to learn in that meeting.

Just the thought threatened her mood.

It was waiting for her, like a fatal diagnosis. Lurking in the shadows, submerged just below the surface of conscious thought.

They had a monster on their hands.

Well, maybe they did, Molly thought, almost physically squaring her shoulders. But before she dealt with it, she was going to fortify herself on breakfast, and then soothe herself with the secrets growing in her basement.

She was just dispatching the last of her pancakes when the phone rang. Patrick, teenager that he was, jumped up to answer it.

". . . yes, ma'am. She's here. One moment."

Molly received both phone and vaguely disappointed scowl. "Hello?"

She'd been expecting Winnie. Winnie wasn't what she got.

"Ms. Burke, this is Donna Kirkland of Action Seven News, and we've had a report that a serial killer is sending you trophies. Would you care to comment on that?"

This wasn't right.

It wasn't the way it was supposed to go.

Kenny paused a moment, his hand still on her head. Her warm head where her brain still fired in sporadic enough bursts to keep her breathing in shallow, gasping efforts. Her soft, sweet head where his own juices now flowed, even if only for a while longer.

He'd pictured it so perfectly in his own head. Dreamed it a thousand times, with her eyes open and smiling, her brain his. Her soul in a perfect, quiet compliance so that she wouldn't leave.

But now she was dead and he still didn't feel just right.

It hadn't taken long enough. She hadn't smiled at him. Not once. Not even after he'd laid her out on the couch and patted her all over like a mother pats a little boy. Or a friend pats a friend. With hands and smiles and conversation.

She hadn't smiled. She hadn't even screamed or begged or cried.

She'd wet herself, her eyes wide and silent, her mouth round like a fish, her fingers spasming, as if she were too far under water to get to air.

Kenny pulled over the tools he'd already laid out with the precision of a scientist to finish the ritual. To keep her there where he'd captured her, his butterfly on the board. His newest, prettiest friend.

Belinda. He liked the name even better than Flower. He would call her Belinda.

He'd wanted so much for Belinda to be the next gift he'd give Miss Burke. The perfect gift, which he knew she'd recognize. Which, soon, she'd understand. He knew she was getting his messages. He knew she was reacting. He knew she thought she couldn't betray that.

But she would.

He'd really wanted it to be with this gift, with this perfect message. And his new friend had ruined it by not cooperating.

Just like Miss Burke, he realized with a funny smile.

Next time.

This time he'd just have to give her somebody else, somebody who had been close, who had, in fact, screamed, although with his hand over her warm, moist mouth, so that no one heard. No one saw.

Miss Burke would see.

Miss Burke would understand, because she was the only one who ever had.

But that was another part of his dream, a part he would plan later.

So even while he picked up his sharpest knife to begin slicing his new friend apart, he began to plan for his next friend. He began to picture it, there in his own mind where he'd kept his pictures for years, rehearsing until the reality could match the visions.

Next time, he swore, stepping aside to avoid the blood. Next time it would be better.

Next time it would be perfect.

i have my own bird now. i
found it in the road. i
put my hands around its
neck and SQUEEzed

it fought me it fought me and then
it flopped.
it flopped and flopped
oh this is better than I
      ever
                  thought

SEVEN

Molly was really beginning to hate the conference room. She never seemed to get out of it. She didn't get any resolution from it. She just kept coming back, with each visit worse than the one before, and Winnie a little more angry, as if Molly had orchestrated this whole black farce just to piss her off.

And now Donna Kirkland had gone and detonated the situation right in everybody's face.

She'd said it.

Said the very words that called up the devil.

Molly hadn't said it, and Winnie hadn't said it, and Rhett hadn't even thought it. But Donna Kirkland had said the words and unleashed a firestorm.

The meeting today had been set up between Winnie and the chief of homicide. It was supposed to include Winnie, Molly, Rhett Butler, Major McConnell, the chief of homicide, and the anthropologist, Dr. DeVries. A simple testing of the waters, so the chief could be apprised of the situation and prepare his department for its impact. So they could quickly garner their forces and coordinate their efforts without interference or notoriety.

Within an hour of Donna Kirkland's phone call, the entire city administration had been mobilized.

So instead of a quiet, controlled businesslike meeting to

review facts and project investigative paths, they were going to be subjected to a classic city dick-pull.

Winnie was all but glowing with rage.

"Well, Ms. Burke," she addressed her from the head of the crowded table. "Because of you, we now have the press on our asses. I know for a fact that *I* didn't call them. Did you call them, Dr. DeVries?"

The forensic anthropologist shook her head so hard her bushy blond hair took on a life of its own. "Of course not."

Actually, the words sounded more like "of corrrz not." Dr. DeVries was from some Danish town where humor had evidently been banished. Horse-faced and oat-colored, she perched on her chair like a guest lecturer at the Inquisition.

But Molly couldn't blame Dr. DeVries, who had really done them a service. She couldn't blame Winnie, who saw a cluster fuck of epic proportions developing before her eyes. She couldn't, in all honesty, blame the lovely and rapacious Channel 7 news anchor Donna Kirkland for calling any city department that might be able to comment on a hot story.

Somebody had told the news anchor that Molly was getting distasteful gifts. And Donna, eyes on that *Hard Copy* anchor seat, had seen the story as her big step up.

Which led directly to altered attendance at today's meeting.

There were nine people crowded into the little conference room. The original list of Molly, Winnie, Rhett Butler, Dr. DeVries, and Major McConnell had been supplemented with Kevin McNally, senior death investigator; Colonel Beck, chief of detectives; Billy Armistead, the ME office's administrator; and Pete Brinkner, the city attorney.

The circuit attorney had also been invited, but declined due to continuing antipathy toward the mayor's office and a previous squash date.

"So where does that leave us?" the city attorney asked, clicking his gold ballpoint and letting it hover over a blank legal pad that looked much like the one still on Molly's kitchen table.

"How about, where do we begin?" Winnie asked in glacial tones.

"That might be the question to ask," offered Billy Armistead.

Seated directly across from Winnie in open-necked polo shirt and pressed jeans, Billy Armistead was a member of one of the city's most powerful and notorious political families. Billy was a nondescript man, middle height and build, with round, fairly blond features. It was his job as administrator of the Office of Medical Examiner to take care that political realities didn't inconvenience Winnie.

"We still don't even know if it's a real problem," the lawyer insisted. "I mean, we only have the one test on the sample, don't we? Shouldn't we double-check it to make sure we aren't getting all worked up over a decorated deer shin?"

Dr. DeVries stiffened so fast Molly could hear wind whistling up her nose. "You would question my results?" she demanded.

Again Billy jumped in, a hand on the anthropologist's arm. "It's a tough verdict to swallow, Puffin, no matter how unimpeachable the source."

Puffin. What a first name. If Molly hadn't gotten that quick warning look from Kevin, she would have burst out laughing.

Dr. DeVries relented a millimeter. "I suppose so."

"Could it be a hoax?" the lawyer asked.

"Of course it could be a hoax," Winnie snapped, her hands slapping flat against the table. "It could also be another Ted Bundy sending love missives to my death investigator."

Molly wasn't sure whether it was the Ted Bundy part or the fact that he was contacting *her* death investigator that had Winnie more riled.

"Bundy never sent trophies," Molly said equably rather than betray just what those once-delicious pancakes were now doing to her stomach.

Everybody glared at her.

Molly glared right back. "And I suppose you all think I'm getting my rocks off knowing that somebody thinks I'm the ideal partner for anato-toss? Invite our friend to lob a few human body parts at *your* dog and see how you feel."

"We know, Molly—" Billy interceded.

"Shut up, Billy," both Molly and Winnie retorted.

Billy just smiled.

"How do we proceed?" the lawyer asked.

Colonel Beck sighed and scratched his chest. Kevin kept very still. Winnie glowered all over again. Molly sweated in silence and fought the urge to run.

She'd opened her textbooks after all. The ones that applied to this situation, anyway. *Sexual Homicide*, by Ressler, Douglas, and Burgess. *Crime Classification Manual.* Same crowd. Any number of others she'd collected through the years.

She'd curled up on her couch by the big back window, out which she could see Magnum chasing squirrels, and she'd read up on the kinds of people who might consider fresh body parts to be party favors. She'd studied what the experts thought an investigation into that kind of person should entail.

So she knew, even before they told her.

"First, how do we deal with the news?" the lawyer asked.

Winnie blinked like a dyslexic in a spelling bee. She turned to Billy Armistead, who was consulting the top of the table.

"Can you deal with that, Bill?" Colonel Beck asked, scratching again, making Molly wonder how much starch his wife put in that white uniform shirt. The colonel was a formal kind of guy, always conscious of his image. An enthusiastically martial man with rigid posture, piercing blue eyes, and iron gray hair that receded at a pace with his chin, he'd managed to reach his position as chief of detectives without once working the streets. Which meant he was way out of his starched and postured league. Thank God Major McConnell, as head of homicide, was there to offset him.

"Deal with it how, Perry?" Billy asked with a half smile.

The colonel rolled his hands, as if that meant something. "Tell that woman to hold the story until we get more information."

"How much more information?" Molly asked.

"What information?" Rhett answered very quietly.

"We can't just let this blow out of proportion," the colonel protested.

Molly couldn't help but laugh. "Considering what I've pulled out of my dog's mouth, I'm not sure 'out of proportion' is possible."

The colonel scowled. "You know what I mean. We need to proceed carefully. After all, what if it is a hoax? The damage to the city could be incalculable."

"And if it isn't a hoax?" Winnie countered with deceptive calm. "Imagine the damage if we don't inform the public that young girls are at risk."

"Not probable," the colonel snapped. "I checked. No unidentified DBs in the freezer missing parts. No big missing persons cases still open. The last one was that woman they found in Forest Park. Shannon something."

"Sharon," Winnie corrected. "Sharon Peters."

"That's right. I mean, we would have heard something if this guy'd been working the area here."

Molly's smile was grim at best. Obviously the colonel hadn't been reading the same books she had.

"We need to liaise with the county," Major McConnell said. "Not to mention the surrounding counties and state highway patrol for missing person reports. There's plenty of places besides the city where this guy could be gathering his collection."

"What if it isn't even from around here at all?" Rhett asked.

Everybody turned on him as if he'd farted "Taps."

"What?" Winnie demanded.

Rhett shot Molly an apologetic glance. "Molly has moved a lot. Who says she met this individual here in St. Louis? Who says he even really knows Molly?"

"They were addressed to her," Kevin said.

Rhett shrugged. "She's a public figure."

"I don't suppose I could suggest Donna Kirkland's name to this guy," Winnie suggested.

Molly sighed. "Trophies usually don't go to strangers."

When everybody stared at her all over again, she flushed,

wishing that somebody else in the room had invested their forty bucks for *Sexual Homicide* like she had.

As if she'd heard those very thoughts, Winnie huffed like an overheated horse. "Didn't anybody here see *Silence of the Lambs*, for God's sake?"

It was the colonel's turn to stiffen. "This isn't Seattle, Dr. Harrison. We just don't get serial killers here."

"We've had a few," Major McConnell said.

"And not one of us was on board when they came through," Colonel Beck retorted, looking down his long nose at his subordinate. "We need to liaise with the men who worked those cases. Somebody who's familiar with serial killers."

Molly actually flinched. Didn't those two words terrify anybody else in this room as much as Molly?

"There were those two women stuffed in packing boxes," Kevin mused, rubbing at his chin with a pencil. "We haven't caught that bastard yet."

"No missing parts," Molly informed him, trying hard to sound offhand. "It's not our boy."

"Can we get on with it?" the lawyer demanded with pursed lips and narrowed eyes. "First of all, we haven't even established that what we have here is a serial killer."

"We don't have the luxury anymore of assuming he's not," Winnie said. "That—*those*—eyes he sent were from a woman. Probably a young woman, since there were no disease processes present. No retinopathy of any kind, no cataracts, that kind of thing."

"You're sure it was a woman?" the lawyer asked.

Winnie shot him a look of pure disdain. "In thirty percent of females, Barr bodies can be seen just at the edge of the nucleus in the epithelial cells. It's the clumping of the XX chromosome, which is more visible than the XY. Barr bodies are never found in the male eye. This eye had Barr bodies present."

"So it was a woman. Okay."

"The eye was also coated in Vaseline and frozen."

Molly almost puked right on the table.

"A very careful preparation," Winnie said, her eyes losing focus. "Not professional, as in a med school. And he didn't get all the optic muscles dissected away, not like a physician would have. But his dissection was precise and . . ."

"And?" Major McConnell asked.

Winnie actually shook her head, bemused. "Courteous."

That brought the table to a full stop. For a long, second-counting moment, full, stricken silence reigned.

Then Major McConnell, ever the professional, took over. "All right. We have a guy who decorates body parts and tosses them over a fence. Somebody who seems to know Molly, because he seems to also be sending her little love notes. We have to assume, since he's tossing them here, that he's doing this from St. Louis. Which means we probably now have another serial killer here."

"We live in a miraculous age," Winnie reminded him. "All he'd have to do to visit is take his choice of planes, trains, and automobiles."

"Motorcycles," Molly couldn't help adding.

"Buses," Rhett threw in.

"Boats," Billy said with a grin.

The collective reproach of the rest of the audience silenced them. Molly fought the giggles, the kind that had always gotten her into trouble at funerals. Better than screaming, after all.

"You mean this guy came to town just to lob eyeballs into Ms. Burke's backyard?" the lawyer demanded with some distaste. Directed at Molly rather than her correspondent.

"From what I've learned about . . . these kind of guys," Molly said, "they don't tend to go out of their way to drop off trophies. If they travel, they do it to hunt or escape notice. He could have just moved here recently, though."

Now even Winnie was looking unhappy. "So he brought his gifts with him from another city."

"That's one Ryder truck I wouldn't want to peek into," Billy offered.

Molly shrugged. "If we really aren't missing anybody locally, it's possible. Although I should remind you that nobody noticed who was missing in Milwaukee until they opened Dahmer's icebox. Same with Gacy's basement. These guys hide their tracks awfully well."

And he was sending his gifts to her.

To *her*.

"We can get an identification off what we have, can't we?" the lawyer asked. "Find out who that bone belongs to?"

"Not with just a femur," the anthropologist informed them. "We need a suspected victim and the good luck to have preexisting femoral X rays to compare."

"What about DNA?" the lawyer asked.

Even Winnie looked pitying. "You're going to run DNA matches on every missing seventeen-year-old in the country? With whose budget? And how long do you want to take to do it? One DNA test takes at least a couple of weeks."

"Which leaves us where?" the lawyer demanded.

"A task force," Colonel Beck offered.

Every other person at the table groaned. "Hand it over to Major McConnell for now," Winnie said. "You throw in special people, you'll just screw it up."

Nobody bothered to mention the fact that the last task force the mayor and colonel had put together had run up an astronomical bill with no results until two veteran homicide coppers had gone back on their own time to recheck the results.

"What about the FBI?" Kevin asked.

Rhett shook his head. "I already talked to the local special agent in charge. A—the government shutdown affects them, too. Behavioral Science Unit can't pull in any more cases, since their support staff is locked out. B—the Behavioral Science Unit can't give us any kind of profile without either a crime scene or a victim identification. I did get some ideas of where to go in the meantime, though."

"Where?" Winnie asked.

Half a dozen pens were poised to take notes. Molly's wasn't one of them. Molly knew perfectly well where they'd have to start. Even so, when Kevin and Rhett both looked her way, she smiled. She knew they weren't any happier about the next stage than she was.

"Molly," Rhett said simply.

The lawyer looked from Rhett to Molly and back again. "Molly what?"

Rhett shrugged. "It's a variation on victimology. If you're trying to find a perpetrator, you can learn as much about him from the victims he chooses as the crimes he commits. We don't know who the actual victims are, but we do know that for some reason he's singled Molly out to receive his trophies. Which puts her in a kind of victimology category. If we can figure out why he's targeting Molly, we might get a better handle on who he is."

"What we think are his trophies," Molly objected.

Rhett grinned like a chagrined kid and nodded. "We need to investigate Molly's background to find out why somebody might want to contact her like this."

Now everybody was staring at her. Molly wanted to hide. She wanted somebody to tell her this was all a big mistake, but these weren't the people who were going to do it.

"Don't look at her as if she's the damn Rosetta Stone," Winnie snapped. "He probably just saw her on television. God knows, everyone else in the bi-state area has."

"Whoever it is," Billy ventured, "you really pissed 'em off."

Molly scowled. "You're making me feel better by the minute, Bill."

"You've been looking into this for a few days now, Detective Butler," Winnie said. "What have you learned so far?"

Rhett didn't even glance at Molly this time. He bent to the cop notebook he flipped open. "Nobody in the immediate vicinity noticed anything unusual. But then, since the neighborhood is gated and adjoins Euclid, it's tough to tell about noise. Lots of foot and car traffic on the other side of her fence. No strangers noted in the side streets, except for Ms. Burke's nephew, who's recently arrived. As for Ms. Burke, her next-door neighbor wants to adopt her, the lady across the street would like her for a gardener, and the family down the street wishes she'd get a better car."

"So does she," Molly said under her breath.

"That's it?" Rhett's superior demanded.

Rhett shot Molly a glance and stiffened like a chastised schoolboy. "Melinda Anne Burke, DOB eight/fifteen/fifty, born in St. Louis, traveled extensively as a child with her parents. Earned a bachelor of nursing from St. Louis University in 1971, enlisted in the Army, where she served for twelve months in Vietnam from 1971–1972, earning campaign ribbons, Bronze Star, and Purple Heart . . ."

Almost embarrassed, he looked up at the group, who were looking at Molly with some surprise.

"You were in Vietnam?" the lawyer demanded.

Winnie slapped a hand on the table. "Unless this guy is an NVA regular she failed to treat, I doubt it's relevant. What else?"

Rhett blushed. "Uh, that's it so far on background. I haven't had a chance to interview Miss . . . uh, Molly. I also just tracked down the FBI guy yesterday. My next step is to sit with Molly and do a more thorough personal and professional history."

"Couldn't it just be somebody mad at her from work?" the lawyer asked. "Like Dr. Harrison said, she has been kind of visible lately."

Rhett cleared his throat. "If she were getting them at work, I'd be more inclined to agree. But she's getting them at home. Besides, a trophy is awfully personal. Most of these guys give them to wives and girlfriends."

Molly felt every eye in the room on her, and saw more than one eyebrow raised. "Sorry to disappoint you again."

Rhett gave her an especially interested glance, but then, Rhett had met Frank. But even Rhett didn't understand the relationship Frank and Molly had. Probably because Molly didn't either. But then, Frank would probably get a huge kick out of being a suspect in a high-profile investigation like this.

"What about surveillance on her house?" Colonel Beck asked.

"You tell us," Winnie answered. "Do we have the manpower and funding?"

The colonel shrugged. "Do we have a choice? Do some more tests on that bone, and that . . . you know. Make sure we're not making a mountain out of a molehill here. In the meantime, I'll apprise the chief of police, and Major McConnell can . . ."

"We'll start canvassing the neighborhood. Look more closely into missing persons. Recheck some files that might be applicable."

Molly saw Rhett's shoulders sag microscopically. For almost seventy-two hours, he'd been handling a potential redball on his own. Now the system was taking it back out of his hands. Even so, he maintained his revered professional demeanor. "I'll talk to missing persons," he said.

Major McConnell shook his head. "You talk to Ms. Burke. Find out what the hell's so appealing about her."

Molly laughed out loud. "Well," she offered drily, "she's quite a conversationalist, and on occasion has been heard to play a mean jazz piano."

The major had the good grace to flush. "You know what I mean," he muttered.

Molly was afraid she did.

"And what about that newswoman?" the lawyer demanded.

"I think we should stonewall her," the colonel said.

"You think you should stonewall everybody," Winnie retorted. "I say we make her inclusive. Ask her silence until we can double-check Puffin's findings, then give her an early exclusive."

"I think that's gonna get us bit in the ass," the lawyer protested. "Full disclosure now."

"And wade through the packs of *Inside Edition* reporters in the morning?" Winnie argued. "Can you spell JonBenét Ramsey?"

"There's also the question of just who leaked the information in the first place," the lawyer said.

"Another reason to keep this business close to the vest," the colonel said.

"You might also want to consider the fact that this guy might be waiting for a news story," Molly offered, her stomach off on a roil again. "If he is, indeed, what we think he is—" Okay, so she wasn't as brave as she wanted to be

"—one of his goals is to relive the moment. Lots of news coverage helps him do just that."

"Fine," the colonel said with a sharp nod. "*You* talk to her."

"She is *not* talking to her," Winnie snapped.

Considering the fact that she'd said about all she wanted to on the subject, Molly sat back and doodled on her notepad, trying to think what she could do. More truthfully, what she could do that would inconvenience her the least.

Inconvenience. Nice euphemism for preventing the shrieks. Molly had to get that new therapist, and fast. She had the feeling her stress level was just about to go critical.

It took Molly a minute to notice that the meeting was breaking up. The chief of detectives shook hands with the lawyer, and the anthropologist nodded curtly to Billy, who seemed tickled. Nobody seemed to feel the need to bother with Rhett or Molly, which meant that they were the first ones through the door.

"When do you want to sit down and talk?" he asked as they walked the short hall back to where Molly shared an office with the other four investigators.

"How 'bout when hell freezes over?" Molly asked. "When the Cubs win the World Series. When St. Louis goes Republican. When the mayor—"

"Molly."

Stepping into the investigator's room, Molly sighed. "What are you doing now?" she asked.

Rhett kind of gaped. "Now?"

Molly glared at him. "Ever had a tooth pulled? Better to slam that door really fast."

Rhett's smile was at once sorry and chagrined. "This isn't going to be anywhere near really fast, Mol."

"Which is why we should do it right away," she said. "If we don't, by the time you catch me I'll have moved to Oregon."

Since Kevin was taking call today, none of the other investigators were on. The room, stuffed with untidy desks, a sprung black Naugahyde couch for night shifts, and a portable black-and-white TV perennially turned to ESPN, seemed unnaturally still. Molly had some paperwork she had to catch up on. She had follow-up calls to make, and notes to transcribe from her last shift. And she had Rhett standing patiently at her side waiting to pick her brain apart.

She wanted to ask Rhett if he could wait until she found herself a new shrink before he started, but as picky as she was, by the time she had any luck, she'd be in Oregon and Rhett would have to get a flight warrant on her.

So she attempted one of those calming breaths, and she picked up the papers she'd left on her desk.

"Come along, Mr. Butler," she said, turning on her heel. "I believe it's our turn to dance."

Rhett didn't get it, but he followed, palming his homicide hat onto his head. "We're not going to sit out in your backyard again, are we?" he asked a bit faintly.

Molly always made it a point to sit in the backyard when talking about cases. She hated to talk about culpability and guilt in that stony house. But the wind was blowing and the temperatures were dropping again. She guessed it wouldn't help to refrigerate her homicide officer.

"You're not going to drag me over to interrogation?"

Rhett's smile was way too old for that face. "Only if I thought it would intimidate you into revealing surprises. I don't think I'd have any luck."

Molly laughed this time. "Once you've had sex in an interrogation room, they just aren't that intimidating anymore, Rhett."

Rhett goggled. "What?"

"We'll go to my house," she said, walking on by. "It's a much scarier place."

"Sex?" he demanded. "At the *station*?"

But Molly decided he didn't need an answer.

On her way by Winnie's office, Molly dropped a set of papers on the desk and kept an identical set in her hand. The party was still breaking up in the conference room. Winnie caught sight of Molly and stopped whatever conversation she was having.

"You refer any questions at all to this office. You understand?"

"With pleasure."

"I want a report—"

"On your desk," Molly told her. "Everything up to and including the call to the meeting this morning. Okay?"

She didn't see Winnie smile. "About time."

"You have a report written up already?" Rhett demanded.

Grabbing the railing and heading down the wide steps, Molly shrugged. "Not much to tell. Six notes, one bone, two alleged eyeballs, no suspects. On my way to pick brain with cute homicide officer. End of story."

As if it were.

"Cute?" Rhett echoed, just like the puppy he was.

Molly laughed.

They'd made it to the bottom of the stairs when the receptionist waylaid them.

"Oh, Molly, you had a call while you were upstairs. Mr. Patterson. He said as soon as you were out, beep him, he'd pick you up at your house."

Molly stumbled to a halt, which made Rhett skid sideways, leaving black marks on the marble floor.

"My house?" she demanded. "What for?"

The receptionist's expression said that she figured she could well guess. "Well, I don't know. He just said it's important, and he knew you wouldn't be able to turn him down. He said he was sure you'd rather see him than Donna Kirkland?"

Molly froze in place. "Donna Kirkland?" she demanded.

"You're sure he said Donna Kirkland?" Rhett asked right behind her.

The receptionist scowled. "Like that's a name I'd mess up."

"He wouldn't have called her, would he?" Rhett asked, his voice all but hushed.

Amazing how fast her temper flared out of control. Molly yanked her keys from her purse and headed for the door. "Maybe it's a good thing you're coming over right now after all, Rhett. That way you don't have to wait to be called for the homicide."

i want somthing. i want something
important, something that will make
me feel better. bigger
bigger than even her, then all of
them. I want another bird. Maybe a
cat. a cat would be good I'd give it
to her on her plate at dinner.
Staring at her.

maybe i'd let it eat her eyes.

EIGHT

Fortunately for Frank, he wasn't at Molly's house when she got there. Come to think of it, neither was Patrick. Not that he'd locked up or set the alarm when he'd left. Just like the teenager he was, he'd evidently simply wandered off. If Molly hadn't on occasion committed the same crime, she probably would have been more outraged. As it was, she double-checked the valuables to make sure Patrick wasn't out getting ready cash and led Rhett to the kitchen.

"What would you like to drink?" she asked as she dumped her magenta down jacket over a kitchen chair and headed for the kettle.

"Oh, uh, nothing," Rhett assured her, adding his overcoat to the pile and setting his homicide hat on the table like a sacred offering. He was looking around, just as he always did—just as everybody did who'd ever been inside or heard about the house. "Do you really think Patterson is the one who tipped off Donna Kirkland?"

Molly set the water to boil and took a peek out the back door to find Magnum's big, ugly face pressed to the glass. She knew it was dumb, but she checked to make sure he didn't have glitter on his lips.

"I wouldn't put anything past Frank," she admitted. "As

fond as he is of yanking my chain, though, I wouldn't jump to any conclusions till he drops the other shoe."

"Aren't you supposed to beep him or something?"

"Nah. He didn't really expect me to beep him back. He'll show up on his own."

Rhett couldn't seem to come up with a suitable comment. Molly, already feeling as hounded as a prison escapee, just went about pulling out her tea supplies with ever-shaking hands.

"Where do you want to start?" Rhett asked behind her.

"With another person."

"I can't, Molly. You know that." He paused, shuffled his feet. Went on in a rush. "Um, about your military history . . ."

Molly looked up and saw something perilously close to awe in Rhett's eyes. It was a look she'd seen more than once in young men who discovered her history, the inevitable reaction from a young male untested in war. That she should see it in Rhett, who had survived over six years in the much more unpredictable street wars of urban America, made her angry.

What did he want? Validation? Absolution? Whatever it was, Molly didn't have any today. Hell, she didn't even have absolution for herself. All she had was the growing dread of what would be left of her when they finished laying her out like a science experiment.

Not even waiting for the kettle to whistle, Molly poured the hot water into mugs. "I sincerely doubt that a Nam vet would just be showing up now as a serial killer," she said, as if that was what Rhett was after. "They're too old. And way too tired."

And most of them, she thought, had far different demons to deal with.

"Even your friend Frank?" Rhett asked quietly.

Molly laughed so hard Magnum barked. "Frank would never go to that much trouble," she assured him. "Besides, Frank's preferred methods of torture are far more subtle and traumatic than mere dismemberment."

Rhett shrugged as if none of it mattered. "Well, I will need to find out all about him."

"Ask him when he shows up," she said, ladling sugar into her mug. "He'd be delighted to be grilled. If he survives my polite questions about Donna Kirkland, anyway."

Molly handed off the mug of tea Rhett hadn't asked for, which he accepted without a qualm.

"Then we'll talk about other things till he comes," he said.

Molly nodded. "Fine. Follow me."

Molly really didn't have to think about where to take this round of *To Tell the Truth*. She headed straight for the basement, where the grow lights hummed and the low ceiling forced Rhett into an uncomfortable stoop.

"You growing marijuana down here?" he asked, only half kidding.

"Why is it that everyone figures if you have grow lights you're using them for illicit activity?" Molly demanded.

Rhett shrugged and plopped down on a high stool. "Because usually that's what they're for."

Molly picked up her mister and went after her seedlings. "I start my annuals in here during the winter," she said. "From seeds. I also grow African violets and some orchids."

Rhett looked over the room with its orderly tables, its thicket of immature leaves, its neatly hung gardening tools, and he pulled out his cop book.

"Where do you want to start?" he asked.

Molly misted her violets, picking off old leaves as she moved. "You decide. It's your interview."

"You know just as much about what I need as I do."

Molly glared at him. "You want to earn those big stripes or not, Rhett? Don't make me do your work for you."

Rhett raised only one eyebrow in reaction. All Molly could think of was how many hours Rhett must have stood in front of a mirror trying to master the muscle control.

"You're not a suspect of any kind," he reassured her. "You know that, don't you?"

Molly kept her attention on her plants and sucked in a tough breath. "That doesn't matter worth a damn. You know that, too? The minute this all gets out, I'm going to be the only meat on the counter. If this guy is as bad as he seems, we're going to have every sleazy magazine and news crew on three continents here. And because we can't give them another damn thing to expose or scoop, they're going take apart my life for the viewing pleasure of all the morons who tune in to that stuff."

Now Rhett's voice was very quiet. "Do you have some things you don't want people to know?"

"The only person my revelations will be important to is me. Which is why I don't think they belong on national news."

"This doesn't involve just you," he corrected her. "It involves everybody you've known your whole life."

For a long moment, Molly didn't so much as move. She just stood there staring at the velvet pink petals of her violets.

"You knew that," Rhett said quietly. Rhett, who was much smarter than he seemed.

"Of course I knew that."

She just hadn't admitted it to herself. Not really. Not even after studying *Sexual Homicide*. Molly compartmentalized because it was easier. It was quieter. It kept her life manageable and her dreams only occasionally terrifying.

And now Rhett was asking her to throw open all those old boxes at once.

"Your military history," he prompted, a new note in his voice.

Empathy. God, Molly hated empathy. Where the hell was Frank with his "who gives a shit" attitude? Rhett was going to strip her raw and leave her bleeding with those John-Boy eyes of his. And there wasn't a damn thing she could do about it, because he was right. They had to stop this guy, and the only way was to find out as much about her as they could.

Somewhere in her past, this monster had touched her. Had smiled or frowned or screamed just for her. And Molly, somehow, had to remember.

"By military history," she said, brusquely tending her overtended plants, "I assume you also mean the information you considerately left out of the summation this afternoon about my various cognitive vacations at Rancho V.A."

Amazing how just the sound of shuffling feet could convey misery. Poor Rhett.

Molly finally faced him. "Rhett, honey, it's okay. Winnie knows all about it."

Rhett looked almost fierce. "Yeah, but the colonel doesn't."

Molly sighed, wondering what she'd done to deserve a watch puppy. "He will."

Rhett looked, if possible, even more miserable. "You want to talk about it?"

Molly laughed. "Don't be stupid, Rhett. Of course I don't want to talk about it. But I'm going to have to. It's part of that deep evaluation, just like both of my marriages and the seventeen or eighteen jobs I've had since Nam."

Rhett blinked. "Both?"

Molly sighed, already tired of this game. "Both. You want 'em alphabetically or chronologically?"

"Will they talk to me?"

"The one who's still alive will. As for the stays at Uncle Sam's Prozac Palace, I'll sign permission for you to check files. Those would be more reliable than my memory."

Rhett bent to his book. "Uh, how many . . . I mean, how often . . ."

"I did four short tours before I found somebody on the outside who understood the concept of a woman having posttraumatic stress. Once I hooked up with him, I managed on the outside much better."

As long as she had her Paxil.

And her silence.

And it wasn't Christmas or summer.

"I never . . . uh . . ." If possible, Rhett was looking even more miserable. And Molly, caregiver since birth, took pity.

"You never thought of women having post-traumatic stress. I know. Nobody really did. It's okay, Rhett. I'm not going to start screaming or pull out an AK-47, if that's what you're afraid of."

He looked as if she'd slapped him. "I'd *never* . . ."

But he sat. He sipped at his tea. He flipped open his book

and thought about things. "I would have thought . . . I don't know . . . didn't your, uh, husband . . ."

"Husbands," Molly amended as she pinched some more leaves and thought about fertilizer. "Make it better? Sex doesn't cure all, Rhett, no matter what Frank tries to tell you."

Rhett, unbelievably, blushed.

"On the other hand," Molly said, just to see him get redder. "It's been so long, I'm not sure I wouldn't mind finding out if it still doesn't make things worse."

Silence. Throat clearing. Molly wondered how he lasted an hour with a pimp in an interrogation room without passing out.

"Two husbands, Rhett," she said, leaning against a high table across from him. "One at a time, of course. John Michael Murphy, 1973 to 1981. We married here at College Church and divorced in Los Angeles. He was a great kisser and wild about the Dead. It's fitting, I guess. He is now himself. Jammin' with Jerry Garcia."

"I'm, uh . . . sorry."

Molly shrugged. "Not as sorry as he was. He was into stoned skydiving. Problem is that when you're stoned you tend to forget what the cord's for."

Pause. Blush. "Oh."

"His mother might hate me, but she's ninety. I doubt she has the energy to chew the meat off bones, much less toss 'em in vats."

"So he was from St. Louis?"

"Went to Mary Queen of Peace."

Which in the small world of St. Louis, told Rhett everything he needed to know about the dear, late, still-lamented John Michael. In St. Louis, a person was defined by his parish boundaries, and John Michael's parish boundaries pronounced him upper-middle-class bordering on pretention, conservative, with parents who were likely Republican, college-educated, and committed to Catholic education, sports, and keeping a perfect lawn.

They'd tried so hard, she and John Michael. Both castoffs from the same war, both trying to outrun their nightmares.

Early on they'd tended to alternate times in the hospital. Then John Michael had discovered the spiritual bliss of chemical oblivion and found another way out.

"After that was Peter Paul Perkins, 1982 to 1985," she said briskly. "I guess I must have been into alliteration. Or big dicks. He had both. Come to think of it, he also *was* one."

"But he's, uh, alive."

"In Idaho somewhere. He bounced in the opposite direction from John Michael. Went from pleasantly interesting lab tech to born-again, militant militia leader. Soldier of the Lord in the fight against UN infiltration."

"What about his family?"

"Happily building the final outposts of civilization in the mountains. They weren't at all disappointed when I declined the offer to join them. I'm tainted, ya know. My brother is in the government."

"Which means?"

Molly grinned. "Why, that he's a lackey for the UN invasion forces. I'm sure the Perkins family would only visit so they could unearth Martin's manual for reading street signs backward for the time he takes over Idaho for the Belgian army."

"What is his official title?"

"Martin or Peter Paul? Peter Paul is, I believe, Colonel Perkins. Catchy, don't you think? My brother Martin is Undersecretary of Commerce, or cattle, or something. He is presently in China finding facts." She grinned briefly again, the image of Martin in blue helmet and camos distracting. "As you might imagine, Peter was as popular with my family as I was with his."

"Would you . . . I mean, consider your ex-husband . . . um . . ."

"A cannibal? No. But then, when I knew him he was a vegetarian. I can't guarantee he didn't give that up with agnosticism. But I do think he's much too busy with the big picture to be this attentive to me."

"Is there any way I can find out about your work history?"

Molly nodded, still focused on her flowers. "I have an extra résumé upstairs. Call away. In the meantime I'll try and remember anybody I worked with who might be angry enough—and crazy enough—to do this. I'll tell you right now, though, with sixteen or so jobs, it's going to be a stretch to remember anybody."

"You'd think somebody like this would be memorable."

Molly thought about that a moment, and then admitted her own misconception. "Just the opposite, actually. People like this don't want the folks around them to recognize them. After all, if they're caught, they have to give up the fantasy."

Rhett frowned. "The fantasy."

Molly nodded, thinking about the dark ruminations she'd been caught in during the predawn hours. "Fantasy, Rhett. This is too meticulous, too complex to be a simple act of frustration. The standing theory is a guy like this is actually acting out a fantasy he's been perfecting since he was about six years old."

Rhett almost choked on his tea. "Six?"

Molly nodded, thinking of all those interviews, all those things only hinted at by other monsters. "The pros think that the signature of . . . this kind of crime, what makes it belong to one particular killer, is the reflection not only of early childhood experiences, but of what his fantasy has been his whole life, from the time he could first put it into pictures."

Rhett actually looked pale. "Oh. And this guy's fantasy is against you?"

Molly turned away. "How the heck do I know? Was Ted Bundy really so angry specifically at those girls he killed, or were they the substitute for whatever he saw in his head when he was a kid? Or maybe the woman who caused the precipitating event that incited him to act out his fantasy the first time?"

"So you think this guy isn't really targeting you because he's mad at you."

Molly stroked her violets again, wishing the petals were bigger, older. Wishing her garden were in full bloom beneath a soft late-spring night so she could lie on the dark earth and smell the life there. So she could be restored.

Now, though, she had to settle for tiny wisps of life, because outside her plants were dormant and the earth was hard.

"I don't know," she finally admitted in a small voice.

"I mean, it's not like you live a high-risk kind of life for this sort of thing," he said softly, almost to himself. "Everybody at work says you're more likely to go out with the moms for hamburgers at Steak n Shake than the swinging singles for slamming at the Toe Tag. You don't date much, do you?"

"I think 'at all' is the more appropriate term."

"You work two responsible jobs, keep a pretty regular schedule, and associate with an old man and a teenage nephew. You don't live the kind of life that should make you show up on a serial killer's radar screen."

Molly scowled. "You're right, Rhett. I don't. I'm appalled to say that I have safely passed through that stage of my life and found it less than enchanting."

"When did you do that?"

Molly rubbed at her forehead and felt the grit of soil on her fingers. "Oh, jobs four through ten, I guess. And then, maybe a relapse around job thirteen."

Rhett scribbled hard. "You're going to be an interesting investigation, Molly."

Molly's smile was wry.

"About your nephew . . ."

"Son of the undersecretary. Here because of parental problems, currently making a living wage bussing tables at Via Venito over on Maryland."

"Not a suspect."

Molly turned on him. "What?"

Rhett's smile reminded her of a Boy Scout getting Granny across the street. "That wasn't a question, Molly. When that last . . . uh, flower box came in. Do you remember the last time you saw your dog before you got home to let him out?"

"Sure. I let him out just before I left for work."

"And you're pretty sure he didn't have the box then."

"If he had, he would never have ever come back in."

"And your nephew?"

"Had already gone. Why?"

"Because I checked with the restaurant. Patrick was there until you saw him climbing over the fence. They remember because not only were they busy and had a truck to unload after dinner, but Patrick evidently . . . well, uh . . ."

"Spit it out. I doubt it's going to be more upsetting than the possibility that he's been chopping up young women."

"He's been on probation because of attitude. Evidently he has trouble following orders from a boss only a year older than he is."

Molly sighed, at once frustrated and relieved. Not that she'd really thought Patrick capable of this, but it was nice to have him safely out of the suspect pool. On the other hand, she'd have to have a Come-to-Jesus meeting with him about responsibility and trust.

"You're sure?" she said.

Rhett raised an eyebrow again. "You were worried?"

"Of course not. I just want to keep my problems on their separate plates. It would be exhausting to confuse the mad killer stuff with the petulant, abandoned teenager stuff. Ya know?"

She wasn't sure he did, but he nodded anyway. "From the condition of the flower box, Dr. Harrison is pretty sure your dog was working on it from the minute he went outside when you got home. And Patrick wasn't around then to toss it."

Molly threw off a quick nod. "Good. Maybe he'll be easier to deal with now."

"I still have to see if Mr. Patterson had an alibi."

Leave it to Frank to know the nanosecond to show up. "An alibi for what?" he asked from the top of the steps.

Rhett damn near fell off his stool. Molly scowled.

"You've come to tell me that your message about Donna Kirkland was another tasteless joke, haven't you?" she demanded without moving.

Neither did Frank. "My jokes are never tasteless, Molly. Above your comprehension, maybe."

Rhett was about to say something, but Molly forestalled him. "Explain, then."

She could hear the amused smile in his voice. "Your

nephew is impressed with his aunt's notoriety. You might want to make sure he isn't so impressed he finds himself wanting to share it."

"You didn't call Donna Kirkland?" Rhett asked, obviously out of patience with subtlety.

Frank's laugh echoed around the basement like cannon fire. "Sorry to disappoint you, Detective."

Molly was perfectly content to continue this way, with Frank perched as close as he could to her basement, and her comfortably settled on her stool, until she heard the staccato of Mary Jane shoes on her kitchen floor upstairs.

She was off that stool as if she'd been spring-loaded.

"Did you bring that pack of wild animals with you?" she demanded of Frank with barely suppressed delight.

"She wants to know if you're wild animals," he said to someone else.

"Yes, Daddy," a tiny voice piped up.

"I'm sorry, Molly," he apologized, his voice echoing faintly down her steps. "I did bring wild animals into your house."

"Well, give them some cookies or something before they chew up my drapes," she insisted, grinning like a kid as she grabbed a towel and wiped her hands. She'd been given a break. Hell, she'd been given a reward.

Molly didn't wait for Frank to come down into her basement, because he wouldn't. She led Rhett upstairs to meet them all.

"How'd you get in my house, Frank?"

"You left the back door open for us, Molly," he said with a sparkling grin, "just like I knew you would. Your kitchen's a mess, by the way."

Molly scowled. "My kitchen has suffered at the hands of a teenager, Frank. Make sure you teach your wild animals the proper respect for a kitchen before it's too late."

He already had. Frank had three children, six-year-old twins and four-year-old Abigail. The twins, a boy and a girl named Tim and Theresa, were intense, active blonds Molly had been told looked like their mother. Abigail, a dead ringer

for Frank, was solemn and sweet. Considering what a wild
card their father was, Molly was forever amazed that his children were so . . . well, normal.

"Cookies?" Abigail asked, raising her arms to Molly.
Without another thought, Molly scooped her up and spent a
moment reveling in the uncomplicated pleasure of a tiny,
sturdy life in her arms.

Abigail was at the pinafore and hair-bow stage, all glossy
dark hair and huge eyes and amazement, and Molly couldn't
get enough of her. The twins, Frank's athletes, were both in
jeans and polo shirts under their bright down jackets, which
was unusual for them. They both preferred the sports uniform
of the day.

"No soccer?" she asked as she headed for the cookie jar
her neighbor Sam had supplied her with since Frank had begun to bring the kids by. Sam might have had Winnie the
Pooh, but Molly had Harry Potter.

Tim proffered a face of long suffering. "Church," he
moaned.

Molly did her best not to laugh. "Church, Frank?" she
asked. "And the ceiling didn't fall in on you?"

Frank settled himself into a kitchen chair and wrapped an
arm around each twin. "Not so much as a rumble from the
skies, St. Molly. But I had my protectors with me, didn't I,
kids?"

"Daddy says God can't possibly get mad at him if we're
there," Abigail announced.

"Using your children as celestial shields, Frank," Molly
admonished, pillaging Harry Potter's head for Oreos. "A
new low."

"I go to church every Sunday, Mol. Don't you?"

"You *need* church every Sunday, Frank. In fact, you could
probably use it every day. Possibly every hour on the hour."

His smile was brash and bright and happy. Molly handed
off cookies and got ready thanks from the kids. Abigail
munched hers like a queen at tea, one arm around Molly's
neck, and for the first time in days, Molly felt better.

"Why do you have ashes on your forehead?" Theresa asked, head tilted to the side. "We don't."

Molly wasn't quite sure what to say. So Frank said it for her. Laughing. "She's repenting for her many sins of slander against me, honey," he said as he walked over to scoop the dishrag from the sink and approach Molly.

Molly took an instinctive step back, but Frank caught her arm and swiped at her forehead. Which was when Molly understood.

"Those aren't ashes," she said with a grin for the kids. "I was playing in the dirt."

"Of course they're ashes," Frank disagreed, throwing the rag back into the clutter of half-empty cups and scraped plates. "Molly considers every day Lent and all her actions penance."

"Don't play over your audience's head," Molly suggested drily.

"Doesn't he get a cookie?" Theresa asked, eyes on Rhett, who was standing by the basement door watching all the action with a cop's quiet eye.

"He doesn't deserve a cookie," Frank said. "He's been asking questions about your daddy."

All three little heads looked his way. "Why, Dad?" Tim asked. "Is he a lawyer, too?"

Molly damn near choked on her cookie. "No, honey," she said. "He has a real job. Rhett is a policeman."

All three sets of eyes widened noticeably.

"What did you do this time?" Tim asked with perfect innocence.

Molly laughed and tossed Rhett a cookie, which he caught one-handed.

"I didn't do anything," Frank assured his son with a nuggie to the top of his head just like he gave Magnum. "I never do anything but what is right and beneficial to my family. But the rest of the world simply doesn't appreciate my special nature."

All three kids rolled their eyes. "Uh-huh."

"I would like to talk to you," Rhett told Frank diffidently.

Frank nodded pleasantly. "Of course. Come see me at my high-priced office tomorrow, so I can intimidate you."

Molly just shook her head. "I thought you guys were going to teach your daddy to play well with others," she mourned to Abigail.

Abigail sighed, as if she were faced with the biggest challenge in the world. "He doesn't listen."

For that she got grabbed right out of Molly's arms and tickled within an inch of her life. Molly fed herself on the delighted giggles that ricocheted throughout her kitchen.

"So what's this important thing I'm going to do for you, Frank?" she asked.

Frank was busy gnawing on his daughter's neck. "Check on Joey."

Some of that peace of mind evaporated. "Why?"

Frank's tone of voice didn't change at all so his kids wouldn't catch his meaning. "He didn't meet us after mass this morning. And he's not answering."

"Joey eats breakfast with us on Sunday," Theresa explained.

Molly knew that. She also knew that Joey was as predictable as the stock market and twice as reasonable. Joey was one of Frank's oldest friends, a pal from grade school when they'd both attended St. Gabriel's in the city. A buddy through high school at St. Louis U. High, where they'd withstood the rites of puberty together, dating best friends and playing pickup basketball on St. Gabe's playground. But that had been a long time ago.

While Frank had come home from Vietnam almost whole, the best parts of Joey had been left behind. Joey now lived in the caves beneath St. Louis, his eyes vacant, his speech slurred, his mind pocked with madness and despair. Joey was Frank's penance, and he'd paid it for years.

"What do you want me to do?" Molly asked, because she knew Joey, too.

Frank didn't face her. "Go in and check on him."

Go down into the cave, he meant. Just the suggestion

made her sweat all over again. "Oh, I don't think so," she said. "I don't do caves."

Frank laughed and shot a look toward her basement door. "We all do caves, St. Molly. Joey's is just more literal than most."

And Frank, brash, bright, fearless Frank, couldn't so much as stand in the entrance to Joey's cave. Frank couldn't even bring himself to set a foot down Molly's stairs into the basement. Molly had never asked why and Frank had never said. But then, Molly respected phobias like that.

"Can't you yell or have somebody else go down?" she asked.

"He won't let anybody else in but you," Frank said. "It's what you get for having been a female medical officer. Even the crazies respect that."

A neat little fact Molly had used to her advantage more than once in her career. Amazing how that military lilt in your voice incited reactions like Pavlov's bell. The odd homeless vet, who listened to no one but his voices and the whisper of Jim Beam, couldn't ignore the peculiar pull a nurse's command stirred up. Molly just didn't want to test the theory today. In a cave.

"You talked to the other guys."

He nodded.

Rhett made a couple quick notes in his book, Molly saw. Probably figuring on checking out Joey, too. It would keep him busy and accomplish nothing. There wasn't enough of Joey left in that wasted shell to summon any emotion, much less revenge.

Molly took a look out her kitchen window, to where the sun shifted among the clouds across a bleak winter landscape. She thought of how the wind would blow down by the river, how the men would shuffle in the shadows just out of sight where they wouldn't have to risk discovery. She thought of Joey, who had a claim on her because of those haunted, hopeless eyes of his.

"Aw, shit," she sighed.

Frank smiled. His kids grinned at catching an adult in a rule infraction. Outside Magnum began to bark.

"You want me to check for surprise packages?" Frank asked.

Molly shook her head. "It's Patrick. Magnum gets this amazing note of outrage when Patrick comes in the front door so he can sneak by without having to pet him."

As if announced, Patrick slammed the front door like a poltergeist in a tantrum. "More news, Aunt Molly!" he yelled, loping over the hardwood floors toward the kitchen.

"What is it, Patrick?"

He arrived in the kitchen red-cheeked and windblown, his coat hanging open and his shoes half tied. When he caught sight of exactly who was there to greet him, he slid to an abrupt halt. "I thought you said nobody ever came to see you," he all but accused.

"You know Frank and the kids," Molly said. "This is Detective Butler. He's helping with the investigation."

Patrick didn't so much as waste a glance on Rhett. He was doing some kind of weird male domination dance with Frank, as if he realized that Frank was the person most likely to threaten him.

Frank just smiled. "I bet you're back to clean up the kitchen, aren't you?"

Molly wasn't sure whether she wanted to express gratitude or outrage. It had been a hell of a long time since she'd asked a man to settle her problems. Longer even since she'd allowed one to simply take over by rights.

"Exerting your territorial prerogative, are you?" Patrick demanded.

Before Molly had the chance to slap her nephew, Frank laughed. "Call me a consultant. Your aunt is a whiz at carnage, but her long-term experience with teenage boys is a little light."

"She's doing just fine," Patrick said, stiff and cold.

Frank nodded agreeably. "Her learning curve is exceptional. I'm just helping fill in a few blanks. See, having been a teenage boy once myself, I know just how far a kid'll go to keep from fulfilling his responsibilities. But I know how much you want to help your Aunt Molly to say thanks for taking you in."

Molly could feel the tension crackle like air around a high-voltage wire. Give those two another minute, they'd be peeing in the corners.

"That's why I came home," Patrick said in a deadpan voice, his eyes flat as rocks. "Because I forgot to finish cleaning up."

Frank's smile was bright as day. "Isn't that what I told you, Molly?"

Molly almost broke out laughing. "You did, Frank. And thank you, Patrick. You know how I appreciate a clean house."

As if pulling a foot from mud, Patrick yanked his attention around to Molly. "Might as well," he said. "You want it nice for when you're on camera."

"When I'm what?"

He waved an arm in the general direction of the front door. "There's a camera truck outside from Channel Seven. They asked me if you lived here."

Molly thought she was going to throw up. "And you said yes."

"Well, sure. I want to be on TV, too."

It was all Molly could do to keep from heaving her teacup at the wall. "Damn it," she groused. "I guess that means nobody got hold of old Donna."

"Well, you might want to talk to her," Patrick said with relish. "Before she talks to the evidence guys."

Now all the adults were staring. "What evidence guys?"

Patrick's grin was sly and triumphant. "The ones digging up your backyard."

isn't it funny? she says i have snakes in my head. she's the one who has them. I can see them. I can see them squirming inside like big, fat maggots and i can see me digging them out and looking inside. i can see me make her quiet so quiet so still i can get the snakes and make them eat her eyes out too.

maybe that will be my next birthday present. when I'm ten.

NINE

They weren't exactly digging up the backyard. They had taped it, the yellow plastic fluttering in the breeze, and the white evidence truck tucked away on Euclid on the other side of Molly's wrought-iron fence. Two blue-uniformed techs with gloves and tape measures stood there eyeing Magnum, who was barking loud enough to set off the seismographs at St. Louis U.

"All this for one funny flower box?" Frank asked.

Molly whipped around from where they'd been peering out the back door and stalked to the front of the house. Everybody joined her at the front window to consider the scene there.

She had a satellite truck parked in front of her big maple tree. Alongside it stood an overdressed, over-made-up woman in Burberry and Brooks Brothers, who was taking a final pat at perfectly groomed blond hair as she conferred with a guy holding a videocam. A couple of neighborhood doors had opened, and Sam stood on his lawn with Little Allen, who looked as if he were posing for a statue commemorating grocery baggers. And inside Molly's house, her guests were all peeking out her windows like settlers setting up shots in an Indian raid. This had to be just about the most ludicrous day of her life.

"No," Molly bleakly assured Frank as she let the curtain fall back into place. "All of this is for two funny flower boxes."

"Those *were* flowers," he protested. "You're not going to get me on that."

"*You* sent me flowers," she said, backing up so fast she almost bumped into Rhett. "My secret admirer sent me another present. And somebody told the news about it. Which is why we laughed so hard about your Donna Kirkland joke, Frank."

Frank's eyes widened. "You really got another gift?"

Molly glared. "Yes, Frank. I did. Makes those flowers really funny, huh?"

For the first time since she'd known him, Molly saw a look of consternation on Frank. Only a flash, of course. Frank didn't waste his time on guilt. "I'm sorry, Mol. I guess I believed you when you said it was all a mistake."

"Why should I be mad at you?" She shrugged. "I tried to believe it, too."

Molly took care of Ms. Kirkland with a call to Winnie. Rhett watched as the CSI guys raked Molly's yard for a sum total of five half-masticated chew toys, twelve cigarette butts (which Patrick had to apologize for), three buttons, and an empty can of motor oil. And after they'd all gone, Molly spent the rest of the afternoon down in a too-small cave by the river making sure that Frank's friend Joey would again come out.

By the time Molly walked into the ED next day at three, she was exhausted and impatient. And then, to make matters worse, she was waylaid by Sasha in the parking garage.

Molly hated the parking garage. It was just like Joey's cave but more dangerous. Fewer lights, lower ceilings, and the sudden scuttle of the kind of unpleasant company that kept to the shadows.

Molly always tried to park on the roof of the garage, where she could at least see the stars. But then, again, every female who didn't want to feel at risk parked in the same place. So tonight, Molly was two floors down and having trouble breathing.

And then Sasha waylaid her.

"Good," she said, shutting her car door and falling into step. "I caught you. It gives me the chance to remind you—yet again—that you haven't attended the class about the new computer system."

"I've got enough on my plate right now, Sash. I add computers to the stew and I might just commit mayhem."

"You have somebody taking apart bodies for you, and *computers* bother you?"

"Computers should bother any sentient being."

"Garbage. You just don't want to learn this system. But may I remind you that with the new mergers, we have to be able to access records from at least four hospitals? Does it occur to your Neanderthal brain how beneficial that can be?"

"Of course. It's just that I know that while we're not looking, those things are conspiring against us."

"You said the same thing about the last class of interns."

"And I was right. They stole every otoscope in the ED and replaced them with vibrators. Or don't you remember?"

"Of course I remember. I'm a huge fan of the electronic age. Which reminds me. I saw your Detective Butler the other day. Have you finished that list of people who hate you yet?"

That got Molly's attention. "No. Why?"

"Well, put me on it."

Molly stared. "You? It's only a computer class, Sasha. Surely that's not enough to make you throw body parts at me."

"No. I'm just intrigued by the idea of being interrogated."

Molly came to a dead stop, not four feet from the safety of the elevator. "You'd hurt him, Sasha."

Sasha's smile was lazy and private. "Only if he asked."

Molly just closed her eyes and shook her head. "Well, at least I've finally found something to think about that's scarier than computers."

"Think of all the research you could do on that computer system."

"I don't want to do research, Sasha."

"Not even to check out the people on that hate list?"

Molly got her eyes open at that. No, she thought. She didn't want to check anybody on her hate list.

Yes, she did.

She wanted to know before somebody brought her the news. She turned and kept on walking. "I'll let you know."

Her decision was made for her not two hours later.

It had been a pretty typical shift, a lot of winter flu, ice accidents, and one candidate for the Darwin Awards. A stupicide they called it in the ED. Death by idiocy.

"Stupicide how?" Sasha asked as the Medical Examiner's transport cart came rolling down the hall toward room three, where the unfortunate nominee awaited.

"He and his friend thought it would be fun to shoot apples off each other's head. The friend sneezed."

"I bet that left a mark."

"Well, at least our man won the bet. The other guy's apple had a perfect hole through it. He gave it to the homicide cops."

"Who probably ate it."

"They'd missed lunch."

"Misch Burke? Isch that you?"

Molly looked up from her perusal of Clarence Jervis's chart to see a couple of men in white shirts and black slacks coming to a halt on either side of an ambulance cart alongside room five. Turning to answer the smiling one, she almost dropped her charts.

"Lewis?" Molly gaped. "What are you doing here?"

Lewis, whom she couldn't imagine being anywhere but in the corner of the city morgue folding body bags.

His shrug was shy and deferential, his smile all but adoring. "They needed some help with the transchport unit. I volunteered."

Molly couldn't think of anything more productive to offer than a small nod. "Oh."

"You're here for William Tell?" Sasha asked.

Lewis blinked like a hypnosis experiment.

"The patient for the morgue," Molly clarified, trying to ignore the long-suffering look of Lewis's teammate, an overweight, undermotivated guy she'd never been overly fond of.

Lewis straightened to attention. "Oh, yesch, ma'am. Isch that your patient?"

"Yeah, Lewis. I'll be in in a minute."

Sasha leaned over so that only Molly could hear her. "You just seem to inspire all men to poetry, don't you?"

Molly glared, but Sasha was looking away toward room three, into which Lewis had disappeared. "What did you do for him, teach him to use a pocket comb?"

Molly deliberately refocused on her work. "He's one of the morgue techs at the office."

Sasha nodded. "He'sch in love," she said, neatly mimicking Lewis's lisp.

Molly laughed. "He's . . ."

What? Semiliterate? Semisocialized? Semitidy?

"In *love*," Sasha repeated. "Just like Frank. And Rhett. And at least one of those poor housekeeping dweebs who keeps asking to pull time down here so he can gaze rapturously at you. You do have the most interesting impact on men."

Molly was quickly losing her sense of humor. "Frank considers me a challenge. Rhett is . . ." She shrugged. "Rhett. As for Lewis, I don't kick him like an oversize poodle, which Winnie has been known to do. I don't have a clue what the housekeeping guy's problem is."

"You're nice to him."

"Well then, I'll stop. Right now. Just point him out to me and I'll sneer at him. I'll sneer at them all. If this is just a reaction to my being a nice person, I'll show them my true colors."

Sasha nodded. "I see. It's not love. Just blind devotion. No wonder you have somebody sending you body parts."

A week ago Molly would have at least attempted a laugh. But this time she grabbed her paperwork and stalked off, figuring silence would be better than an anatomically impossible suggestion.

"Molly Burke, outside line one. Molly Burke . . ."

Molly grabbed the phone next to the copy machine. "This is Molly Burke."

"Ms. Burke, this is Sheila, Mr. Phillips's secretary?"

Molly almost said, "Who?" It took her several long moments to pull the name out of her memory banks. But then, she shouldn't have been surprised.

Mr. Phillips was Molly's investment broker. The investment broker who took Sam's suggestions and put them to such solid use for her retirement account. In the five years Molly had been home, Mr. Phillips had never once found need to call her at work. Molly forgot the chart she was copying.

"Yes, Sheila?"

There was a little nervous silence, a brief clearing of the throat. "I thought . . . that is, Mr. Phillips wanted me to call you. The . . . the *police* are here, Ms. Burke. They want to look into your *finances*."

Molly shut her eyes, tried to block out the sounds in the work lane. Retirement accounts were not a normal part of victimology—at least not any she'd ever studied. Which meant that somebody suddenly considered her more than a victim.

"Who's there?" she asked. "Detective Butler?"

"Uh . . ."

"Cute, puppy dog kind of guy, blond?"

"Oh no. This man is . . . well, he's, uh . . . *black*." Whispered, as if she should have been embarrassed to notice. "He says he can come back with a court order."

Which meant he didn't have one yet. Molly could stand on her rights and dick the guy around. She should, damn it. He shouldn't think he was dealing with an amateur here.

"Let me talk to him."

It took only a nanosecond for the change of voice. "This is Sergeant Davidson. Miss Burke?"

Davidson. Aw, hell. Molly did not like Sergeant Davidson, a too-handsome, too-groomed, too-controlled cop with a gleaming bald pate and the kind of tailored suits that cops only wore on TV.

"What are you doing?" Molly demanded.

"Using my best judgment in investigating this case, Ms. Burke. The major asked me to take over."

Molly's blood pressure skyrocketed.

"And Rhett?"

"If you have any problems, you can come to me."

"Problems like you investigating my finances without a court order?"

"Problems like that."

Well, at least he didn't play any games with her.

"Have you even bothered to talk to Rhett, who already has my financial information?" she demanded.

"He has the information you gave him."

Her field of vision was going red. She was shaking. For the first time since this whole mess started, she was beginning to feel violated. Donna Kirkland was going to leave her bleeding. This guy was going to tear apart what was left.

Molly swore she hadn't been really mad until then. Which was undoubtedly why she almost broke the phone in half.

"So what do you think?" she snapped. "That I'm working with somebody else to create a sensation in my backyard, from which I collect cash and the other person collects . . . what? Notoriety? A souvenir concession? And I get my shot at Larry King as the only recorded serial killer who's left body part trophies to *herself*?"

Oh, great. She was so mad, he'd made her say the word. Which made her even more furious. "If I wanted to do that, Sergeant Davidson, I probably would have manufactured miraculous visions of the Virgin Mary in my fishpond. No need for evidence at all, ya know? Not to mention having to deal with all that Soilex and paint."

"You must understand why we—" Even that sounded suspicious and patronizing at once.

Molly squeezed her eyes shut against the blinding rage she couldn't seem to control anymore. "Give me the goddamn secretary," she ground out.

"Ms. Burke—" he objected.

"You asshole," she all but whispered, so terrible was her need to destroy something, "I'm giving you your wish. Check the records. Impound every goddamn check I've written in my fifty-two years on this earth. And then get the fuck out of my life."

He handed over the phone. Sheila took Molly's permission and then bade her good-bye in hushed tones, leaving

Molly just standing there, the phone to her ear, the dial tone buzzing like a faulty circuit, her whole body shaking.

"If you really need to break something," Sasha said quietly behind her, "may I suggest that blanket warmer? It's nice and big, and it isn't working anyway."

Molly couldn't even face her friend. There were tears of rage in her eyes, and her hands still shook. She couldn't even seem to put the phone down, no matter how crazy that damn buzzing was making her.

"I'm all right," she managed through clenched teeth.

"Uh-huh. While you're waiting for your temper to catch up with the rest of that 'all right,' you want me to give your little friend from the morgue his chart so he doesn't come over and ask in person? I don't want to be the one to explain to Dr. Harrison why we sent her transport tech back to her inside out."

Molly nodded. Sasha gathered the chart up and departed, somehow keeping other humans out of the little cubicle until Molly managed to get the phone safely back into its cradle and her temper under marginal control.

"Now," Sasha said, her self-preservational sense of distance perfect. "Who can we have castrated for you?"

Molly's laugh was a surprised bark of frustration. But she didn't answer her friend just yet. She put in a call to Rhett.

Who didn't answer, just like Sergeant Davidson said he wouldn't.

And Molly had thought finding Donna Kirkland on her lawn had felt bad. She couldn't stop shaking.

"I have a bad feeling," she said, eyeing the phone as if it were at fault.

This time Sasha laughed. "*Now?*" she demanded. "You just have a bad feeling *now*? Where have you been the last week or so?"

Molly turned on her, her own brain awash in white noise. "I don't suppose you know any good psychiatrists."

Even Sasha was sometimes surprised. "Does this mean I can't count on you for the rest of the shift?"

"It means that if I'm going to make it through this without racking up my own body count, I need to get some help. I'm feeling awfully out of control all of a sudden, and this thing's just beginning to heat up."

Sasha tossed a small wave at the phone. "What was that all about that it sent you into hyperspace?"

Molly sucked in a very deep breath. God, she wanted some vodka. She was suddenly so scared. "Davidson has taken over the investigation," she said. "And I have the feeling that he doesn't want me in the loop anymore."

"Because?"

"Because somebody thinks I might be involved?"

"Ridiculous."

Molly just shrugged.

"What are you going to do?" Sasha asked drily.

Molly faced the wall, the blank, worn wall with old tape marks where outdated lifesaving posters had once resided. She fought to control the hot rush of outrage and desperation that still threatened to swamp her. She tried like hell to convince herself that confronting the problem was better than having it force her back into darker and darker alleys. She promised herself, standing in the shadowless lights of the ED, that she wouldn't let the shadows bother her.

"I think," she said anyway, "that I have to start doing what I should have from the beginning."

Was Sasha smiling? "Yeah?"

"Take control of my part of the investigation." She closed her eyes, hating this. Hating what had happened on that phone worse. "I have to go back over the same ground I just slogged with Rhett."

"Uh-huh."

"I have to make that goddamn list, and include every goddamn man I know."

"Uh-huh."

Molly's sudden scowl was so ferocious that one of the techs scuttled all the way to the other side of the hall. "And then I have to learn how to use those goddamn computers so I can check on everybody I know who might have been treated or worked in any of the hospitals in this system."

Sasha actually smiled. "I may weep with joy."

Molly laughed. "I really can do that with just my ID number, right?"

"You would have known that if you'd been to the class . . . well, you would have known about getting medical records. I know about getting work records."

Molly's eyes popped open to see Sasha grinning like a Cheshire cat.

"You're going to help?"

She shrugged. "Nothing like a little larceny to brighten a boring day."

"This isn't like you, Sash."

"I know. I amaze myself."

The bubble of panic began to deflate a little. Molly nodded.

"Thanks, Sash," she said with a weary grin. "I needed that."

"Yes," Sasha agreed. "You did. Between Christmas and all this hoopla, you've been no damn fun at all. By the way, the next class is at nine A.M. tomorrow."

Molly sighed. "Can't be worse than talking to Davidson."

"That's the spirit."

Molly shook her head, exhausted before she ever sat down at a keyboard. She wished she could have said she was happy. She was at least calmer. She was, for better or worse, girding for battle.

She felt better right up until the moment she arrived home four hours later to find a policeman perched on her front porch looking for Patrick.

Kenny held his breath. It was so quiet in the room. So dark and silent and warm. He shouldn't be here yet. It wasn't time. He needed to get to know her better before he began his ritual. This time when he took her brain, it had to be already his.

Just like she was now. Tucked into bed, safe in the shadows, her breath breaking like waves on the beach. Kenny opened the door just enough so the light from the hall spilled across the floor, but it didn't reach her feet. He tiptoed in, just to hear her. Just to smell the sleep on her. Just to imagine what it would feel like when her life ebbed away beneath his hands. God, he was ready to come just thinking about it.

This time, he thought with such anxiety he had to put his hand over his mouth to keep silent. This time would be perfect. This time, now that he had her in his place, he would own her and keep her in the dark where all his dreams lived.

His feet quieter than her breath, he stepped up to the bed where she lay, silent under the weight of the sedatives. He saw that she wasn't perfectly covered. Her foot had escaped, pale white flesh at the edge of the light like a fish on the beach. Calling to him. Wanting him to touch it. To claim it.

Kenny whimpered with desire. His head pounded with urgency. His hand reached out, almost by itself, to find her foot. Her ankle, where it peeked from the cover. And there, in the silent hours of the night when he could do anything, he touched her.

He claimed her.

He felt her skin beneath his, warm, warm skin. Smooth skin, soft skin. He grew bold with his touch and moved to her head.

Her head.

Oh, her head.

He reached out, his fingers as white as her skin in the night, and he touched her hair, her dark, thick hair that felt like cotton wool. Her hair that was warm from the scalp beneath it, that shone as if her dreams had painted it.

Her head.

Oh, Kenny could hardly hold still. He wanted her now. He wanted her head in his hands where it belonged. Where she would belong to him.

But he knew it wasn't time, no matter what he wanted. Kenny moaned, trying to hold in his laughter, and she stirred.

Sighed.

Kenny froze. She wasn't supposed to see him yet. Not his face. It would ruin it. He had to be no more than a whisper in her dreams.

As she settled back to sleep, not even knowing he'd been there, Kenny crept out of the room and thought about exactly what would happen next. Especially now that Miss Burke would know.

I'm writing it all down.
Everything i feel,
everything i want. I
don't think anybody has
any idea what i really
want, but I'll write it
anyway, for her. Because
she's the only one who
doesn't run away. She's
not like HER at all
but I can't tell her
that. i can't tell
anyone, or they'd know
about my birds
and the cat in the closet

TEN

"I'm just making inquiries, ma'am," the officer assured her as he stood there on her porch at one in the morning.

Short, thin, and blond, his posture stiff enough for the Marines, he bore his pressed and polished uniform like sacred vestments. He wore the earnest eyes of the young.

Molly's insides clutched up as she imagined the worst.

"Is there something wrong?" she asked.

It was cold outside, and he held his hat in his hand. "Well, uh, if I could talk to the boy . . ."

Molly looked around, as if expecting to see Patrick materialize. "He's, uh . . . at work. Or Sam's. My neighbor. He goes there after work."

Opening the door, she let the officer in while she called Sam. Who was playing chess with Patrick, just as Molly had hoped.

"Now," she said, as Patrick came clattering in the front door at a dead run a few minutes later. "What's the problem?"

"You've been at your neighbor's all evening?" Officer Matthews asked Patrick.

Patrick, chapped by the cold and rubbing his hands, nodded. "Got off work early. Why?"

The poor cop actually looked relieved. "We've had reports

of someone peeking in windows in the neighborhood. It was mentioned that you were new to the area. Just checking."

Somebody standing in the shadows. Molly shivered.

Patrick didn't seem to notice. He just kept bouncing and rubbing. "Can I go back now? I'm about to checkmate Mr. Spiegel."

Officer Matthews nodded, then paused. "You, uh, know somebody named . . . um, Little Allen?"

Patrick did a credible double-take. Molly just nodded. "He's a delivery boy from Straub's, why?"

"Another name mentioned. What can you tell me about him?"

"He's weird," Patrick offered.

"He's in the neighborhood a lot because he delivers to Sam, and Sam makes his shopping list in five-item increments," Molly amended.

"He knows the area, though?"

"Sam's not his only customer."

Matthews nodded, jotting in his notebook. "If you don't mind, I'd like to go over and talk to the neighbor. Just to check."

"Uh, before you go," Molly said, wishing with all her heart that her friend Dee had been on tonight instead. "I've been receiving some . . . uh, unpleasant gifts. Rhett Butler down in homicide knows about them. Just in case this is re-lated, would you mind letting Rhett know?"

"Gifts, ma'am?"

Screw Davidson. Let him play catch-up this time.

"Detective Butler will fill you in."

Officer Matthews just nodded, jotted, and buttoned his notebook away in his shirt pocket. Then, with no more than regulation pleasantries, he headed back out the door.

Patrick was about to follow, when Molly made a mistake.

"Patrick . . ."

It must have been in the tone of her voice. A question. A request for reassurance. Patrick, having the sonar every teen possesses for distrust, picked up on it and spun around.

"I've been with Sam," he snapped. "You can ask him."

Molly sighed, heartily wishing for that brief camaraderie they'd shared over pancakes. Wishing she had the time or energy to explain right now how much her life had changed, just since the report had come back on those body parts. "Let's talk later, okay?"

She saw his eyes shutter. Saw him slacken with rebellious indifference. "Sure. Whatever."

And then Molly was left alone in the hallway with the cold ghost of his resentment and the mounting acid of her own unease.

"So," Molly greeted Winnie the next afternoon as she stalked into the mask-decorated office. "Can you talk to me, or do I have to reach you through Davidson, too?"

What she wanted to say was, *Do you know a good psychiatrist? Hell, a half-decent psychiatrist? A psychologist with experience in PTSD and teenagers? A voodoo priestess with a good line in protection against psychopaths?*

No, Molly thought. After the morning she'd spent at the hospital education department, what she needed was an exorcist who could ward off computers. But that wasn't going to happen either.

Poised behind her desk like a queen considering a recalcitrant subject, Winnie lifted an eyebrow. "You seem to have made the point moot, haven't you?"

Molly slid her rump into one of the hardback chairs and sighed. "I'm sorry. Did you know that there's a new gunslinger in town and he's doing more than a victimology on me?"

"Of course. The major puts a lot of faith in Davidson's investigational skills."

"Let's hope they're better than his interpersonal communication skills. He might have let me know what's going on."

"And have Donna Kirkland find out that this investigation hasn't been thorough and unbiased? She would spread that information like an evangelist."

So she wasn't just concerned. She was trapped like a rat in a cupboard. Definitely time for Molly to take her initiative back.

"I've also been talking to Billy Armistead," Winnie continued, "and we've decided that for the present you shouldn't be put into a position to worry about facing the media."

Molly straightened. "Which means I'm on suspension."

"Which means you will work out of this office on the problem at hand." Winnie's eyebrow was up again. "The effects of having that teenager in your house are beginning to show, aren't they?"

Molly didn't bother to be pleasant. "You mean I'm short-tempered and surly? Yeah, I guess I am. But don't blame it on Patrick. Blame it on my shy suitor. Better yet, blame it on the fact I'm beginning to feel like a big beach ball at a Dead concert all of a sudden."

"I told you—"

Molly's smile was as grim as Winnie's had ever been. "Yeah. Everybody told me, Winnie. Well, I'm here to tell you that if you want my cooperation, you'll have to cooperate back. All of you. Bureaucratic games aren't going to help us on this one."

"You seem to have changed your mind" was all Winnie said. "It wasn't that long ago I couldn't even get a list out of you."

"If you think this is easy, I invite you to change houses for a while. I'll even throw in all the support I've received from everybody else as an added bonus."

A simple tantrum shouldn't have caused fresh shakes. It did, though. Molly stood, needing to get finished and then get away.

"Everyone is doing their job."

"Everyone's forgetting that I'm the one getting the body parts. I'm the one who has all the answers to the big questions." *I'm the one who needs the answers most and wants them least.* "Trust me. I want this over faster than anybody, and I'll do everything I can to help that. But I can't do it blindfolded and isolated. So either Rhett starts answering his phone, or from now on, I stop answering mine."

She'd almost made it to the door when Winnie pulled her up sharp.

"Clear your cases with this office," she said. "Then get to work on whatever it is you plan to do."

Molly turned on her. "You mean what I plan to do once I know what the police are doing?"

"Don't sulk. After that tirade you just subjected me to, I assume you have some kind of plan."

After a second, Molly nodded, surrendered. "I have a plan."

"Good. As long as you understand that anything you learn is immediately shared with the homicide team. Including Sergeant Davidson."

Molly nodded with less grace than Patrick agreeing to clean his room.

Winnie gave her gold Cross pen a couple of brisk clicks and consulted the neatly arranged folders on her desk. "Now, do you have any cases you want to hand over to Kevin?"

Molly took a second to change gears. "I'm pretty much behind the scenes on everything I have. I can keep up on those."

"Even the Wilsons?"

Ah, the Wilsons. Mrs. Wilson had gotten the local chapter of the NAACP involved in the cry for justice for her murdered daughter, and Molly's name was still the most frequently invoked.

"I've already made my news there," Molly said. "I promise to stay out of sight. Besides, Wilmetta Wilson is going to have something else to think about pretty soon. The lab called today. They have viable DNA from that skin we got from under her daughter's fingernails, and it isn't the girl's."

Winnie's smile was sudden and terrible. "They getting a warrant for blood from the boyfriend?"

"That's what I hear."

"Good. Very good. I want to see the report when it comes in. Anything else?"

Molly almost asked it. *Help me here, Winnie. I'm tap dancing ahead of the flood, and I don't think I can swim.* Instead she tossed off a weak grin. "You want a teenage boy?"

"Good God, no. I already have one."

"Then timely advice would be appreciated."

"Too late. My advice would have been never to let him in your front door."

"That's what Frank says."

"Patterson? The lawyer? I can imagine. If anybody would understand the machinations of a teenage boy, he'd be the one. Now, is there anything else you need to know from this office?"

Alphabetically or chronologically? "Do you have any more info on my body parts?"

Winnie betrayed her frustration. "Nothing. Whoever he is, this guy is using dime-store acrylic paint and glitter, dime-store letters, and easy-to-obtain chemicals. There aren't any saw marks on the bones, which might mean he's trained in anatomy."

"Or he's already had a lot of practice."

Winnie did not appear pleased. "Something I'm sure you'll consider as you make up your list."

"I have made up my list."

"Who do *you* think it is?"

Molly gaped at her boss like a landed fish. "Who do I think it is? Shit, Winnie, *I* don't know."

"You just said you've been making up a list. Surely you have some kind of idea. What about a profile?"

"It's too soon for a profile. You know that."

"No I don't. I don't waste my time with that nonsense. You're the one who sits at the feet of those Behavioral Science guys and laps all that mumbo jumbo up like chocolate mousse. So, what good is it if you don't even have an idea where we should look?"

Belatedly Molly realized that Winnie was serious. This wasn't one of Winnie's intellectual challenges. She was upset. Sincerely distressed. And she wasn't even getting the anat-o-grams.

Molly couldn't so much as move. This was what she got for sounding so damn sure of herself.

"A spider." Just the word sent ripples of unease through

her. Still, she held Winnie's gaze and took that big leap. "A trap-door spider who sits tucked away in his hole and only comes out to hunt."

"Explain."

Molly wrapped her fingers together, as if anchoring herself. "We have body parts from women we don't even know are missing. Carefully culled and presented. That's a Dahmer kind of thing. Bundy just tossed his women away like so much trash. Dahmer and Gacy hid their victims away like secrets.

"We have meticulous planning and excellent camouflage. The whole business is personal and private, and I think it's carried out within a specific comfort zone. This isn't the kind of guy who moves around. He's not the kind of guy who's into slash and trash. The kind of guy who likes to be in our faces and grandstands for the crowd. I think this guy only came out because he needed to get some message to me."

"What message?"

Molly's temper flared. She battled the red haze for a second before managing an answer.

"I don't know."

I don't want to know.

"Let the cops figure out why," she told her boss. "I don't care."

Liar.

Winnie considered her a moment in silence and then pulled over a pad of paper. Without looking back at Molly, she began jotting her own notes, and Molly realized that for all her vaunted knowledge, the Medical Examiner had really needed Molly's information. But then, Winnie's brilliance lay in tangibles. Repeatable scientific truths measured in millimeters and liters and parts per million. The core of what they needed to stop this monster lay well beyond a measurable boundary of any kind. It lay in the mind and the heart and the soul, and Winnie was singularly unqualified to interpret any of those.

And Molly didn't want to.

But she was going to have to. She'd made that decision last night. Then she'd spent the rest of the night regretting it.

She'd walked the red mud of Pleiku over and over again in her dreams looking for a face she should have recognized and somehow, couldn't.

"So what are you going to do?" Winnie asked without looking up, as if she'd heard Molly's thoughts.

Molly damn near laughed. Good thing Winnie hadn't asked her what she *wanted* to do. She answered the Medical Examiner like a pro, though. Chapter and verse. And Winnie listened until Molly mentioned her new skills in the world of technology.

"It's illegal," Winnie said.

"Tell that to all the credit companies and HMOs who tap into computers every day," she said. "I'm just looking for names. Places. Dates. Patterns."

Patterns.

"And then?"

Molly thought of all those damn psychological boxes she'd tucked away in her brain, their lids askew, the past whispering out of them like weary ghosts, and she fought the shakes all over again.

"Then I share what I have with Rhett and Davidson and crew and see if we can find a match that rings bells. That shows us . . ."

Patterns.

Her voice stalled. She caught her breath, because she'd just figured out how she could get the information the police needed without having to face the demons she didn't want to.

It was so simple. So obvious. Surely after all these years she couldn't be wrong. Not after she'd played so very many rounds of The Game and lost.

"Shows us?" Winnie prompted, pen poised.

"Patterns," Molly said, still thinking.

"What?"

For the first time since she'd walked in the office, Molly smiled. "All that mumbo jumbo, Winnie. It's going to show me how to track a killer right to my back porch."

"And?"

Molly finally made it to the door, still smiling. "And I now have the means to do just that. Bye, Winnie."

As she was headed down the hall, she heard the dry voice behind her. "Glad I could help."

Molly went home first, because the next job on her list was her own victimology, and she wasn't about to do that in front of witnesses. She'd expected to have to at least face Patrick, but Patrick had forestalled that by leaving her a note saying he'd gone in early to work. Molly felt guilty with relief.

She told herself it was because she didn't want witnesses for what she had to do. She knew better.

Still, she didn't take any chances. Before anyone could interrupt, she sat down with her research books, her work résumé, and her revulsion for self-revelation, and she set about reconstructing her own history. And within five minutes, she found herself forced to admit that Rhett was just as good an interviewer as everybody claimed.

When Rhett had compiled her victimology, he'd bounced his questions all around so they had seemed less overwhelming. Where had she gone to school? Did she still have friends she kept in touch with from childhood? From her other jobs? From other cities? It must be tough to keep track of all the people she'd worked with. Did she enjoy moving around, or was it tough for her?

Molly looked at the range of areas Rhett had investigated to complete a thorough victimology and thought how easily he'd gleaned his facts. Looked at in a stark succession, it made her choke up. Asked in that guileless way of his, as if he were doing nothing more than filling time on a first date, it had been bearable.

Well, bearable or not, Molly had to ask herself the same questions. She had to evaluate her lifestyle, her employment, her personality, her friends, income, family, alcohol or drug use, dress, handicaps, transportation used, reputation, marriage and dating history, habits, fears. . . .

She had to fillet her life like a dead fish and find the bones that lurked inside. And she had to do it as dispassionately as possible, when she had enjoyed it all so much in the first place she'd made it a point over the years to completely shut it away.

Had she had addictions? Of course she had—although the other people she knew with PTSD tended to call it self-medicating. Molly had spent years on that roller-coaster ride trying to numb a pain no one else seemed to know how to exorcise. Even after a good doctor and an introduction to the newest generation of antidepressants, Molly still had to acknowledge that her alcohol intake rose appreciably during the summer. Not enough to interfere. Not enough so far to inhibit those self-preservational drives that keep everyone chugging along. But enough, sometimes, to make her less careful. Less perceptive. Less hopeful.

She still had nightmares on a regular basis, and, on occasion, flashbacks. None of that should have any relevance to the investigation. But Rhett had asked what her fears were, hadn't he?

Her other habits were unremarkable. She might live in a fancy house, but she sure couldn't afford a fancy life. She worked two jobs, had a dog, several friends, and an adopted Jewish grandfather. She rarely saw her own family and preferred to see them even less. She read a lot, vacationed a little, and drove around in a beat-up, paid-off 1988 Toyota Celica GT because she liked the speed and handling and couldn't afford a real car.

She had no criminal activity in her past beyond the odd antiwar demonstration and one case of trespassing that had involved an ED party, a goat, and a hospital CEO's swimming pool. Nothing, certainly, that would put her in a high-risk behavior category like solicitation or felony drug possession.

Her illicit drug possession had all been of the misdemeanor variety. Her addictions had been prescribed or toted in brown paper bags, not tiny plasticene baggies.

She was, Molly knew, boring. Her likes included both her jobs, her friends, Frank's kids, and, most of all, her gardening, which she'd raised to the status of minor religion. Her dislikes: insurance companies, hospital administration, BMWs, and her family. Her lifestyle changes had, unfortunately, included that family, but Patrick could only be considered an added stressor. He hadn't been there long enough to be considered anything else.

Which brought Molly to the categories she thought most pertinent. What the pros called precipitating events.

In the career of any serial killer, there were precipitating events that seemed to propel the killer over the next, higher wall of restraint. Maybe a breakup with a girlfriend pushed the killer from the fantasy stage to his first kill. Maybe a loss of job pushed him into a faster cycle, or more violent crime. Maybe a direct challenge or desertion pushed him into multiple murder. Whatever, each precipitating event could be plotted against an escalation in antisocial behavior like a chemistry reaction.

The question was whether Molly would find any incidents on her own graph that might correspond to blips on the killer's. So she wrote down the events that had been recently noteworthy to her.

If she just tracked the last two years, she could include getting sued, losing her job and life savings, meeting Frank, finally securing her job at Grace Hospital, the very last hospital in town in which she'd ever considered working, and her job at the ME's.

Molly looked at that list and laughed. Too bad they weren't hunting a mass murderer. Based on that list of stressors, she would have been a prime candidate. But then, her entire life had been comprised of ridiculous little clusters like that.

Okay, next. She had gone to work at the Medical Examiner's office as a part-time investigator. That had translated into a little more pay, a lot more stress, and several shots at public exposure. It had also led to a case just this last summer that had sent a half dozen people to prison and tumbled a few political figures in St. Louis. But any threats she'd received from that had been direct and simple. And not one had involved body parts—other than hers, anyway.

Her most recent appearances in public had involved the Wilsons and Sharon Peters, both of whom she'd spoken to news crews about. But both had been uninvolved, impulsive acts of rage and control that would never have fit the profile of this kind of serial killer. This guy wasn't impulsive at all.

Molly stopped there and looked out her window.

Serial killer. She'd said it again. She'd admitted it as the fact she knew it to be.

The phantom they'd all been trying to wave back into smoke was fast solidifying instead. And nightmares and superstitions be damned, Molly had the most unholy feeling that this was what he wanted her to do. He wanted her to bring him out of the vapors.

He was looking for a sense of himself, and she was obliging.

But he *was* a serial killer. Molly could no longer deny or pretend. She knew just what kind of serial killer she was dealing with the way she knew all hell was about to break loose in her ED. Her gut was churning. Her chest was tight as a tripwire. She could feel feet dancing on her grave, and she never ignored feelings like that.

So he was real. He was looking for her. She had to stop him, no matter what anybody else did. And even with all the data she and Rhett had compiled, she still had no idea of where to start.

Without realizing it, Molly turned back to consider her résumé. Eight pages, thirty years, at least seven cities. Too, too much data to comb through in the time they had, with the dearth of information they had. Too many people to consider.

Most of whom had no idea where she was.

That stopped her cold. For a long moment, Molly could do no more than just look at the list she'd compiled, the names of just about every man she'd ever known scribbled in haphazard fashion.

Still with an eye to that list, Molly got up to let Magnum out the back door. Then, refilling her straight tea, she sat back down, stunned by such a simple revelation.

They had no idea where she lived.

Most people didn't. Molly wasn't in the phone book. Both the hospital and the Medical Examiner's office protected her private information like the palace guard. She hadn't kept track of anybody she'd worked with from the other cities, which meant they wouldn't have easy access to her address. Besides, if they'd come back into her life, she would have recognized them. She would have at least been assailed by that "out of place" feeling one gets when one sees someone in the wrong environment. But she hadn't felt that at all.

She'd lived in St. Louis off and on until her twenty-first birthday when she'd gone to Vietnam. She'd come home three times since, once to marry and twice more when her options elsewhere had run out. She'd come home to stay five years ago. And each time she'd worked in a hospital in the metropolitan area. Two of those hospitals were now joined in the merger that had eaten Grace.

Molly could look back at every single person she'd met all those years on the road. She had a feeling it would be a waste of time.

Her answer was here. In sight. Close enough that something she'd done within the last few weeks had set the person off.

The person here in St. Louis. The person who knew not where she worked, but where she lived.

Molly took a quick look at the rambling list of names on her yellow legal pad and knew she could take off about half. At least for now. Which meant she had a place to start. As soon as she could get in to work and ask Sasha for time on her computer.

Sasha might very well drop dead from the shock. For the second time that day, Molly smiled.

It figured that once she found a viable direction to follow, Molly didn't get the chance to take it. As if hearing her plans, the city went nuts and poured, in toto, into her ED.

The weather was bouncing around, which set off pulmonary problems like the spring spread thunderstorms. The people who weren't hacking were either brought in back-boarded from post–Christmas-party demolition derbies, or hunched over and puking from the Yule cheer they were spreading around. And Molly, who so enjoyed the season anyway, found herself immersed in its celebrants like a monk at black mass.

The only time she got at the computer she spent limbering up her skills, which resulted in no more than humiliating re-buffs from an inanimate object that considered itself smarter than Molly. That probably, in all fairness, was.

By the time Rhett finally returned her call the next after-noon, Molly was surly and tired. Rhett promptly made it worse when he gave his update on police activity.

A detective was checking Soilex and hydrochloric acid suppliers. Another was double-checking missing persons re-ports from as far away as Springfield, Illinois. A third, the canvas on Molly's neighborhood. But the current consensus remained that they were going to need another bone to point their way.

Molly arranged to get Rhett her notated list of names, sug-gested her own theories, and returned to practice her com-puter scales in Sasha's office.

"Do you know I pulled up my own psych records?" she demanded of Sasha as they were changing at end of shift eight hours later. "Anybody with a pass code could find out all about my past."

Brushing her hair into a perfect pageboy, Sasha shrugged. "As any third grader with a TV could tell you."

"I need you to teach me how to get those work records."

"And we're looking for what, exactly?"

Molly smiled and leaned against the sink, her new sense of direction exciting her. "What is the point of The Game, Sasha?"

"The Game?" Sasha asked, now focused on lipstick. "To see who we can save, of course."

"Uh-huh. And what about the ones we can't?"

Sasha's eyes met Molly's in the mirror. "You're playing The Game?"

"Nope. I'm taking it to the logical conclusion. What we

know about serial killers is that the press always interviews the wrong person. They always get the neighbor, who says—"

" 'But he was always such a quiet man,' " Sasha responded in dramatically astonished tones.

Molly nodded. "They never ask the old juvenile officers, the teachers or social workers or psychiatrists. You and I know damn well which one of these kids is going to the big leagues, and we only see them in short bursts. They have an escalating relationship with psych and penal systems you can trace back like footsteps in the snow, and I'm going to follow them."

Sasha had forgotten about makeup. "How's that?"

Molly shrugged. "Well, if he knows me, like everybody thinks he does, I might just find him in that computer system you're so hot about. I can double-check anybody's record for past psychiatric or work-related problems, notations that might indicate trouble with the law, prior violent or voyeuristic behavior, problems with women, that sort of thing. This guy's experienced. He's been there building his repertory for twenty years, maybe from Peeping Tom to rape to murder. His footprints will be somewhere in the computer, and the cops can't get in it without a search warrant." Molly's smile was terrible. "I can."

Sasha tilted her head in consideration. "You'll let me help."

Molly's smile got bigger. "Actually, yes."

Sasha finished with a flourish and the two of them headed out of the bathroom. "Where do we start?"

"I have a list I'd like you to take a look at," Molly admitted. "All the guys I've known in my St. Louis jobs who are now at least thirty."

Sasha raised an eyebrow. "Thirty? Why?"

"Average age at first human kill is twenty-one, although I really think that number's going to go down. This guy's proficient enough to have been doing it awhile. And a guy, because statistically, chop-shop killings just aren't a woman's signature, unless she's just trying to hide evidence."

The two of them walked down a hall that was still hopping. "You have way too much information, if you ask me," Sasha said.

"I have to," Molly informed her. "I'm the one getting the body parts."

"And an escort home again, it seems."

There, lounging against the triage desk at the far end of the hall in Icelandic sweater and khakis, was the ever-smiling Frank. Just as she'd found him the last three shifts.

"He's trying to annoy me to death," Molly informed her friend. "As well as he's doing, I may not last until we find out who my secret admirer is."

"You have to be the only woman alive who'd consider that man annoying."

"Why, Frank?" Molly demanded as she approached. "Why do you persist in harassing me?"

"You can harass me any time you want, honey," a voice floated out of one of the rooms.

"I'll let you know!" Frank called back.

Molly wanted to laugh. She wanted to scream. She wanted to run, because she had a terrible feeling that Frank was about to demand things from her she simply couldn't give. He was going to try and give things he couldn't.

She should have known better. His smile was knowing, even as those who looked on thought he was professing something wonderfully romantic. "Don't waste your maidenly nerves on me, Miss Molly," he assured her. "You of all people know what I am. I trust you not to expect more, which is why I'm so comfortable doing this little extra for you. You know it's about all I can manage."

She did. Frank—handsome, deadly, driven Frank—was no Prince Charming. Heck, he wasn't even Prince Charles. Somehow this bright, breezy, beautiful man had only been given a half cup of humanity, and he wasted it all on his children and his friend Joey. A little, perhaps, on her, when he could. It was all she'd ever wanted. All, in reality, she could handle. She needed Frank to be Frank. So she shouldn't regret it when he was.

Molly gave him a smile, which everybody on the hall misinterpreted. "All right, if you're going to be that way about it. See if I don't make you pick up the next bone."

Sasha just shook her weary head and led the way up to the garage, where Frank regaled them both with lawyer jokes. It wasn't until much later as he walked Molly up the front steps to her house that he remembered to ask how her day had been.

"I evidently insulted Patrick again without knowing how," she admitted, opening her front door. "So when he isn't at work or Sam's, he's taken to spending most of his time in his room calling his friends around the country. On my dime, of course. But he says that's necessary because I don't have the Internet."

Frank was greatly unimpressed. "Uh-huh. Check the heirlooms."

"You really don't trust Patrick, do you?" Molly asked.

The kitchen light was off, which meant Patrick hadn't come home yet. Since Sam's lights were still on, Molly wasn't terribly worried. She punched in the numbers to turn off her alarm and led Frank into the house.

"I recognize him," Frank said. "He's a sixteen-year-old me."

Shucking her jacket as she walked through, Molly considered Frank. "I would have thought that would make you two bond."

Frank's smile wasn't as bright as usual. "It wears better on me. Now, we going bone hunting?"

It was a joke, the same one he'd made for the last three nights. The same kind of joke that had propelled him to send the roses and hold her hand in the parking garage, scaring off the dark for her. Molly headed for the kitchen, ready to play along.

And then she realized what was wrong.

The house was silent.

Empty.

Molly knew where Patrick was. She just didn't know where Magnum was.

"If that boy has just left my dog out in the cold, I'll clock him," she snarled, heading for the back door.

Magnum wasn't there either. Molly went straight from annoyed to scared. Magnum should have been waiting for her. He should have been barking in indignation. She couldn't see him. Without bothering to reclaim her coat, she opened the door.

"Magnum?" she called, her voice echoing off buildings a block away. "Honey—"

"Molly—" Frank protested, trying to head her off.

He never stood a chance. Molly had finally seen what she was afraid of. A large, dark body on the back lawn.

Silent. Still.

She stepped off the porch to run for him and almost put her foot right through a human skull.

I can see her
there   in   the   window
brushing her   hair   her
hair her hair over her
head.
i watch her and I pretend
its HER
I watch her in the dark,
in the safe dark where
she can't see me, and I
pretend
i plan
what i'm going to do
when   i   stab   out   the
maggots behind her eyes

ELEVEN

The good news was that Magnum wasn't dead.

"Hamburger," Frank decided from where he was crouched over the lump of matter he'd found within a few feet of Magnum's snoring body. "My guess would be that somebody stuffed sedatives in it, and your not-too-bright watchdog gobbled it down."

Molly, huddled and shaking on her small back porch, nodded blankly. "Should I call the vet? See what an overdose is? God, I'm not putting an Ewald tube down that dog's throat to pump him out."

Even to her ears her laughter sounded way too shrill. She just couldn't hold her hands still.

"Call the vet," Frank agreed. "Right after the police."

The bad news was that the skull was real. Obviously human, painted a funny kind of marbleized gray with stars and circles circling the sides and back of the head, almost as if somebody considered it a doodling pad. And, of course, an address.

THIS IS FOR MOLLY BURKE

Right across the forehead, so it wouldn't be missed.

But this time it had come with a note.

And eyes.

Brown eyes.

Watching Molly in the dark from within those cavernous orbits.

Molly was sitting on cold concrete in her lab coat and scrubs holding the note she'd pulled from beneath the left eye with ungloved hands. Just like an amateur.

Hey, she thought inconsequentially. *I defy any cop to stumble over this little treat in his own backyard and remember the rules of evidence.*

"Oh, God," she moaned on a fresh shudder as she scanned the note. "He wants me to understand him."

Frank looked up from where he'd been trying to shake her dog awake. "What?"

Molly couldn't take her eyes off the paper. Better than looking at the skull that seemed to be watching her, as if waiting for her to recognize something. "My little buddy has stopped relying on the post."

Frank was alongside her in a flash to peer over her shoulder. "Boy, Mol, when you have an event, you really do it up right."

Molly shook some more. "Shut up, Frank."

What Frank did was ease her to her feet, leaving the skull where they'd found it at the edge of the porch like a left-over Halloween treat. "First we prevent frostbite," he commanded. "Then we still have to call the police."

"We have to make sure Magnum doesn't get to it," Molly protested. "Magnum has a taste for eyes."

She was laughing again, high and sharp.

"Magnum's not going to wake up till Tuesday. Come on, St. Molly the Morbid," he coaxed, his arm around her as he guided her inside. "You're not that surprised."

"I'm appalled, Frank. But hey, I'm glad you're having a good time."

"I know you always try and make my visits special."

And damn it, she laughed. Even more shrilly, a hair's breadth from hysterics, but it was still laughter. She had a skull painted like a paperweight and accessorized with brown eyes in her backyard and a fresh love note from a psychopath, and she was giggling like a teen on a date. That is, she was giggling until she seized over and threw up in the grass.

"The evidence crew isn't going to like that, Miss Molly," Frank admonished, pulling out the pristine handkerchief Molly should have damn well known he'd carry.

She wiped her mouth and struggled to regain her dignity. "I wasn't particularly wild about it either, Frank. Although I'm amazed you didn't take pictures to mark the occasion."

"It will always be a fond memory, Mol."

Molly grabbed the door rather than look back at all she'd left on the lawn. "Right after we call the police, get on the phone to Sam and see if he or Patrick heard anything."

"You're sure Patrick didn't do this just to piss you off?"

"If it'd been beer cans and cigarette butts, I'd say yes. But he's been at Sam's since just after I left for work."

And so he was. Of course, after that call, both he and Sam appeared in her kitchen, neither of them remembering a coat, and Sam suggesting tea for the humans and a blanket for the dog. By the time Dee arrived, the kitchen looked like a coffeehouse, but at least Molly had regained a measure of control.

"He came right up to the door," Patrick was saying again in tones of outrage and dreadful fascination.

Molly knew how he felt. She wanted to bathe. She wanted to curl into a ball and become catatonic. She settled for pouring a little more Stoly into her tea. Hell, she let Patrick have some.

"I'm sorry, Molly," Dee said by way of greeting, his large uniformed frame filling the doorway.

Molly got her tea mug to her mouth without spilling more than an ounce and tried to give a smile for her favorite policeman. "You didn't leave the damn thing, Dee."

"Did you notice the lower jaw and teeth are missing?" Frank asked.

"That's to prevent identification," Patrick assured him.

All the adults stared.

Patrick stiffened. "I saw it on *American Justice*, okay?"

A skull, Molly thought again, squeezing her own eyes shut as if it would force out the image of those other eyes. Blank, staring eyes, delicate and sad, somehow. Such a small thing, pretty and exotic. Finally, truly, human.

Molly thought of the light, the spirit, the animation that had once made that skull such a miracle. The dreams carried in whispers, the triumphs touted in smiles, the small, petty jealousies compressed in pursed lips. All gone, now. Scooped out like a bad melon and then painted like a craft fair project. Left to communicate with Molly.

And for the first time, Molly forced herself to think past age and sex and death to the real question. *Who were you? What have we lost with your death? What terrible, despairing thoughts were your last?*

What should I see that I don't?

"Molly?"

She startled. "Sorry."

Dee frowned. "I been trying to tell you the bad news. About the skull. The dispatcher spilled the beans."

Molly felt the blood leave her face. "Over the air."

Dee damn near dug a foot through the tile. "Big as life."

Molly dropped her head into her hands. "Every camera truck in the state of Missouri will be on my block within the hour." More tea. She needed more tea. Hell, forget the tea, she needed a good long slug from the Stoly bottle. "You'd better call your boss, Dee. I'll call mine."

Not only every camera truck ended up blocking her street, but damn near every police car, most of them with their lights flashing so nobody could miss the show. Molly sat in her kitchen amid a growing pile of half-empty coffee cups and McDonald's wrappings and patted her dog, who was still groggy enough to not give a damn that dozens of strangers were stepping over him on their way by.

This time, even Winnie put in an appearance.

"You look all right," she greeted Molly.

Molly didn't bother to lift her head from her hands. "It's a talent I have, Winnie. In fact, I've seen it on several evaluations. 'No matter what, Molly looks all right.' "

Winnie's eyebrow slid north. "You've been drinking."

Leave it to Sam to go toe to toe with a woman six inches taller and forty years younger than he. "A little tea. For shock."

Winnie looked down on that thatch of white hair and nodded. "You got some of that tea for me?"

Sam beamed. "What a question."

Sergeant Davidson glided up from a chair like Taye Diggs with a badge. Winnie never looked at him as she took his place.

"You know Sergeant Davidson, Winnie," Molly introduced them. "He's investigating me."

Winnie ignored innuendo and introduction. "I hear we have no teeth."

Molly flashed on that skull again, now safely hidden away in the evidence van. "But we do have a note."

"Like the others?"

"Oh no. This one is different."

Winnie paid attention. "How?"

Sergeant Davidson handed it over. Instead of noticing the evidence bag into which he'd safely sealed it, Molly noticed that his hands were manicured. Some cop.

Winnie read the message. And smiled.

Smiled.

"Our friend is finally getting thoughtful."

More than one head turned her way.

"That's certainly how I'd put it," Molly retorted drily.

Winnie was completely unruffled. "We can reconstruct a skull. Even part of a skull. And the more words he puts on a page, the better our chances of finding out about him."

Not so many words, Molly thought muzzily. More than usual, though. This time he'd said, *If anyone should understand, it's you. You SAW me.*

Volumes. Implied meanings Molly should have been getting, according to her friend. This same friend who had been telling her to drop dead for the last month.

Molly wanted another drink. All of that enthusiasm about digging into computer files to unearth a spider disintegrated

like personal courage at the sound of a gunshot. This note put
them right back on the "why" square, and Molly didn't want
to sit there.

She didn't want a relationship with this guy, no matter
what he thought. She didn't want to recognize him when they
finally forced him out of the dark. She most certainly didn't
want to know why he was so sure she should understand him.

And, God, oh, God, she didn't want to meet the girl that
skull had been.

"I'm sure you'll tell me where the police surveillance
was," Winnie said to the detective.

Davidson actually flinched. "You'd have to take that up
with my superiors, Doctor. That wasn't my responsibility."

"Let them know for me that I'm convinced it's necessary
now. Understand?"

"Yes, ma'am."

"I don't imagine it occurred to any of them that serial
killers tend to return to the scene of their crimes to relive the
experience," she said in that "lecturing the illiterate fresh-
men" tone she got. "And that, quite possibly, our man might
feel compelled to revisit my death investigator to witness the
effect of his gifts."

Molly was more surprised than Davidson. That little
speech was a long way from that "I don't know nothin' 'bout
no serial killers" stance Winnie had taken until about two
days ago.

"I'm not sure, ma'am," Davidson grudgingly admitted.

"Or that, in fact, he might just be outside right now in the
shadows watching us all career around Ms. Burke's yard like
the Keystone Kops?"

"There was a prowler in the area the other night," Molly
offered lamely. "An Officer Matthews took the report."

Davidson straightened. With no more than a quick glance
out the back window, as if verifying the allegation himself,
he yanked out his cell phone and made for the front yard.

Left behind, Molly considered her boss in amazement.
"You've been up late reading, haven't you?"

Winnie glared at her. "What makes you think you should have all the fun?"

Oddly enough, Winnie was the second person to make Molly laugh tonight. "I bet Donna Kirkland's pissed, huh?" she asked.

Winnie actually smiled. "Furious. *C'est la guerre.* Has this stirred any ideas in you?"

"Yes. A vacation in Hawaii. Maybe Tahiti. No, Tibet. I hear they still frown on freedom of the press there."

Winnie waved off her objections. "You've been through this before. Stop whining."

This time, it was Patrick who laughed. Curled up on the floor in the corner where he could watch the proceedings but stay out of the way. Wide-eyed and pale, as if this were too much for him, which Molly sincerely hoped it was. It was sure too much for her.

Of course, seeing him over there in his oversize khaki sweater and worn jeans made her realize that this was no longer the best place for him to be. Even if his parents weren't home, he should go there. He should go somewhere the press couldn't corner him. Another vote for Tibet, it seemed.

But she'd deal with that after the police cleared out.

"There is an upside to all this, Patrick," Molly said abruptly. "After seeing what the cops have done to my kitchen, I have to admit that you aren't quite so messy after all."

His head jerked up and Molly was even more unsettled. His pupils were dilated. His nostrils were wide, and he couldn't quite keep his hands still. Even so, he managed a grin that looked too tight. "See? Told you I'd make a perfect cop."

"You, a cop?" Winnie demanded. "God help us all."

Which, oddly enough, made him smile even more.

"Well," Winnie announced, standing back up. "I'm going to personally take this little beauty and wake Puffin out of a sound sleep so we can get started on a computer-generated model. And I expect you'll get some time today with Officer Butler so you can discuss your . . . feelings on this little incident."

"Anybody know where Detective Butler is?" Molly asked.

Most of the people looked around the kitchen as if they'd misplaced him under the dishes.

"Not on call," somebody offered, which seemed to satisfy the rest.

Winnie turned her attention to one of the cops. "Please remind Sergeant Davidson that for now he'll leave at least one officer outside to prevent problems."

The uniform, a wrinkled, deflated veteran of the street wars, nodded with some satisfaction. "I'll do it. Better than dancing with the Deuceboys down the block."

Winnie swept out, and the rest of the cops followed. Molly, left in her tumbled, littered kitchen, decided it was time to take care of everyone else.

"All right then," she said, climbing to her feet. "Frank, I know you wouldn't mind walking Sam home. It's way past our bedtime."

"*I'll* take him," Patrick protested, lurching to his feet.

Molly took a considered look at him—her lonely, angry, impressionable, teenage nephew, who had come to her for stability. She shook her head. "No, Patrick. You need to get to bed, too. Frank deserves to be shoved by a cameraman or two. You don't."

He stiffened. "You can't—"

Sam cut off his protest with a hand. "You obey your aunt, young man. I'll see you tomorrow."

Patrick saved his flash of resentment for Molly. For Sam he succumbed with no more than a curt nod. "Yes, sir."

"Go on to bed, Patrick," Molly said softly, forgiving him. "You're exhausted."

He didn't even protest. Just headed for the stairs. Molly caught him on the way by, her hand on his arm. She could feel the tension in those young muscles, the tremors of dying adrenaline. "I'm sorry about this, honey," she said gently.

There was so much she wanted to say, but no words to really convey it.

"What for?" he asked with a shrug, not bothering to face any of them. "This is more entertaining than *Faces of Death*."

Molly heard the residual quake in that voice and reached up to give him a hug. Some kind of contact. But again he skittered away, his hands up as if to apologize, his eyes hooded and hidden. And before Molly could try again, he skipped up the steps and she heard the door slam.

"Give him time," Sam advised with sorrowful eyes. "He's a troubled boy."

A master of understatement, Molly thought, and wondered at the secrets Patrick hid behind his abortive attempts at socialization. But for Sam, Molly smiled. "I know, *zeyde*. Thank you for being there for him."

"*Feh!*" Sam sighed with a wave of the hand. "He's good company."

Busy draping his own topcoat over Sam's shoulders, Frank lifted an eyebrow. "You want me to come back and stay? See if we get a return visit? Maybe a hank of hair to go with those bones?"

Molly unlocked the back door. "That happens, you'll be the last person I'll tell. Go home." She accepted a buss on the cheek from Sam and managed one final smile. "Thank you, both."

And then she stood aside and let Frank lead Sam out into the early morning cold.

The temperatures were so low and the night so still that the clatter and murmur of the people in Molly's front yard echoed off buildings two blocks away. Red and white strobes shuddered through her trees, and the impatient chatter of the police radios had awakened the birds. Molly stood in the doorway, chilled to her toes and unable to move. She wasn't going to get any sleep. She wasn't going to get any peace. She wasn't at all sure she was going to wade through this nonsense intact.

"Aren't you afraid?"

Startled by the sound of Patrick's voice, Molly turned around. Her nephew stood at the doorway to the stairs, his posture uncertain, his attitude aggressive, impatient with all those untidy teenage emotions he hadn't allowed before strangers. Molly shut the door and leaned against it, wishing like hell for inspiration.

"I'm not sure," she admitted truthfully.

That evidently wasn't what he'd been looking for. "But you've been threatened, and you're getting . . . like, dead people in your backyard. What does it take to get to you?"

Molly damn near told him the truth. That teenage boys with hair-trigger tempers and a lifetime of resentments got to her. That old memories got to her when they wouldn't rest quietly. That the risk of losing everything all over again got to her. But Patrick wasn't looking for the truth. He was looking, she thought, for reassurance.

"I'm not happy here, Patrick. I sincerely doubt anybody in a situation like this would be. But I'm not afraid. Trophies usually aren't threats. They're more like gifts. Messages of some kind. I'm much more afraid for whoever this guy's victims really are."

"Then why have you been having nightmares? You yell in your sleep, ya know."

Molly nodded. "I know. I'm sorry. That's old business. It doesn't mean I'm afraid, though. It means I'm worried. And I am worried." Was this the time to tell him? Was any time? "One of the things I'm worried about is you."

Patrick straightened like an outraged debutante. "I'm not going home."

Molly sighed. "I can't say I haven't thought of it."

"Any excuse in a storm?"

"Any way to protect you. I think I'm safe, but I just don't know if you are. I sure as hell know you didn't sign on for this."

Molly couldn't have said anything more wrong if she'd told Patrick she'd bought him passage to China.

"Sure, why not?" he demanded, white-faced and rigid. "You never wanted me here in the first place."

She'd had a bad enough night. Now he was giving her a headache. "Patrick, think. The press are about to overrun this house like rats on a grain barge. I'm getting visits from a psychopath, whom I'd much rather you didn't surprise coming over the backyard fence. And I'm the center of the investigation. That means I have to be there to help the police. I just can't do that and be here to protect you. It's not fair, don't you see?"

He just glared, looking, somehow, triumphant, as if she'd just proven some point of his. "To who?"

"Whom," she automatically corrected and lost more points. "It's not fair to you."

That quickly, his face went blank, the questions and demands clamped down tight. Molly looked for reaction, for objection, and saw nothing. Just a bland, beautiful teenage boy with soft eyes and a hard mouth. She had to say it anyway.

"Honestly?" she said. "I think you should go home. It's not great there right now, but it's not dangerous. And you can always come back when this is over."

The smile she got reminded her of that first morning, and the call to his parents. "Of course. Any time. When you'll remember to teach me about law enforcement. Like you promised."

Like she'd promised before Davidson had peeked into her financial file and shoved everything else into the background.

"Patrick—"

Behind her, the door swung open, shattering the standoff. Molly jumped like a gigged frog.

"I thought you were in bed," Frank greeted Patrick.

Patrick leveled one fulminating glare at Molly and hit the stairs, which left Molly behind wondering exactly what would have been the right answer.

"Aren't you glad I came back?" Frank asked.

Molly scowled. "I have a Taser, you know."

He stepped into the warm kitchen, his heavy winter coat thrown over a shoulder like a toreador's cape. "I know. That's one of the things I love about you."

Sighing in capitulation, she walked back to join him. "You have children to go home to, Frank. It's almost Christmas, for God's sake. Go hang tinsel or something."

Frank dropped his coat over a chair. "You all right?"

Picking it right back up and offering it to him, Molly laughed in disgust. "I thought we'd already established that."

He just stood there. "You're planning on doing this all alone again, aren't you?"

Molly glared up at him as if he'd just accused her of cowardice. "Didn't you see all those people in my kitchen?"

Frank turned around with a smile and began picking up coffee cups to drop in the sink. "Seems to me the notes weren't addressed to any of them."

"You're not trying to take care of me again, are you, Frank?"

God bless him, he laughed. "Good God, no. But I have some resources you might be able to make use of."

"A good shrink?"

"As a matter of fact, yes."

Molly stared again, stunned, but Frank was neither embarrassed nor reticent. "A person without a shrink in this day and age is a person with nothing to say at a cocktail party."

Molly just shook her head. "I need one who would understand what nightmares in a jungle mean."

"Vietnam is only going to play so long, St. Molly."

"The dreams are about Vietnam, Frank," she informed him drily, his coat now gathered to her chest like a security blanket. "I didn't say the problem is."

He nodded briskly. "Then he can help. I also happen to play squash with an FBI agent who is sorely underutilized right now."

Molly looked around for something to do and realized that Frank had already done it. He even had a rag in his hand to clean the marks off her table.

"Stop this," she insisted, shoving his coat at his chest so he'd have to catch it. "You're getting worse than Sam."

Once more Frank turned on her. He tossed the rag in the sink and slipped into his coat, all the while smiling that infuriating, Frank Patterson smile. Then he simply opened his arms wide and stepped up for a hug.

Molly knew damn well this wasn't an invitation. She knew just what it was. Somehow, though, Frank didn't manage to get his arms around her. Molly backed away at the same moment, and Frank was left in the cold air with an arm full of nothing.

"You're going to have to accept help sometime," he said, still smiling as he let her open the door.

Molly faced him down, even though she felt oddly impatient and unnerved. "Don't be silly, Frank."

And finally found herself alone in a silent kitchen, in a silent house, with only her dog to comfort her. She knew what her dreams would be that night, but she went to bed anyway.

Nobody knows anymore who
I am
they can't stop me
here in my special dark
place
in the dark where i rule

TWELVE

"I'm sorry," Rhett said.

Molly sighed. "Everybody's sorry, Rhett."

He'd shown up at her door about three minutes past dawn bearing a box of doughnuts and a hatful of sincerity, and Molly, against her better judgment, let him inside. The good news for the day was that so far most of the news crews had only responded to one skull appearing in an urban yard, and were treating it like the latest "Satanists in St. Louis?" scare. Molly was still holding her breath for Donna Kirkland to blow open the door on the rest.

The bad news was that Rhett still wasn't telling her much more than he had.

"I thought we had this cleared up, Rhett," Molly said as she prepared the obligatory coffee to go with the sinful doughnut hole long johns. "Winnie promised that the next time you talked to me, you'd actually talk to me."

"She's still discussing it with the brass. They, uh, still . . ."

"Wonder if that stupid little detective from the Fifth District is right and I'm doing this to myself for the attention. Well, I'll tell you what, Rhett. I am. As you can tell, I've never been happier. I spent the night passing coffee out to the television crews, and after you leave, I may bake pies."

Standing uncomfortably by the door to the hallway, Rhett blushed. "I'm—"

Molly nodded impatiently. "Sorry. Yeah, I know. Sorry doesn't get you shit, Rhett, and I don't have the luxury right now to be wasting time."

At least Rhett was more polite than Winnie and failed to mention Molly's about-face. As frantic and fidgety as she felt this morning, she probably would have decked him for telling the truth. She'd definitely had jungle visits the night before, nightmares she could still taste on the back of her tongue like bad meat. And doughnuts and coffee weren't enough to wash it away.

Well, she couldn't get through it until she got started with it. Pouring out the coffee, Molly sat down with hers and waited for Rhett to do likewise. "I hope you've had some luck with my list, Rhett. I started checking work and health records."

"We have a couple detectives on it."

She picked up her second doughnut and devoured half in one bite. "Anything raising flags with missing persons yet?"

Rhett played with his cruller. "No. We've been in touch with all the surrounding counties and every one of the city districts."

"The districts? The district detectives do missing persons?"

"Yeah. Missing persons is only a couple guys in a basement downtown. They get the files when they go inactive. You know. Dad missing for a year with entire bank account, that kind of thing. Kids and high-profile stuff stay out of the basement for a long time."

Molly sighed. "Who can I talk to?"

"Baitshop Caletti."

Molly's eyebrow raised. Not at the nickname. Every cop had a nickname. But this was a beaut. "Baitshop?"

Rhett grinned. "Long story."

"I bet. I need to contact him."

"Her."

Molly nodded, now sure of it. "Her. Has anybody even talked to the FBI about possible plans of investigation?"

"The government's on budgetary shutdown."

Molly's patience suffered another setback. "We all know the agents in the area well enough to buy 'em a beer, Rhett. Hell, Frank offered me a squash buddy. Come on. This is a serial killer we're talking about. One good enough that he's teasing me with parts of bodies we don't even know are missing."

"I'm trying to get hold of somebody," he protested. "I'm also trying to bone up on my own. Just in case I can get a word in edgewise with Davidson."

Molly was again struck by the disparity in the Beaver Cleaver tone of Rhett's manner and the meat cleaver sharpness of his brain.

"I'll lend you some of my stuff, if you don't already have it," she offered.

He smiled like a kid getting a puppy, and Molly hoped she'd discovered his secret agenda.

"We're still perilously short of a direction," she reminded him. "And not just because I still don't think I fall into the 'most likely to receive a serial killer's trophies' category. I've never heard of people getting trophies and death threats in the same mailbox."

"You think this last one was?"

Stirring her coffee, Molly focused on the soft swirls of steam that lifted to obscure her kitchen window. She could see eye sockets in the swirls. She'd seen eye sockets in her dreams last night. "I don't know. This last one sounded more disappointed, ya know? As if I should have figured this out. But I haven't. I can't."

So she climbed back to her feet and headed in for her personal library. She'd made it to the door of the playroom when she heard Patrick clamber down the steps.

"What are you doing up, Aunt Molly?" he asked, looking veiled and surly. "Checking up on me? Or phoning for those cheap airfares to Washington?"

Which was just about the last straw on Molly's haystack. Even so, she managed to keep her temper. "Detective Butler finally put in an appearance. He brought us doughnuts. Have a couple."

Patrick took a quick look toward the kitchen and all but sneered. "This guy's a detective, and I'm not allowed to walk into the morgue?"

Molly began pulling out forensic texts on serial killers. "Yes, he is. Undoubtedly because he treated his older relatives with respect when he was a teenager. Police forces value that trait highly in their detectives."

Patrick just snorted. "Well, if that's all it is, I'm going back to bed."

But not before Rhett had had a chance to follow Molly into the playroom. He greeted Patrick with a shy, quiet smile, that Tom Sawyer front he preferred. "Morning, Pat. How are you?"

Patrick stiffened. "Patrick," he snapped.

Rhett shrugged agreeably as Molly turned back, weighed down with tomes. "Patrick. Sorry. Busy night last night, huh?"

"How would you know? You weren't here."

Molly sighed. "Please excuse my nephew," she said to Rhett. "If he didn't have the manners of a goat, I'd probably ask you to grant his fondest wish and talk to him about police work. But I think even Patrick knows better than to ask a favor like that now."

Rhett was perfectly copacetic. Patrick, on the other hand, went absolutely white and bolted right back up the stairs.

Molly sighed. "Back to that manual on teenagers for me."

Hands out for the books Molly had picked off the shelf, Rhett chuckled. "Aw, don't worry about him. He's just being sixteen. If you meant it, I'd be happy to talk to him when this is over."

When Molly smiled this time, it was with true relief. "Thanks, sweetie. You're a gem."

Oddly enough, that was what got the reaction out of Rhett. Even odder, it was a grimace of distaste. "Yeah, that's me. Everybody's favorite pet."

Fighting a surprised grin, Molly decided that this wasn't the time to pat his head. "Figure this out before the brass, and you'll be the big dog," she suggested.

"Or the dead dog."

But he took the books anyway and escaped before Molly could press him for any more information.

Molly spent the next hour trying to get Patrick to come out of his room, but all she ended up with was a locked bedroom door and a concert by Marilyn Manson. Molly found herself standing out in the hallway looking at the old hunting prints that marched down the wall like well-mannered retainers and thinking how badly Patrick's rage and frustration fit into this house.

Which made her wonder, considering how Patrick's poltergeist energy wore on her, whether she was so different from the people in her life she'd most resented. After all, the Burkes had had their problems. They'd just had them sotto voce, the traumas carefully controlled and contained, as if to protect the eggshell of their house. Even Molly had saved her real moments of disorder for outside the house.

The music in Patrick's room screeched on about death and despair and the hormonal privilege of rebellion, and Molly stood outside on gleaming hardwood and thought that maybe she'd succumbed to the place after all. Maybe she should take a page out of Patrick's book. When he left for work, she might just sneak into his room and unearth the various tools of his teenage rebellion and see if she could make them work for her.

Maybe it would help protect her from facing the situation she was in. Maybe old Marilyn Manson could tell her how to ignore those sad, empty eyes that already followed her to sleep. Maybe he could show her how to avoid all those ghosts she was forcing out of their boxes so they could chase her down these eggshell white hallways like untidy children seeking to be heard.

Smiling wearily to herself at the concept of childish ghosts, Molly turned and walked on back downstairs. How long would it take, she wondered, before they were unearthed as well?

"You offered to help," she said to Sasha the next afternoon. "Now, pay up."

Molly should have been doing her research down at the Medical Examiner's office, but the local press had already staked it out. So Molly opted to take advantage of some extra hours at the ED and Sasha's free computer time.

"Catch that kid," Sasha snapped at one of their techs as a naked, shrieking toddler raced by. "Help how?"

Molly pulled her hands through her hair and stretched out some of her late-night kinks. "I spent yesterday morning in an exercise that made me question my judgment, so I want you to double-check the list I made up of possible suspects. Guys I know are over thirty, who I'm checking for . . . problems. The ones you might know from Grace are in red."

Sasha slid her elegant self into the other chair. "Problems like a fondness for other people's postmortem remains?"

"Yeah. Like that."

Sasha scanned the list. Molly closed her eyes as if that would protect her from Sasha's too-acute perception. It didn't keep her from thinking of the list she'd collected like a confession of treason.

It was too long. Too general. Just from this hospital Molly had too many names. Men she'd met by chance. Men she'd worked with, socialized with. Liked and disliked and actively loathed. Nurses and physicians and impatient spouses. Paramedics who brought them all manner of disaster and indignity, and then partnered them at parties. Police who protected them, and security guards who didn't. X-ray techs and at least one pathologist who liked to peek into women's rest rooms to see visitors squeal in surprise.

And that didn't even take into account the names written in other colors.

"Quite a list," Sasha said, actually sounding a bit abashed.

Molly didn't bother to open her eyes. "Tell me about it."

"You put in those housekeeping guys?"

"Yeah. Even the one you pointed out, although you seem to see him more than I do. John Martin. Fourth from the end."

"What about that morgue guy? Lewis."

"He's in green. ME's office."

"As long as he's there. Any other weird guys pop to mind who aren't here?"

"Well, Sam's over thirty. You think he has big blue vats full of Soilex in his basement?"

"Even if he did, he couldn't get down the steps to fill 'em. What about somebody else who made an impression on you?"

"There's a guy who delivers Sam's groceries. Little Allen something, there in black. The police are checking him out first."

"Anybody else?"

Molly opened her eyes to see Lorenzo, their best tech, trying to placate an angry mother. Thank heavens Lorenzo was only twenty. She didn't want him on the list. Not with those sweet, chocolate eyes and fierce young mind. Not when he had the patience of a saint and the smile of a child.

"Hey, there, Miss Molly, I knew that was you!"

Molly turned around to find herself faced with a short, round, bald, black elf bouncing on the tips of his toes. For the first time since waking up, she seriously smiled. "Hi there, James. You got something for me?"

"What, my polished head isn't enough?" he demanded with a saucy grin, bouncing in time to some rhythm only James could hear. As evening pharmacy supervisor, James should have been perched behind his window somewhere two floors down between a disused laundry and the power plant. But sometimes James made special appearances to personally bestow his more prized wares to particular clients, like Molly.

James fed everybody's jones for junk food.

"Your head's beautiful," Molly assured him. "But I have money. I have stock shares. Hell, I have a house in the West End I'll trade you for one lousy Twinkie. Come on, James."

James's grin grew impossibly wider. "I ain't tradin' nothin', Miss Molly. You earned it. Skulls in the backyard's better'n anything James ever done to get hisself on the news. But you think of me, you need an on-air quote 'bout how wonderful you are, hear?"

Molly laughed. "I hear. Now, give."

It wasn't Twinkies. It wasn't Ding Dongs. It was Hostess Cup Cakes, the most decadent of James's treats. Molly held out her hand like a supplicant at communion.

"How old are you?" Sasha suddenly asked James.

Molly snatched her hand away, almost losing her treat. "Sasha," she warned.

"Wayne Williams," Sasha said simply.

Fortunately, James didn't understand the reference to the nation's most notorious black serial killer. "Thirty-five. Why, Chernobyl? You lookin' for a date? James'd show you a fine time, I can promise you that."

Sasha took one look at James's favorite gold canine and offered a frosty smile. "I'll let you know."

James hooted in delight and dropped the snack treat in Molly's lap before sashaying on down the hall to spread medication and benevolence like a hip-hop St. Nick. Left behind, Molly reluctantly scribbled his name at the bottom of her list.

"Now what?" Sasha asked, watching.

"You're going to show me that illegal stuff. And then, if we're slow enough, I'm taking a full lunch break to get started on the computer in your office. Okay?"

"Certainly. Just don't tell me."

And so Molly spent her break poring over hospital and employment records she had no business accessing. She was looking for patterns, because if there was one thing she understood from her research, every serial killer followed an inviolate pattern that only ended in his or her death. Maybe the specifics were different. Maybe his parents were drug addicts instead of alcoholics. Maybe the abuse suffered was psychological or merely the most awful abuse of childhood, the unfillable void of absolute neglect. Maybe the psychopathic triad of bed-wetting, fire-starting, and animal abuse was incomplete. But there were always markers along the way. Markers that were absolutely obvious to everyone who ever saw the child as he grew inexorably toward his destiny.

Molly knew of at least a half dozen juvenile officers who kept files of kids they were just waiting to see appear on the

NCIC computer. She knew teachers and social workers and psychotherapists who watched a child progress from maladjustment to rage to predatory behavior and played the same game Molly had all these years. Everyone who touched the children who had been hurt knew that they were watching the progression of a terrible disease of violence they had no way to prevent.

Molly didn't have access to any juvenile records. They were still closed and expunged in Missouri. But she had work records. She had the knowledge of how evaluations were worded to avoid blatant accusations. And she had the understanding that a person caught in the thrall of serial offense was an uncertain employee. No matter the image, like Bundy or Gacy with their bright smiles and public personae, the serial killer never really succeeded at anything as well as his crime. And the more the obsession controlled him, the more energy he drained from the rest of life to feed his primary goal. The stalking and killing of humans.

Molly looked in the files of her candidates for interpersonal problems. For questions of misbehavior. Angry outbursts, difficulty dealing with other employees, suspicions of sneakery of any kind. Voyeurism, harassment, patient abuse. Any or all could show up on a serial offender's work record. And all could be and had been tolerated by hospitals too short of staff and too afraid to face the consequences of a precipitate firing. In fact, much to Molly's chagrin, they had been tolerated in five out of the first twelve names she investigated.

Well, that made her feel safe, she thought as she stretched out new and crankier kinks. If she'd seen a pattern of escalation in any of the men, she would have called Rhett right away. As it was, it seemed more a chronic problem than an acute one. A chronic problem the hospital was already liable for, since at least one of the men had been caught in inappropriate behavior involving female patients. But nothing so far that rang the big bells.

The good news was that James the pharmacy supervisor had come up absolutely clean. Dr. RattleSpizer himself, on the other hand, seemed to make a few ICU nurses uncomfortable. Considering the fact that he had a widow's peak like Wolfman and a leer like Jack Nicholson, Molly could imagine why.

Molly spent her shift at the sinks where she helped cool off every screaming child in the city with a temp and took her breaks in Sasha's office. And then, because she'd finally figured out how to coerce her information from the computers she so loathed, after clocking out she adjourned back to Sasha's office until it was too late to see Donna Kirkland let the psychopath out of the bag on the ten o'clock news.

Molly had told Patrick that she wasn't afraid. But she was. She was terrified.

And it wasn't just body parts and methodical murderers that scared her. It was news. Notoriety.

More than once Molly had found herself at the mercy of the mini-cam, and it was still enough to traumatize her. Her face on the news, her past tossed up like compost to explain her behavior. Her follies and frustrations the Tinker Toys of a media's need for quick explanations. It had been tough enough seeing Rhett's reaction to the ignoble idiocies of her past. She couldn't bear it on the fatuous faces of media stars.

Finally, though, Molly knew she had to get home to at least check on Patrick. Stretching out every tired and cramped muscle she had, she shut down the computer, closed Sasha's office, and headed back to get her stuff for home. Tomorrow was soon enough to see if any of her possible suspects also had psychiatric evaluations or court-ordered care.

She knew it was necessary. She even knew she was doing it for a vital cause. It didn't make her feel any less soiled.

Which was why, of course, it was so appropriate that she walked into the lounge to find Frank settled on the couch like one of the inmates.

"What are you doing here?" she demanded. "I got off three hours ago."

Considering the fact that she'd had a sum total of about two hours' sleep the night before and no memory of grooming, it seriously displeased her to see him looking so neat and slick.

"Why I'm checking up on you," Frank said happily, never taking his eyes from the television.

"This grisly discovery in the Central West End is, evidently, not the first . . ."

Molly heard the all-too-familiar excitement, the almost moist pronunciation of the words of outrage, and faltered to a halt. She hadn't waited long enough after all. There was Donna Kirkland plastered all over the lounge TV, which meant that all hell was about to break loose.

"Oh, Molly, you *are* still here," Lorenzo said behind her. "I thought you'd gone home."

Molly turned around a little too quickly, much preferring Lorenzo's sweet smile to Donna's barracuda intensity. "I'm going now. I don't suppose you could keep Frank here till I get away?"

"You don't want him to," Frank said, his eyes still on the TV. "Frank has a present for you."

"I don't want any more presents from you, Frank."

"Sure you do, Mol. St. Molly of the Masses, meet Kathy Kinstle."

At which point Molly noticed the quiet, middle-aged woman seated next to Frank. Soft, she thought. Comfortable. Kind. A pretty face, cropped chestnut hair, and a mother's figure. A wardrobe that looked to include the same kind of suits Molly wore to the ME's office. Turning from the televised images of Molly's backyard, she offered Molly a kind smile.

"Hi, Kathy," Molly greeted her. "What awful thing has Frank done to *you*?"

"Molly, excuse me," Lorenzo interrupted behind her. "I have to get back. There was a message for you, but I thought you were gone. They said you'd understand."

Molly's stomach lurched. There were so many messages Molly didn't want. Beginning, she thought, with the fact that Donna was even now unleashing reporters toward her house like clouds of flying monkeys.

But Lorenzo surprised her again. "It's about the Water Child?" he asked, understandably confused.

The Water Child. It actually took Molly a second to comprehend. To remember, briefly and vividly, the frail, limp weight of him in her hands. "What about him?"

"The NICU nurses wanted you to know that he sank. Is that supposed to mean anything?"

At first, Molly could only blink. All that work. All that fierce, focused hope. Sasha would have said he was lucky. Sasha was probably right. After spending the evening searching for the detritus of abused children, Molly almost agreed.

Almost.

"Come on, Frank," she said, grabbing her coat off the rack and turning for the door. "Let's get out of here."

"But Donna's not finished," he protested, hand out to the television.

"She'll never be finished."

"In which case," he said with a bright smile as he and Kathy got to their feet, "you'll be more than happy to talk to Kathy."

Molly stopped and considered the small, kind woman. "Are you the psychiatrist?" she asked.

Kathy laughed. "God, no," she said. "FBI."

It figured. "Well, come on," Molly suggested and turned for the door.

Along the hallway, the spate of baby fevers had, if anything, grown worse. In addition to all the traumas and chest pains, the place still overflowed with fretful, flushed toddlers, all up to their navels in stainless-steel sinks filled with tepid water. Staff scooted around like bumper cars, and at least half the parents were complaining in voices only a bit more fractious than the kids'.

Molly led her little gaggle through them like Moses through the Red Sea. And then she went the hell home.

Kathy Kinstle and Frank followed right behind.

Patrick wasn't home again. The alarm wasn't set. The kitchen, however, was fairly tidy. Molly spent a moment letting her excited dog out of the house and casting her by-now obsessive peek at the porch for surprises.

"Your answering machine's blinking," Frank offered as he slid off his jacket. "You want me to check it?"

"No. It's undoubtedly somebody I don't want to talk to. Sit down, Kathy," she suggested. "I'll make us something hot so we can talk and Frank can go home, like I'm sure he wants to."

"Not on your life," he said. "I provided the entertainment, I get to stay and enjoy it."

Kathy smiled like a mother.

Molly slammed her teapot down on a burner. "I hope he didn't drag you over to see me against your will," she said.

Kathy was still smiling, her hands folded neatly on the table. "Not at all. This isn't an official visit, but when Frank told me what was happening, well . . ." It was just a small shrug. A glitter in the eyes. That quickly, Kathy went from Betty Crocker to Janet Reno and back again. "I'm in between assignments and can't get into my office until the support staff gets back from shutdown, and I admit I'm a little antsy. It also looks like you've stumbled over something interesting."

Molly handed Kathy her mug and ignored Frank when he absconded with hers. "Stumbled being the operative word. I almost put my foot right through it."

Kathy spooned in sugar and nodded. "Yeah, I heard. Would you like to tell me about it?"

Molly took a considered look at the notes she'd compiled that sat at the side of her table and then at Frank, who was standing over by the door as if Molly wouldn't see him. She didn't want to offer this stuff up to him. She didn't want his help or his sporadic concern. But he *had* been the only one in town to provide an FBI agent.

"You're local?" Molly asked Kathy.

"I am now. I came in from the Norfolk office. But I've done profiling on a part-time basis the last ten years." A quick shadow passed over the complacent features and was gone. "I don't have the stones to do it full time. Too many kids."

Having just done the research, Molly nodded. Seventeen-year-olds were bad enough to deal with. She couldn't imagine facing what was happening to the real children.

Easing herself into a chair, Molly pulled over her legal pad. It occurred to her in passing that a lot of unpleasant business had taken place at this table lately.

"So far we don't have enough for anything definite," she said. "No victim. No murder scene. Not enough to start a real profile of any kind."

"Tell me what you do have."

As concisely and dispassionately as she could, Molly did just that. She mentioned the victimology both she and Rhett had done without actually showing it. She shared the list she'd made up and what she was discovering on it. She even alluded to her illegal computer work.

"What about me?" Frank demanded from where he leaned against the wall, unsipped tea in hand. "Aren't you investigating me?"

"You're despicable, Frank," Molly assured him. "Not malevolent."

"Why, Molly," he sighed. "I'm touched."

"May I see the notes you've compiled?" Kathy asked. "While I'm looking at them, I'm sure Frank wants to be getting home."

After a couple more cups of tea, Molly was going to have to ask Kathy how she could get quite so much unchallengeable command in such a soft statement. Frank didn't like Kathy's complacent smile, but he put down his mug anyway and slid into his coat.

"I have the most overwhelming suspicion that you don't trust me," he protested with a grin.

"It's not that," Kathy said, patting him like a grade-school teacher. "It's just that Molly has some things to tell me she doesn't want you to know."

"You sure you're with the FBI?" Molly couldn't help but ask.

Kathy just smiled and walked along with Molly as she led Frank out the front door.

"You don't appreciate my help," he objected on the front porch.

Molly laughed. "I do, Frank. I do. But Patrick's due home

soon, and Kathy's here. And you only have three shopping days left till Christmas. Buy me something nice."

"Only if you buy me something nicer."

"After you sued me, I don't have the money for nicer."

Frank's grin should have been a misdemeanor. "Then I'll just have to settle for naughtier."

Molly ignored him. "Say hi to the kids for me."

The night wasn't quite as cold as it had been. Up and down the block, Christmas lights flickered and shone, fireflies in the winter, the only thing Molly liked about Christmas. Challenging the dark and all. The city, for once, was quiet, and Molly found herself wanting to just stand out in the night.

Pulling his keys from his pocket, Frank walked off the porch. "You sure you don't want me to stay, St. Molly? I'd never forgive myself if something happened to you."

"Nothing's going to happen to me, Frank," Molly said, following him down the walk toward where his bright red Mercedes sports coupe upstaged her faded little Toyota in the driveway. "There are cops watching my house, and I have an FBI agent on my porch. Besides, my friend's never come two nights in a row. Excitement's over for a while."

As if in punctuation, Frank lifted his hand and did that little wrist flip he did so that everybody knew that the car that was about to start was his. Then, with that shit-eating grin of his, he punched the little red button on his keychain.

The night disintegrated. There was a flat crack of noise, a shot of light, and Molly found herself airborne. She was still trying to figure out what the hell happened when her head hit something and all the noise and lights just stopped.

it isn't enough
animals are just animals

I want to do it to a
girl

THIRTEEN

"Incoming!"

She wasn't going out there. She wasn't.

"Burke, come on! They're walking the rounds right toward the triage area!"

She shivered, sick, exhausted, scared. It didn't matter what was happening. She wasn't moving. She wasn't walking out into a shower of shrapnel for anybody. Not anymore.

Another round hit closer, tossing her cot a little and her stomach more. She was so hung over. She was blind with a headache, and the shells were thumping closer and closer. Louder, more deadly. And her best friend was standing there, waiting for her to do the right thing, just as she'd always done.

"I'm short, Sally," she objected. "I'm so damn short we had my going-away party last night, or weren't you there? I'm not gonna ruin it by going back to the world in a body bag. Now go away!"

Shouts, now; screams. Pulling at her even harder than Sally's hands. Sally who had only been in Nam four months. Who had been such a good friend. Whom Molly was going to miss when she got home.

Home.

The mortars came, and she thought she should just crawl

*under her bunk. The mortars were thumping closer, walking
right down the main street like shattering footsteps, and
Molly shook, sick, curled into fetal position.*

Four days. She had four fucking days left.

*She found herself on her feet and running before she even
knew she was going to do it. Helmet in one hand, boots in the
other, running toward that hailstorm of misery, toward the
screams and shouts, eyes closed, head bent, legs pumping.*

*It wasn't a shell that dropped her. She tripped. She just
tripped, right there in the middle of the dirt, sprawling in the
road with a mortar storm raging around her.*

*It was when she opened her eyes to go on that she saw
what she'd tripped over. Round, rolling, no more than inches
away, dirty with the impact of her fall.*

"Sally!"

*She picked it up. She picked her up, stunned to silence.
Sally's eyes were wide, surprised, sad. Accusing. Bleeding all
over Molly's hands and arms, mouth open as if to make one final plea for help. If only Molly had gotten up and run with her.*

But how could a skull call for help? How could a face with no
jaw, no teeth, beg Molly to run fast before it was too late?

"Molly, are you all right?"

"It's her head. It's Sally . . ."

Hands on her shoulders. Gentle hands. "Molly?"

Molly saw now. She wasn't in the dirt. She was on her lawn.
On her back, in the dark, with the edges of the night flickering
like a mortar attack. And she hurt. She hurt everywhere.

But her hands were empty. Sally had been gone a long time.

"Molly?"

Molly blinked to find that it wasn't day, it wasn't hot and
thick and terrible. It was a cold winter night, where Christmas
lights held off the dark, and Kathy was crouched over her, patting her cheek. "You got knocked out, Molly. You okay?"

"I know this is a cliché—" Molly began, struggling to sit up.

"Car bomb," Kathy offered. "I need you to help me."

Molly heard Magnum now. Maybe her ears were clearing,
maybe just her brain.

Her eyes focused, and she saw the scene in her driveway.

Frank's car was a funeral pyre. Molly's car smoked with the debris from Frank's car that had pocked the ragtop. The night was washed in red and yellow, sirens already keening down the road. Molly blinked, saw what else she'd missed, and scrambled to her feet.

"Oh, shit," she moaned. "Oh no."

There was an untidy pile of winter coats crumpled on the ground not ten feet in front of her.

"Frank!" Molly yelled, crouching by his side, hands on him, focus on his ashen face, the rivulets of blood down his cheeks, the patches of burn on his cheek, on his gasping, uneven breaths. "Don't do this, Frank. I only have one lifesaving attempt in me per friend." And she'd used it up this summer, which was still close enough to give her the big shakes.

If it hadn't been Frank, Molly would have been amazed at his aplomb. He opened those stunning eyes and grinned. "I live . . . for . . . moments like . . . this, Mol."

He'd been thrown against one of the steps on her walk, and lay there, just a little bent by the impact. Molly unbuttoned his coat and checked his pupils, which were fairly sluggish.

"Give me the full scoop," she commanded, ignoring the rising wails that approached, ignoring even Kathy, who stood thoughtfully to her side. "What hurts? What feels like it's not working?"

"I'm . . . afraid . . ." he said with a wry grin, his eyes fully open and still a little dazed, "I've breathed . . . better."

"Left or right?"

"Left."

Molly palpated his chest to a few surprised grunts of pain and grimaced herself. "You've crunched some ribs, you idiot. Why couldn't you start the car from the porch like you're supposed to?"

His grin was lopsided. "You . . . distracted me. You said there wouldn't . . . be any . . . excitement . . ."

Molly felt hot tears drip down her nose. "Shut up, Frank."

Emergency equipment swept up and people tumbled out like clowns from Volkswagens. The paramedic team was one of the best, and they wasted no time on Frank's jokes. Hooking him up to monitor, oxygen, and IV, they ignored his pleas for his million-dollar Armani suit as they sliced through his clothes like pizza and laid him bare on the lawn. Molly helped, and then Molly stood back, and then Molly fought off fresh shakes and nausea.

Her car was being drenched by a high arc of water. Frank's was a hunk of eviscerated and charred modern art. At least one of Molly's house windows had blown out, and the stink of oily smoke and gasoline congealed in the air.

"*This* is the kind of stuff you've been dealing with?" Kathy asked in her quiet way, hands tucked into her winter coat.

That was when Molly noticed that Kathy had somehow gotten a coat draped over Molly's shoulders. When she turned to answer, she saw Sam and Patrick standing poised at the other edge of her lawn, waiting for the moment they could step forward and assert their rights to the victims. Molly waved them over.

"Not exactly this," Molly admitted to the FBI agent. "But it is one more weird thing to add to the tally."

Kathy nodded, bemused. "Then I definitely think I'd like to hang around."

"Who would do this?" Sam all but keened as he tottered closer. "*Gottenyu!*" And then, the situation obviously overwhelmed him, because he sank straight into Yiddish, his words coming so fast Molly wasn't sure whether he was praying or cursing, even as he held on to her, patting and clutching, to make sure she was whole.

Molly felt far from whole. Blood trickled down her neck, and bruises were rising in at least half a dozen places. Her ears still rang, and her stomach wasn't sure which way to heave. But Sam didn't need to get that whole story.

"I'm fine, *zeyde*," she assured him, hugging him back. "Just a little shaken up."

"How's Frank?" Patrick asked, the whites of his eyes showing.

Molly took a quick look back to where they were loading

Frank onto a stretcher. "Frank's made it through worse than this," she assured him with a pat to his arm. "Although I'm not sure if he'll survive the loss of both his Mercedes and Armani in the same night. Can you say Kaddish for inanimate objects, Sam?"

Sam's laugh was a bark. "Such a thing to say, *taibeleh*." But he patted her cheek and panted, tears in his old, bright eyes.

"You're coming with us, aren't you, Molly?" one of the paramedics asked.

Molly looked around, trying to assess with only half a brain.

"Go," Sam commanded. "You hurt your head. I'll watch Patrick and make sure the police don't *mutshe* your poor dog."

Molly knew she had other things to think about, but she saw the first news truck pull up and made up her mind. "Patrick, go with Sam and keep the newspeople away from him. I'll call from the ED," she said, then pointed to the approaching caravan. "And don't let one of those *momzers* in my house."

Molly spent the rest of the night acquiring four staples on the side of her head, a salesman's sample of painkillers, and the acquaintance of the local bomb and arson guy who showed up with Rhett Butler. She held them off until she'd gotten in touch with Frank's mother-in-law to explain that Frank was going to do a little hospital time after having a chest tube stuck in him to reinflate his collapsed lung.

"It was a pipe bomb," Rhett told her as he patted her hands. "Rigged to his automatic starter."

Molly tried not to scowl. "I guessed that, Rhett. Right about the time he pressed the starter and his car blew up."

"Actually, you were both lucky," the arson guy said. "The explosion was rigged to go straight up. Nuts and knees kinda thing."

Molly just stared at him, sure somebody in arson academy must have trained him better than to be so blunt.

"Any idea who it might have been?" Rhett asked.

Molly blinked at him, and then blinked at the bomb and arson guy, who stood alongside. "Like, have I been hanging around with anybody from the Lebanese Mafia lately? What's the matter, didn't Davidson finish his report on me yet?"

"Molly—"

But Molly had just about had it. "I'm going up to see that Frank isn't harassing the nurses, Rhett. And then I'm going the hell home. If anybody has anything of interest to say to me, you can just wait until I'm damn well ready, because you sure as hell haven't said it yet."

And, much to everybody's surprise—especially Molly's—she did just that.

Fortunately for Frank, he was way too sedated to notice how agitated Molly was. She left him humming sleepily to himself. Unfortunately for Molly, she made it back down to the ED just in time to remember that she had no way home and it was three in the morning. Which was why she didn't bite Rhett's head off when she saw him perched on one of the work lane stools waiting for her.

"You could have told me not to make an idiot of myself," she groused as she neared.

His grin was sweet. "You could have told me the same thing. I'm sorry."

That brought her to a dead halt. "Real cops never apologize, Rhett. Didn't somebody tell you that?"

"Homicide cops never let arson cops overrule them. For penance I thought I'd give you a name. Micklawski. Mean anything?"

"Polish sausage."

"Only if it's delivered. It's Little Allen's name. Allen Walter Micklawski."

Molly managed to get her eyes marginally bigger. "Find anything on him yet?"

"Nope, but there was another peeper call in tonight. They're checking real hard this time."

Molly nodded, briefly distracted by the urge to sneak into Sasha's office and boot up the computer. "I don't suppose we have any news from the cops who were supposed to be watching my house."

Rhett shrugged diplomatically. "I haven't been . . . uh, included in that particular discussion. You ready to go home?"

So much for urges. Molly took a look around an unusually quiet work lane and sighed. "I guess so. I imagine I still have a fair amount of charred metal and hand-sewn leather to move out of my driveway."

Rhett held out his arm like a cotillion date. "That's what he gets for driving a status symbol."

Molly slipped her arm through Rhett's and walked out the door. "I don't suppose my little Toyota escaped unscathed, did it?"

"Almost. Your backseat's a little wet, and your convertible top is air-conditioned. You think this is related to your thing, or is somebody pissed off enough at Frank to follow him to your house just to blow him up?"

Molly had thought of little else, especially as she'd stood in the shadowy edges of Frank's ICU room watching the monitors blink.

"Well, if anybody could piss a person off that badly, it would definitely be Frank."

"But you don't think so."

She sighed. "Somebody who's mad at Frank has the rest of the city to blow him up in. Why would they pick a place that's suddenly in the news all the time?"

"To get their message home?"

"Go ahead and investigate him. I'll go talk to my FBI agent."

They walked in silence out to the ambulance bay where Rhett's car waited.

"What if it is the guy who's visiting you, Molly?"

Molly thought until she was seated and belted in his unit. Then she shook her head. "It still doesn't make sense."

"It doesn't make any sense," Kathy said when she showed up at Molly's door later that day.

Molly rubbed a hand over her face and thought she should probably open her door. The agent was standing out on her porch in her best London Fog coat, looking more like a soccer mom than an FBI agent. Molly still had destruction art in her driveway, a glazier in her living room, and another round of yellow police tape in her yard, over which some neighborhood wag had draped red ribbons and a couple of ornaments. And that didn't even take into account the size of her headache.

Happy Holidays.

"Agent Kinstle," she finally greeted the woman. "What can I do for you?"

Kathy didn't even try to look uncomfortable. "You doing anything right now?"

Molly laughed. "I'm waiting to talk to Patrick's parents, Frank's insurance agent, *my* insurance agent, my nephew, and my neighbor. I have half a dozen camera trucks in my street wanting to interrogate me, and an even dozen forensic and police authorities waiting downtown for the same privilege. And then I have to go see Frank and comfort him for the loss of his nearest and dearest. Why? You need something?"

"I've been thinking about your little problem." Kathy flashed a quick, unrepentant grin. "As a matter of fact, while everybody was crawling over your driveway, I was in your kitchen reading your notes. I'd like to get some more information, if I could."

Way too tired to resent the intrusion, Molly opened the door the rest of the way to let Kathy in along with a fresh blast of arctic air.

"I was wondering if I could see the notes you've been getting," Kathy said as she shrugged out of her coat to reveal slacks and sweatshirt cross-stitched with holly and kittens.

"They're at evidence," Molly said, limping into the kitchen. "But there are copies in the ME file."

Magnum gave Kathy a few suspicious sniffs and a half-hearted growl and settled by the stove. Molly thought of putting on tea and decided she'd just had too much damn tea lately.

"How's Frank?" Kathy asked behind her.

"Annoying."

Kathy smiled. "And your nephew. Is he still next door?"

Molly looked up to see Kathy considering the CD player on the counter. "Yeah. At least till I can get him back to his parents."

His parents, who were not returning the call she'd first placed at four-thirty this morning. "Tell you what," Molly decided, swinging instead to the phone. "Let me tell Sam where I'm going and I'll take you to the ME's office. Do you have a car? The heater in mine isn't quite working right now."

Not to mention the fact that there was half an inch of ice on the floor of the backseat.

Kathy smiled again. "I have a car."

Molly found the file labeled MOLLY'S SECRET PAL on Kevin McNally's desk.

"You the castle guard?" she asked him. "Or is this to ensure I stop by for a chat?"

Kevin smiled, looking far too peaceful for what was going on. But then, Kevin probably had a car without its own koi pond in the backseat. "We decided that all files should stay here for now. To prevent leaks. You okay? You look . . ."

Molly grinned. "I feel. . . . I do have a present for the office, though. An out-of-work FBI profiler who wants to help. That okay?"

Kevin's bushy red eyebrows lifted. "I'm not sure what the protocol is on that. I'm not even sure what the law is. But what the hell? Nobody else is coming up with anything."

"You talked to anybody else?" Molly demanded. "Nobody's saying anything to me but 'what's your financial stake in all this?' "

"Not me. But don't take it too hard that Davidson's involved. He really is the best."

Sighing, Molly scratched at her staples and rubbed at her very sore and tired face. "I hope so. Our friend isn't any amateur." She gestured to the overstuffed, oversize file. "So, is it okay if I do a little end run?"

"Do a quarterback sneak if you want. We need help."

He handed the thing off like a Torah in temple, and Molly turned for the door. She was halfway out the door when Kevin cleared his throat.

"One more thing, Mol. In the file."

Molly turned on him.

To anyone who didn't know him, Kevin would have looked passive. Molly saw distress. "Winnie wanted you to see it when you got in. Before we began to circulate it around the street. It's in the file."

"What?"

He had the grace to face her head on. "Your latest victim."

For a second, Molly could only stare at him. Then she just walked out.

Back in the investigator's pen, Kathy was being entertained by Vic Fellows, one of the other investigators.

"We're on *Hard Copy* watch," he was telling her with great relish as he groomed the seven remaining hairs on the top of his head. "Human bones, firebombs, drugged dogs. It's a natural. I'm going from here to get my hair cut so I look good on camera."

The minute Molly dropped the file on her desk, the party broke up. Kathy made a grab for the threatening notes that sat at the top of the pile. Coat off, pencil behind one ear, the FBI agent bent over the pages like a teacher grading tests. Vic huffed a couple of times and stalked out of the room. Molly carried the rest of the file over to the windows.

She knew where to look for the information she needed. She just didn't want to do it. Her hands were clammy, for God's sake. Her heart was actually pounding. She felt as if she were playing a bad scene in a worse movie. She couldn't stop flashing on the sight of her friend's head in her hands so many years ago. Those eyes staring hard at her, just as those new brown eyes had. Even so, she opened the file to the back. And saw who had belonged to her skull. Or part of the skull. The upper half, drawn as if peeking over a fence, so the missing jaw wouldn't matter.

She should have known.

It was the eyes. Wide, soft, dark eyes. Beautiful eyes. Young eyes. Molly wanted to cry. The computer generation was flat, unspecific, merely adding millimeters to bone structure, flesh to form. But somehow, the magic had happened anyway, and Molly saw a young girl with wide, sweet brown eyes and delicate cheekbones.

Asian, Dr. DeVries had written in her note. *FORDDISC computation based on gross morphological and metric analysis suggests race to be Indochinese, possibly Vietnamese; well nourished, age approximately eighteen, of small stature, female.*

Molly wanted more. She wanted a name. An address. She wanted the rest of this girl, who only lived now in the pixels of the Video Image Capture and Reproduction programs.

"Molly?"

Startled by the sharp note in Kathy's voice, Molly looked up. Kathy was smiling, which meant she'd been trying to get Molly's attention.

"The notes came in the order I have them here?" the agent asked, displaying them on Molly's desktop.

Molly took a distracted look. *Just die. Fuck you. You'll scream. Bitch witch. Die Bitch. YOU DESERVE WORSE.* All scrawled, heavy-handed and urgent. Furious strokes for furious emotions. And then, printed, as if the bones themselves had sapped out the rage that demanded personal force, the last note. *If anybody should understand, it's you. You SAW me.*

"Yep."

"And the last note was the only one that came *with* a bone."

Molly's hands were beginning to sweat again. Maybe because she'd never seen the notes all together, like a truculent gang gathered at the edge of an alley.

"Yes."

"And then the bomb."

"Uh-huh."

Kathy took one final look at the notes and scooped them into a pile. "Who's the homicide team on this?" she asked, shoving the pile into the folder right over the young girl's face. "I'd like to compare some ideas."

Molly's attention was still on the file, on the tumble of threats she'd received. On the feelings of helplessness they'd generated.

She hated that feeling. She hated the fact that she'd been backed away, chased down, threatened. She hated feeling so responsible for that soft-eyed girl on the bottom of the file.

That soft-eyed girl.

Suddenly Molly swept the notes aside to look again at that single sheet with its summation. The summation, which suddenly meant more to her than those empty eyes.

Asian . . . possibly Vietnamese.

It meant something. It meant something particular in St. Louis. At least, Molly truly hoped it did.

"Molly."

Molly started again. She blinked up at the agent and found a half smile. "I wonder if the homicide guys saw what I did," she said.

Now it was Kathy's turn to blink in confusion. "Pardon?"

"It may be nothing," Molly said, getting to her feet, then pushing the notes the rest of the way off that young girl's face. "She may be from Seattle or New Orleans for all we know."

Now Kathy was taking a serious look at the vacant-eyed image. "Yes?"

"But we do have a couple of areas in St. Louis with a high concentration of Asian immigrants. Especially," she said, finger to the last supposition, "Vietnamese."

Kathy straightened like a shot and took a long look at the page. "And you said the homicide team is who?"

"Headed by a Sergeant Davidson. Who, unless they're doing doughnut duty, should be next door. Wanna go?"

Kathy's flashing smile said it all. "Oh, yeah. I think I would."

Molly was finally reduced to just nods. She was walking

into Kevin's office to return the folder when she heard a chair crash over behind her.

"We're famous!" Vic Fellows yelled, delighted. "*Hard Copy* on line one!"

"Aren't you supposed to be chained to the office poring over mug books or something?"

Molly rubbed at her head again and settled into the most uncomfortable visitor's chair in the universe. "Shut up, Frank."

"She always says that," Abigail announced from where she was perched on the side of the bed, her father's arm around her waist.

"That's 'cause she loves me, honey," her daddy assured her, his voice still breathy with discomfort.

The twins were standing on the other side of the bed, taut, careful of going anywhere near the tube that snaked out from beneath the covers to the bag that hung in front of them.

"But you said 'shut up' was a bad thing to say," Abigail insisted.

Frank tousled her hair with a hand that shook just a little. "I give Molly special license for putting up with me."

"We put up with you," his son said with an embryonic version of the famous Patterson grin.

Frank scowled. "Remind me to smack you when I can get out of bed in under twenty minutes."

He got a snort of derision. "You'll need a twenty-minute lead to catch me on a good day."

"Then I'll have Molly do it."

"No thanks," Molly demurred. "Molly doesn't smack."

"Even Patrick?" Abigail asked.

"Especially Patrick. He's bigger than I am."

"He's at work," the little girl informed her father in a breathy whisper as if it were a secret. "I kissed him good-bye when we dropped him off."

Frank gave her his best outraged father look. "That will be quite enough of that, young lady," he objected. "No kissing boys until you're at least twenty."

"Oh, Daddy," both girls protested in disgust.

"Make that thirty," he amended. "Now, I need you to go buy Tim a soda. He had soccer today and needs the nourishment."

The two girls scowled at Molly. "Can't *you* tell him we're big enough to stay?"

Molly shook her head. "Your dad's right. Tim looks positively peaked."

There was grumbling, but the kids finally ran out, which gave them no more than a few minutes' grace.

"So, what's on your mind, St. Molly?" Frank immediately asked.

Molly gave him a grimace. "I came here for a little escape, Frank."

She hadn't started out with that in mind, of course. She'd meant to come warn him off. To tell him to take his beautiful, normal children and get the hell out of the city for a while, away from her before it all got a lot worse. But then, somehow, she'd ended up picking up his children, because their grandmother didn't like driving in winter, so here she was.

Frank just grinned. "You came to ask if I could think of anybody—besides you, of course—with reason enough to toast my beautiful Lauren."

Leave it to Frank to name his car after Lauren Bacall. Because it was fast, sweet, and seductive, with a low growl, he said. And here Molly had thought calling her Toyota "good car" was enough.

"Well, can you?"

His smile was easier than hers would have been if she'd been laid up with a tube in her chest and a face that looked like overdone chicken. "Nope. Everybody I deal with fights back with briefs and countersuits. But then, if you'd talked to the arson guy, you'd know he already asked me that."

"It doesn't mean you told him the truth."

Damn him if he didn't think that was funny. Molly got her revenge when he laughed before remembering how compromised his chest muscles were. "This time, I'm afraid I did. You having any luck with Kathy?"

"Oh yes. The homicide guys fell all over her like a beer truck in the desert. We spent a lovely afternoon sharing evi-

dence, and then she and a couple of them went off for drinks.
I decided I'd had enough fun and borrowed her car to run the
Grace Hospital carpool instead. That way I could play with
your kids and visit you. Then, maybe I'll do more computer
time."

His eyes widened. "You? Computers?"

Molly scowled. "I'd say you're the last person to tell me to
blow off anything that can help us nail this guy, Frank."

Frank's smile was way too knowing. "I'd say I couldn't
stop you if I tied you to a chair and gagged you, St. Molly.
But computers. This *must* be serious."

"That's what I've been trying to tell everyone," she said
with a grin. Still creaking like an old screen door, she got to her
feet just as the kids tumbled back into the room. "I'll be back to
pick you up in a bit, kids. Till then, do me a favor. Tickle him."

"You didn't ask, Daddy," Abigail protested as Molly
lurched toward the door.

"You're right, sweetheart. But Molly won't say yes to me.
She'll only say yes to you."

Chagrined, Molly turned to find those wide brown eyes
lifted her way in the kind of mute appeal four-year-olds had
used all down the ages to get whatever they wanted.

"We talked about it," Abigail said, "and you and Patrick
don't have any kids for Christmas."

Molly's stomach plummeted. "I usually work on Christmas, pumpkin."

But the kids weren't buying. "We want you to come,"
Theresa said. "Since you keep saving Dad and all."

Since she kept almost getting him killed.

"I'd be honored to come," Molly said, knowing there was
no way out. "One condition, though. Until then, you keep
your daddy at home. Or better yet, take him on vacation
somewhere."

"Molly . . ." Frank all but growled.

Molly glared at him with all the meaning they couldn't
share with children. "For my Christmas present, take care of
your most cherished gifts."

"Dinner's . . . oh, uh . . ."

Molly heard the scuffle of shoes behind her and turned to find her housekeeping guy standing in the door, looking even more disheveled than usual and struggling with Frank's dinner tray as if it had a life of its own.

"Uh . . . hi," he greeted her with his half smile.

Molly smiled back and pulled the kids aside to make room. "How ya doing, John?"

He just tucked his chin in his chest, dropped the tray onto Frank's bedside table, and backed out the door again.

"He's scared of you," Frank accused with a grin.

"I think he's been drinking," Molly accused back. "Couldn't you smell it?"

Frank scowled. "All I can smell is disinfectant and the chocolate Abigail won't share with me."

Abigail immediately climbed up on the bed, and Molly took her own temporary leave for some computer work, so Frank could spend a little time alone with his kids. And once she made it out of the room, she pulled the floor team leader aside to report the hapless housekeeping tech. She did it quietly and calmly. The nurse, an average talent with a too big workload and too little trained help, promised action as if Molly were cutting the ground out from beneath her feet. Molly smiled in commiseration and then got the hell out before anybody could think to ask her to fill in.

Much later, when it was completely dark out and Molly couldn't put off going home anymore, she shut off the computer, picked up Frank's kids, and headed homeward.

Which was where she found Kathy. Not at Molly's house, of course. The agent had evidently checked in and decided that a course of tea and Jewish sympathy would be the best alternative for an extended waiting period. By the time Molly waded twice through the quicksand of microphones and shark smiles to track her down in Sam's flea market of a kitchen, the agent's cheeks were rosy, her posture a bit sloppy, and she was telling Sam a rather ribald joke.

"Oh, Sam," Molly mourned. "You've debauched an FBI agent. I think that's a federal offense."

Kathy, unbelievably, giggled. Sam waved Molly off like an offending fly. "*Feh!*" he snapped. "A little tea."

Molly didn't take her eyes off the usually very upright agent. "I'm not sure she can get to her feet, Sam."

"Of course she can," Kathy said with a tidy wink. "She'll have to. She needs to talk to you."

"Good news or bad?"

"Both."

Molly almost walked out of the room. "Good first."

Kathy nodded in approval. "I am considerably heartened by the police attitude. Evidently they have decided to ignore certain chiefs and political appointees. They have, I believe— and barring surprises—a workable plan."

"Uh-huh. Then the bad news is?"

Kathy stopped blinking. She watched Molly with disconcerting intensity. "In my opinion you definitely have a serial killer delivering you trophies."

"I knew that, Kathy."

Kathy shook her head. "He's not sending you the notes, though."

Suddenly the only noise in that kitchen was the loud ticking of the yellow plastic daisy clock on Sam's wall.

"What?"

Kathy looked apologetic. "You have more than one person trying to get your attention, Molly."

Kenny never watched the five o'clock news. Never. But after what he'd heard today at work, he knew he had to make an exception.

He should have been so happy. He had been happy. Had it only been two nights ago when Donnatheanchor had begun her story with "A grisly discovery in the Central West End . . ."?

He had seen Miss Burke's face, there on the television as she'd run past the microphones on her way into work. He'd heard all about how the police were concerned, how she was mystified, how sources had admitted that this wasn't the first discovery of its kind, how experts were trying to examine the bones to find clues. It should have been so perfect.

But this was wrong. This wasn't the way it was supposed to be. She was supposed to understand. Be surprised, maybe even sorry. He would even understand if she were worried. After all, Kenny knew that his hobby wasn't usual.

But to be afraid. Afraid for her life.

For somebody to try and hurt her.

For her to think it was him *who was doing it!*

This was supposed to be between Miss Burke and him. Nobody else. Nobody had the right to interfere.

My God, he thought, picking up his beer with shaking hands, she could have been killed by some stranger. She could have died alone, and all because he'd done something wrong. Given the wrong message, or done it at the wrong time or the wrong way so that somebody thought it was a game Kenny would share.

He had to think. He had to prepare. He had to make her understand, so she didn't suffer at someone else's hands.

So she didn't leave.

Kenny was all set to get up when the picture stopped on Miss Burke's face, and he saw it. There in her eyes, surprised by the bright lights and some smart-aleck camera guy.

Fear. The confused, kind of hollow look of somebody who thinks they're being hunted and doesn't know why.

Scared. The one person who knew him. The one person who'd tried to help.

And it was his fault. It had to be.

Kenny didn't remember putting his beer down. He didn't know if he turned off the TV or put his friend away. He just knew that suddenly he was in his dark place. Curled up tight on the floor, his eyes closed, his heartbeat louder than thunder, his cheeks and hair wet. He just knew he was where he belonged for what he must have done, and he knew he was scared.

She couldn't leave. Please, please, Miss Burke, don't leave. You're all I have. You're the only one. The only one.

If you leave me, there won't be any of me left.

And so he cried and he rocked and he knew that when his punishment was over, he would prepare another way.

I snuck in when she
wasn't looking, when she
was asleep
it would have been so
easy to just reach over
and
touch
                her
hurt her

but I didn't. I watched,
holding   my   breath,
holding myself
 tonight because
knowing was
enough

FOURTEEN

All Molly could think was that she'd had such a bad day she was automatically hearing worst-case scenarios. Even Sam was quiet, his eyes wide, his breathing quick and raspy. Molly so wanted to just slump into one of his bright blue kitchen chairs and make a grab for the vodka.

Two people. Two entirely separate threats, both of them deadly. And here she'd been thinking that they'd finally made some headway.

She should have known. She *had* known, down there where the little whispery voices lived. Where the notes and bones had never quite fit into a perfect match, no matter how hard they all tried.

"You look like you need to vent a little, *taibeleh*," Sam sympathized, patting her arm. "I have a whole houseful of awful ceramic doodads my Myra bought when we traveled. They're all very ugly. Go break them in my fireplace."

Molly knew all about the ceramics. A good half dozen resided in her family room. But that wasn't what she'd been considering.

"Sam," she said, dropping into that chair after all so she could take his hand. "I had a thought. How about if we call your daughter? She would so love to see you for Hanukkah."

Sam stiffened as if she'd questioned his honor. "And leave Myra alone?"

"Okay then, what about staying with *her* for a few days? Only till things settle down. I'm sure they'd be able to let you stay there with her. You know, away from all this noise and bother."

"Away from these *momzers* who attack you?" The old man made Molly frantic when he smiled and took hold of her hand. "Molly, my dear, sweet girl. I am eighty years old. I have blue ink on my forearm that won't ever wash off, and a wife who doesn't know me from a plant who I still visit every day. And you think one dybbuk crazy man is enough to send me running away from you?"

Molly never gave way to tears. They were in her eyes now. "I couldn't bear anything happening to you because of me."

"And what should become of Patrick if I disappear? You know he can't stay in that house of yours with those *pishers* out front."

"I'm sending him home as soon as I can get hold of his parents."

Sam shook his head. "He'll never forgive you."

"I don't care if he ever forgives me! I just want him to be alive to make the choice."

"Talk to lovely Kathy here first," he suggested. "Let this all sink in, so you can think right. It's too much of a shock." His eyes brightened and he gave her a little shake. "Some tea," he suggested and made a move to get to get to his feet.

Molly eased him right back down with a grim attempt at a smile. "And have *Hard Copy* get a shot of me falling flat on my face in your driveway? No, Sam. But thank you."

"*Feh!*" he snapped, waving her off. "As if you're afraid of those toothless jackals. I swept four off my porch before dinner!"

"Nonetheless, I don't think I want to incite them." Especially since they'd go into a feeding frenzy when they got hold of this latest bit of gossip. "I think it would be better if Kathy and I go someplace and talk."

Kathy frowned a little. "The press isn't going to ignore me going into your house much more."

Molly straightened as if she'd been shot. "Not my house. I've spent too damn much time there. Besides, I need to fortify myself."

Kathy scooped up her purse and scraped her chair back. "There are a couple of quiet bars in the neighborhood if you want."

Sam actually laughed and patted the agent's hand. "You don't understand Molly's idea of fortification, young lady."

Molly gave Sam a kiss on the cheek as Kathy got her coat. "Please, Sam," she begged. "For my Hanukkah gift. Think about it."

She was about to lead Kathy out the back door when Sam took hold of her arm. "Molly, a moment . . ."

Molly knew that tone of voice. She bent to her old friend, as if that could provide confidentiality. "What happened?"

He puffed a little in distress. "I hate to bother you now. It's such a small thing."

"Don't make me go out the door worrying, Sam."

His smile was brief and relieved. "Little Allen's money . . ."

"Again?"

"I had him get it for me. I was wrapping something, and well, the tape . . ."

"Allen looked in your jar and told you your money was missing?" Molly asked, not at all happy. When Sam nodded, she felt worse. "And you got him money from your stash, didn't you?"

He nodded again. "I'm sure I didn't misplace the money. I saw it just this morning. Where could it go?"

And Molly had thought her head hurt before. "Do me a favor. Move your stash. I'll call Straub's in the morning. I don't want Allen back here. There have been some questions, Sam . . ."

Sam clucked in distress. "Not Little Allen."

"Could it be Patrick?"

Sam's expression froze. "I'll call Straub's tomorrow."

Molly took hold of his hands. "I want you to be safe. I promise, if we're wrong, I'll apologize myself. Till then, you don't need to keep losing money, okay?"

She actually saw tears of distress and shame in his eyes. He'd been afraid his mind was slipping, stuttering away to decay like his beloved Myra's.

"*Zeyde,*" she said, squeezing those gnarled old fingers, "your mind is as sharp as glass. Please, believe me. Now, lock your doors and let nobody in but me or Patrick." He allowed Molly's fierce hug as long as he could return pats on Molly's back.

"I'm sorry, Sam."

"*Gottenyu, neshomeleh,*" he whispered. "Don't ever be sorry. You've made my old life a joy. Now, go."

And then she led Kathy out the back door.

It was actually painfully easy to elude the press. While they watched the street, Molly and Kathy crept back through Sam's darkened backyard to the Roberts' yard beyond. A quick hop over the fences, and they got to Molly's Toyota, which she'd left parked on the much busier Euclid. Waiting only long enough for a full-lights-and-siren fire truck to pass, Molly waved to her plainclothes baby-sitter stationed up the block and drove up to Taylor to turn left onto Kingshighway and head south.

Uncle Bill's Pancake House had sat on the west side of South Kingshighway as long as Molly could remember. One of the first twenty-four-hour pancake joints in St. Louis, it had always been a local favorite for late dates, after-prom parties, and late-shift breakfasts. Molly had attended her share for tradition, kitsch, and chocolate chip pancakes.

The customers hadn't changed much, and the display case in the front still boasted glittered ceramic crèche figures for sale. Inside, a decor that had begun as Black Forest half-timber now boasted a veritable symphony of wood panelings. Add to that the brown-pattern carpeting, the faux-wood

Formica-and-Naugahyde booths, and Uncle Bill's was the epitome of South St. Louis decor.

Kathy, obviously a veteran of local food joints the country over, gave a half smile as she slid into the booth. Molly inhaled the bouquet of coffee and syrup and sighed in relief. Whatever she needed to hear, it would sound better over pancakes. Apple pecan, she decided, checking the place-mat menu. Sausage and hash browns. Biscuits with grape jelly. Maybe a couple of eggs.

The hell with vodka. What she needed right now was a big, honkin' dose of cholesterol.

"Been a while, Molly," the waitress said with a smile. "The usual?"

Molly smiled right back at the polyester-bedecked woman. "Hi, Fran. Yeah, the usual. Apple pecan tonight."

She grimaced in disappointment when Kathy ordered nothing more than fruit and coffee.

"All right, Kathy," Molly said softly after the waitress had departed, pencil over ear. "What the hell were you talking about?"

Kathy concentrated on mixing cream into her coffee, as if it were a ritual for dispensing bad news. "Off the record," she said.

"If you write anything down, I'll eat it before I leave."

"I'd let you, but then I'd have to kill you."

Molly's laugh was a little sore. "Actually, it'd sure be a lot more restful than any of the other alternatives."

Kathy's smile was softer than Molly had ever seen on an investigator. "You're taking on too much, you know."

This time Molly couldn't manage more than a stunned blink.

Kathy wasn't at all insulted. "I may not be able to help everything," she said. "But I can give you a couple pieces of well-earned advice."

Molly snorted rather unkindly. "Oh, why not? After all, Frank's not available right now."

Kathy still smiled. But then, Kathy knew Frank. "Your

only real responsibility is your nephew. Everybody else can take care of themselves."

"But . . ."

"They're all perfectly aware of how dangerous it might be," Kathy said. "They're your friends, Molly. Whether you like it or not, you're going to need them to get through this."

For a minute Molly couldn't even answer. She wasn't sure if it was bile or high dudgeon that lodged in her throat. It was bad enough the agent was so presumptuous. Did she also have to understand so well? Molly refused to look at her.

"And the other piece?"

"Don't take her home with you."

Molly did look up then. "Pardon me?"

Kathy watched her carefully. "The young girl who belongs to that skull and those eyes. Becomes personal when you see a face, doesn't it? Well, don't let it. He's not killing them to get back at you. He's doing it because he's been wanting to do it since he was six years old. And he'll probably kill again before we can find him. You're going to have to live with that."

For a minute all Molly could manage was a tactless stare. Then she laughed, although it sounded a little sharp. "You sure you're not a shrink?" she asked.

Kathy still smiled. "I've just spent my share of time at this particular dance. Why do you think I'll only do it part-time?"

Molly watched the eddies she'd created in her own coffee. She thought of those soft, dark eyes that had ceased to exist because of a psychopath's obsession, and she sighed. "It's been so long since it affected me like this. I thought I'd . . ." She shrugged, knowing there were too few words for too many years. "I don't know, built that wall high enough, ya know? But then, I've never had a victim come personally addressed to me before, either."

"It's not your fault."

Molly's smile wasn't any happier. "I'm sure you told yourself that a lot over the years."

Kathy didn't need to say a word.

Molly wished she'd waited for vodka after all. "You want to tell me what you think?"

"I have no crime scene and no victim," Kathy warned.

"Which means I can't hold you accountable for your hunches. I know. Come on, Kathy. We all have a pretty damn good idea of what's going on. If we're too chicken to put it into words, this guy's gonna decimate South St. Louis before we get him."

Kathy just nodded. "Your friends the homicide officers agree with you. They said that the Vietnamese community tends to live in two areas, Olivette in the county and the South Grand area in the city. Do you know them?"

"South Grand much better. And if our girl's really Vietnamese, this perp couldn't have picked a more perfect victim. The Vietnamese community down there is pretty insular. The local gangs hold a heck of a lot more sway than the cops do, since the immigrants don't trust the police enough to talk to them."

"Which means the girl probably hasn't even been reported missing." Kathy kept looking into her coffee. "But if they're as localized as you say, it could give us a possible hunting perimeter for our man. Guys like him . . ."

Kathy's training stopped her short of a supposition. Molly waved aside the pause. "Guys like him have a very specific comfort zone. Which means he's playing his game straight from the Dahmer Manual."

Kathy looked up.

"Just because the chief of detectives wouldn't know a serial killer from a cereal bowl, doesn't mean the rest of us don't," Molly informed her, leaning forward. "There are certain similarities that can't be discounted. The bones I'm getting are decorated, just like Jeff decorated his shrine. They've been prepared with Jeff's favorite chemical cocktail. The only obvious unsolved serial killer we've had in the area was a guy dumping prostitutes along the highway in big boxes. Not at all our boy's signature. So he's been hunting in the area for a while without anybody knowing it. No skeletized remains in wilderness areas, no bodies in drainage ditches. Just, suddenly, body parts. Which means he's probably taking care of all his business close to home and being real careful about disposing evidence. And, if our Vietnamese girl is any indicator, he's picking marginal, easily controlled victims whose disappearance wouldn't cause an immediate outcry. Just like Jeff. So, what would this guy *not* do if he's been studying at the Dahmer Academy of Toxicology and Taxidermy?"

"He wouldn't travel." Now Kathy was leaning forward as well, her eyes sharp. "He's got a well-defined comfort zone, and he's acting within it. He's hiding his victims, not dropping them. He's cherishing them, which means he's keeping at least some of them close. And his trophies are extremely personal. It sure looks to me as if he's adapted to his needs pretty damn well."

"And, if he has picked South Grand," Molly added, just as intensely, "he's found the perfect victim pool. South Grand is a marginal neighborhood. It's ethnically diverse, which means lots of people who aren't on comfortable terms with English, much less the local law enforcement community. It's a rehab area sprinkled in among a high-crime zone. The business strip, which has lots of restaurants, coffee shops, and retro shops, also happens to be a magnet for some of the more disenfranchised youth who come seeking entertainment, outrageous attire, and seditious discourse."

"Would you be willing to give me a tour?"

"After I get some food in me. Sure."

Which was, thankfully, just about the time Molly's breakfast showed up. She knew she should have been too sick to eat. Unfortunately, Molly had never been too sick to eat. She slammed into those pancakes as if they were the last grain products in North America. Kathy took one wide-eyed look at the food piled on Molly's plate and dipped into her fruit like a debutante.

"If we're very lucky," Kathy said as she speared a melon chunk, "this may just give us our first insight into our man's pattern. If we're even more lucky, he should be very predictable, which means that every scrap of information we learned from the Dahmers of this world will come in handy."

"Why did he change now?" Molly asked, scooping up eggs to follow her pancakes.

"Why send you the bones?"

Molly nodded.

Kathy leaned back. "Because of a greater need than he's had. Or a change in availability of his fantasy. The truth? I think he just realized you were around and couldn't wait to contact you."

All of a sudden, Molly was way behind again. "He *just* . . . ? What do you mean, he just realized it? Isn't this somebody I know?"

Kathy shrugged. "Maybe. But I think more important, he's somebody who knew you before. Remember the wording of his letter? 'You saw me.' The word *saw* capitalized. Not a sophisticated note, but heartfelt. You say you've done the research on these guys, Molly. What does that kind of note sound like to you?"

It sounded like he wanted to send her pretty bones. What the hell did Kathy think it sounded like?

"Come on," Kathy urged, voice taut, suddenly as much like a soccer mom as a sniper. "You've read the histories. You've probably heard the interviews. What's a frequent theme in the growth and development of the serial killer?"

Funny, Molly was sweating. "You're not talking about that stupid, 'she's the only teacher who tried to help me' stuff."

"It's quite a recurring theme, Molly. Usually in their childhood. About the time the obsession is taking over and the killer begins to disappear beneath his facade. One person stands out as 'seeing' them. 'Knowing' them. One person recognizes whatever humanity is left and tries to help. And if this guy is a Dahmer type, then he spent his life being abandoned, ignored, and, ultimately, invisible. He just disappeared from human radar until the only way left for him to have a social circle was to create it with hydrochloric acid and Soilex. But somewhere as he began to disappear, maybe somewhere about the age of ten or so, I think you were there, and you were the only one who tried to pull him back."

Molly's reaction was instinctive. "Don't be—"

Kathy didn't have to say a word.

The Game. Molly had played The Game for so long. Praying so hard that she could make a difference to those silent, shattered children. Inch by inch giving in to the inevitable decline of hope until she just watched. Just counted. Just wished she knew what to do when there was nothing to do.

She wondered suddenly if she was coming down with something. She felt light-headed and even more sweaty. She couldn't take a deep breath. She felt as if she were caught back in one of those damn small dark corners and couldn't get out.

"He's sending eyes," she whispered, wondering why she didn't vomit.

Kathy nodded. "He's sending eyes."

Molly didn't know what else to say. She didn't know how to get those wide, empty brown eyes out of her head.

"Serial killers often send their trophies to people they're attached to, or people they want to impress," Kathy said. "I haven't yet seen them send any to an early influence. Especially with a note. My God, Molly, do you know what this could mean?"

No question what it meant to Kathy. Her eyes suddenly glittered, and she couldn't seem to keep her hands quite still. The hunter had finally banished the quiet urban mom.

Well, that made Molly feel a hundred percent better. "It means I've become part of the fantasy," she snapped.

But Kathy shook her head. "You've always been part of the fantasy. This has been part of the plan since he first met you years ago. Maybe to show you. Maybe to thank you. Who knows? The point is, we could find out vitally important information from this. The problem is that I don't know what pro-active behavior would guarantee the best results."

"You mean, do we let the press know or not? Do we correct his spelling and send the note back? Do we just ignore him altogether?"

Kathy's smile was deprecating. "Something like that, yeah. But that's my problem. Yours is to try and figure out who this is."

"But I don't have any children," Molly objected. "I never had any relations with children. Hell, I never even had any over for the night. How the hell could I have affected anybody like that?"

"What about the kids from the hospital?"

Molly was already shaking her head. "I've always worked in an ED," she said, "and we live there by the three-hour rule. You have three hours to be better, dead, or out my door. Not much time to build up a rapport."

"What if he showed up more than once?"

Kathy was stealing Molly's breath again. "Well, in that case, we don't have a chance in hell of finding out who this guy is. I might have been able to identify somebody I know now. I couldn't tell you the name of one kid I took care of in the last thirty years."

"Even if you went through the records?"

Molly laughed. "You know how many patients I averaged in a shift? I think we'd better concentrate on the here and now."

"And if he hasn't shown his face lately? What then?"

"Hope he comes back to visit when the police are there."

As if in punctuation, Molly returned her attention to her sadly decimated dinner, wiping up leftover egg as if it alone would hold off the problems at hand.

Kathy contemplated her own empty bowl and the smear of yolk left on Molly's plate. "Before we drive down to South Grand, you might want to talk about your other problem."

Molly found herself looking at her empty plate, as if she'd forgotten something on it. What she'd almost managed to forget was the second part of this evening's joke. The fact that she'd been right all along. Trophies and threats usually didn't show up from the same address.

Giving in to the inevitable, she set down her knife and fork. "My other letter writer, you mean?"

Kathy didn't move. "Actually, I'd be more inclined to call

him or her letter writer number one. I'd also have to say that in that case, you're definitely the target."

Molly just sat there. "Delightful."

Kathy's smile was a bit effacing. "I'm surprised one of the police didn't catch it sooner. If you look at all the correspondence together, it's obvious it doesn't fit. The only note that doesn't seem a direct threat is the one that came with the skull. It was also the only one that is meticulously printed, which probably means the sender understands forensics enough to try and camouflage his handwriting. Obviously a different correspondent, both in text and execution."

"Been there, Kathy. Go on."

Kathy nodded. "Your first correspondent hasn't taken the time to consider being caught. I'm afraid you've really fired somebody up, and they were mad before those bones started showing up."

Molly's head was beginning to hurt. Much more of this and she'd enjoy a revisit from the pancakes she'd just enjoyed. "And the bomb?"

Kathy looked pensive. "The most interesting piece. Definitely not our killer. Once you have a serial killer at this level of proficiency, he's completely focused on his art. The idea that he'd take a jig over into bomb making is pretty far-fetched."

"An angry note writer, on the other hand, might not be so averse to the idea."

Kathy shrugged. "The tone of the notes didn't escalate, but the later the note, the more rips there are in the paper."

For a second Molly just closed her eyes. She thought about running away again. She thought about how much fun she had in store for her now. "Which means we're back at square one. Except we have two guys to look for."

"Maybe a guy and a girl," Kathy said. "Women are much more prone to those distanced forms of murder than men, you know."

Molly opened her eyes. "Bomb making?"

She shrugged. "I'd have to check with ATF on that, but I do know that women account for a higher percentage of arson than other crimes."

How liberating for our gender, Molly thought sourly. "How do you rig a bomb like that anyway?" she asked.

"You can learn it on the Internet, Molly. Where've you been?"

"In a perfect, Luddite world where computers haven't been invented yet."

Kathy smiled and patted her mouth with a paper napkin. "You have any ideas who's mad at you?"

"I gave that list to the police a long time ago. It hasn't changed any."

"What about somebody who's mad at both you and Frank? That was his car that blew up."

Molly had been thinking about that. "With the assurance that he wouldn't be in it when it went."

Kathy crooked an eyebrow.

Molly's smile was dry. "The point of a remote control car starter is that you aren't in the car when it starts. And the arson guy said the bomb was directed straight up. 'Nuts and knees,' he called it, which I'd think would limit damage to people standing alongside. Or, in fact, on the porch, which was where Frank usually is when he uses it."

"So you think the bomb was rigged to go off to *prevent* injury?"

"Yeah," Molly said, suddenly sure. "I do."

"Which means it's just another, more impressive threat."

Molly nodded. "Done with enough skill that the cops watching my house didn't realize there had been somebody messing around under Frank's car."

Kathy actually looked uncomfortable. "Well, that might not be so surprising, since the cops were sitting out behind your house on Euclid."

Molly almost let her temper go, until she realized the logic to it. Only on TV did cops have the manpower to do a thorough stakeout. So, if the police only had the manpower for one team, where would they put it? In close enough view of the area the killer had visited three times before, of course. The back of her house. Where the cops couldn't see Frank's car.

"They've, uh, increased the surveillance," Kathy said with a small smile, which made Molly laugh.

"They don't have to. They have at least a dozen camera trucks doing it for them."

"Which you're going to have to deal with," Kathy said quietly.

Molly sighed. "I've done it before. Not on quite a national scale, of course . . ."

And not with an unpredictable teenager in the house. She wondered, in fact, how long it was going to be before Patrick slipped the bonds of good sense and trotted out to the *Inside Edition* van for a chat.

"If you're right," Kathy said, absently stirring her own coffee, "you have to consider the fact that your bomber has been watching you. At least enough to know Frank's habits."

Molly nodded, amazed she could feel worse. "We've had a peeper in the neighborhood."

"Might answer."

"In the meantime," Molly said with sudden decision, "you want to see South Grand."

Better than thinking of somebody waiting out in the shadows.

Molly had just waved for the bill when she saw a suspiciously familiar face in the doorway.

Finally, something to smile about. "You looking for me, little boy?" she demanded.

Rhett immediately brightened and bounced over, a friend in tow. Molly was going to say something scathing, when she caught sight of all of him. She couldn't quite manage to speak or close her mouth.

"Happy holidays, Special Agent Kinstle," he greeted Kathy. "And you, of course, Molly."

Molly's reaction was a gurgle of laughter. Because, amazingly enough, it was the first time Molly had seen Rhett out of homicide uniform. And it had to be in a six-foot-tall green-and-red elf's costume, with pointy shoes, bells hanging off his collar, and mistletoe tied to the top of his head with a red pipe cleaner. Molly damn near choked. Especially since his companion, a five-foot-three-inch blond girl about his age and half his size, was dressed as Santa.

"Christmas party?" Kathy asked with an admirably straight face.

Rhett scowled heartily. "Almost. I called Sam, who said I'd find you either here or Cunetto's. I tried here first."

Molly was still struggling with her control. "Where do you have your gun?" she demanded, her voice high and silly.

Rhett scowled, at which point the blonde dug into her big, Santa belly and pulled out not only one gun, but two. "Tough to get a concealed holster in those tights," she said with a sly grin.

"Oh, good," Molly giggled. "Then he *is* just glad to see me."

She thought Rhett would go down for the count. Waving him over, she made him bend way down so she could grab him by the ears and soundly kiss him on the mouth. "Thanks," she said sincerely. "You don't know how badly I needed this tonight."

Rhett's face outshone the bright red collar with the bells on it. "In that case," he managed. "I might as well give you the rest of the news."

Molly let him go. "I've had my quota of bad news today," she said. "I'm only accepting good news. If you have good news, pull up a chair. If not, take a hike. But leave Santa. I could use two guns right about now."

Thankfully, both Rhett and his friend sat down.

"We could delay this until we get into the car," Molly suggested. "I'm about to show Kathy the South Grand area."

At that, the blonde perked up noticeably. "Really? Good. That's just what I was thinking."

Molly didn't want to be rude enough to ask why, so she turned to her favorite homicide officer. "You were about to introduce us to your jolly friend here, Rhett."

Rhett scowled. "I was getting to that. Lucia and I were just at the Third District Christmas party. We figured we might as well, since we wouldn't have anything else to do till tomorrow, what with them trying to figure out the search warrant for those old hospital records. . . ."

Molly glared. "Hospital records?"

"You left before we got to that part," Kathy said without so much as a blink.

"Which ones?" Molly retorted. "I worked in about ten, you know. All over the country."

And damn if Kathy wasn't in the least upset. "We thought we'd start with St. Roch's. If we're right about our boy's age, he was born between '66 and about '72. You were back in St. Louis at St. Roch's between '76 and '81. As good a place as any, don't you think?"

Molly couldn't even manage an answer. God bless Rhett, who continued his thought as if nobody had interrupted. ". . . and since Lucia's our missing persons contact, we thought we'd share notes."

Molly scowled. "I assume this is the introduction I was asking for before."

The blonde held out her hand. "Lucia Caletti."

Molly started smiling again. "Baitshop?"

The girl's responding grin was easy and bright. "The same. I asked Rhett if I could come along. I've been dying to talk to you."

Molly shared a hearty handshake. "Feeling's mutual."

She liked the girl. Half her age, still hungry, still quick and alert. A jock. The kind of girl who would have been on all the teams, with a natural sense of balance and self-confidence that translated into aggressive agility, and a brain that obviously clicked along even faster than her reflexes. Not a natural blonde. But a cute one, with big brown eyes and a mobile, bow-shaped mouth. And, of course, the restless attention of a good cop.

"Baitshop?" Agent Kinstle echoed a bit more uncertainly.

Caletti grinned like a pirate. "I was undercover at Bill and Barney's Bass and Bud Bargain Basement down on South Jefferson. Ran a meth lab in the back."

"She could bait a hook faster than anybody else in narcotics," Rhett gloated for her. "She also took the place down with nothing more than a bullhorn, a fishing creel, and a popup display of Ed McMahon."

"But that's a story for another time," Baitshop demurred.

"I bet you'd like to come along and help tell Kathy all about South Grand."

Baitshop damn near wiggled on her seat. "Love to. There are a couple of theories I want to share."

"Like why nobody paid attention to girls going missing in town?"

"About who the girls are."

Molly nodded, ready to get up.

"Not yet," Rhett protested. "Not till you hear my news."

The three women looked at him like teachers waiting for a fourth-grade book report.

Rhett all but preened. "It's just this, Molly. We got a good hit on somebody on your list."

Molly sat abruptly back down. "What do you mean, a hit?"

"Escalating pattern of offenses from weenie wagging to serious peeping to B&Es, to molestation, to suspicion of arson. Juvenile file. Possible psychiatric history."

Molly sighed. "Little Allen."

Rhett's grin was huge. "Nope. Lewis Travers." He waited, but there was no answering light. "The morgue attendant down at the ME's office."

I have her head in my
hands because it flops.
her tits, soft tits,
in my teeth
and her eyes?
maggots
cut 'em out

FIFTEEN

Molly put her head straight down on the table, barely missing a plate puddled in syrup. "I can't take much more of this," she moaned.

Rhett patted her on the shoulder. Kathy moved Molly's plate so she wouldn't wear the rest of her breakfast home.

"Evidently when they checked Lewis's desk at work tonight, there were several notes about you in there," Rhett said.

"Death threats?" Kathy asked.

Rhett sounded uncomfortable. "Not exactly."

Molly groaned again, refusing to lift her head. Lewis, Patrick's new best friend, who had shown him bodies. Who had been so polite and called Molly "Miss Burke" with that damn lisp and blushed. Lewis, who had access just about anywhere, and certainly the exposure to not only surgical instruments but practices.

Lewis, who thought the bones were so nicely decorated.

"What kind of notes?" Kathy asked.

Rhett actually blushed. "Um. Complimentary ones, okay?"

Molly groaned all over again.

"There's only one problem," Rhett said.

Molly shot to her feet so fast she almost dented the top of her head on Rhett's chin. "No," she snapped. "No problems.

Tell me later. Right now we're going to take Kathy on a tour of the city."

"Whose car?" Rhett asked.

"Yours," Molly said, shrugging into her coat. "I refuse to be seen chauffeuring around an oversize elf and an undersized Santa."

"Better they drive you," Kathy said with a complacent nod. "It's easier to hide if I don't have to keep my hands on the steering wheel."

Rhett was, of course, driving a Chevy Caprice, with plenty of seat belts, legroom, and a police radio. Molly slid in behind Santa and buckled up.

"By the way," Rhett announced as he backed out of his parking spot, "just so you know. There's a press conference being held tonight down at city hall."

"Telling everybody they have a suspect in mind?" Molly asked, well familiar with the politics of public pressure.

"Trying to explain to all the parents of missing teenage girls who've been beating down the mayor's door, why they didn't hear the news sooner that a possible serial killer might be dropping an unidentified girl's bones on your doorstep."

Molly's grin was almost feral. So the "let's bury it" attitude had come back to bite the colonel in the ass. "Press found out, huh?"

"Yeah. All hell's breaking loose. That minister who was egging on Mrs. Wilson is running this photo op, too. Police ignoring the concerns of disenfranchised citizens, that kind of thing."

"Sometimes teenage girls *do* run away," Lucia said pensively.

"Not, evidently, all of them. Not this time anyway."

"Why aren't you down at the press conference, Lucia?" Kathy asked. "You're the missing persons person. Aren't you?"

Lucia's expression was not pleasant. "I am the unplanned second missing persons person. The real person got the nod to press his detective suit."

"So missing persons' not your usual gig?"

"No. There was a small misunderstanding with my last lieutenant."

Since the South Grand area was actually east-northeast of Uncle Bill's, Rhett turned north on Kingshighway. Molly absently watched car dealerships and light industry give way to a section of tree-lined residentials just south of the highway.

St. Louis city proper was a patchwork of prosperity and poverty, where lush parks and solid, white-collar neighborhoods lay within blocks of crack houses, and rehabbed Victorian communities sat cheek-by-jowl with boarded-up flats. Molly's neighborhood was one such, her own house in a sometimes precarious island of security in a still-unstable neighborhood. South Grand was another.

To get there, Rhett turned east on Magnolia, which, in the four miles from Kingshighway to Grand, ran between two of the city's most beautiful green spaces, Tower Grove Park and the Missouri Botanical Gardens. Both were ringed in substantial, landscaped residential streets that screamed security and solidity. The gardens were closed this time of night, but Tower Grove was swathed in holiday lights.

Molly hadn't really noticed before how the patina of security wore thin the closer they got to Grand. Fewer trees maybe, the houses a little more careworn and more often divided into flats. From real stability to simulated stability. A toehold on normalcy only blocks from some of the more notorious violence of the city.

"Molly?" Rhett said, pulling her attention back.

"Sorry. What?"

He swung the car south onto Grand and slowed for the traffic waiting to see the light display in the park. "Don't be surprised if you get another whole spate of questions from the press."

"How delightful," Molly retorted drily. "I do so love bantering with them. And when they ask about the bomb, what do I tell them?"

"That Detective Davidson is the person to talk to."

Molly stiffened in outrage. "Davidson? That jerk?"

It was Baitshop who turned around. "Ah, you fell victim to his charm, too, huh? If it makes you feel better, he is relentless."

Molly snorted. "He has his nails manicured. Jack Webb would have had a stroke. Was he at the Christmas party?"

"Sure. Everybody who wasn't tucked up behind the mayor was."

"What'd he come as?"

"The Grinch."

There was a profound silence in the backseat. "Repeat that."

Baitshop was laughing. "Actually Rhett would have looked better, but Fuzzy said he had a reputation to uphold."

Molly leaned forward, sure she was hearing wrong now. "Fuzzy?"

Lucia was grinning. "As in, 'Warm and'?"

"Uh-huh."

Rhett finally wove past the traffic and headed south toward the next expanse of Christmas lights that had been strung along the business fronts south of the park.

"South Grand really starts about here," Rhett was saying, motioning to the area just beyond the residential streets around the park. Only a few miles from downtown itself, South Grand had once been a thriving community. Like many of St. Louis's neighborhoods, it had seen boom and decline and rebirth since its first houses had been built in Victorian times. Now the area supported a rich mixture of residents, from rehabbers to immigrants to blue-collar families to a variety of less-stable inhabitants.

The business district itself, which consisted of the section of Grand Boulevard that stretched from Tower Grove Park to Pius X Catholic Church, was comprised of a potpourri of shops, restaurants, and family businesses. The keystone of a revitalization move in the area, the business district looked shiny and busy and marginally prosperous, selling everything from books to bongs to any variation of ethnic food and cutting-edge retro.

The side streets to the west retained the tree-lined sense of stability, with either single- or two-family dwellings. To the east, though, as Grand moved south, the side streets quickly degenerated from large brick Victorians to row after row of low-rent multifamily dwellings, identical and uninspiring, as if Grand itself were the icing disguising an uninspired cake.

"It's kind of quiet here now," Baitshop was saying. "But in the summer, the sidewalks are usually pretty active. Lots of diversity. Vietnamese grandmas outside Jay's International Foods selling trinkets from blankets to yuppies, all the way to slackers cluttering up the coffee shops and retro shops."

"Any prostitution?" Kathy asked, her head swiveling to take in the few people strolling through frigid streets, the traffic slowing and circling, the restaurants full and the banks empty.

"Yeah, sometimes, although it's better controlled than before," Baitshop said. "It had been one of the three big areas down here. This, Cherokee, and Jefferson. They kind of move in a constant triangle when the cops and the Asian gangs toss them out. But around this area the prostitutes have been mostly gays. Tower Grove Park was kind of a traditional gay meeting place."

"Well, that's one chapter I don't think our friend copied from Jeff's handbook," Kathy said. "Our boy does seem to like girls."

Even in the winter, Molly could see some of the more marginal kids hunched over scratchy tables at the coffeehouses. Spiked hair, pierced lips, hungry eyes, and anxious hands. There were really two places in the St. Louis area kids hung out in concentrations. University City Loop, where protected kids celebrated safe rebellion, and South Grand, where kids really knew what living on the edge meant. Molly explained as much to Kathy, who nodded absently and watched the traffic.

"So it wouldn't be that much of a surprise if a girl did, possibly, run away from an area like this."

Baitshop shook her head. "Not at all. I checked my files when I heard about the Vietnamese victim, and I have at least twenty open files on kids who were either last seen down here or had lived around here. Twelve of them girls."

"Were any of them a surprise?"

Baitshop shook her head. "Every one of them has a history of juvy stuff and delinquency. I'm not at all surprised the local dicks put them off as runaways."

Kathy nodded reflectively. "Then I think you're right, Molly. Immigrants and chronic runaways, maybe a hooker or two. It's the perfect victim pool. Has anyone talked to the parents yet?"

"I think they're still at the press conference."

"How 'bout the local detectives?" Molly asked. "They only give the missing persons files to you when it's too cold to care, don't they?"

"Yeah. I'm in frequent contact with the Third District guys, and I think they do a good job. They also have lots of support in the area: community commitment, community policing, that kind of thing. The civilians are trying hard to hold on to the turnaround in the neighborhood. But there really is only so much you can do if you have kids in chronic trouble."

"And a killer who's perfected the art of invisibility."

They passed Pius X with its gray granite front and Right to Life sign, and the street deteriorated from active to struggling economy in a few blocks. The housing looked tattered and the storefronts half empty, with men loitering in untidy clumps in doorways to share their smokes and forties.

Rhett turned off Grand proper and wove in and out of the side streets, where much of the Third District violence was spawned, until they turned back onto Grand by the blue awning of Grand Books. Molly noticed as they passed that the front window was decorated to advertise a book signing by a local mystery writer. A bloody mannequin in green scrubs was sprawled across sheets. In the mood she was in, Molly didn't quite appreciate the image.

"We're going to need to talk to somebody who's inside the Vietnamese community if we're going to get any info on the girl," Rhett said, pulling her attention away.

"Nobody reported any missing Vietnamese teens?" Kathy asked.

Baitshop shook her head. "Nary a one. Not that I expected any. There is a Lutheran minister hereabouts who works with the community, though. He's a Nam vet. We could talk to him."

"What about the Olivette area?" Molly asked. "Anybody from county canvassing that?"

"Not one missing person from the area," Baitshop said. "South Grand is our baby. We just need to do some questioning."

"You know Vietnamese, don't you, Mol?" Rhett asked. "I mean . . ."

"If it comes down to that," she said, "I can ask about their health and their animals."

"How would you like to talk to the other parents, too?" Baitshop asked.

"That's why they pay you the big bucks, honey," Molly said.

"They don't pay me enough for any of this shit," the young woman suddenly snapped. Just as quickly, she sighed and yanked off the scruffy little beard she'd been wearing hooked over her ears.

"You aren't enjoying your stint in missing persons?" Molly asked.

The girl's scowl was impressive for somebody her size. "If I can help break this, maybe they'll finally see my goddamn transfer requests and get me back on the streets."

"You prefer the streets?"

Rhett laughed. "Baitshop was born for the streets. I'd rather have her than an entire canine team back me up in a crunch. The nine mil she pulled out of her belly is mine. The three-fifty-seven is hers."

When the little blonde smiled, it looked like the entire front seat lit up. Rhett, concentrating on avoiding that Tower Grove traffic, missed it.

"Of course," Rhett amended, "she's also one of the best missing persons dicks I've seen."

"Fuck you" was her only answer.

He grinned. "You want to hear the bad news yet, Molly?"

And here Molly thought he'd forgotten it. "Sure. I've just

about had all the fun I'm gonna have tonight. Tell me the bad news."

"Well, we found out about Lewis."

"Uh-huh."

"We just don't know where he is."

The city hall press conference wasn't the worst part of the news that night. The worst part was the film somebody had shot of Molly giving Kathy a leg over Sam's backyard fence to escape the press. The inference was made, of course, that she had something to hide. The result was that the effort to talk to her redoubled, and her house was summarily surrounded. Not only that, but as she sat in her back room trying to ignore the assault outside, her phone rang.

"We have touchdown!" came the voice of one of the death investigators on her answering machine. Molly sank into her couch like a drowning victim. "The tabloids have hit town."

". . . in an effort to find out why Ms. Burke should be receiving such gruesome gifts," Donna Kirkland continued with barely concealed delight on the TV, "the police have been looking into her background. Sources close to the investigation admit that Ms. Burke has a history of problems stemming back as far as her service as a nurse in Vietnam."

Molly took one look at the avid delight in the newsanchor's eyes and knew there was no way of ever getting her boxes closed again and tucked back into the attic. Not only would all her friends know her past, but the entire country, courtesy of Donna and her source, whom Molly would some day cheerfully throttle.

Added to that, it was just about time for Molly to make another run out into the gauntlet to get Patrick from work. God, what she'd give for one good night's sleep and a name nobody knew.

"Next up," Donna was saying with that bright plastic smile of hers, "the final end to a congressional standoff on the budget."

The phone rang, just as it had been doing all evening. Molly let the answering machine handle it—until she heard her brother Martin's voice yelling at her from seven thousand miles away.

"Where have you been?" Molly demanded without preamble when she grabbed the phone.

"In China," he reminded her acerbicly. "I think I told you that. What the hell's going on there, Molly? We saw on CNN tonight some mention of a . . . serial killer or something?"

Great. Not only the country. The world. No wonder Molly hated technology. "That's why I've been trying to get in touch with you, Martin. It's just not safe for Patrick to be here anymore. I'm being stormed by the press, I'm stuck in a pretty bizarre investigation, and I've had death threats."

"You'd better not have let anything happen to that house, Molly," her brother warned.

Molly was damn near struck dumb. Sliding onto the family room couch, she laid her head back and closed her eyes. She couldn't face all that Picasso rage and anguish while she dealt with her brother.

"Thanks for the filial concern, Martin," she snapped. "Your next question, of course, was going to be, 'My God, Molly, is Patrick safe?' "

That got her a couple seconds of static. "Well, of course it was. But you would have said something right away . . ."

"Nice try. I've been calling you because I have to send him home, Martin. I know I promised to keep him, but he just shouldn't be in the middle of this. He's not safe here. Maybe when things settle down—"

"Uh, I'm afraid that's not possible."

Molly stopped. Opened her eyes. Communed with Picasso's furious woman. "Why?"

"Well, with Patrick out of town, and the mission here dragging on, well, we just figured . . ."

And Molly thought her brother couldn't have upset her more. "My God," she breathed. "You had Sean come to China."

"I'm really sorry, Molly," he apologized at light speed. "If we'd known, but, well, you know, with the boys gone, we gave Juanita time off. The house is closed till New Year's."

Molly closed her eyes again, mostly to help suppress the rage. She counted. She struggled past the wash of red that stained the edges of her vision. She prayed. She came close to sobbing with the struggle against the obscenities that choked her.

She'd been battling with a serial killer. She'd been matching wits with a bomber. She'd been balancing her job, her nephew, and her sanity on a pinhead. And it was her brother who was going to shove her over the edge.

"I know you'll understand, Molly," he was saying. "You know how easily stressed Mary Ellen can be, and well, this last year with Patrick, she's been . . . well, it's just better this way. At least until we can get him to military school."

Molly hit critical mass.

"You self-serving, sanctimonious, sack of shit," she breathed. "You piece of toxic waste crapped into a diplomatic pouch! You—"

She got no further, because her brother simply hung up on her. Like that was going to settle things. "You worthless excuse for a human being," she whispered, finally washing her hands of him. Of all of them. Of all of them except for Patrick, to whom she'd have to explain this.

"I see the parents have run true to form," he said in that atonal voice of his.

Molly jumped off the couch as if she'd been hit by a live wire. Lounging in the doorway, Patrick didn't so much as smile.

"Patrick! I was just coming to get you from work."

She got a shrug. "No need. I was on the track team. High hurdles are my specialties." He must have seen Molly's unconscious reaction, because his expression grew cold. "Sam asked me not to talk to them. So far, that's been a more compelling motive than embarrassing the parents. I do, though, see the undeniable attraction of communicating with the old man via CNN." Lifting himself away from the wall, he shook his head. "So the brilliant Sean is in China, is he? Good. Sean loathes Chinese food."

Molly took a step forward. "Patrick—"

It was all there in her voice, all that fury and betrayal and anxiety that swirled like acid.

Patrick was having none of it. "It's actually not a problem," he said indifferently, hands shoved in khaki pockets. "I'd much rather have the house to myself for a few weeks. Juanita's cooking sucks, and Sean is forever waving his achievements in my face."

"You can't go back there."

"I can't stay here," he retorted, neatly throwing her challenge back at her. He looked so much older than he should. Looked less betrayed than Molly felt. Maybe he'd played this scene more times than Molly had, which said something else about her esteemed brother and his twitchy wife.

"What I was hoping," Molly said, sucking in a calming breath, "was that you'd stay with Sam. I can't be around all the time to protect him from those assholes out on the lawn, not to mention whatever the hell this bomb business is, and he won't go anywhere to be safe. Would you?" she asked. "For Sam?"

Patrick's expression never changed. His shoulders never eased as he made a show of thinking about it. "For Sam? Yeah. For him I guess I would."

Molly nodded. She felt suddenly so distant from him, so useless, as if in the last few days while she'd been tap dancing to keep ahead of disaster, she'd missed some vital chance to keep him from slipping away from her. So they stood before each other, cold and silent, and only one of them caring.

"Would you like something to eat?" she asked.

His smile was even older. "Always the answer, huh?"

She shrugged. "Better than drugs. Cheaper, anyway." Molly had taken a couple of steps toward him when she recognized a very familiar scent. "Patrick, your restaurant doesn't serve mesquite grill. What is that?"

He stepped back a bit, as if afraid she'd reach out to him. "Nothing. We had a small fire tonight in the restaurant . . ."

"Oh, my God," Molly breathed, distressed all over again. "That's where the fire truck was going. Are you okay? Was anybody hurt?"

She did reach out. He flinched away as if she were contaminated. "No. It was more smoke and excitement than anything. I won't be going into work for a few days, though."

Pulling her head back, Molly turned for the kitchen. "Well, no kidding . . ."

Fire. Arson. Criminal records.

Molly faltered to a sick halt, Rhett's voice all but sounding in her ear. It looked as if she was going to have to talk to Patrick about Lewis sooner than she'd thought.

"Patrick," she said, turning carefully. "You struck up a friendship with Lewis down at the morgue."

Patrick went pretty quiet. "Who objects? You or the great protector of the rice tariffs?"

Close up she could see that his eyebrows had been singed a little. His face was flushed and his hands were sooty. Molly didn't want to think how close it could have been. She didn't even want to think of how hard she was trying to protect him from the unimaginable, when it could well be the capricious that hurt him.

"No," she disagreed, "it's not that I object. I mean . . . well, you were being nice and all. It's just that . . . well, you haven't talked to him lately, have you?"

"No. Why? He in trouble?"

Well, there was a question for the sages. "I don't know. I just know that the police need to talk to him, and they can't find him. It seems he put a fake address on his employment form."

And damn if Patrick didn't smile. "That's because he was homeless when he got the job. He told me. He didn't want people to know he was living in a box."

Molly all but held her breath. "Do you know where he lives now?"

For a minute she really wasn't sure whether he'd help. He seemed suddenly so closed off, his beautiful hazel eyes cold and wary. Molly wanted to appeal to his altruistic side, but after what he'd heard this evening, she wasn't sure he'd respond to it. There was only so much kicking a kid could take without wanting to kick back, just to know he could.

"I think he lives down in a flat on Michigan somewhere."

Michigan. No more than four blocks east of Grand. Great. Molly nodded and walked on into the kitchen. She'd have to call the police, but she didn't have to do it right now. Right now she had to remind her nephew that there was at least one person who gave a damn about him. She just wished she knew how to do it without screwing up. Molly had the unnerving feeling she was running out of chances.

"Oh, one other thing with Sam," she said, stopping again. "He really depends on you, ya know. Could you make sure Little Allen doesn't get into that house again?"

"Sam finally figured out the little *pisher*'s been stealing his food money?"

Molly almost grinned at the unconscious Yiddish. "Yeah. It's killing him. He likes the little *pisher*."

Finally, briefly, she got a smile and felt a little better.

Rarely had Molly been more glad to be scheduled to work. It was the only thing that prevented her from spending her day down in the records morgue of St. Roch's Hospital. The search warrant for the records search came through at noon, by which time Rhett had let Molly know he was at her disposal whenever she could meet him at the hospital, where they had to hand-search charts too old to be in the computer. Molly, meanwhile, spent a near-quiet morning getting Patrick settled into Sam's and doing her best to ignore the tide of press that threatened to trample her beautiful lawn.

When she heard ex-husband-number-two, Peter Perkins, on her answering machine, she headed down to Jay's International Foods on South Grand in search of a crack in the closed walls of the Vietnamese community. Hooking a basket over her arm, she strolled down aisles packed with lemongrass, a hundred kinds of rice, a dozen kinds of soy sauce, couscous, and falafel, and she listened to the lilt of a dozen different languages. When she heard Vietnamese, she spoke up, diffident and polite, to ask questions. She spent over two hours there, talking about food and health and animals and, occasionally, children. She learned nothing, she bought fifty dollars' worth of spices she'd never use, and then stopped for Chinese takeout.

From there she headed straight into work where she could hide away in Sasha's office until her shift started.

"Well, if it isn't the notorious 'Necro-nurse,'" Sasha greeted her.

"Please tell me you didn't make that up," Molly begged, never taking her eyes off the screen of Sasha's computer as her supervisor divested herself of coat and scarf.

"How dare you? It was in the *Star*. Front page. I'm collecting all the tabs for your scrapbook. You don't have to thank me."

"I won't. I'll give them your name."

Sasha simply gathered her supplies for work. "You have no sense of adventure. After all, it could be worse. According to the accumulated press, you're probably the psycho dream date, whereas the St. Louis police are a cabal of ineffectual co-conspirators doing their best to ignore the plight of lower-class kids and their grieving parents."

"You're right," Molly agreed. "Given the choice, I'll take psycho dream date any day."

"You're just saying that because none of your psychos can get through that crowd of reporters around your house."

"Who are all psychos in their own right."

"Some of whom pull in quite a good paycheck," Sasha mused. "Might be worth considering."

"Frank makes a good paycheck. If I wouldn't consider him, I'm not considering bottom-of-the-food-chain tabloid reporters. Ya know, I hate to say this, but this computer stuff is pretty amazing."

Sasha plopped, openmouthed, into a chair.

"Oh, shut up," Molly chastised, then waved at the screen. "No, I mean it. It's frightening, of course, because with the right employee ID anybody could access every byte of usable information about me, which terrifies me to my toes. But with my own ID, I've been able to access almost everybody else's medical and employment secrets, and that might save me some . . . time." She'd almost said pain and suffering. But there was no way she'd tell Sasha what it would cost her to wade through twenty-five years of records.

"Like who?" Sasha asked, leaning closer.

"My morgue buddy, Lewis. He has not only a pretty impressive rap sheet, he has more than a nodding acquaintance with shrinks. Although, truth to tell, I haven't found antisocial behavior listed among his evaluations. Just arrested psychological development and a bit of obsessive ideation. On the other hand, my local grocer boy has lots of antisocial behavior, and I think he's been trolling the neighborhood for open windows. I wonder if he has a rap sheet, too."

"Who else?"

"Well, I have a list from St. Roch's and, of course, the people here. John Martin, by the way, that housekeeping tech, doesn't have any psych history. Just a bit of sneaky-peeking when he works nights. He works better by himself—which would make him much better at housekeeping than patient care—and has been suspected of substance abuse."

"Pretty normal stuff around here," Sasha admitted. "I'm disappointed."

"I know. You really wanted him to be our man."

"It would have gotten him out of patient care, anyway. I thought I smelled alcohol on his breath the other day.

Molly looked up. "You, too? I reported him the other night. He damn near dropped Frank's dinner out the window."

Sasha wasn't quite as amused as Molly expected her to be. "What do you do now?"

"I pop up to visit Frank, start my ten hours saving lives, and then come back to this when I'm finished."

Sasha got to her feet and grabbed her lab coat. "You do live an exciting life. Are you really in as good a mood as you seem?"

Molly shut off the computer and climbed to her feet. "Don't be absurd."

"You're getting too famous for me," Frank greeted her. He was scratching at the stitches they'd taken in his side when they'd pulled the tube, and fidgeting with his remote control. Definitely time to dispatch him to his family.

"It's been my dream all along, Frank," Molly informed him. "To be too famous for you."

"You okay, St. Molly?"

"I suck, Frank."

"How?"

"Alphabetically or chronologically?"

If it hadn't been Frank, she probably wouldn't have told him. But Frank understood about Patrick, and knew all about Molly's aversion to past-life regression therapy. So he got an earful. Then he got another when he made several objectionable suggestions about how he could make Molly feel better.

"Once you leave here, you can't even come near me," Molly reminded him acerbically. "It isn't safe."

"If I liked being safe, St. Molly," he retorted with that sinful smile of his, "I wouldn't play with you in the first place."

But for once, even Frank didn't improve her mood.

Fortunately for her peace of mind, at least, the weather went sour about four o'clock, which meant that the place was too busy for her to worry, and the roads too awful for the press to make an attempt to storm the proverbial hospital gates. By the time Molly finished work, the only way to get home was by emergency vehicle. So she curled up in one of the empty call rooms and called it a night.

Molly never had a problem sleeping in the hospital. There was just something about the syncopated dings from elevators, the murmur of the paging system, the slap and swish of running shoes on the halls that lulled her to sleep more completely than the silence at home. And she was so tired tonight, it worked even better. No more than three minutes after her head hit the pillow she was sucked so deep into an exhausted sleep that even the nightmares failed to follow her down. Which was why when something woke her in the early morning hours, she surfaced like a drowning swimmer.

Molly startled awake so fast she felt sick. She didn't move, couldn't think past the idea that something was wrong.

That she was afraid. She wasn't quite sure what it was, but something had happened that had yanked her straight out of oblivion.

She was in the hospital; she knew that. She remembered tossing to get comfortable on the ill-used mattress and trying to ignore the smell of old aftershave on the covers.

She could still smell it. She could hear the hospital noises, and they were no different. There wasn't even a Code Blue page, which might have dug through to deeper instincts than exhaustion.

Maybe it was the fact that the call room door was cracked open. Molly never slept with the door open. Hospital lights were too stark to induce sleep, and Molly didn't like the idea of people peeking in.

Maybe it was just the fact that her bare foot had somehow escaped the blanket. Considering how cold her feet usually were, it wasn't a place she encouraged them to be.

Or maybe it was just the lingering feeling that she'd missed something, like catching movement out of the corner of her eye. The side of her ankle was tingling, as if it had just brushed against something, and her stomach was doing flip-flops.

For a second she just looked at her foot, as if it were an alien life form grafted onto her body and sending strange signals. The tingling was spreading, a shiver of dread, of distaste. Of inexplicable familiarity.

Molly sat up in bed and looked around, but there wasn't anything there. Not a whisper of movement in the room or out in the hallway. Not even the feeling that somebody stood in the dark or around the corner, waiting and watching.

Still, she just couldn't shake the feeling that somebody had been there.

Somebody who had touched her naked foot and then left.

"You look like shit," Marianne the secretary greeted Molly when she stumbled back out onto the work lane later that morning.

Molly rubbed at her face, wishing like hell she could rid

herself of that creepy feeling she'd been watched the night before. She knew damn well it had probably been somebody who'd been fascinated by the notoriety, but even so . . .

"For a change I'm going to make your day and agree with you, Marianne," Molly said. "I feel like shit. I have any messages?"

"This isn't a fuckin' hotel," the girl sneered.

Which meant that there were messages, but Molly was going to have to work for them. "I'll make you a deal. You give me my messages, and I promise not to work your shift today. How's that?"

With any luck, Molly'd be able to look outside and find she couldn't get to St. Roch's. Of course, if the roads were bad, Marianne would be the last person at work, but there was hope.

Marianne just kept shooting those "fuck-you" glares, so Molly cinched up the drawstrings on her borrowed scrubs and walked on by. Green scrubs, she thought inconsequentially. Just like the ones on that bloody mannequin in the bookstore window the other night.

Molly fought a new set of shivers and hoped that what she was feeling was just the creeps, not prescience.

"Detective Butler is here somewhere looking for you," Marianne finally conceded just before Molly made it out of earshot. Molly battled the chronic urge to strangle the secretary and waited for the punch line. "Said he knew you wouldn't want to worry about how to get up to St. Roch's, so he came to pick you up."

Well, there went the rest of Molly's marginal mood.

"Hey there, Molly," the annoyance in question greeted her from the other end of the hall.

"And you got another delivery," Marianne said.

No, *there* went the rest of Molly's marginal mood. She was sorely tempted just to keep on walking, but so far that hadn't solved a damn thing. So she gave Marianne the satisfaction of turning around. Marianne rewarded her by making a big show of pulling out the mystery delivery and setting it on the top of her desk.

What a surprise. A big, brand-new, shiny flower box. Square, this time. With a red ribbon.

"You want to check it for bombs again?" Marianne asked.

Molly sighed. She knew darn well that Frank had ordered it after getting a taste of the mood she was in the night before. Even so, Molly just didn't have the patience for it.

"It's all yours, Marianne," she decided. "Just do me a favor and write Frank a truly tasteless note thanking him, because this time it's probably water balloons."

Marianne's laugh betrayed how stupid she thought Molly was for turning down yet another box of flowers. Molly turned on her heel and faced her next problem.

"Hey, Officer Butler," Molly greeted him, on the move again. "What do you know that will brighten my day?"

"As a matter of fact," he said, ambling her way, "we do have news. Turns out that more than half a dozen of the parents who showed up last night about missing teens happen to have femur X rays of their daughters. Although why all those girls would need femur X rays doesn't make sense to me . . ."

"Sports," Molly conceded, scratching at the side of her head, where she'd had one of the docs pull her staples the night before. "Which means we should go now and offer up a mass for those parents who push their children to excessive athletic achievements—"

She got no further. Behind her, Marianne began to scream. Molly shut her eyes, praying for rodents. For flashing house doctors. For the second coming of Christ in her work lane. When Marianne kept screaming, Molly knew she wasn't going to be so lucky.

I didn't mean to do it
I didn't, i swear.
Now they'll catch me.
They'll know i hurt her.
I feel so sick
I feel so
     strong

SIXTEEN

"You gave me that box on purpose!" Marianne shrieked for the thirtieth time in two hours.

Molly ignored her—again. She was much too preoccupied with the fact that she'd once again underestimated her correspondent. After all, it had been the only reason she hadn't run screaming into the street the minute that first news van had parked out in front of her house. She'd figured that no self-respecting serial killer would chance showing up on the ten o'clock news trying to drop off a trophy.

What Molly had stupidly overlooked was the possibility that he might be more motivated than intimidated. Which meant he'd found a way to leave a box at the triage desk without anybody remembering how, or by whom. And Marianne had opened it to find another skull. Another note. Another paint job.

Eyes watching in terrible silence.

Marianne hadn't stopped screaming for twenty minutes. By that time, there wasn't a person in all eight stories of the hospital who didn't know precisely what was going on.

Which also meant that the cops and Winnie had to wade through a fresh sea of newspeople to see what it was Molly had received.

"I hate Christmas," Molly was muttering to herself as she stared at that very gift.

THIS IS FOR MOLLY BURKE

In red this time, right across the forehead. The forehead that had been painted so that it looked like gray marble. Tucked in glittery cotton and surrounded by dime-store gold stars, the kind teachers put on good reports.

Sitting beside her on the lounge couch, Sasha tsked. "You wouldn't have minded so much if he'd just succumbed to crass commercialism and gotten you a bottle of perfume."

"True," Molly sighed, shaking with the effort to quell hysterics that would have silenced even Marianne. "I guess one person's art is just another person's . . ."

"Cranium?"

Molly giggled. She was having way too much trouble controlling herself. Probably because of the letter she held in her hands. Her gloved hands. It was, after all, one of the benefits of receiving viable evidence in a hospital.

"Pretty personal, huh?" Sasha asked as if knowing.

Molly couldn't look at her. She couldn't look at the note. She didn't want to admit yet that Kathy had been terrifyingly right. That Molly was going to have to go down into the basement of St. Roch's whether she liked it or not, and that she was going to have to pick through a couple of the worst years of her life so she could try and remember a kid she hadn't managed to help.

Dear Miss Burke,

Miss Burke. Molly flashed again on Lewis with his lopsided grin and untidy uniform. Did she remember him from another, smaller life when she'd tried to save him? Did she really believe he could have searched for her for twenty years with the sole purpose of having her remind him he was real?

After this new letter, she had no choice.

It's his fault, whoever he is. He doesn't understand and he's interfering. I didn't do that. I wouldn't do that. I would never bomb people. It's stupid. Besides, this is between you and me. I wouldn't hurt your friend. Or

*your boy. He's real handsome now, isn't he? Real
smart. I remember wanting to be him when I saw you
before. I wanted to be your baby, Miss Burke. But I
wasn't. I was theres, and they made me nobody. Here is
another one of my friends for you, her name is Flower.
So you know. So you remember. So you'll know me,
too, when you see me*

"What do you think?" Kathy asked quietly, looking over
Molly's shoulder at the hastily printed words that seemed to
have been spilled, impatient as children, across the page.

"I think," Molly said, closing her eyes against the fire this
new note lit in her chest, "that he's just told us where we'll
find him."

Kathy straightened like a hound on scent. "What do you
mean?"

"He'll be in the St. Roch's records somewhere in 1979 or
early 1980."

She could hear Kathy go very still, and beyond her Sasha,
Rhett, and Winnie. They were so still in fact, that all Molly
could finally hear was her own heart.

"Why is that, Molly?" Winnie asked, her own voice oddly
gentle.

Molly shook her head, not wanting to concede to the old
grief that clogged her throat. It was the box she'd kept closed
the tightest. The one she hadn't looked in since shoving that
lid down the day she'd buried her first husband, John Michael
Murphy. It was the box in which lay the last of the ashes of
their struggle to recover what they'd been.

"Because I was pregnant in 1979."

"You were pregnant four times," Sasha said, as hesitant as
the rest, as out of character. "You've told me that before."

Finally Molly opened her eyes and faced her friends. "I
miscarried three times," she said. "But 1979 I . . . 1979 was
the only time he could have seen that I was going to have a
baby and wanted to be it. It's why he thinks Patrick is my
child, because Patrick looks about the same age as Johnny."

The rest of them left it to Sasha to ask. "Johnny?"

Molly tried so hard to smile as if it were a joke. "I actually managed to enjoy the special delights of labor."

But Johnny could never have been mistaken for Patrick. He never would have grown to be as beautiful, with soft hazel eyes and a poet's face. Johnny had been born acephalic. Molly's baby had lived but a few days, gasping and fragile and misshapen, doomed from the moment Molly and John, both exposed to Agent Orange, had conceived him. He was buried in Calvary Cemetery, next to the father who would follow him no more than six months later.

Handing the letter she'd received over into Kathy's gloved hand, Molly managed a stiff smile at the appalled discomfort on her friends' faces. Then, she got up and walked out.

No, she didn't just walk out. She ran. Just as she always did. As she always had, from home to the military, from city to city, from friend to friend without settling, as if that way, neither could her memories settle on her.

The problem was, she realized as she hurried down the hall to the elevators, she couldn't run this time. She had to turn around and face what hurt the most, or somebody else would die. A lot of somebodies would die, fragile, wide-eyed children on the brink of adulthood who had committed no greater crime than being confused and unpredictable.

Another skull. Another little girl who had smiled at the wrong man. Molly barely made it to the heliport on the roof of the fifth floor where the wind snapped the windsock and snow swirled and glittered in a winter sun. And then, wrapping her arms around herself, Molly just folded down into the corner of the roof where she knew she'd be safe, and she stayed there, wishing like hell she couldn't yet, after all these years, feel that soft, misshapen body in her hands. All those soft, sad bodies she'd lost and couldn't get back.

She shouldn't really have been surprised that they refused to leave her alone.

"Go away, Frank."

He crouched right beside her, coat flapping around him,

hair tumbled and dusted with snow. "Sasha would have my liver if I went back inside."

Molly steeled herself against the pity and looked up.

Thank God they'd thought to send Frank. "It's perfectly all right to make people feel bad because they can't do anything to help," he said easily. "But you probably don't want to scare them."

Molly managed a grin, teeth chattering and arms blue. "They all too chicken to face me?"

"Nope. Kathy thought you'd be more comfortable if you made your surrender to the inevitable by easy stages. I'm stage one, the prudent approach."

Molly frowned. "Inevitable?"

His grin was brash, his eyes just a bit less. "That you have friends who might take the trouble to worry about you."

Molly dropped her head back into her crossed arms as if she could ignore him. "No wonder she's a profiler. I guess this means you won't go away until I bare my soul."

"Don't be stupid. It's freezing out here. I'm just the silent support stage. You know better than to think I'm going to compare scars with you."

That got her head back up to surprise the brief, tiny flash of pain in Frank's eyes. His own ashes. Frank's lovely young wife had chosen Abigail over treatment for leukemia and died soon after giving birth. Frank, from all reports, had handled it with exceeding bad grace. And Frank, if he was out on this windswept roof, now knew all of Molly's story.

Odd, that that alone should make her feel a little less lost. She guessed they were right. This stuff was tricky.

"Let's go back in before you get dismissed just in time to catch pneumonia," she suggested, climbing to her feet.

He scowled up at her a moment. "You're not going to wait till I'm inside and toss yourself off into traffic?"

Which was why Kathy had thought to send Frank. He made Molly laugh. "It would be far too mundane," she promised him, holding out a hand. When he took hold and stood, she flashed him a grin. "I'll wait until I can land on your car."

She was heading through the door when she heard the real grief in his voice. "I don't have a car . . ." And she smiled, despite herself.

"We have an ID on one of the victims!"

Molly looked up from the stacks of logbooks and ED charts that surrounded her to see Rhett waving a paper at her. She'd been stuck in the station for three days now, trying to pull protoplasm from old ink, and it was giving her the headache of the century. Not to mention the fact that she'd simply stopped sleeping. She dreamed when she slept, and she dreamed about her friend Sally, except now Sally spoke to her from the dirt, and Molly didn't think she wanted to hear any more accusations.

So she took some of the folders home, and then she came down to the station to read the rest, hoping against hope that she'd suddenly be struck by insight without actually having to wade through the tales of mayhem that had been visited on children two decades earlier. Wishing like hell her list of names was shorter, or that she could put a face and voice to just one of them.

And when the children weighed on her too heavily, she stepped back out to Jay's International Foods store and practiced her Vietnamese, without any better results.

"Winnie get a hit on our latest skull?" Molly asked, taking the time to rub at the ache behind her eyes.

"She just released the damn thing two hours ago," Rhett reminded her. "No, as a matter of fact, the anthropologist—"

"Puffin." Probably the only amusing point in her day.

"Yeah." His grin was no more respectful. "Anyway, she and a radiologist managed to match up one of your femurs to some X rays. Delighted the hell out of her. Is that creepy or what?"

Molly forbore reminding Rhett that most of the things that delighted him in the course of his work were at least as creepy, and reached for the paper. "So, who is it?"

"Crystal Marie Taggatt, 3217 Hope Street, Arnold, Missouri. Seventeen years old, five-foot-seven-inches tall. Blond and blue, if that makes a difference."

Molly looked up. "Arnold? Then . . ."

"She didn't live in or near the target zone." His sudden grin was surprisingly feral. "The last place she was seen, on the other hand, was at the Mean Bean Coffeehouse on South Grand Boulevard."

Should she feel better or worse? Considering the condition of her stomach and head, tough to feel worse. On the other hand, given a chance, Molly was sure she'd manage it.

"Somebody going to talk to the family?"

"Baitshop and me."

Molly looked up, amazed. "The big boys are letting you loose?"

Rhett's grin was understandably proud. "I'm now on the starting line-up."

"Then let me go with you," she begged like a beagle. "Please?"

"But you need to—"

Molly scrambled to her feet. "I *have* been. I have been for three fucking days, and I'm about to lose my mind. Let me out for a little fresh air, for God's sake."

Rhett actually grinned. "You sound like we keep you in a cave."

Molly made it a point to look around at the interrogation room they'd offered her with its scarred, soundproofed walls, its tang of old cigarette smoke and sweat. Its table that was buried beneath a layer of fast-food wrappings and congealed grease.

Rhett lifted an eyebrow. "Hey, you were the one who chose this room."

"That's so nobody could hear me screaming. Come on, Rhett. I can help. I do these interviews all the time."

"But nobody else can interpret those charts."

"An hour isn't going to change anything. I doubt I'm going to be struck with inspiration before you get back. Trust me."

Rhett took another uncomfortable look at the untidy

mountain of records they'd carted away from the hospital in a van. "What have you found out so far?"

Molly took her own look and sighed. "I found out I worked way too much and got way too little out of it."

Rhett didn't bother to comment.

"I think it was the hormones," Molly said. "I seem to have been on a mission to save every bruised kid who hit the door."

"That was unusual for you?"

"You want the truth?" Molly rubbed at the gnaw in her epigastrium even White Castles couldn't cure. "I don't know."

Now Rhett did comment, all with his eyes.

Molly shrugged. "I don't remember. I don't remember much of what's in that stack at all, no matter how many times I signed my name. Just the outrageous stuff. The frat jock who entered the fart lighting contest and our burn unit in the same day, the crazy who really did cut off his nose to spite his face, the woman who was valet parking Hot Wheels in her very own subterranean garage. But the everyday stuff?" She shook her head. "It doesn't pay to remember that stuff. It just gets me mad all over again, and I've had my fill of mad, thanks."

"So you can't put any memories to any of the possibles you've listed?"

A list of thirteen so far. Boys, all of them, questioned abuse. Neglect. Trauma. Possibly, now that they'd finally learned to diagnose it, Munchausen by Proxy, by which a parent got attention by making her own child ill. And every one of those names meaningless. It was only the lesson that had remained, an awful brew distilled from all those sad, empty eyes.

The Game.

And, evidently, one little boy who had remembered better than Molly. But if Kathy was right, while Molly had tried to save them all, only Molly had tried to save that one little boy.

Rhett picked up Molly's list. "Well," he said. "We can at least start running these while we're gone."

Molly had her coat on before Rhett could argue. "Good idea."

Sasha was fond of saying that one could tell exactly where one was in the social structure of St. Louis by the Christmas lights in the yard. If this was true, the Taggatt neighborhood sat solidly in white trash central, where the lights probably confused overhead airliners, and the seasonal lawn orna-ments represented every Christmas cliché but Jingle Barney.

At the Taggatt home, the lawn held a plastic manger, Santa, deer, candy canes, lights, and Homer Simpson. Multi-colored lights were strung from the roof out to the lawn like a spiderweb, and a big HAPPY HOLIDAYS sign hung over the front porch. The house beneath the lights was small, shabby, and sagging. So was the woman who answered the door.

"Yeah?"

Rhett and Baitshop flipped badges. "Mrs. Taggatt? May we talk to you, please? We're from the St. Louis police."

Molly just stood behind with her hands in her coat pockets while Mrs. Taggatt assessed the situation.

"About fuckin' time," she finally said and pushed the door open. "You here about Crystal?"

The inside of the Taggatt home looked no better, with a pink Christmas tree fighting for space with a big-screen TV tuned to soaps, and tables cluttered with Busch bottles.

"Could we sit down?" Rhett asked. "Is Mr. Taggatt in?"

Mrs. Taggatt laughed like an air horn and reached for her cigarettes. "That asshole ain't never in. Now, you gonna tell me where Crystal is? She in trouble again? If she is, I'll blis-ter her little ass." She lit up and sat, and everybody else fol-lowed, the three of them tucked into a dingy blue couch that smelled more than faintly of cat. "I'll tell you, that girl's been trouble since the day she grew tits. Always wants her own way. Like she knows better. Well, I'll tell you, she's sure as shit gonna know better now."

Molly simply sat by while Rhett waited for an opening into which to insert his news. As pissed as Mrs. Taggatt was at her daughter, at the police, at Mr. Taggatt, it could take a while.

In the meantime, Molly did what she did every time she entered a home for an interview. She looked for pictures. Evidence of what kind of family might dwell in the house. Did they arrange their memories, or save them at all? Did they keep the faces of the people they loved close at hand, clustered like bouquets, or did they just forget?

There were a few pictures arranged on the far wall in a triangle. Mrs. Taggatt in a better time, leaning back against a fairly good-looking guy with high cheekbones and small eyes. A boy seated in a Sears-type pose with football and fall leaves. A girl, looking old and hard in a Glamour Shot pose with sequins, too much makeup, and teased, stiff mall-hair. One of those child-women who didn't know quite where she belonged anymore, her expression a dead cross between fear and bravado.

The face, Molly knew, of one of her victims.

"Mrs. Taggatt," Rhett said, his tone of voice pulling Molly's attention back. "I'm afraid I have some bad news."

The woman stopped dead in the middle of a drag, the smoke curling up beyond her straw yellow hair like a small barn fire.

"No," was all she said, going pale.

The three occupants of the couch tensed to react.

"I'm so sorry," Rhett said softly, reaching for her hand.

She jumped as if he'd scalded her. "No!" she shrieked, on her feet so fast she almost sent the tree over. "You get outta here with that shit! They told me she run away."

"I'm sorry." The litany of homicide. Of death investigation. Of trauma. "We're virtually sure that your daughter Crystal was the victim of a . . . murderer in the area."

"No . . ." Tears blurred exophthalmic blue eyes. "She's not dead. If I see her, I'll prove it. Show me that girl you found. Show her to me and I'll . . ."

Rhett just shook his head. It was better than explaining that all that was left to identify was a painted bone. "I'm afraid there isn't any question, Mrs. Taggatt. We matched her with those X rays you provided the police last week. Please, won't you help us find who did this? Would you answer a few questions?"

The tears came fast now. Real tears, silent, blinding, streaking Mrs. Taggatt's makeup and running down her neck. "Aw, God, no. Who would . . . who . . ."

Molly made it to Mrs. Taggatt before either of the other two. And then she just held her. Just let her sob. Closed her own eyes, trying to close her ears against such furious, keening grief. Understanding perfectly well why she hadn't remembered any of the people she'd seen in the ED twenty years ago.

Baitshop found the Kleenex, and Rhett got his interview. Molly held on to Crystal's mother until she finally pulled herself to her feet and lifted that Glamour Shot picture off the wall to hand to Rhett.

"You told the police you heard her making a date that last night," Rhett said in his most compassionate voice as Mrs. Taggatt sat back down, the photo still in her hands, her thumbs on her daughter's cheeks.

Mrs. Taggatt nodded, snuffling. "I told her not to go. I told her I hated that crowd she hung with up there. They talked her into dressing like a whore. And she was piercing every fuckin' thing she could find. Tell me, what the hell does that mean?"

"She'd tried to run away before, hadn't she?"

"Three times. We got her back every time. She didn't mean it. Not really. She just doesn't get along with her dad, ya know?"

"We know. Kids just do that sometimes," Rhett said with a soft smile. He didn't say that usually they did that because there was abuse somewhere in their life. After all, it would take a pretty awful home to be worse than the streets in winter. "Is there any reason to think she meant to go again?"

Mrs. Taggatt looked down at the face on her lap. "No. I really don't think so. She . . . she usually got real antsy when she was thinking about it. Bitchy, like nothin' we did was right. She wasn't doin' that. In fact, after she was sick, she really seemed happier."

"Sick?" Molly asked.

Mrs. Taggatt couldn't quite look at her. "She . . . well, she didn't mean to really hurt herself. I mean, who tells you that Tylenol shit can kill ya? She was just bein' dramatic. That's what Lou says."

"Of course. How long was that before you last saw her?"

"Only a few weeks. But she seemed better."

"Do you know who she met that last night?" Rhett asked.

"Kenny. She said his name was Kenny. That they was just gonna have coffee."

Molly knew for sure then how good a cop Rhett was, because he never reacted to the fact that they now had a name. "How'd she get up there, ma'am?"

Another dip of the head. "I don't know. I told her she couldn't go. She had to baby-sit her sisters. I just don't know how she got there."

"But you never saw this Kenny."

"No. She wouldn't tell me where she met him or nothin'. Just that he was real nice." She shrugged. "Harmless."

"But she went up to the Mean Bean a lot?"

"Yeah. Said she felt normal up there. Whatever the hell that means." She was shaking her head, eyes unfocused, hands trembling. "You couldn't be wrong . . . ?"

"No, ma'am," Rhett told her, because that, in the end was all they could give her for closure. "We couldn't be wrong."

Molly enjoyed that trip so very much that when she got back, she packed up her pile of charts and she just went home. She brewed up more tea, she called Sam to find that Patrick had gone down to the local cyber café to contact his friends, she changed from jeans and T-shirt into a flannel nightgown, as if that would simulate sleep, and she sat down to more long-forgotten mayhem.

She got her first nibble about three hours later.

She'd been digging through the various and sundry disasters of October 1979 when her attention was caught by a nurse's note on the chart of a ten-year-old named Peter Wilson. His father had brought him in for a sore throat. There was nothing on the face of the chart that should have stopped her. No injuries high on the abuse-suspicion category, no mention of multiple visits or signs of neglect. But she checked anyway, just as she had every chart, for a pattern she might only later recognize.

And there it was, and in her own handwriting.

Kenny appears to be anxious and alert. No apparent distress. Vague about symptoms.

Kenny. Molly checked the face sheet again to find that no middle name was listed. She read the disposition on the chart to discover that none of the physical findings supported the child's complaints. She saw that two other times she'd referred to the child as "Kenny" as opposed to "patient," which was the traditional appellation.

Peter Wilson.

Molly reviewed the list she'd begun. Names she'd suspected of obvious abuse. Repeat offenders with obvious problems. The name wasn't among them. She certainly didn't remember the name or the child. But something about the careful notes made her uneasy. She had to get back to her previous logbooks and see if the name Peter Wilson showed up. She had to look ahead.

Well, she could start with what she had, which was October.

Molly was so deep in her research, that it took her a minute to hear the tapping. She looked up and shrieked. There was a face at her window. Then she recognized Rhett's abashed smile and damn near killed him.

If only Magnum hadn't adopted him, just like all the other people in her life. Molly stalked to the back door and threw it open, ready to rip the officer several new orifices. The worry lines between his eyes stopped her.

"No," she said, turning away before the videocams lurking on the other side of her back fence caught her in her nightie. "No more bad news. I already told you that."

"I'm sorry, Molly."

She didn't even bother to turn around. "Don't be sorry, Rhett. Just be gone."

He followed her into her family room where all the charts were strewn across the floor and tables. "I can't."

Molly sat down and pulled over the October logbook. "I'm ignoring you," she informed her very uncomfortable friend. "I'm looking to see if I can find a repeat visitor named Peter Wilson. Wanna know why?"

"You were the one who wanted to be kept in the loop," he reminded her, "and you haven't been answering your phone."

Molly waved him off. "You want me, beep me. I stopped answering the phone."

"I know. The answering machine's full, too."

Molly snorted. "Mostly hang-ups, since I won't give quotes."

Rhett wasn't going to be deterred. "Molly, you need to know this."

Molly closed her eyes and sighed. "Sit down then, and get it over with. Then I'll tell you the interesting stuff."

Rhett sat. He shot a longing look over toward the teapot, but Molly was way past playing hostess.

"Your neighbor's grocery guy—uh . . ."

"Allen."

"Yeah, Allen. It's an alias."

Molly sat down on her own chair at that. "What's his name?"

"Everett K. Thorne—K for Keith, by the way. We can't be quite *that* lucky. Anyway, he's got a pretty interesting rap sheet all full of B&E and petty theft charges that go back to California and Washington. He's only been here three or four years."

"No sex stuff?"

"Not that I've found. But then, we, uh, can't seem to find him, either. He has an address in Maplewood, but evidently, he's rarely there. Nobody's seen him in the last few days."

"Him, too? What about Lewis from the morgue? Have you caught up with him, yet?"

"Yeah. We found him. He's creepy, but there's nothing more concrete than that yet. Winnie sure doesn't like us accusing her dieners of serial murder, does she?"

"She's funny like that. But you think Allen bears more watching." Molly waited for a nod and looked back at that chart she hadn't let go of. "I don't suppose his name was ever Peter Wilson."

Rhett frowned. "You really want me to pay attention to this Peter Wilson thing, don't you?"

"What a bright boy you are. I know you'll figure it out for yourself." She handed over the chart. "Note the name. Note what I called him in my notes. Specifically. Several times."

Rhett skimmed the chart once, then again. "What do you think?" he asked, looking up.

"Do you respect nurse instincts?"

"Every bit as much as I respect cop instincts."

"In that case, it means something."

"Great. I can run it tonight. Davidson's still down at the office."

Molly climbed to her feet, suddenly shaken by the idea that she might actually be able to put a face to her correspondent. That she might have to face him and admit she knew him.

"Then that demands a celebration."

She'd barely gotten hold of the Stoly she hid in the broken coffeepot when Magnum jumped up, barking. Somebody started pounding on the back door.

Magnum backed up, barking like a real guard dog. Rhett reached for his hip holster and bolted for the door. Molly jumped so high she dropped the bottle. It shattered, spraying the floor with vodka and glass, and all Molly could do was stare at it.

"Molly?"

She looked up to see Rhett poised in the open doorway, his expression caught between dread and exhilaration, a uniformed officer standing just outside on her step.

"What?"

"They caught somebody prowling the neighborhood. He has two pair of women's panties and won't give them his name. You want to see if you know him?"

No. She didn't. She wanted to finish her Stoly, but it was all over the damn floor.

Dear sweet Jesus, she thought in sudden terror, let it be a serial killer in her backyard. Let it be Kenny come to call so the police could just sweep him up like trash.

"Aw, hell," she capitulated, a shaking hand to her epigastric area. "Why not? The way things are going, it's probably Sam."

She heard the escalating noise of discovery, the proverbial baying of the newshounds out front as they caught the scent of something happening. She stood stock still in a widening pool of vodka as a cadre of patrol cops tumbled in her back door, their captive caught in unyielding hands and hooded with one of their jackets.

Molly felt unaccountably afraid and backed away. No, come to think of it, she didn't want to know. She wasn't ready for this.

And then, like David Copperfield at the sound of a drum-roll, one of the cops lifted that jacket, and Molly felt another big rock hit her head.

Blinking in the fluorescents of her kitchen and smiling as if he'd pulled the biggest prank of his life, there, in the middle of her kitchen floor surrounded by scowling police, stood Patrick.

They don't know. They
never found out. They
don't know what I can do,
what I want to do.
What I will do.

I'll take their eyes
scoop out their eyes
stab out their eyes I'll
eat their brains i'll
fuck their brains
I'll make it slow so they
know what they are

ALL OF THEM

SEVENTEEN

"Hi, Aunt Molly," Patrick greeted her with the nonchalance of a carny.

Rhett gaped. Every one of the patrol cops flushed. It was nothing compared to what Molly was feeling.

"You want to explain this?" she demanded.

One of the cops stepped forward, but Molly waved him off. "Not you. Him."

"Can I get these off?" Patrick asked, lifting his arms a little to remind them all that he was cuffed.

"No. Talk."

"Were those her . . . uh, things you had?" one of the cops asked.

Patrick, unbelievably, laughed. "You hosin' me? What the fuck would I want with my aunt's underwear?"

Molly actually spent a moment fighting dizziness. Just how absurd could this get? "So you *have* been playing Peeping Tom?" she asked, knowing the answer from his smirk. "I don't suppose you shoplifted the panties."

His gaze was level. "What fun would that be?"

Molly closed her eyes for a second and thought how profoundly silent that kitchen was for all the cops in it. "I guess I can't hope you guys would just look the other way while I strangle the life out of him, would you?" she asked.

"Be tough to get the body past all the camera crews," Rhett objected.

Molly snorted. "That's what basements and potting soil are for."

"Works for me," one of the patrols said. "I hate paperwork."

Molly opened her eyes. "In that case you're going to hate this. I'm sure Patrick will remember that I warned him about this type of behavior. He is, proverbially and in any other way possible, all yours."

She got not a few scowls from the cops. "You sure?" one asked.

Patrick was literally agape. "You're going to let them just arrest me? For this! It's only a couple pair of panties. I never touched anybody."

"If you didn't get them off a clothesline, that's breaking and entering, Patrick."

He paled as if she'd hit him. "Do you know what this is going to do to the parents?"

"You don't care what it does to your parents," she snapped. "But you should care what it's going to do to Sam. I asked you to protect that old man, Patrick. How could you do this to him?"

"Well, let me go and I'll make it up to him," he wheedled.

"Call Frank," she advised instead, deliberately turning away. "I hear he's a good lawyer."

"He doesn't even like me."

"Fortunately, you don't need a lawyer to like you. Even better, he was released from the hospital today."

"But Aunt Molly . . . !"

She turned back on him from a safer distance. "You want to tell me what else you've been up to? These nice men and women are going to find out sooner or later anyway. Which means you'll probably lose that job we worked so hard to get."

For that she got a sneer. "Spare me. I ditched that chicken-shit place two weeks ago. Like you give a damn."

Molly just slumped into a kitchen chair and laughed. "Of course you did. I'm probably not even surprised. Should I send this crew upstairs to search for stolen goods?"

Patrick huffed. "I don't live here anymore, remember?"

Molly glared at him. "If you've done anything to compromise that old man next door . . ."

"You know better than that!" he protested, for all the world looking seriously outraged.

Molly wasn't sure she could buy it anymore. "I don't seem to know better than anything tonight."

"You know this'll go on my record," he whined. "I don't need that right now, Aunt Molly."

Molly considered him a moment, those beautiful, liquid eyes and angelic beauty. The mercurial mind and heartbreaking self-destructiveness. God, she wanted to get her hands around her brother's neck, because he'd been the one to create this mess and then leave it in her lap without any kind of instructions. All she had was the increasing conviction that no one in Patrick's life had taught him the consequences of his actions. That even now it might be too late. That she still didn't have a choice in the matter.

"I told you," she said sadly. "My rules are simple and inviolate. You broke them. You broke the law. You have to figure out what that means. This, I'm afraid, is the way you do that."

Patrick didn't say another word. Neither did Molly. But it was as they were spiriting Patrick back out the door that Molly flashed on the moment four nights earlier when Patrick had walked in the house with singed eyebrows and a tale of a fire at the restaurant where he worked. Where he really hadn't been working after all.

And she didn't know what to do about it.

"Molly?" Rhett asked softly behind her. "You all right?"

Molly sprang to her feet. "You want some tea, Rhett? I want some goddamn tea."

What she pulled out was another full bottle of Stoly.

At least they got a solid handle on Kenny. It was the next day after Rhett had brought Patrick home to Sam's and the old man had sufficiently harangued the apparently chastised child, all the while patting the boy's hands as if to cushion the blow of his anger. Molly slipped out Sam's back door and carried her charts and hip flask down to the station and holed up in that airless, soundproof room with several cups of Sam's tea to warm her and logbooks to distract her.

She needed to do something about Patrick. She'd made a quick recon of his room the night before to find another half dozen pair of panties and a stack of old *Hustler* magazines, but no items purloined from either Sam or herself, and no hydrocarbon residue of any kind. But Patrick's parents were seven thousand miles away, and his housekeeper wasn't talking about what he might have been running from when he'd strolled into Molly's house.

Sam prescribed *nudging* and watchful support. Frank recommended the Alcatraz Summer Camp. And Molly, who had once again lost contact with the entire country of China, could only hesitate, because she simply didn't know.

So she sipped her tea and leafed through her logbooks and ignored everything but that one name that should damn well have meant more to her than it did.

Kenny.

She found him again in late September. A thin chart about a bike accident resulting in an injured elbow and some faint bruising along the chest. No scrapes, which one would have thought would have shown up from a bike accident. No cooperation from the mother, who'd brought the child in.

Peter K. Wilson. Molly actually smiled. At least she hadn't been completely nuts all those years ago.

After that, it was easy, because Peter had come often. And not just for injuries, although those were certainly represented. For possible asthma attacks, for sore throat, for fever. Mostly brought by his mother. Most injuries significant and suspicious, most medical complaints benign. Real hurts and manufactured ills for clandestine attention. All seen by Molly.

And one chart that sent absolute chills through her. The last chart. That chart recorded bruising on that young body, possible ligature marks at wrists and ankles, and the worst. The most horrific.

Cockroach bites.

At least thirty inflamed cockroach bites.

Just how long would a child have to be tied down, where would he have had to be, to suffer more than two dozen cockroach bites without being able to get away?

What in God's name would it have done to him?

Molly collected all Kenny's charts, every one to the last, and sat staring at them, knowing with absolute certainty that she was looking at the tracks of their killer. She saw the nurse's notes trace his changes from hesitant, pleasant child, to the kind of specter she could almost see through. Silent, empty-eyed, still. As if he were becoming invisible before her eyes.

Which was precisely what he'd been doing. Just like Kathy had known all along.

The only problem was that Molly couldn't remember a thing about him. Not even, God help her, a small body full of cockroach bites. She sat for a good two hours, sipping at the Stoly-enhanced tea until her eyebrows got numb and staring at the old face sheets, but she couldn't pull up a single image or thought or impression to go with those sparse facts.

Kenny was right. He was invisible. He'd grown to adulthood with the belief that only one person in the world, like a psychological Topper, could see him. The only problem was that, after all was said and done, she'd lost him, too.

"Aren't you getting tired of this place?" Kathy asked, leaning in the doorway.

Molly blinked a bit at her. "What are you doing back here? I thought you were busy putting your new office into shape, now that our federal government is back in business."

Kathy grinned. "Been there, done that. It's after six, when normal people go home to their pets and exercise machines. The government has decided that I can pull extra duty on your team."

Molly just nodded, as if she'd figured that out already. "Wanna read some charts? Tell you everything we know about Kenny?"

Kathy took another step in and cadged a peek at Molly's high-octane tea. "Enjoying your stroll down memory lane, huh?"

Molly sighed and rubbed weary eyes. "That's just the problem. There is no memory. I don't remember him." She gestured to the charts she'd fanned out on the table. "Considering the fact that I reported that family to DFS three times, you'd think I would, wouldn't you?"

Kathy slid into the other chair. "What'd you report them for?"

"Suspicious injuries. Failure to thrive. Lots of mentions here of alcohol on the parents' breath. Pretty classic stuff. The parents must have finally caught on to what I was trying to do, because there's a late note on the last chart that when DFS went to check the home, the family had disappeared." She sighed, tapping the chart. "Abusers might be assholes, but they're not idiots."

Kenny's last ED chart was dated a week before Molly had gone on maternity leave. By the time she'd come back, she'd probably forgotten all the effort she'd made on Kenny's behalf. Just like all the other efforts she'd forgotten.

"Your charting is pretty clear here," Kathy said, taking her own look. "No mistaking your impressions . . . ah, he was eleven, huh? We're right on target. Poor kid, look at all those injuries."

"Which should have left pretty big scars for somebody down the line to recognize," Molly said. "He had keloid scarring, which is obvious and never goes away. It also looks like he was already forming some pretty interesting personality disorders."

"You can see that here?"

Molly smiled and pointed to a particular set of medical initials in her notes. "W.L.K.," she said. "Weird Little Kid. It was kind of a catch-all description for nondiagnosable bizarre behavior. We also had F.L.K., which meant Funny Looking Kid, meaning something was physically or genetically wrong, we just couldn't pin it down."

Kathy nodded. "Uh-huh. You notice he also manufactured problems just to come see you." Her eyes soft, she shook her head. "Can you imagine how horrible it was if an emergency room nurse seemed to be the only person he could turn to?"

No, Molly thought, she couldn't. She didn't want to. A person simply didn't hurt for a guy who was chopping up bodies to build his friends with. But looking down on the traces of the desperate, hunted little boy he'd once been, she did.

"The cops are out there running down any records there might be of Peter Wilson," Kathy said, back to business.

"Like if he has any recognizable aliases?"

"Like that. Rhett's doing a microscopic check on your friends Lewis and Allen, but nothing's ringing bells so far. And we haven't found any local hits on a Peter Wilson after the age of seventeen when he would have come out of juvenile blackout, which means he probably did leave town when he was eleven and come back a lot later as somebody else. On the other hand, I don't think he went alias by the time he was seventeen, so some kind of record should show up. I'm hoping hard for B&E, weenie wagging, and sexual assault." Kathy unfocused, the predator's eyes going vague with odd yearnings. "God, what I'd give for anything in those early years. Anybody who saw the fantasy before it became the crime scene."

"There isn't a box to check off on ED charts for that, I'm afraid."

"They would have been cementing into his sexual impulses about then, ya know. All that rage and terror and need for control pairing up with the most powerful impulse known to the universe to set his pattern." Kathy sighed, the archaeologist trying to pull juice and substance from bits of distant stone. "One of these days, we'll have the sense to ask those questions before a kid gets to the active participation stage. One day we'll be able to circumvent the process."

One day. Not this one, though.

The door opened and Rhett popped his head in. "Molly? There's somebody here who wants to talk to you."

Looking up, Molly caught the look on Rhett's face and thought maybe numb eyebrows weren't enough. "Who? And why?"

He just pushed the door open farther and motioned with his head.

Molly's visitor was small, thin, precise, and Vietnamese.
A young man in neat khakis, pinstripe shirt, and tie, he had
well-trimmed black hair, delicate facial bones, and eyes as
restless as a cop's. He stood at Rhett's desk like a wading bird
at the water, which Molly understood perfectly. After all,
she'd caught sight of the tattoo when he'd reached up to
brush at his hair. Five blue dots in a circle in the web between
thumb and forefinger. An Asian gang member had broached
the police station to see Molly.

She smiled a quiet greeting. "Can I help you?"

His attention zeroed in on her with chilled intensity. "You
are Molly Burke," he said with a nod, his accent faint. "I understand now your sudden taste for curry and ginger."

Molly nodded. "You also know what I was trying to find
out. Why don't you come back here where we can talk?"

Without even waiting for Rhett's invitation, she led the
man back to the interrogation room so he could see the work
she was wading through, and she sat him down.

"My name is Luc Trang," he said when she followed suit.
"I've come to you because my mother insisted. You were a
nurse in my country?"

Again she nodded. "In 1971 at Pleiku."

He nodded. "That's what my mother said. She spoke to
you a few days ago. She likes your eyes. She has this thing
about eyes . . ."

For a second, he looked almost callow, the face a mother
might see. And then the vulnerability disappeared. Molly
more than understood the need to protect pride. She never
moved to acknowledge his distress.

"It's about the picture the police have been passing around
in your neighborhood," she said very quietly. "Your sister?"

His head came up, but Molly was ready with a soft smile.

"You look very much like her," she said. "She was a beautiful young woman, Mr. Trang."

"We don't usually let others do what we can," he said, his
eyes on Molly instead of Rhett, who had followed them in
like a polite shadow. "But I think . . ."

He didn't even shrug. He just stopped. And Molly, who

had experience not only with the Vietnamese but with grief, recognized the glint of it in his rigidly contained fury.

"We have some information on the man who killed your sister—" Molly began.

"Lilly," he said starkly. "Her name is Lilly."

Molly nodded. "We think the man who killed Lilly has been preying on others in the South Grand area. We know he's been seen at the Mean Bean. We know he's taken at least one other girl from the area. Do you know, or could we talk to your mother, about the people Lilly knew?"

"My mother wouldn't know. Lilly moved out last year. She's been going to school and working at one of the restaurants. The Little Saigon. My mother has seen reports on the news that this man is targeting prostitutes and runaways, and it hurts her to have people think of Lilly like that."

Molly nodded. "How long has Lilly been missing?"

He shrugged. "Four months. She'd had a fight with our mother and we thought she'd gone to visit family elsewhere. By the time we realized she wasn't . . ."

Another small shrug. Another flash of rage.

Molly leaned forward, wanting to be the one to ask him everything and knowing she wasn't thorough enough. Knowing that her job was to get him to allow Rhett the access he needed. "Mr. Trang, I think you know that what is happening is beyond a neighborhood's capability to control. The police have a team working just on this . . . person. If you could tell us everything you know about Lilly and her friends. Where she went, who she saw—"

"I know the routine, Miss Burke."

Molly flushed and smiled. "You're right. I'm sorry. But you can also help us gain access to the neighborhood. That seems to be where he's preying, which puts girls in the Asian community at the highest risk. If you could work with Rhett here, maybe encourage the people to talk to the police, we might get a picture of what this guy looks like."

"Now?"

Molly felt Rhett stir behind her and knew she was giving away too much. But then, Rhett's sister hadn't ended up a sketch on the ten o'clock news. "It's your neighborhood, Mr. Trang."

He said nothing, but she saw his posture change a fraction.

"We think we have an idea who he is," she said, "but we don't know what he looks like. We just know that he might very well go by the name of Kenny."

She watched hard for a reaction, but she didn't get it.

"You've never heard of him."

"No."

"Did your sister date Caucasians? Did she have friends you might not have known about?"

A loaded question, since it was Luc's business to know everything that went on in his neighborhood. "She knew people. From school. From work. She never talked that much about them, because my mother didn't understand."

"One of those people killed her, Mr. Trang," Molly said, again fighting the urge to comfort him. "Will you help us?"

A taut pause. "What if we find him?"

"We'll have enough to convict him."

The young man's eyes were like black ice. "And you think that's enough."

"Enough isn't the question," Molly said. "Getting him off the street before he can hurt another Lilly is."

Luc challenged her a long moment in silence before the small sag in his shoulders betrayed his decision. "I will tell you about Lilly. The police who are canvassing the neighborhood will have cooperation. As long as they don't play games."

"This is too important." Molly wanted to reach out to him. Even that small a gap was inexcusable to a nurse who'd spent thirty years delivering bad news like a toxic stork. She didn't, though. Luc was not a toucher. So she nodded to Rhett, who stood quietly by. "This is Detective Butler, Mr. Trang. Would you talk to him?"

"What about Baitshop?" Luc asked. "Is she here?"

Molly admitted surprise. "You know Baitshop?"

Luc brightened a little. "You kidding? She's a legend in my neighborhood. You'll be there, too?"

"There's something else we need Molly to do first, Mr. Trang," Rhett said from where he was lounging in the corner of the room.

Molly looked up, surprised.

"Special Agent Kinstle needs you to go with her about another identification."

So much for hope. This was getting to be a good news/bad news joke. The good news was that their pattern was tumbling into place at light speed. The bad news was they had to wade through a morass of grief and rage to get to it.

"One more thing, Miss Burke," Luc said, a shadow of a smile touching his eyes. "My mother wanted me to tell you that she doesn't believe what they say about you on *Hard Copy*."

Molly stiffened like a burglar hearing sirens. "What did they say about me on *Hard Copy*?"

Luc was actively grinning now. "Why, that you're killing the people who show up in your backyard."

He was probably disappointed when she laughed in relief.

"So you didn't just come to share tea and hospital charts with me, huh?" Molly greeted Kathy when she finally made it out to find the agent by the bullpen coffeepot.

"Sure I did," Kathy said. "I also knew you'd want to share the next victim with me."

"Who?"

Kathy straightened and grabbed her coat. "The second skull. The homicide task force has already notified family. What I'd like to do is talk a bit more to the young woman in University City who did the ID."

Molly frowned. "Another devotee of the Mean Bean?"

"Evidently not. That's why we're headed up there. So far, they can't find any connection with South Grand."

Molly grabbed her coat and followed Kathy out the door.

The house was small, brick, and quaint, the kind of place indigenous to a college area. Bare wood floors and art show posters on the wall, overflowing bookcases and garage sale furniture. Incense coated the marijuana in the air, and half-burned candles cluttered the windows where two women had shared class schedules, love lives, and dreams.

Only one woman was present when Molly and Kathy showed up, a postgrad student named Petra, who studied at Washington University down the block. And she wasn't handling her friend's death well at all. Considering the fact that her friend hadn't even been reported missing yet, Molly wondered why.

"She always does this," the girl wailed, thick, kinky black hair bouncing in time with her words. A stick of energy, the girl tapped and swayed and blinked like a semaphore when she spoke. "And Jesus make me a garbageman if I'm supposed to let her parents know. 'Oh no, Dr. and Dr. Pierson. Amanda's around here someplace. I can't imagine what's keeping her.' Like, maybe sex with some Nicaraguan poli-sci major, or a tequila run to Tijuana. Shit, fuck, fratmonkeys, what am I going to tell them? 'Sorry, we misplaced Amanda for a minute or two, and now she's some guy's TV dinner'? Oh, yeah, that'll be fuckin' brilliant!"

Molly and Kathy had been there for ten minutes, and so far hadn't gotten more out than their identifications. As if she'd been waiting for that very thing to uncork her reaction, Petra Ojibma spewed outrage, astonishment, and annoyance at them like an out-of-control fire hose. And Molly and Kathy sat side by side on a brown corduroy couch and simply filtered out the bits they needed.

"Like I'm supposed to monitor all her flea-bitten, butt-brained friends and lovers. Motherscrew, I'd have to have a gig of memory in my hard drive just for her black book!"

"Which means you might not have known whether she'd gone down to South Grand for anything," Kathy ventured.

"South Grand? She hated South Grand. *Loathed* it. Called it pretentious, self-indulgent, self-abusers and losers with all the culture of yogurt. Art majors can be *such* assholes, ya know? She was doing her bit down on Washington and Grandel, supporting the cause, wallowing in all that bullshit meaning-of-life stew. No, Tijuana she'd goddrivel go to, but not fuckformed South Grand. Go fuckin' figure."

All Molly could figure was that she'd had too much Stoly and Petra had had way too little lithium for this conversation.

"Did she mention anybody named Kenny?" Kathy asked.

"Kenny?" Now Petra was adding cigarette smoke to the mix, puffing as if punishing the cigarette. "Kenny? Sure. Maybe. I mean, she just loved to shove her conquests in my face like rotten grapefruit, didn't she? But they were usually named Serge. Mario. *Illya.* Kenny's so fuckin' tame, I figured she was just yankin' me. She said she might try him for a difference—which meant, I guess, that he didn't bring a baseball bat to bed with him, ya know? Amanda couldn't get off without it, which I figure translates to dear old Mister Doctor playing house with his kid. You think?"

Molly didn't answer. "Did she ever describe Kenny to you?"

"Harmless. That's all she said about him." Petra gave a snort like an overheated horse and shoved open the window to let in a little subzero air. "She'd last ten fuckin' minutes with harmless."

"You didn't meet him?" Kathy asked.

"God, no . . . God, God, no. Not for me, thanks. I like one guy at a time, ya know? I'm not into mercy missions. Besides, that way I stay out of hospitals."

"She was in the hospital?"

A laugh, strident and tight. "Which time? I told you, she liked playing doctor. The real kind, where they had to stitch her up and try and convince her not to go back to that . . . oh, let's see, what's the term? Oh, yeah, 'nonproductive relationship.' Matter of fact, last time I saw her was when I drove her home—*again*—from the cracksnackin' hospital listening how this time was gonna be different because she thought she'd try this *nothin'* guy."

"How long ago was that?" Molly asked.

"Oh, shit, who knows? A couple o' weeks? She's been gone about that long I think. I don't know for sure really. I have other things on my fuckin' plate, and like I said, she's done it before."

They stayed another few minutes, but they didn't get much else. The cops had Amanda Pierson's address book, her class books, any scrap of paper they'd managed to vacuum from her room, and Petra had the Piersons to deal with.

As they were standing to leave, just for the hell of it, Molly smiled. "What's your major, Petra?"

Petra dragged a hand halfway through her tangle of hair where it got caught. She just stood there, impaled on herself. "Psychology."

Kathy kept her mouth shut until they were outside the building. "Too fuckin' cliché" was all she said.

Molly just laughed.

"Frank, this is a police station," Molly greeted him wearily when he breezed through the door of the interrogation room later that night.

"To which you're going to have to start paying room and board soon," Frank assured her with a glance around the littered, fuggy little room. "Contrary to popular opinion, St. Molly, earthly penance does not have to resemble actual hell."

Molly barely looked up from the notes she was making. "It didn't resemble anything more than a college cram room until you showed up, Frank. Now it's at least purgatory."

"Not quite."

She hadn't realized how hungry she was until he pulled out a bag from Steak n Shake and plopped it on the table. Molly actually felt dizzy from the temptation. "Oh, Frank . . ."

His laughter probably could have been heard down the block at the ME's office. "You know, I'd hoped you'd reserve that particular tone of voice for the first time you saw me naked."

"I have seen you naked," she scoffed, reaching for the bag with trembling hands.

"Splayed out on a hospital gurney with tubes in me and a hole the size of Iowa in my chest isn't what I had in mind," he mourned, and then reached over to pick up her tea. One good sniff had his eyes watering. "Still in the market for a good shrink, huh?"

Molly gave all her attention to the siren song wafting from the crinkled white bag on the table. "Good shrink is an oxymoron, Frank. I'm just trying to make the statistics taste better."

"Yeah, I know, Mol. I've drowned my share of statistics in my time. Here. Obviously these cops don't know what really makes you feel better."

And like a sleight-of-hand artist, he pulled out a tall, covered to-go cup.

"A shake?" she asked, nearly overwhelmed.

"Chocolate."

Molly sighed with all the pent-up anxiety of the day and almost cried. "Too bad we'd kill each other in a week if we actually lived together, Frank. I could almost offer to marry you for this."

Frank's grimace was artful. "Heaven help us both, Molly. Can you imagine my kids in your house or you putting up with my mother-in-law? I say we just visit in sin and share birthday parties."

Her mouth full of steakburger, Molly looked up to see that behind all that insouciance, Frank was making a real offer. And Molly, who had held him at arm's length for so long, stopped chewing.

"Why?" she asked.

Frank grinned. "Because I'm too old to play all those stupid courting games. Because airheads make me dizzy, and having to cross the cultural barrier between generations makes me exhausted. Because, somewhere in that rigidly button-down temple to survival you call a personality, I have a feeling rages a core of frivolity just aching to get free, and I'd like to see it happen." He shrugged, for the first time since Molly had known him, just a little self-conscious. "Because my kids like you."

Molly damn near choked on her burger. "I'm not sure I was looking for anything quite so involved, Frank. I was just feeling a little frumpy."

"You look a little frumpy," he agreed heartily. "In fact—"

Molly waved him off. "This is not the time to get enthusiastic on me, Frank."

"I don't keep coming back to your house because I like the neighborhood, Molly," he said, sounding amazingly sweet. Reaching over, he wiped a dribble of mustard that dotted the corner of Molly's mouth and proceeded to shatter the mood with a big, Frank grin. "Although I do admit I'd like visitation rights to that artwork . . ."

Molly chuckled, inordinately relieved that Frank had pulled back behind the lines. She was so tired, so frightened, so overwhelmed. And suddenly, sitting here in this scarred, cluttered little room that seeped futility and rage, she surprised herself with an urge to just curl up in Frank's lap and let him make her laugh. Let him . . .

Molly sucked in a breath and almost inhaled the second half of her burger. If there was one thing she was good at, it was compartmentalizing. And the illicit acts she'd just imagined had no place here. She had made use of interrogation rooms for fun before, but now just wasn't the time. So she settled for getting to her feet and leaning across the table to give Frank the kiss of his life, vodka, steakburger, mustard, relish, and all.

And briefly, before she clamped down everything but what she had to do, Molly admitted what she'd been denying herself all this time. Frank, the bastard, tasted damn good. He'd probably taste even better in bed. And one of these days she was going to find out.

"Thanks for the compliment, Frank," she said, and, still startled by her own impulsive action, sat down with a thump.

Fortunately, Frank understood impulse as well as Molly, and settled for a smug smile before settling back on his chair.

"So, what's the status with your friend?" he asked, stealing a couple of fries.

Molly licked her lips to reinforce that tiny moment of freedom and forced herself back to work. "We think we know who he was. Well, we know his name and his parents' names. We know he left the state a while back as Peter K. Wilson and came back as the ubiquitous Kenny, although he hasn't applied for any kind of official document that would show up in a computer under either name."

Frank sat, waiting for more. "You did take care of him, then?"

That quickly, the rest of the fun disappeared. For the first time in her life, even the hamburger lost its appeal. "I did," she said, her focus on the residue of Kenny's childhood that lay across the table. "Evidently, I tried to intervene on his behalf, and, as so often happens, failed miserably."

"Evidently."

Her smile was sad. "All he wants is for somebody to know he really exists. For years he's been manufacturing his own permanent fan club, but even he knows the difference. When he saw me somewhere, he figured he found an actual person he didn't have to chop up and eat to recognize him. Only, once again, he didn't have any luck. I can't remember him at all."

Frank stole a fry and chewed. "His instincts were still good, Molly. He picked a warrior saint to protect him."

Molly damn near cried. "Knock it off, Frank. I'm nothing of the kind."

Frank's answering smile was softer than she'd ever seen. "You're who I would have looked for at that age."

Again, Molly was struck silent. If she weren't such a damn good nurse, she wouldn't have caught it. Frank, after all, let less out than she did. But there it was anyway, a whiff of old, old, pain. A long-familiar blip on an otherwise normal screen.

"You needed somebody?" she asked quietly.

Frank's smile was brighter than ever, which just put Molly in mind of novas. "None of us are the way we are because of accident, St. Molly. We're all making up for something, even if we don't grow up to be warrior saints. My guess would be that your friend Kenny was never given another chance to grab the life preserver. Maybe if he'd hung on long enough, he would have found that strong male role model who could have pulled him out."

Molly absolutely gaped. "What are you talking about?"

She knew, of course. She just didn't think Frank would.

Frank did. She could see it way back in his eyes, no matter how brash his smile. "Don't tell me you haven't read Ressler, St. Molly of the Morgue. You told me yourself that you studied under him. He's the one who subscribes to the theory that a serial predator is made by the age of six, but if between the ages of eight and twelve the child can come into contact with a strong, positive male role model, he can be turned away from his anti-social behavior."

Molly was nodding. "He won't be normal, necessarily. A sociopath's still a sociopath. But he won't be a predator. Of course I know that, Frank. Why should you?"

Frank kept looking more and more delighted, as if Molly had discovered his talent for moneymaking. "Who was it who said, 'Know thyself'? Ressler's right. It's amazing what a difference it can make at that age if just one man thinks you're worth molding into another man."

Molly was breathless. She'd known Frank, certainly, understood his limitations and his strengths. She'd still never guessed at the real rot that lay in the shadows beneath the bright flame of his personality. Seeing Frank now in his shiny facade of brass and conspicuous consumption, it was almost impossible to imagine the kind of pale, trembling little boy who would need a defender. Who would be so trapped that he'd never made it completely away.

She couldn't reach out to him. He'd bolt like a spooked horse. She couldn't share her understanding in any kind of concrete way. All she could offer him, in the end, was a concession.

"I wonder if this means there's still hope for Patrick."

Frank's grin was brash. "Well, he'll never be as handsome as I am."

"No one is, Frank. No one is."

That made him even happier. "Speaking of incorrigible delinquents," he said, literally and figuratively leaning back. "How is the demon spawn today? Write any good jail poetry?"

Molly sucked in an unsteady breath, hid behind a couple good hits on her shake, and let Frank lead the subject safely away. "He's at Sam's. I'm waiting to talk to his father, but I have a feeling the family housekeeper has tipped off the perpetrators and given them the chance to hide behind a wall of Chinese obscurity."

Frank's frown was real. "I know a good Jesuit we can inflict him on."

Molly shook her head. "He had the Jesuits. They gave him back."

"Smart priests." He grinned, but Molly saw little humor. "You know he's headed for big trouble, don't you, Mol?"

She sighed, forgot her milkshake. "I know. Am I too naïve to think that Sam and I can at least keep him from felony first class while he's here?"

Frank shrugged. "I don't know. Sam does seem to gentle him somehow. And he came to you for a reason."

Molly's smile was wry. "He showed up for the same reason you do. My artwork. He has been better since the arrest, though. Maybe he just needed somebody to put a foot down."

"You mean somebody to give a damn, don't you, St. Molly?"

Molly understood every nuance of that statement and ignored them all. She looked at her steakburger, but couldn't actually pick it up. She reached for her teacup, only to realize she was out of Stoly again. God, she thought, trying like hell to hide her shakes from Frank, she wasn't going to make it much longer.

And what was even worse, she'd forgotten how to anticipate the quiet time after Christmas. All she could see was this cluttered, dismal room and Patrick's hostile eyes.

I can't do this, Frank, she wanted to say. I can't keep digging into my past, just to remind myself of every failure I've ever committed, every mistake I've made. Every loss I've suffered. Isn't Christmas bad enough without rubbing my face in everything I've given away over the years?

Tears, she thought in terrible amazement. I'm going to goddamn well cry if I don't stop this. And I'm going to do it in front of Frank Patterson, God help me.

"What else do you have to do here before you're ready to go home?" Frank asked as if he'd heard her.

Molly looked up to see him lounging complacently across from her nibbling on another of her fries. "You're not going to start following me around again, Frank," she warned with a scowl. "You still look about as healthy as Rasputin pulling himself out of the Volga, and you have kids to think about. Besides, aren't there Christmas parties to go to or something?"

"I only go to Christmas parties to make business contacts, Molly. And nobody wants to trust a lawyer who looks like he lost."

The reason Molly knew it wasn't Rhett barging in on them was because he didn't knock. Instead it was Baitshop, who looked as pulled and drawn as the rest of them, her attire at this time of night an academy sweatshirt and baggy jeans. "We have news . . . well, hi there. You're new on the force. You come to make my life happy?"

Frank was already on his feet. No matter how thankful she was for the diversion, Molly offered a huge scowl. "Baitshop, this is Frank Patterson. To be safe, don't touch without proper protection. That being a whip and a chair."

"Who wants safe?" Baitshop demanded, already having succumbed to the Patterson pirate smile.

"You want to impart something?" Molly asked. "Or simply bask in the glow of Frank's charisma?"

"Let her bask," Frank said, taking hold of Baitshop's hand as if he were asking her to dance. "It's my small contribution to the war effort."

Molly just put her head down on the table.

"I have bad news," Baitshop said, blinking like a photo op survivor.

Molly's head came up. She would have been furious if the look on Baitshop's face didn't want to make her laugh. "Sometime today would be nice."

Baitshop blinked a couple more times. "Uh-huh. Well, I'm afraid our two favorite suspects have washed out. You know, Lewis Picarkie—whatever, the guy in the morgue. And Allen the bagboy. Lewis's folder of weirdness looks like it goes back to birth right here in town under his own name. He lived in North County, by the way. And, uh, Allen . . ."

"Stop stroking her wrist, Frank," Molly suggested drily. "She's losing oxygen. Allen the bagboy?"

"Yeah. Has alibis. Davidson wants you to start looking further . . . uh, afield."

Instinctively Molly reached for her tea, only to remember its deficiencies. She reached for the chocolate shake instead. They were back on square one. Dead center on whom she knew. Whom she'd known and forgotten.

"Thanks, Baitshop," she said and fought another round of nausea as she turned back to her folders and lists.

With a snap, the young officer pulled herself out of Frank's range and wiped her hand on her jean leg. "Davidson also wanted me to tell you that even though those two are off the hook for baggin' body parts, he's still eyein' 'em for the man with the timer switch. He has DNA off those threatening notes, and he plans on matching it somewhere. But considering all the people you pissed off, he can't narrow it down yet. Which means we're left holding our dicks in our hands looking for a place to piss." That quickly she grinned, a cop still very high on her job. "Wish my life was as exciting as yours, Molly."

Her eyes on those damn lists, Molly actually laughed. "Anytime, Baitshop. Anytime."

Baitshop left, and Molly stared at the stuff on her desk.

"Get your things together, St. Molly," Frank said, smoothing down his gray Icelandic sweater. "I'll carry your schoolbooks home."

Molly sighed. "I'm never going home, Frank. Not till this makes sense."

"Explain it to me on the way."

Molly couldn't move. So Frank walked around the table, tucked his hands beneath her arms and lifted.

"Stop that," she snapped, pulled out of her paralysis, just like he knew she would. "You just got out of the hospital."

The son of a bitch tweaked her nose. "Then get moving. You're going home. And you're going to tell me what you know. It'll help. I promise."

"It'll end up on *Jerry Springer.*"

Frank's smile was salacious as he gathered up the folders she'd just spread. "I'm holding out for Barbara Walters. Now, come on. Tell me what you're thinking."

By the time Molly could actually manage forward momentum or thought, Frank had everything under his arm. Molly sighed and picked up her jacket. "You know way too much already, ya know."

"I know."

She slung her purse and climbed slowly to her feet. "And somebody's sure to point out the fact that a serial killer's second favorite pastime is making sure he's in on the investigation."

Frank held out an arm. "You said it yourself, St. Molly. I'm despicable. Not malevolent. Spill it."

Molly headed out the door as if she were on her way to hell and sighed. "We have three ID'd victims. Two of them spoke of a Kenny. Two of them were last seen in the South Grand area. Problem is, they're not the same two."

"You sure you're working on the right common denominator?"

"What, South Grand? Yeah, it fits the profile."

"What about the gal who didn't go there? She know Kenny?"

Molly sighed. "Yes. At least that's what her friend said, but I'll bet my Picasso that somehow she ended up down there anyway."

"Anything else show up more than once in your files?"

"No, and we looked. Completely different backgrounds, lifestyles, friends, and family. Only the fact that they tended to fall into higher-risk categories united them. Crystal was a chronic runaway, Lilly was hidden in a community that refused to contact the police, and Amanda preferred her dates rough. Then, of course, there's the fact that with all the manpower out on the street asking questions, not one other person in these women's lives remembered ever seeing a Kenny. It's like he's—"

Frank said it for her. "Invisible."

"But he shouldn't be," Molly insisted, rubbing at her gritty eyes before she remembered that she still had salt on her fingers from the fries. "He has keloid scarring around his shoulder and back from early injuries, and that's unusual in a white guy. People would remember. It raises a welt, like a red leech sitting on your skin, and he . . ."

Molly slammed to a halt six inches into the hallway and didn't even feel Frank rear end her with her own pile of paperwork.

Something.

Something . . .

"Yoo hoo," Frank nudged gently. "You channeling Miss Marple in there or something?"

Molly squeezed her stinging eyes shut, her hands clenched, her memory flighty. She was so goddamn tired, so completely washed out and frantic. And suddenly she couldn't breathe, as if the rest of her statement were caught in her chest and she couldn't free it. The room was so silent, Frank's breathing like a quiet wash on some shore somewhere.

It was the keloid scarring that suddenly set her mental slot machine spinning. Maybe because Frank had shaken up her brain cells. Maybe because she'd been forced to jettison Lewis and Allen from the suspect pool. Maybe it was just the time for it to make sense.

Whatever it was, it was something she should have known all along. Something right in front of her eyes.

"Molly?"

Her breath all but whistling past the terrible constriction in her chest, Molly grabbed the interview folders out of Frank's hands and stalked back into the interrogation room. The slots had clicked into place. Three girls all in a line. Three girls united by their lack of discretion. Their susceptibility to a harmless-looking guy.

And maybe one other thing.

Molly ran a quick eye over Crystal's notes, and then

turned to the homicide team's initial interview with Petra about Amanda. She looked for what she thought she'd find, and damned if she didn't find it.

Suddenly, she really couldn't breathe. Could it be that easy? Could it be that obscene? She pulled out Lilly Trang's file, however, and came up empty.

"I have to call Luc Trang," she said, checking her watch as she bolted out the door.

If they hadn't had a sea of reporters outside feeding public frenzy, the homicide floor would have been all but empty at this time of night. Instead, there were cops on half the phones, and pictures and graphs decorating blackboards and walls. Molly found Baitshop hunched with Rhett by the back of the room.

"I need to talk to you," Molly said, interview in hand as she bore down on them, Frank hot on her heels.

Rhett looked up, eyes bloodshot and hair fingered into dreadlocks. "Oh, hi, Frank. You joining the force?"

"You don't pay enough," Frank assured him.

Molly scowled. "Rhett!"

Rhett blinked again. "I should be having sex right now, ya know. Hot, nasty, sweaty sex. The kind you should have with a blindfold on because you're just so embarrassed you're doing what you're doing. Since I'm not getting that, though, go ahead and tell me what you want."

It was a measure of how distracted they all were that nobody mentioned how out of character Rhett sounded.

"Did Luc Trang mention anything about his sister being sick or injured recently?" Molly demanded instead. "There's nothing about it in the interview."

Rhett blinked a couple times. "Don't think so. Baitshop?"

Baitshop shook her head.

"I need a number to call him," Molly said.

Rhett laughed. "You kidding? It's damn near one o'clock. He's doin' business. Try his beeper."

Molly tried his beeper. He called back within five minutes.

By the time she hung up again, Molly's hands were sweaty. They'd been right and they'd been wrong. South

Grand was important. It was probably where Kenny lived. The problem was, it wasn't where he'd been casting his web.

Molly stood ten feet from the victim photos that had been taped to the wall and simply stared at them.

"Molly?" Baitshop asked quietly.

"Amanda Pierson wouldn't be caught dead in South Grand," Molly said.

"Well, that's what Petra said, of course."

"And yet Amanda met Kenny."

Baitshop was getting quieter. "Yes?"

Molly nodded. "I know where."

That even brought Rhett to attention. "Molly?"

She looked up at them, certain now. Sick and afraid and ashamed, because she hadn't seen it sooner. "He isn't picking his women on the street at South Grand," she said. "That's just where he's hauling them in. He's making his selections at work."

A dark call room. The uncomfortable feeling of being watched. Being touched. Molly wanted to vomit.

"I know who Kenny is."

It was so easy, really.

Too easy.

She saw Kenny coming and she sneered. She stood there in the parking garage and she sneered like he was nothing.

"Hello, Marianne," he said, smiling.

Nobody ever pays attention to a man who's smiling.

"What do you want?" she asked, too busy looking in her little mirror to see the knife.

Until Kenny had it at her throat.

He usually didn't do it like that. He was usually so much more subtle.

She smelled just right, though. Panicky all of a sudden.

She peed in her pants. Kenny saw it running down her leg, her eyes wide, her head shaking like Katharine Hepburn.

"I bet you know where you're going," Kenny smiled, and then smiled again.

And this smile she didn't ignore.

She started to cry, big sobbing gulps nobody would hear, and suddenly she isn't so pretty as she thought anymore.

Oh, this will be the best, because she already smells afraid, and he hasn't even started yet.

i did it oh, i did it
I followed her
smelling   her   hair,
hearing her breath
I hid in the dark where
she didn't see me
stupid bitch
and i jumped her

EIGHTEEN

Molly might as well have lobbed a mortar round straight into the center of the room.

"Who is it?" Davidson demanded, on his feet.

"How do you know?" Baitshop asked.

"The keloid scarring," Molly said. "I've seen it. I've seen *him*. And they're right. He's completely forgettable." She couldn't seem to stop shaking. "Unless, of course, you happen to set him to stuttering. I should have connected it sooner, but his hospital record wasn't that bad yet. He didn't show up anywhere, and I just got focused on Lewis and Allen, ya know? I mean, it was so much easier that way."

Certainly easier than suspecting someone to whom you've entrusted your patients.

A forgettable nonentity you just wanted to ignore.

A shy, stumbling man with earnest eyes.

She was going to vomit all over Sergeant Davidson's shoes. She should warn him, she guessed.

"His name is John Martin," she said, closing her eyes against the surge of nausea. "He's been working at Grace Hospital. He'd been hired for maintenance and then cross-trained to do patient care—I'd bet my ass without anybody rechecking all his references and qualifications."

"Grace?" Rhett asked, hushed.

"You're sure?" one of the other cops demanded.

Molly nodded. "I got the key from Luc Trang. He didn't tell you that his sister had been in the hospital just a while before she disappeared. She'd had an abortion and developed complications. She was at Grace. So were Crystal and Amanda. I think John took care of them, and then used his hospital ID to get access to their personal information. Then he just picked his victims and lured them back down to his neighborhood. After all, the women referred to him as harmless. It wouldn't have been tough."

"Do you know whether he'd be working now?" Rhett asked.

Molly checked her watch. "I'll find out."

"Keloid," one of the detectives said. "What is that?"

Molly pulled out a couple of Kenny's old charts. "The scars are easily identifiable," she said. "Like red ropes. The problem is going to be matching Peter Wilson with John Martin."

"No sweat. We'll do a local and national search. We'll get another warrant for hospital charts of anybody else on our missing persons list. See if his name shows up. . . . Bait-shop?"

"I'm on it," she said.

"If we can do that, we can get a search warrant for his house. And if you and that fibbie are right, that's where we'll find all the rest of the evidence we need."

Molly reached for Rhett's phone and dialed the hospital.

"Bert?" Molly greeted the night supervisor. "This is Molly Burke, from emergency. Could you check for me and see if John Martin might be on tonight?"

"John Martin? What's up, Molly? You want to kick him again?"

Molly froze. "I beg your pardon?"

"Okay, so the guy's almost useless. But do you know how short-staffed we're getting because we keep losing those damn housekeeping people? He was at least willing to stick it out."

"Bert, you're not making sense. What did I do to John?"

"You got him fired, honey. That's what you did."

Molly wasn't sure how, but suddenly she was sitting down. "How did I do that?"

"The report you made about his drinking on duty. You and that bitch supervisor of yours. It was a final straw. He'd been pulled in before, ya know."

Molly shut her eyes, sure she was going to throw up. "Great."

"Yeah, no shit. He wasn't so bad. And now I'm scrambling to cover some of his shifts."

After that, there just wasn't much to say. Molly hung up and stared at the phone. Things were about to get worse in ways they hadn't even anticipated, and Molly knew without a doubt that Kenny would hold her responsible.

"This asshole really is invisible," one of the detectives said behind her. "He doesn't come up anywhere. Not even a driver's license."

"No big surprise," Rhett offered, enlightened as he was with information from Molly's books. "He probably rides the bus. It'd fit the profile."

"Well, good," the guy said. "We can just wait for the little wanker at the hospital bus stop, can't we?"

Well, Molly thought bleakly, you don't get a better cue than that. "Not tonight, you can't."

"He's not on, huh? When's his next shift?"

She was feeling worse by the minute. "From the gist of the conversation I just had, when hell freezes over. He was fired for being drunk on duty."

And she'd been the one to get him fired. The one person in the world he seemed to think would protect him. If ever there was a definition of a precipitating event, that was it.

To his way of thinking, Molly had betrayed him. She might have been able to deny responsibility for the girls who'd already died. She had a feeling that that had just changed.

"You might want to call Kathy," she suggested, battening down her own urge to hurry. To run in any direction just to move before it was too late. It was probably too late already, and there wasn't a damn thing she could do but keep going so they could catch him for good. So she could betray him one final time. "Kathy would have a good idea how to proceed so that by the time we toss his house we can bring him down in one try."

So they could betray him again. How could she possibly feel elated and ashamed at the same time?

One of the detectives peeled off like a fighter jet after Jeeps. Davidson, his tie pulled and his hands in his pockets, paced a short track around the partitions. "We need to put a description out for the guys canvassing South Grand. Molly, can you get us a likeness?" He didn't even wait for her answer before hitting the next corner. "We also need an address. We can at least keep a close eye on him till the info comes in."

"No phone, no license," a chunky redhead provided.

Molly checked her watch again. The cops would, in the end, get John's address. Molly could just get it quicker. Picking up the phone, she dialed Grace and asked for the other night supervisor.

"Clare, I have an emergency," Molly said. "I know this isn't kosher, but I need John Martin's address . . ."

"This have something to do with his being fired?" Clare asked.

"It has everything to do with it. Please?"

There was a pause, and then Clare put her on hold. Molly held her breath. Behind her, Frank stirred.

"Too bad I can't get this guy my card first," he said with that predatory grin of his. "What a cherry case this'd be."

"You don't do criminal law, Frank," Molly reminded him drily.

"It'd be worth it to try."

Molly would have been happy to dispel that particular fantasy, but Clare made it back on the line. "You be careful with this, hon," she said. "Johnny gives me the creeps, and he was pissed when he walked."

"I promise."

"Okay, here it is."

Molly wrote down the address with a growing sense of fatalism. Another nail in the coffin. Another piece of circumstantial evidence that would convict Kenny anywhere but in a court of law.

"Thanks, Clare," she said. "And I'd really appreciate it if you'd keep this to yourself for now, okay?"

"This doesn't have something to do with the news trucks that have been circling the hospital for the last few days, does it?"

"It has to do with my getting him fired" was all Molly said. "Thanks, Clare. I owe you."

Molly handed off the address, and the head guy whistled. "So he lives on Juniata. Dead center in the ten ring of South Grand. I think we have a winner, folks. Let's get this asshole."

Two more detectives peeled off for the phones. Molly took time with the Identi-kit to construct as close a likeness as she could to a basically forgettable face, and then, giving in to the inevitable, let Frank help her on with her coat.

"And now, fellow babies," she said. "I'm going home to bed."

"We're going to need you to help us go through the other hospital charts when we get 'em," the head guy said.

Molly nodded. "Call me when you do. Right now, I have a nephew to see to and a dog to feed. Besides, if I don't show up at least once tonight, the camera crews are going to come looking for me, and you don't need them asking tricky questions right now."

"Just make sure you don't detour down to Juniata on your way home," Rhett suggested drily. "He probably knows what your car looks like."

"I bet he knows what your cars look like, too," she retorted, and then shook her head. "It is a temptation, though, isn't it? We're so close."

Ambivalence at its finest. She could find the answer, end the terror.

It would mean confronting the biggest failure in her life. It would mean facing Kenny and finally seeing for herself the end score of The Game.

"We think we're close," Davidson amended.

"Trust me," Molly said, turning for home. "I'm never wrong about guilt-inducing traumas. We're close."

As much as Molly kept trying to push Frank to arm's length for his own safety, she had to admit that she appreciated his undemanding company as they walked out of the police station into the frigid night air at the edge of downtown. The lights flattened a cloudy sky, and off in the distance, the arch light blinked. Uplink trucks took up much of the city hall parking lot across the street, with a few hardy souls still awake. They must have caught sight of Molly, because a couple of people tumbled out of truck doors and began to sprint. Luckily, Frank was faster.

"So that's why you came by," Molly said with a weary grin as they made the Medical Examiner parking lot half a block ahead of their pursuers. "You're showing off again."

He hit his car starter, and the brand-new candy-apple red BMW purred to life without a hitch. "You want a ride? Bogies closing fast at three o'clock."

"My car's fast enough, Frank," she said, sliding the key into her scratched and dinged faded red door. "But thanks anyway. Now, go home before something else happens to you."

She'd just locked her doors when she caught a movement in the shadows at the edge of the parking lot. She froze in place. It was somebody out to get a smoke, she thought briskly. A news guy watching the back door.

Even so, it took a full minute to regain enough coordination to flip on her headlights. By then, she could hear feet pounding onto the asphalt from the street. She saw the form at the edge of her lights.

He moved. Molly saw the sloppy posture, the lank hair, the fatuous smile. And she saw that he was waiting, there in the shadows, for one of the newsmen to come to him.

Molly almost choked on her surprised laughter. So that was where at least one leak was coming from. She couldn't be happier. She wished Lewis fame and fortune and the sharp edge of Winnie's tongue. And then she backed out, her hands so sweaty she almost missed a gear.

Frank followed her home, just because Molly had asked him not to, but he did have the sense not to face the other gauntlet. Molly did that alone to finally reach an empty house and whining dog.

She hated this house. But, oddly enough, with the reporters swarming over the rest of the city like red ants, she was beginning to look forward to at least the peace here. The cool silence of stability.

God, she thought in distress as she poured out Magnum's food and let him out in time to chase off a couple of cameramen. I am getting old. I'm even getting too tired for mutiny.

Maybe, she thought, eyeing the bottle of Stoly she'd left on the sink, I'm just at the numb level. Sensory and emotional overload, like the latter days in Pleiku. She'd simply reached critical mass and refused to react anymore.

Which meant, she realized as she turned for the phone, that she'd just react to them later.

Look for a goddamn shrink she wrote on the scratch pad next to the receiver.

The answering machine was blinking. What a surprise. Undoubtedly Ted Koppel and Geraldo Rivera and more tabloids than she knew existed wanting the details of her secret satanic relationship with the Missouri Muncher.

Since Patrick had been here, he'd taken to wiping off the machine, jotting down any pertinent messages. A small favor, but one Molly appreciated. She would have appreciated it tonight. Putting the teapot on to boil, she hit the replay and waited.

"Oh, hi . . ." Girl's voice. Breathy. Sweet. "Paddy? Is that you? It's Tracy. I've missed you."

Molly's eyes widened. Really.

She got through three more demands for interviews, two having to do with Patrick's contretemps with the cops, before she got her second surprise.

"Hey, man, this is Scott. You comin' over or what? Amber's here and we're headin' for some action. Ya know?"

There were three others, people Molly didn't even realize Patrick knew. She was going to have to ask. Pry in Patrick's affairs even more and see if these were people she should worry about. She was pulling out a mug when the last message beeped.

"Uh . . . hello . . . are you . . . are you there . . . ?" Molly spun around, the mug shattering on the floor. "Just checking in, Pat. I haven't talked to you in a while."

Molly froze. She'd just said she couldn't take any more. Stupid, stupid her.

Suddenly, she remembered what she should have seen. What she'd put down to wishful thinking.

It hadn't been. My God, oh God, it hadn't been.

He's real handsome now, isn't he? Real smart.

She'd thought Kenny had just made his assumptions about Patrick after seeing him on the news. Maybe in the distance as he'd waited to plant his bones. But he hadn't. He'd known because he'd talked to Patrick. The hang-ups on her answering machine hadn't all been the press. They'd been Kenny looking for somebody to talk to.

Evidently he'd found somebody.

Molly stumbled over the broken crockery to get to her phone.

"Homicide," Rhett answered on the second ring. "Detective—"

"Rhett?" Molly interrupted frantically. "He's been calling here. He's been fucking *calling* here!"

"What?"

"Kenny. He's been talking to Patrick. I've got to get over to Sam's and find out about it, but I'm telling you I've got Kenny on my goddamn answering machine!"

"I'll be right there."

"Don't be stupid. I have the Super Bowl of videocams out here. I'll call you from Sam's."

Molly barely got the phone hung up before spinning for the door, her heart hammering, her palms sweaty. She realized she was running when she got a look at the reporters doing recon at her fence edge. Deliberately, slowly, she opened the gate and yelled to them that she was going to visit her friend and leave the old guy alone, please. Then, as if that was really what she was doing, she knocked on Sam's back door.

"I didn't know!" Patrick cried, standing in Sam's bazaar-decorated living room like an innocent at a witch hunt. "My God, Aunt Molly, *he's* the guy who's been . . . he's been leaving those *eyeballs*? *That's* who John is?"

Molly stood nose to nose with him, shaking as hard as he. As frightened, more outraged. Even more unsure. "How long has he been calling you?"

Patrick threw off a shrug like a wrestling move. "I don't know! I've only talked to him a few times. He seemed . . . I don't know . . ."

If he said harmless, Molly was going to have to kill him.

"What did he talk about? What did you say?"

Sam took her by the arm. *"Taibeleh*, hush. You're both screeching like owls. That won't settle anything."

"Settle?" Molly screeched at him. "This isn't about settling, Sam! That bastard's been calling my nephew. My God!" She actually had tears in her eyes, she was that furious. "He's been insinuating himself into my house like one of the family!"

"Shush, shush," he soothed, guiding her to a couch, settling Patrick a safe distance away. "Calm down and maybe Patrick can offer you something you need. He didn't know who the man was."

"I'll tell you anything, Aunt Molly," Patrick offered, his posture as rigid as an embassy guard's. "But he didn't . . . you know, say anything. Certainly nothing that made me think he was a serial killer, for God sakes. Don't you think I would have told you?"

Molly struggled for sanity. She just didn't know what she thought anymore. Except that she just wanted to stay in Sam's house, with its comfortable furniture and capricious, gypsy-caravan decor. Forget serial killers and marginal teens.

She just wanted to curl up amid those ugly tchotchkes and
bright silk pillows like Alice at the end of a long day in the
rabbit hole and sleep.

"Has he been here?" she asked. "Have you met him?"

"No. Only over the phone. I told you."

"Tell me again."

"I mean it," Patrick said, leaning closer. "I'll tell you every
word I remember. I know I've disappointed you, Aunt Molly.
I know I've hurt Sam, but I swear I never meant to!"

He was the picture of anguish, self-condemnation. A week
ago, Molly would have hurt for him. Now, she was afraid.

"Then tell me," she demanded.

He couldn't seem to meet her eyes. "John never said who
he was or I would have told you. I'm sorry. I really am sorry.
I'll do anything to make it up to you."

Molly looked at his impatient hands and fought the urge to
hold them. She was so damn tired. So pulled and frightened
and outraged. And she was most afraid that she just couldn't
trust Patrick's promises anymore.

"I have to call Officer Butler," she said, winding her fingers together to keep them still. "I want you to tell him everything you know. And I want the truth."

Patrick looked up, his mouth open for rebuttal. Molly
didn't say a word. She saw the flush that shot up his neck and
wondered what he really wanted to say.

"Okay," was what he did say. "Whatever you want."

They talked for at least a couple of hours, and in the end,
Molly knew nothing more than she had before. Kenny—
John—Peter had simply told Patrick about work, about know-
ing Molly. He'd asked Patrick about himself. They'd never met.
They'd never planned to meet. It had begun as a call about a pa-
tient Molly had seen and continued in complacent friendship.

"What patient?" Molly asked her suddenly tongue-tied
nephew. "You didn't tell me."

Another shrug, Patrick's only currency tonight. "I . . . he
said not to worry about it. That he'd catch you at work. I
thought . . . I thought he did."

Molly called Rhett with the information and made Patrick

sit down and write out every word he could remember. And while he was writing it out, Molly fell asleep on the big red sofa under an afghan of orange and green squares as if nothing else mattered.

"We've got him!" Rhett crowed the next afternoon when he slammed into the Grace medical records room where Molly was scanning charts.

She shoved the hair out of her eyes and blinked up at him, dazed and confused even before the morning she'd spent culling information about the women who'd had the misfortune to step straight from Grace Hospital to the missing persons file.

Nine matches so far. Five who had notations in John's hand. Other cases would have to be compared to his schedule and workload to see if he had proximity.

"You have him how?" she asked. "I'm not finished here yet."

Rhett beamed like the only kid in class to get the answer right. "Peter Kenneth Wilson, aka John Martin. Shows up on the rolls of the justice hit list first time at the tender age of seventeen, when he still appeared as Peter K. Wilson. In Akron, Ohio. Assault, weenie wagging, possible arson. Most of them settled, pled out, or arranged for psych counseling and probation. Worked his way up to a sexual assault and battery by twenty-two. Did eighteen months of a three-to-five. Model prisoner."

Molly rubbed at her eyes and wished Rhett were as sensible as Frank and had brought her food. Maybe she'd go out for it while Rhett continued reciting the life and times of Peter K. Wilson like epic poetry. Hamburgers. Cheeseburgers. Bacon cheeseburgers with fries and onion rings.

For the second time in her life, the thought of food didn't soothe her. That unnerved her almost as much as the brand-new wiretap on her phone to catch Kenny. Kenny who hadn't called again since.

"Oh, yeah, and I forgot," Rhett said. "Before the felony count, what do you think shows up?" Rhett asked, grinning.

Molly rubbed her eyes. "An attempt at the Army."

Rhett whistled. "You *are* good. Did a year, less than honorable discharge, alcohol, drugs, and psych problems noted. Did his felony stint at the Ohio farm system and then disappeared off the face of the earth as if he'd never been born."

"And then popped back up as John Martin?"

Suddenly Rhett looked unhappy. "In Cincinnati. Unfortunately, he didn't do that for five more years. I have a bad feeling we have another alias somewhere with a body count attached. We've already apprised both Akron and Cincinnati that they'd better start rechecking all their missing girls. You can imagine how popular we are with them."

"What about his parents?"

"Divorced, father dead, mother relocated. We're still trying to track her down. No living sibs."

"And Kenny has a record as John?"

"Of course. Theft, assault, possible sexual assault, the last at the hospital where he worked in Cincy. Nice, huh?"

Molly just shrugged. "Just the history *I'd* want in a guy I let loose around patients. It's enough to bring him in for questioning. Is it enough for a search warrant?"

"It is if you have some hits for us."

Molly looked down at the charts she'd set aside. Records of dead women who'd put their trust in her hospital and lost. "Five definites. I'll have to dig for the other four. That good enough?"

Rhett gave her a smacking kiss on the top of the head. "That is so good enough you're my hero. Wanna go watch?"

Molly squinted up at him. "The search warrant?"

Rhett nodded like a puppy. "After this it should take about an hour to put it together. The plan is to pick him up, turn that house over like a scene from *Twister*, and hold a news conference right in front as haz mat hauls the blue barrels with the Soilex and hydrochloric acid out the back door."

"Can I sit back in one of the cars?" she asked. "I don't want him to know I'm involved yet."

Since she already knew how he would feel about it. Since

she'd spent the night before dreaming of Nam and Johnny and Lilly Trang.

Rhett looked a little bemused, but he dropped her another kiss. "You're the monster killer, you know, Molly."

Molly sighed and got to her feet. "Remind me of that when I'm spending my hard-earned money getting my nephew counseling because he was chatted up by a serial killer."

Rhett helped Molly store the hospital records back in the box, collected the ones they would use, and helped her sign them out as they left. "Patrick's that upset, huh?"

Molly shook her head. "The minute he finished talking to you, he clammed up like a Mafia witness and hasn't said a word since. Not even to Sam. I'm really worried."

Rhett chuckled. "Aw, heck, Molly. He's a teenager. Give him one interview on Larry King and he'll be right back in form."

He might have been if his father hadn't finally called back. If it had been Molly listening to the frosty disapproval that man had dumped on his son's head, she would have hung up a lot faster than Patrick had.

Molly and Rhett were heading out the emergency door when Sasha intercepted them. "Well," she said drily. "There are my two favorite people. I hear you've been having assignations down in medical records."

Molly damn near fell down when Rhett gave Sasha a kiss, too. Only it wasn't the same kind of kiss he'd given Molly. Not the same at all. "You're just jealous," he assured the blonde, his hand still on her ass.

Sasha scowled. "I'm frustrated," she said. "All that leather and whipped cream, and nobody to use it on."

Molly simply shut her eyes and walked past. A serial killer who dismembered his victims was one thing. This was way too weird for words.

"Molly," Sasha said. "Before you blush yourself into unconsciousness. Did Nancy find you? She heard you were here and went off like a crusader in search of Moors."

"It's been me and the records kids all day," Molly said. "Do you know what she wanted?"

"Yeah. Something about a kid both of you saw? Little 'life basketball' by the name of David?"

"Life basketball" being Sasha's quaint term for the kids who got slam-dunked on a regular basis. It took Molly a minute to make the connection. When she did, it wasn't pleasant. A small, thin, pale specter of a child with the eyes of inevitability. A soccer player. The latest contestant to sign in for The Game.

"Yeah?" Molly asked, not surprised that her voice sounded sharp. The very last thing she needed to hear today was that David had come in dead or in handcuffs.

Sasha surreptitiously popped one of Rhett's shirt buttons with a perfectly manicured nail. "Nancy wanted you to know that she won. That the kid's been pulled from the home and placed in a good foster house. Evidently she went there herself to check it out."

Molly stared as if waiting for Sasha to translate. "You're kidding."

Sasha shrugged. "If I remember correctly, sometimes youthful idealism actually can produce results. Not that I've tried, mind you. But I think I've read about it once or twice."

"Yeah." Molly wasn't sure whether she felt better or worse. She didn't know whether she dared hope David could have the chance to get a hold on that life preserver and find a good man to haul him to adulthood.

Oh, what the hell? She didn't have anything else to hope for right now.

"Tell her I'm proud of her. And I'll listen more next time."

Sasha stared with some astonishment. "She's getting delusional now, little Butler. Get her back into the real world before she forgets what it looks like."

Rhett crooked an arm as if he were leading Molly to a cotillion. She deliberately refused to notice the gap in his otherwise pristine shirt. "I think I can find you some leather, Detective Butler."

Half an hour later Molly found herself sitting in the backseat of a black Crown Vic listening to Davidson and another cop tell her that evidently a ghost had been sending her notes and blowing up her friends' cars. They told her that the parts to the car bomb had been bought at Radio Shack, which meant it could have been anyone, up to and including the Mafia, who liked reliable technology as much as anybody, and that of all the people they'd interviewed, only Latesha Wilson's mother had expressed enough of a desire to really do away with Molly. The problem was, Mrs. Wilson wouldn't have been able to wire a bomb if her next welfare check depended on it, and besides, some press asshole would have noticed a skinny-ass black woman trying to get under the car.

Molly didn't even bother to thank them for their diligence. She just watched as the rest of the team swept up the quiet street and skidded to a choreographed halt in front of Kenny's house like a synchronized arrest team. The neighborhood was old, sedate, and marginal, a checkerboard of rehab and old stability and overburdened boardinghouses. Comfortable square brick houses marched along the street like stolid soldiers, with postage stamp yards and mature trees that would soften all those unrelenting facades come spring.

Kenny's house was as unprepossessing as he. Square, solid, with a thick concrete porch and carefully clipped yard, leaves raked and sidewalk cleaned. An anonymous face among all the other anonymous faces, with nothing to mark it as the place that harbored atrocities.

The first wave of invasion consisted of the detectives, who marched up to that nondescript porch alongside Kathy like the Magnificent Seven in their blue jackets with POLICE emblazoned on the back. A few patrol officers supported them by marking the borders of the yard and keeping away the neighbors, who even now peeked from cracked doors.

Molly watched them mount the stairs. She waited as a few circled to secure the back, and then as they knocked, polite as Mormons on a mission, at the front door. She held her breath, waiting for Kenny to appear. For it to be real.

She waited and nothing happened. Somehow, with all

their watching, they had reached the house to find that Kenny wasn't home.

One of the uniforms provided the battering ram, and they took down the front door just as reinforcements arrived. More cars, more lights, more uniforms. More neighbors, now out on lawns. One with a videocam, preserving it all for his shot at national exposure.

Molly waited, not even realizing that the other two officers in the car were as deathly silent as she, and she prayed.

Evidently she prayed for the wrong thing. Rhett walked back out of the house, his Kevlar vest looking oddly grown up on him, and he stalked over to the car.

Molly rolled down her window.

"Nothing," he said simply. "They're tearing the place apart, and there isn't a fucking thing in there."

"That's impossible," Molly protested, as if that could make all the difference.

"You wanna come look?"

Molly knew it was a rhetorical question. Even so, she stepped out of the car and followed him into the house. And found, just as the team had found before her, that the house was neat, old, doilied, and well cared for. And completely empty of anything that might lead them to where Kenny might be really doing his business.

"Take me back to the hospital," she said. "I have some work to do."

Rhett sighed. "We all do."

Molly checked the records. She talked to anybody she could find who had worked with John Martin to see if he might have mentioned anything about himself that would lead them to another house. She reported in to Rhett and learned that the cops were canvassing the neighborhood with a fine-toothed comb and hadn't been able to come up with more than the fact that John Martin had been an unexceptional neighbor since he'd inherited the house from his grandmother three years before. Considering the state of some of the other houses in the area, the residents considered him a plus.

It didn't take that big a leap to see them all on the five o'clock news as they declared, wide-eyed, "But he was such a quiet man."

Molly went back to the hospital computers to find that nothing had changed. John Martin had been hired at the hospital a little less than a year earlier and worked without too much notice in housekeeping on the top three floors of the hospital. Minor infractions, complaints of laziness, disorganization, inability to work well with others. Medium work evaluations across the board.

And then, with the big buyout in early spring, the downsizing had begun, the cost-cutting, the look to maximizing existing personnel. Somebody up in corporate had decided that it wasn't that big a leap from mopping floors to mopping fevered brows, and corralled the housekeeping crew to do patient care.

And so, without a more thorough background check, John Martin had been given access to not only vulnerable young women, but all their personal information. The administration, in its all-out run to minimize cost, had blithely handed a serial killer his very own, fully equipped playground.

"I'm going home now," Sasha told Molly as she swept into her office, where Molly was staring at the computer. "And so are you."

"No I'm not. Not till I find out what we're all missing."

"You're not missing anything. This guy's just a little smarter than you thought, and he's found a hidey-hole somewhere. The way this hospital's been closing departments, probably the laundry."

Molly looked up, stunned at the thought.

Sasha sighed. "What a stupid thing for me to say. Now we're going to have to go on a tour before we go home."

"You don't have to. I'll do it."

"Don't be ridiculous. You need more authority than that ferocious frown to open the rooms. Besides, security's much more afraid of me than they are of you."

"Especially if they heard that leather and whips statement."

Holding the door open so Molly could precede her, Sasha scowled. "Leather and whipped *cream*," she corrected frostily. "No wonder you don't date. You have no sense of style."

Sasha was as good as her word. She, Molly, and a sweet but dim ex-halfback from Southwest High School opened every long-locked door they could find. But in the end all they could come up with was a couple of trysting nests with hospital blankets and Safeway liquor, and dust-covered, outdated equipment that hadn't been sold off yet. No blue Dahmer barrels. No dungeons of torture. No surprises beyond the fact that there seemed to be renovations nobody had heard about going on in the old obstetrics unit.

Exhausted, disheartened, and an inch past panicked, Molly gave in and gathered her things to follow Sasha out to the garage.

"You will get him," Sasha said. "It's just a matter of time."

"I hate to mouth clichés," Molly objected, "but time is what we don't have. If he's running to profile, he's just about to escalate."

"Why? Because you got him fired?"

Molly stepped into the elevator and punched the garage floor, her movements slow and heavy. "Because I got him fired. The last person on earth he trusted not to desert him has just drop-kicked him over the fence. To tell you the truth, I'm surprised I haven't heard from him by now. He's gotta be pretty upset."

"Well, he hasn't sent anything to the hospital," Sasha said. "And if he tried to get within two miles of your house, all the cops and reporters would use him for a rugby ball. They are still watching you, aren't they?"

Molly nodded. "The house, yeah. I sure don't know why. All they have to do is catch the latest report on *Hard Copy*."

"Who do you think's tipping off *Hard Copy* when to show up?"

It was closing in on midnight, which meant that only the ED was still running full tilt. Up on the med floor, which had the walkway to the parking garage, the halls were half lit, the conversations held sotto voce. Only the elevator dings and a few confused patients disturbed the quiet.

"You're on top again, aren't you?" Sasha asked, wrapping her mohair scarf tight around her neck before hitting the open walkway.

"Isn't that what you've trained me to do?"

"In sex, hon," she scowled. "Not parking garages. It's too damn cold up there."

"It's too damn close anywhere else. Stress gives me claustrophobia. Add that to the paranoia, and I'm a fruit salad of fun."

"Well, enjoy the weather. Sane people park out of the wind."

They parted at the stairs and Molly went up. She kept her face to the sky and her hand on her purse, wherein lived her Taser and pepper spray. Just in case she needed to use them.

She needed to use them.

She just never had the chance to.

She had just climbed into her car, her attention again diverted by the problem at hand, when the problem addressed her.

"Your friend needs you," he said from her backseat.

Molly shrieked like a banshee. She grabbed for her purse. Before she could get there, something very cold, round, and familiar pressed against her neck.

"Please," Kenny said, sounding so very polite. "You have to listen to me. Nobody is ever going to know where she is unless you come with me."

Evidently the gun he nudged against her neck was meant to emphasize the point. Molly stopped breathing. She struggled past the frantic acceleration of her heart.

"What friend?" she managed.

"Why, Marianne."

Marianne? Secretary Marianne? Marianne who couldn't find a nice word for Molly if it meant the fate of the free world?

That Marianne?

Molly damn near laughed.

It was better than thinking about what she was facing. Who she was facing. There in the backseat with a gun to her neck, his voice as calm as Sunday, his hands steady.

Kenny. Kenny, whom she'd evidently tried to save.

Kenny, whom she'd betrayed.

Kenny, whom she couldn't remember. Whom she wouldn't remember still if not for an obscene worm of scarring on his neck.

Kenny, who would have sat on her cart all those years ago looking pale and bruised and hopeless, just like David, whom Nancy had saved.

But Molly hadn't saved Kenny.

How did you feel outraged and lost at the same moment? Molly wanted to puke until there was nothing left in her stomach but lining. Instead she forced herself to suck in a steadying breath.

"Why should I believe you have Marianne?" she asked carefully.

"Because you know me," he said quietly. "Better than anybody."

Molly squeezed her eyes shut, desperately unsure. Convinced more by that soft, certain voice than even the pressure against her neck that Kenny wasn't lying. He had Marianne, and Molly was the ransom. If she ran now, he'd probably just kill her. And then he'd saunter home and kill Marianne and hide her away where the police would never find her, just like the others.

And no matter how surly and antisocial Marianne was, she simply didn't deserve that.

Cursing herself for seven kinds of fool, Molly started the car.

just once I want her to
come into my room when
i'm getting off.
once I want HER to see.
jesus, can you see her
face when she sees them
all with no eyes and no
fuckin tits?
where are the maggots
now, mommy?

NINETEEN

Molly decided she was an idiot. A raving, half-brained, self-absorbed fool. How the hell could she not figure Kenny would do this?

Because it didn't fit the profile. Killers like this didn't make grand gestures. They didn't change their signature just because a precipitating event made things suddenly worse. They shortened their cycle. They increased their violence. They lost control. They didn't get confrontational.

And yet, it seemed that Kenny had.

"I'm sorry, Kenny," Molly said, backing her car out of the parking spot. "Really. I didn't mean for you to get fired."

"Then you did finally figure it out," he said quietly. "Do you remember me?"

This was all going way too fast. What was she supposed to do? Lie and stick it out? Tell him the truth and hope he didn't decide that enough was enough and blow her to hell just to do it?

Molly finally reached the overload point. Too many lives on her conscience, too many surprises and too much guilt. She went numb and stupid and silent when she should have been working her mouth like an Amway salesman.

Still, she had to do something. The parking garage was empty and the hour too late to expect help on the streets.

"I do remember you," she said, praying. "You were such a quiet little thing. I . . . I tried to help, you know."

Her own personal apology to every child she'd lost to The Game.

"I know you did," Kenny said, his voice deceptively reasonable. "It's why I'm going to take you to see Marianne."

"That's good."

Down one floor of the parking garage she drove, then two, the screech of the slow-moving tires echoing against all the concrete.

"You know, they're going to be missing me at home," she said. "My dog hasn't been fed tonight."

"Patrick will do it."

"Who's going to take care of Patrick?"

Make them think of you as a person, the hostage negotiators said. Make sure you aren't faceless so it's harder to kill you.

"Patrick will end up just fine," he said, his voice muffled by the backseat. "He'll go back to Washington and send Sam Hanukkah cards and go to school, just like you wanted."

"He's not going to make it without help."

"He'll be fine. I'm really sorry I mistook him for your baby. Johnny, wasn't it? I mean it. I didn't know."

"It's okay. It's been a long time."

And, bizarrely enough, Molly realized it was. She'd expected the usual rage, the dizzying grief that always accompanied Johnny's name. But it seemed that finally she'd found greater rage, deeper grief to eclipse it. Besides, whatever she had or hadn't done for her baby, she'd at least given him more care and comfort in his twenty-three days than this poor bastard had had his entire life. Than had any of the victims of The Game.

Counseling by psychopath. What a concept. Molly wanted so badly to laugh, to cry with the absurdity of the whole thing. She was still so distracted by it that by the time she reached the ground level she almost missed the sight of a tall blond woman checking something in her trunk.

It dawned on her so suddenly, she almost locked her brakes. Molly sneaked a look in the rearview mirror to see that Kenny was still below the line of sight. She took another look at the red Grand Prix to see the trunk lid up. She tried to ignore the geometric increase in her heart rate.

She already had one co-worker in jeopardy. Should she risk two? Should she try and get Sasha's attention, flash her the ED's universal sign for distress?

"Is Marianne okay?" she asked, her hands suddenly trembling.

"Oh, yeah," Kenny said, his voice like silk. "She's fine."

"Good. That's good," Molly said, willing Sasha to look up. To wave. Anything.

But Sasha seemed intent on whatever it was she was looking for in her trunk, and Molly wasn't sure how slowly she could go before Kenny would notice.

"We're about at the street," she said. "Which way then?"

"Over to Highway Forty-four," he said.

Please, Sasha. Please. Just look. Don't make me tap my horn and give us away. I've got a goddamn gun at my neck and a victim sitting somewhere on the spit.

I've just met Kenny for the first time in twenty years, and it's not going to end well.

Just as Molly was pulling even, Sasha looked up. Molly lifted a hand and flashed her the peace sign. In the brief instant she could hold her friend's gaze as she swept past, Molly silently begged for recognition. For reaction. Sasha just lifted a hand in response and turned back for the driver's door. Molly surprised herself by damn near sobbing in frustration.

"Who's that?" Kenny asked.

"Another nurse from the ER." *Work on keeping your voice level. Kenny's your friend. Kenny's all right. It's the rest of the world that's crazy, or you're never going to get out of this.* "We just walked out together. You can leave her out of this." *She isn't your type.*

Actually that almost made Molly laugh, thinking of a matchup between Sasha and Kenny. Sasha would make such mincemeat of him, all the other serial killers would end up laughing at him.

Adrenaline, Molly thought, struggling hard to focus. She

was pumping with adrenaline and it made her want to giggle when what she needed to do was get help. When what she had to do was get Kenny to offer up Marianne like a game-show prize.

Molly checked her rearview mirror. Still no flurry of movement. No Sasha standing flatfooted in the middle of the lane trying to figure out what was wrong. And no Sasha following right on her bumper. Molly was alone, but Sasha was safe. And Marianne was still sitting somewhere in limbo waiting for Molly to show up.

Which meant that Molly needed to go to game plan two. Or three or twelve. Hell, what did she know? One simply didn't make plans for the moment a serial killer chose to introduce you to his sport.

Except never, never get into the car in the first place. Oh well, too late for that. Besides, there was Marianne to think of.

"So, what's the plan?" Molly asked.

Her hands were sweating so badly they were slipping off the wheel, and her heart was slamming around inside her chest like a landed fish. She knew she should be subtle and manipulative. She should slide into Kenny's delusion and reinforce it so she could ease his secrets out of that muck like old artifacts from the ocean floor. Hell, she probably should have a tape recorder so she could get this for evidence.

But when she should have been coming to grips with the fact that she was finally faced with the boogeyman who'd been rustling under her bed for the last four weeks, all she could think about was Marianne. Marianne and, oddly, Johnny. The baby this monster had wanted to be.

"The plan?" Kenny asked. "There isn't a plan. I knew you'd want to come help your friend."

Another rush of acid up her esophagus. Another dump truck load of guilt on her head.

"Why Marianne?" she asked, wiping her hand on her slacks.

"Because it would help me get close to you. I had it all planned out, ya know. But then . . ."

"But then I went and spoiled it all. I meant it, Kenny. I

didn't intend to desert you like that. I'm afraid the truth is that I just didn't understand your messages quickly enough."

Molly swung south onto Jefferson and headed for Highway 44, for the first time in her life, barely doing the speed limit.

She could smell him. Somehow, she'd never noticed before, or maybe he'd been more careful while he'd still practiced anonymity. But now, caught in a small car heading for disaster, Molly was caught by the almost feral scent in the air.

Gamy. Not quite human. Coming from the very quiet man who was finally poking his head up from the backseat, his hand still absolutely steady where it held the very cold little revolver at right angles to her carotid artery.

"You can't go faster?" he asked a bit petulantly.

"I've got a gun against my neck," Molly said, wondering how the two of them could sound so reasonable. "It makes my driving a bit iffy. I don't think you want me to attract attention."

Of course there weren't any police cars out there. Molly had at least hoped for a reporter waiting to ambush her on the way home from work. The highway was absolutely empty, though, as if everybody had pulled back to give her room.

She took another peek in the rearview mirror, and this time found Kenny there. Composed, quiet, his eyes flicking over the traffic. Nice eyes. Light blue, softened with long lashes.

Why hadn't she realized that before? He was actually good-looking. Square of chin and straight of nose. He should have caught women's attention. He should have been sketched in sharp, swift lines with solid shadows under his cheekbones and brow. But somehow he'd been softened into inconsequentiality, as if wearing a Romulan cloaking device to hide his threat.

Had other women seen the potential of his looks? Had he gotten them to adopt him, as some women would, certain they would be the ones to bring the butterfly out of this cocoon? Or had he traded on his innocuousness, so that they didn't notice the odd glint in those soft blue eyes?

"You want me to head for your house on Juniata, don't you?" she asked, trying so hard to sound calm and interested.

She wanted him to look at her. She wanted him to lock eyes with her so she could see what everybody had missed. What she had missed all those times she'd worked with him on the floor.

They'd had a serial killer walking the halls of their hospital, and the only way they'd discovered it was the keloid scarring he'd forgotten to cover at his neck.

There should have been more. But then, John Martin wasn't the kind of guy you wanted to look in the eye. John Martin may have counted on that.

"My grandmother's house," he said softly, denying Molly that look now.

"The police searched it, ya know. They didn't find anything."

"They won't. I made sure."

Maybe, though, somebody would still be there, on the lookout for their prime suspect in a series of grisly murders. Maybe somebody would see her in trouble.

Grand was so close, only an exit up. Molly swung off the highway south toward Reservoir Park. The traffic on Grand at this hour of the night was virtually nonexistent. Molly swung south past the park water tower. Past side streets with stately, rehabbed brick homes, silent and dark at this time of the night, the Christmas lights off, the only blinking lights the traffic reds that stretched down Grand. Molly had made it almost all the way to Tower Grove Park before she realized that Kenny was talking.

". . . can't believe they didn't see me that last time. I came right up to your door, and there was a police car sitting out by the back fence. I figure they were shoving doughnuts in their faces and talking about blow jobs, ya know?"

She had to pay attention. She had to use whatever he said to her benefit. She had to reassert some kind of control before she just shook apart like an outhouse in a tornado.

"You have been amazing," she said quietly as she watched the streets, watched for cops, watched for Kenny to give something away. "I mean, how many girls have you . . ."

God, what had she said? How subtle was that? Her statement was met by silence, she knew she'd screwed up already.

"Kenny?"

"You really don't know anything, you know," he said, and
Molly heard the first traces of anger in his voice. Still quiet,
as if the anger were miles away. As if he were watching it
through glass.

"I know I don't," she said. "That's why I came along."

"I figured you came for Marianne."

"Well, yeah. That too. But I figured you really wanted me
to understand, or you never would have contacted me in the
first place. Where do you want me to turn?"

"Right up here."

She followed his directions and found herself turning a
block away from Juniata. "If the police are in this neighborhood they're going to spot my car, Kenny. I work with the
ME's office, ya know."

"It's all right."

Anticipation. Molly heard it. She smelled it, laced into
that otherworldly scent of his, as if he put out some other
species' pheromones. She wondered if any of the other
women had smelled them? She wondered if they'd been this
terrified?

Probably not. Probably not until he'd drugged them to the
point they couldn't move and then brought out the toys.

Molly's heart rate was way past aerobic, and she was having trouble coordinating the clutch. Just how smart was she?
She knew perfectly well what Kenny was, and she was deliberately driving to his place.

But she knew how he worked. She knew what to expect, so
that maybe she could anticipate it. She had to take the
chance.

"Here," he said. "Pull into the alley."

Another innocuous house, brick, square, porched, with a
boarded-up house across the street and a Volvo parked two
doors down. "This isn't your house," she pointed out unnec-
essarily.

"Yes, it is," he said as Molly pulled the car into an open garage and stopped. "I used my army pay for it. Not a bad deal, either. The lady who lived here before had cats. About a hundred of them, I think. You can imagine what it smells like."

That one took Molly's breath away. They said that the one thing a serial killer was good at, no matter how ineffectual he was otherwise, was his craft. Kenny had deliberately bought a house with a revoltingly pungent odor. Just about the only odor Molly could think of that might mask the ones he was planning to create.

"By the way," he said before she had the chance to get the door handle and run, "even if you show the police this house, they won't find her either. I promise. I've had five building inspectors in here already, not to mention the police who were asking questions today."

Okay, so she'd been thinking of running. Just taking a dive to the grass and rolling out of the way of a shot and heading for help. That is, if Molly discounted the fact that bullets ran faster than creaky nurses.

"Open the door."

She sucked in a breath. She did as she was told, stepping into a clean, well-ordered garage. Kenny popped the seat forward and climbed out behind her, the gun steady, always at her back. Molly looked around, wondering why nobody saw what was happening.

It was then she realized how truly well-thought-out Kenny's venture was. The house they were about to enter stood directly behind the one the police had raided just that afternoon. Kenny, the trap-door spider, had made sure nobody would stumble over his nest.

Which meant, she had to think with a sinking heart, that Marianne was tucked away someplace beneath the two yards.

"Caves," she breathed in stupefaction.

He actually chuckled. "I found it when I was ten. Right in between the two houses. Convenient, huh?"

She could get away, Molly thought. She could run for help now and just have them dig.

If she couldn't take out Kenny quickly enough, not only would she be dead, but Marianne, too. And Kenny would simply pack up his things, move to a different town, and leave his evidence, undiscovered, a few feet beneath the yards of South Grand.

"Door's open," he told her, the gun making impressions on her skin. "Go on in."

"You just leave the door open?" Molly couldn't help but demand as she climbed the steps to a tidy back porch that held nothing more noticeable than one of those flags people hung by their doors. Kenny's was a bluebird. Cute.

"Nobody really wants to come here unannounced," he said. "I can hardly get them to stop by if I ask. The cat smell, ya know. It's really tough to get out."

Molly opened the door and agreed. Her eyes started to water. She tried breathing through her nose. "Doesn't anybody wonder why you live here?" she demanded.

His laugh was quiet and controlled. "I got it for about twenty thousand dollars. Nobody wonders. And they don't think I actually live here yet. I'm a rehabber from the county named Tony."

"Nobody recognizes you?"

"I look different."

Molly instinctively nodded as she took in the kitchen. Well-scrubbed blue linoleum floors, old white wood cabinets. Toaster covers and plastic flowers in a pink depression-ware glass. All neat and tidy and unexceptional, just as they'd found Dahmer's apartment those times the police had responded. Just as they'd found in Kenny's other house.

And then Molly saw what was sitting on the little dining room table. What Kenny had brought her to discover.

Marianne. Bitchy, impatient Marianne, eyes wide, mouth gaping, dyed blond hair straggling across the dining room table because there was no more left of her than her head and the blood that pooled beneath her severed throat.

Tucked in a bowl on the dining room table like a bloody pile of fruit.

Molly heard herself howling.

She was swinging around even before the sight sunk in. A hand out, a foot, anything to trip him up. To get back out that door and run screaming down the block until somebody heard her.

But Kenny had anticipated it all. Before Molly could get a toe on him, he slammed the gun against the side of her head and took her straight to her knees.

She was shaking her head, struggling to get her limbs back under her, when she felt the sting of a needle at the side of her neck.

"Oh, God" was the last thing she said. The last thing she thought was that she shouldn't have wasted all that time on computer classes. She should have taken martial arts.

And then she just melted to the floor.

FUCK THIS
it isn't enough. it's not
right. it's not like what
i have in my room.
I WANT it to be perfect
maybe for this birthday
now that I drive
I can really hunt

TWENTY

Molly was still thinking how stupid she was when she came to. Well, kind of came to. She couldn't seem to coordinate her limbs. She couldn't think or see very clearly. And she thought she was paralyzed, because she couldn't move.

Molly knew it was cold. She knew it smelled worse than even the cats, a smell anybody who worked in a morgue would have recognized in a heartbeat. Her heart slammed into action, and her brain followed a couple lethargic clicks behind.

Thorazine. Molly recognized the cotton candy feel of it, the drug taste in her mouth, the ataxia in her limbs. Stupid thing to be conversant with, but at least Rancho VA had taught her some things. It had also, fortunately, taught her how to function while half-bagged.

Comprehension followed shortly thereafter, such as it was. She'd been dropped with a load of tranquilizer and transported out of the dining room. She was sitting on a chair, her arms behind her, a rope around her wrists and again around her chest. In a cold, dank place that smelled of earth and death.

Great. Another setting for nightmares. Especially after what she'd seen on that dining room table.

She must have groaned again, the closest she could come to that primal scream of rage she'd let loose with upstairs.

"You're here with me now," Kenny said behind her, his voice dreamy.

Molly tried to turn around, couldn't quite manage it. She wrapped her tongue around her teeth and attempted to get some feeling into it. She was at least beginning to focus now.

"You killed Marianne," she accused, seeing again the obscenity on that table.

"Of course I did. What did you expect?"

Please, she thought. Don't give me the damn scorpion on the turtle analogy. It'd be worse than finding my own head on the dining room table.

Molly had no more than completed the thought when it finally sank in just what her surroundings looked like. And finally the urge to laugh proved too strong.

"What's so funny?" Kenny demanded.

Molly just shook her head, wondering if it was possible for a heart to just fall out and flop around on the floor. Hers sure felt like it was. But she couldn't help it. She'd just awakened in the biggest cliché in the world.

What is this, she wanted to ask, *shock theater?* Kenny had fashioned the cave straight out of a cheap B movie thriller, the kind where the set decorator had obviously been inspired by the more lurid Dahmer stories. But Molly had seen the Dahmer crime-scene photos. She knew that the blue Dahmer vats where he'd soaked the flesh off those bones hadn't been underground in a basement cut out of a low-ceilinged cave. His workshop had all been tucked into that tidy apartment right along with his Sears artwork and television. Didn't Kenny get it? It was much scarier that way.

Which was why she was so sweaty and sick, she was sure.

Of course, the fact that he'd put his workroom in a cave didn't help. Kenny hadn't even thought to whitewash the walls or install grow lights so he could pretend it wasn't a cave after all. He didn't bother to do anything to wipe out the terror that seeped from the earthen walls. Molly was sure she was going to vomit, and she hadn't ever gotten around to eating anything.

But then, she figured she had a right. After all, it wasn't every day a person got to see someone she knew staring at her from the top of a dining room table without benefit of so much as a neck. It was almost right up there with rolling in the dust with one.

Oh, God, Marianne. I'm sorry.

Sorry for another one. Sorry for everyone.

"You've been doing your research on Jeff Dahmer, haven't you?" she asked, struggling for coherence.

Kenny didn't seem particularly put out. "I wrote to him in prison."

"Of course you did."

"You don't understand."

On which level? she wanted to ask. On the "I just want somebody to notice me" level? Sure, she understood. She'd gone to Vietnam on the strength of that particular sentiment. She'd spent her entire life doing what people thought was appropriate so her parents would finally say they were at least aware of her. Hell, wanting to be noticed fueled more good and evil in the world than sex, no matter what Freud said.

But killing people and chopping them up so they'd notice?

"I'm trying," she said.

This time Kenny laughed. "No, you're not. If you'd tried, you wouldn't have betrayed me."

"Like your mom betrayed you?"

"Too late to play party games, Miss Burke. That's been tried before."

Yeah, Molly bet it had. The problem was, if she didn't find the right party game, she wasn't getting out of this basement except in a vat.

She wanted to laugh again. This was the point in the movie where the heroine wormed all the details of the crime out of the bad guy, since he thought she was going to die anyway.

Oh, what the hell? She had to try something to stall until she could think better. Until she could at least move.

"It's a pretty sophisticated setup you have here," she tried.

Unlike the movies, though, real serial killers didn't feel the need to confess. "I think you need more sedative," he mused.

Molly tested the knots at her wrists to find them competent. Her legs were free, which made her believe that Kenny intended to keep working from behind. It only made sense, after all. The point of this exercise was to get the woman under perfect control. Make her what you want, which meant stay as far away from the real her as you could. If Kenny was doing Dahmer time, he'd get Molly at least to the point of total paralysis, if not death, before playing his real reindeer games. That way she could be his friend completely by his ground rules.

How the hell was she going to prevent that?

Molly took another look around the cave that seemed even closer, even darker and more sinister. It seemed she could hear old screams, hopeless cries for help that never came. Every image she'd ever held while walking a crime scene, all packed into this little cave like rancid meat in a can.

A place of extremity, she thought as she listened to the clink and ring of metal beyond her head as Kenny set up his tools. A hell the likes of which she couldn't even have imagined in her worst nightmares. And all born of a small boy's need to be seen.

It must have been the effect of the Thorazine, she thought, because all she could feel was sad.

"It'll be soon, now, Miss Burke," he said. "You're going to be part of me, you know."

Yeah, she thought, squeezing her eyes shut to keep from doing something stupid. Stomach contents.

She was not going to end up on a table. That was all there was to it. She just had to figure out how.

And then came the most awful sound she'd ever thought to hear in her life. Molly almost passed out. Half a foot from her head, Kenny was testing a power drill.

"You don't need to stuff anything in my head to make me your friend," she said, wishing she could keep her voice from rising.

The sound stopped. It was like sitting in a dentist's chair and hearing that high-pitched whine stop and knowing you were only getting a reprieve. One more round of that and she'd wet the chair.

"That's what I thought," he said. "I really did. But I'm afraid I just don't believe that anymore."

Get your feet under you, Molly thought, trying to make them work in tandem. Pitch the chair backward. Somersault right through his instrument tray.

"You never gave me a chance to explain," she insisted as her feet slid along the floor.

A silence. She could almost hear him think. She could smell the rising anticipation on his skin. She'd never forget that smell. Not if she lived to be a hundred. She'd do a paper on that smell. A symposium. Molly Burke standing up in front of the FBI Academy with graphs and charts and pointers defining that smell. *Mark it well, ladies and gentlemen. It's the last thing a victim is going to notice before her skull gets aerated.*

"It's not going to change anything," Kenny said.

"Maybe it will," she offered. "You've practiced this a thousand times even before you did it the first time. And I bet it's never enough, is it?"

Silence. Molly squeezed her eyes shut for a second, praying for inspiration. Then she faced the shadowed steps that seemed to lead nowhere and saw what was tucked along the walls on either side. Altars. Altars decorated in bones. Jars full of floating, watching eyes.

She closed her own eyes again. "If we could talk a little more about what it is you dream about . . . what you want. Maybe I can help make it right. Maybe I can explain why I did what I did. I didn't betray you, Kenny. I swear I didn't. Can't we talk about it?"

Silence. The deathly sibilance of an indrawn breath. "Not anymore."

Molly drew her own breath to argue. To plead. Jesus, she'd weep if he wanted her to, just to distract him enough that she could get a chance to slam back into him.

She didn't get the chance.

She felt the rush of air first. A river of cat piss sinking into the stench of death. Another smell she'd do nightmare time over.

Kenny heard it, too. Molly heard him catch his breath, lift something off whatever was behind her.

She did her best to focus on the stairs, praying.

"Of course it'll help," she said, just a little more loudly. Announcing her presence to anyone who might be there.

Maybe Sasha had seen after all. Maybe she'd alerted the cavalry. The Mounties. The fucking Marines. Whoever it was, Molly meant to help them all she could.

"It's just been so long since I'd seen you, Kenny," she said, a little louder. "I wasn't expecting you to turn up in my life."

He slid something very sharp along the side of her neck. "Be quiet."

Molly was quiet. She tensed every muscle in her legs and back, ready to spring at an instant. She kept her eyes on the edge of the basement. She prayed for a uniform. A voice of authority.

There was no uniform. What she saw instead were Bruno Maglis, and Molly's brain froze.

"No, Patrick!" she screamed, straining against the ropes. "Get out of here! Go get help!"

But Patrick didn't get out. He kept walking right down those perfectly carved steps.

Stupid idiot, Molly thought, truly sobbing now, struggling against the ropes even with that damn knife slicing into her neck. What the hell good was he going to do against a serial killer? What kind of penance was he thinking of paying?

But he kept coming. He reached the bottom of the steps and stooped beneath the low ceiling.

"Patrick, please," she begged. "Run!"

Kenny lifted the knife away. "Hello, Patrick."

"Hi, Kenny," he said with a slow smile. "Am I in time?"

And instead of running to help her, Patrick simply shucked his coat and sat down.

IT'S TIME

TWENTY-ONE

"You don't want to do this," Molly begged.

"But I have to," Kenny said.

"She's talking to me, Ken," Patrick said, his voice quivering, his eyes wide, his skin a little wet. "I have to, too, Aunt Molly, don't you see? He told me he'd do it. I had to know for sure."

"Why? Patrick, go. God, please, just go."

"I can't, Aunt Molly. It's a chance I'll never get again."

Footsteps? No, it was her damn heart again. It was her conscience wondering how the hell she could have missed this. How anybody could actually believe any kid who'd flipped pancakes with such heartbreaking panache could court this kind of insanity.

"Are you surprised to see Patrick here?" Kenny asked, running the flat of the knife along her neck like a vibrator.

"Yeah," Molly managed, her focus, such as it was, on Patrick. "I am."

Amazing how terror and shock could dispel the effects of a sedative. She was thrumming suddenly, every nerve on alert. Sweat dripped down the side of her throat . . . or was that blood? she didn't care. Faced with this latest surprise, it didn't really matter.

"You have to tell me, Patrick," she pleaded. "Why?"

Patrick jumped as if she'd pulled him out of a dream. Then, amazingly, he grinned. "You should have seen your face when that bomb went off."

Maybe she was still more affected than she thought. It took her at least a full minute to make the connection.

Well, if you're in a cave full of nightmares, why miss one? "You were sending the notes."

He laughed, that bright, boy's laugh that was so rare. "Do you believe how good my timing was? Jesus, I just wanted to scare you out of the house, and here Kenny's going me way one better." He licked his lips, shrugged, his movements sharp and almost frantic.

"But the notes were from St. Louis."

His laugh was as sharp as his movements. "If you had a computer, you'd figure out how easy that was. I have friends everywhere, Aunt Molly. Just everywhere. It didn't take much to get 'em to help me scare you shitless." Another tic, a flash of resentment. "You really don't deserve that house, ya know."

"I don't have it," she reminded him. "I'm borrowing it."

He shrugged. "Old argument. Old news. Kenny's the new news. You really goin' through with it, man?"

"Didn't you see what was on the dining room table?" Molly demanded, and almost lost her left carotid to the knife.

"She's already back where she belongs," Kenny informed her.

"Who?" Patrick demanded in a rush. "A friend of hers? She's one of your girls?"

"Patrick, please," Molly begged. "Think about it. You can still turn back and figure things out. I mean, you didn't rig the bomb to hurt anybody. You were just mad. This is . . . this is . . ."

It was there again, that same agitation Patrick had betrayed the night he'd first seen a bone. White-faced, trembling, his eyes dark. Compelled by the lure of something Molly would never understand, as if he couldn't believe he was here but he couldn't leave. Hell, he looked as if he were crouched at the back of a porn theater hoping he wouldn't get caught.

Sweet Jesus. Molly had known he had problems. She'd suspected a real river of rage seething deep through him. But this . . .

Was this what every parent thought when they stood in the police station trying to find a defense lawyer? This urge to rewrite reality into something more palatable? It sure as hell put to rest her own belief that she could play the parenting game better than her brother. It blew to hell her blithe belief that any parent should be able to pick the sociopath out of her own litter.

She hadn't known. No matter what Patrick had put her through, she simply hadn't guessed he could have already made it this far down the path to obscenity.

After all, Molly had only played The Game in short innings, witnessed only the embryonic stage of this kind of malice. And when Patrick had come to her, she'd wanted it to be for help. So she'd seen what she'd wanted to.

She should have listened to Frank. She would apologize to him if she ever got away. She'd let him say "I told you so" as often as he wanted.

If she got away. If she got Patrick away before he had the chance to succumb to the addiction he couldn't survive.

His eyes were getting glassy again, and his gaze was on the knife. On the blood, Molly thought, that was trickling down her throat.

"Patrick!" she tried again.

He startled.

Kenny damn near growled. "Miss Burke, I've tried to be fair, but you have to be quiet."

Patrick shuddered, an almost sexual languor in his eyes. "You just don't understand, Aunt Molly."

Molly shut her eyes, not wanting to see anymore.

"What about Sam?" she asked very quietly.

"Sam will never know. I'll be surprised when you don't come home, and I'll stay with him until the parents come get me. He'll *never know.*"

"Oh, he will," she said softly, then opened her eyes to face him. "And it'll kill him."

Patrick lurched to his feet as if she'd backhanded him. "You leave him the fuck outta this!"

"Don't talk to her that way," Kenny said. "She's my friend."

Patrick's laugh got a little angrier. "*You* talked about her that way. Especially after she got you canned."

"My game, Patrick," Kenny said, his voice abrupt. "My rules."

Patrick bristled. Molly felt Kenny twitch. Maybe that was the angle she should take. Set the two of them against each other. Another one of those old movie clichés. If only she could think fast enough to make it work. To make them go for each other's throats and leave hers alone.

If only it weren't Patrick she was thinking this about.

This from a nurse who played The Game like a track bookie. Molly laughed out loud.

Patrick stared at her. "You nuts?" he demanded. "He's about to make soup out of your brain. What's so funny?"

Molly shrugged and felt the ropes bite. "Me. I can't decide if I'm a fatalist or a pessimist."

He laughed back, but it sounded scratchy. "Sure as shit tough to be an optimist about now."

It was like watching a movie with the sound track off, or the reception faulty. Molly saw familiar expressions, heard familiar words, and yet saw something beneath it all she'd never seen on Patrick before. As if the protective veil had been stripped away.

There was such cold malice. Such fury.

What had Patrick's parents done to him? Those parents Molly had mostly disdained. Mostly avoided. Mostly dismissed. What had they taken away from him that could only be reclaimed in the corner of a cave that smelled like cat piss and death?

"You can't do this," she said, even knowing how clichéd that one was. "Patrick, please. Put a stop to it now."

"I'm not doing anything," Patrick retorted, an arm thrown out in Kenny's direction. "He is. I'm just . . . studying."

"You're not going to be if you both don't shut up," Kenny snapped. "Now shut up or I'll make you. I'll make you both!"

"Not what your fantasy of this moment was at all, is it, Kenny?" Molly tried.

She'd expected argument. She hadn't expected him to slam her in the head again. Lights exploded behind her eyes. The floor tilted and all those barrels tucked away in the corners seemed to dance along with that ossuary in the corners. Floating sculptures, skulls, and femurs and tibias in delicate weavework that put an end to the hope that Kenny hadn't had much practice at this. In a thousand years would archaeologists dig this up and mistake it for an old monastery?

"Now you'll be quiet," Kenny panted in her ear. "Now you'll do what you're supposed to do."

"Her head's bleeding," Patrick objected.

"Get back," Kenny demanded, pressing the knife closer, as if to establish ownership. "I told you. You can watch, but just this once. And you have to do it the way I tell you."

"What makes you think he won't tell on you, Kenny?" Molly demanded, fighting the nausea and dizziness to get her feet planted firmly on the floor. She wasn't sure what she was going to do, but she had to do it. She had to do it before Patrick was able to feed at Kenny's table and find out he liked the fare.

"He said he wouldn't."

"He also told us he didn't know what you were doing."

There was a pause. Patrick looked over Molly's shoulder as if to assess something.

"You told them you'd talked to me?" Kenny asked.

"You were on the answering machine," Patrick said. "I had to tell them something."

"You promised."

Molly held her breath. Could they come to blows? Could they really forget she was there for a minute?

Long enough for what? Her to chew through the ropes and run up the stairs? To change Patrick's mind with the strength of her moral reasoning and yank him after her?

"I helped you, man," Patrick objected, instinctively stepping closer.

Kenny stiffened, and Molly thought the knife made another nick. "I told you. Stay back where you belong or I'll ask you to leave. I'm not so sure about this anymore. I mean, it just doesn't seem right to me."

"Me either," Molly offered, trying to think. "I bet he didn't even think to tell you the truth. Didn't you hear him, Kenny? He's the one who blew up Frank's car. He's the one who's been interrupting your attempt to communicate with me."

"It's not going to work, Aunt Molly," Patrick objected.

"And you," she couldn't help but say. "What have I done to you but help you, Patrick? What exactly have I done that's so awful you'd come to see my brains be scooped out?"

Nothing. No reaction. Just the twitchy, sweaty anticipation layered over cold, lifeless eyes. Beautiful eyes. Terrifying eyes.

"Shut *up*," Kenny ordered, smacking the side of her head again with his fist. The same fist that had the knife. Molly felt it brush through her hair.

Once she got out of this, she wasn't going to so much as slice tomatoes anymore.

Once she got out of this.

She was an idiot. She was a babbling, sweating, terrified fool.

"I'll shut up," she assured him, shaking her head to clear it.

"I need to give you more Thorazine."

"No . . . no, really."

Or maybe she should let him. Wait for him to draw up a big, honkin' dose and then knock him over onto the syringe. Dose himself. She'd seen it happen on a TV show once. Maybe *Magnum*. She seemed to get most of her life lessons from *Magnum*.

She wasn't getting out of this. After all she'd been through, she was going to end up on the menu at the Serial Killer Café, and Patrick was going to watch. Was it too absurd or too awful? Did she care?

God, she did. And damn it, not just to save Patrick's soul. To save hers.

Her life didn't exactly flash before her eyes, but Molly did seem to see all her past traumas in a different light. It was easy to wallow in misfortune if you had the luxury of time. Suddenly Molly found herself with no more than about fourteen minutes left to worry about anything, which put every one of her lost chances into perspective.

She had tried her best.

It should be enough. It should go on her tombstone.

In a moment of amazing clarity, Molly realized that it *was* enough. She had done her best and be damned with the rest. It was just too bad she wouldn't get a chance to tell Frank or Sasha or Sam.

"I'll be quiet," Patrick whispered, backing for the stairs. "I swear. Just don't throw me out."

"You can't trust him," Molly insisted, unable to quit trying.

Kenny answered with another jab in the neck. This time, the needle again. Molly all but groaned in frustration. Seconds. She had seconds to do something before she couldn't so much as blink her eyes anymore. She'd been so busy laying her ghosts to rest, she'd missed her chance to save herself.

Well, screw it, she thought. It'd probably only end up hurting worse, but she wasn't going down without a fight, Thorazine or not. The chair wasn't that sturdy. Maybe she could knock it over hard enough that it would smash against the floor and loosen those damn ropes. Maybe she could knock Kenny out. Maybe she could fly.

She had to do something.

Footsteps again, she thought. But it wasn't her heart this time. She could hear that banging away at hyperspeed. Besides, the feet were shuffling, trying to be quiet.

No, she thought, blinking a couple of times. She had to be nuts. She was imagining help because she so desperately needed it.

Please, God, she thought, breathless with sudden, stupid

hope. Don't let me waste this effort on a Thorazine-fed hallu-
cination.

"You'll be just fine soon—" Kenny began to say.

Molly heard a whisper of movement behind her from
Kenny, saw Patrick's eyes dilate. She couldn't give them the
chance to finish.

Then she saw the shoes on the steps above Patrick. And
damn it if she didn't know those shoes, too.

"Oh, fuck!" she cried in instinctive anger. "Frank, get out
of here! Get help!"

He was walking right down into a cave just for her.

"Down here!" he yelled and began to run.

Patrick lurched to his feet. Kenny hesitated a fraction of a
second. Molly bunched her muscles, pushed off with her feet,
and slammed the chair straight backward.

The chair flew over. Kenny flew over. The table of instruments flew over. Molly's head slammed first into Kenny's
chest and then the stone floor. Sparks shot across her field of
vision, and she thought she heard elephants. She actually felt
the chair sag, like sat-on glasses. Moving on reflex and instinct, she struggled to roll, to impede Kenny's movements as
he hollered and flailed like a tipped turtle.

Molly heard Patrick break for the knives that slid across the
floor. From the sounds of the scuffle, Frank caught up with
him just beyond where Molly was fighting for her life. And
damn if Frank wasn't laughing when he brought Patrick down.

Were there more shoes on the stairs? Molly heard something. Her field of vision encompassed the floor, a side wall,
and a scatter of shiny surgical instruments.

And Kenny. Wild-eyed, spitting, cursing Kenny, who
smelled worse than cat piss and had somehow found his gun
again.

Molly saw him get hold of it and turn toward Frank. She
was not going to let him kill Frank. She wasn't. Even as
the new round of Thorazine settled on her like thick soup, she
fought like a dog, trying to tangle Kenny up enough that he
couldn't get a shot off.

"Get Patrick . . . out of here!" she gasped, head-butting

Kenny into a bloody nose. Hers. It cleared her head just enough to enable her to roll right over on him.

Kenny reached out his fingers and Molly kneed him in the groin. She figured the coffee drinkers on South Grand could hear him shriek. She kept trying to free her arms even as she was becoming convinced they didn't belong to her. She was running out of breath. She was running out of time. And Kenny was going for the gun again.

"Frank, dammit! Get out of the way!"

That wasn't her voice, was it? She wasn't sure. She was busy trying to find that soft center on Kenny again.

"No!" he was screaming in her ear like an animal. "No, you can't do this! No!"

She was face-to-face with him now so she could see the spittle at the corners of his mouth, the stark whites of his sclera as he pulled himself free of the chair and came into contact with her knees, her feet, any part of her she could delay him with. She saw the glint of metal instruments scattered over the floor and refused to consider what they'd been for.

Except for the drill, halfway beneath Kenny's shoulder. She knew damn well what that drill was for, and she meant to keep him away from it.

Another solid roll into Kenny and the chair began to disintegrate. The ropes sagged, and Molly fought harder. Kenny scratched at her eyes, pummeled her face. Bit at her like a cornered cat. Molly didn't feel any of it.

"Frank!" somebody yelled. "Look out!"

Molly was distracted just long enough to give Kenny leverage. She should have known better than to worry about Frank. When she caught sight of him, he was tossing Patrick aside like a bad date and spinning toward her. And the maniac was laughing again. He was in a cave, cuing up to dance with a psychopath, and he was laughing.

"We got him, St. Mol!" he called, hands out.

They didn't get him in time. Frank froze no more than two feet away. Molly felt a slither of steel alongside her throat and stopped breathing. Kenny rasped loudly enough for them both.

Molly was amazed. She was furious. She finally caught sight of more feet, more legs, and saw that some of these were in uniform. And there in the front she saw a flash of Baitshop's anxious face.

God, Molly thought. She's in her pajamas. Doesn't she ever wear anything normal?

And then, almost too close to losing the fight against the Thorazine to care, Molly remembered that Kenny didn't consider himself finished.

"Get outta here!" Kenny screeched in Molly's left ear as the knife lifted away, just enough.

"No!" she heard Baitshop scream as the footsteps thundered. "Don't!"

Molly turned too late.

Kenny had evidently decided that if he couldn't have Molly be part of him, she couldn't be part of anyone else, either. Molly had figured he'd make the statement with a gun. She should have known better. She'd read his history, after all. She'd read all their histories.

He made it with a butcher knife.

He slammed it straight into her chest.

Molly felt the jarring impact all the way to her spine. She heard the yells. She saw Kenny straighten, a look of pure triumph on his face, and she heard a gunshot. Kenny's chest exploded and he dropped like a rock.

Molly lay in a heap, still tangled with the chair, knowing vaguely that something was very, very wrong inside and remembering almost as an afterthought that there was a knife in her lung. She managed to tell somebody to make sure they left that knife in until they got her to somebody's ED. Frank, maybe. Looking as panicked as she'd ever seen Frank, which made her want to tell him it was only fair. God knew she'd spent enough panic on him. She apologized instead. And she thanked him for braving that cave, just for her.

And then, just as the Thorazine pulled her away from the comprehension that the knife was suddenly hurting like hell, she saw what she'd come to see.

Frank moved a little to the side, and Molly realized that

she was lying eye to eye with Kenny. And no matter what anybody else believed later, she saw the life go out of those pretty blue eyes.

What she saw there, she realized, was the logical end to The Game. When Kenny died, his eyes looked no different, because the light there had died years ago.

EPILOGUE

By the time Molly came off the respirator she missed most of the postgame activity. Kenny had been autopsied and sent to his mother in Akron for burial. His mother had given several interviews about her perfectly normal son and blown her cover when Kenny's history of child abuse was discovered. Frank had gone back to work, Kathy settled into her new office in the St. Louis office of the FBI, and Rhett into his new role as ex-lover of Sasha Petrovich.

As for Sasha, she had, after all, recognized the distress signal Molly had flashed. Being a smart girl she knew better than to hie off into danger without help. She'd called 911 from her cell phone. An APB had gone out and all Molly's friends had joined forces with the police to search for her little Toyota.

It had been Frank who had broken it. He'd been heading to Sam's to notify the old man when he'd seen Patrick sneak out of the driveway in Sam's car. And Frank, who knew more about troubled boys than most people should, had notified the troops and followed.

It was Baitshop who had fired the fatal shot, and Baitshop who admitted that what had saved Molly's life had been Frank's quick reaction and the fact that Patrick had left Kenny's trap-door ajar.

Kenny had been right. If they hadn't seen it, they never would have found his special hiding place until they'd brought the dozers to the backyards. So far, twenty-four skulls had been discovered.

Molly learned all this when Sam invited them all to her hospital room to celebrate Hanukkah with him. He brought dreidels and kuchen, and the staff fashioned a no-smoking-area menorah out of penlights to decorate Molly's room.

The next day Frank brought his kids, mother-in-law, and a tree to pass out gifts. Any other year, only the fact that she still sprouted tubes would have prevented Molly from running down the hall to escape. This year, she sang the "Dreidel Song" and "Deck the Halls" and allowed the kids to supply her with party hats.

Her gift from Sam was more tchotchkes from his collection, and from the kids macaroni Christmas tree ornaments. Her gift from Frank showed up her first day out of ICU, when Molly woke up to find a chubby, cherubic, blond guy sitting at her bedside watching Jerry Springer on TV.

"Hear you're looking for a good shrink," he said.

Molly glared at him. "What are you, twelve?"

His smile was older than pain. "Twelve and a half. But I'm not in any twelve-step programs, I've never been accused of sexual misconduct, I don't find myself fixated on articles of women's clothing, and I believe that electric shock therapy is medieval." His grin suddenly reminded her a lot of Frank. "I also did my postdoctoral work on 'Post-Traumatic Stress Disorder in the Vietnam Era Veteran.' Questions?"

Holding on to every staple in her chest, she laughed. "Alphabetically or chronologically?"

So she told him about a little boy named Kenny. She talked about sad John Michael Murphy, and his sweet-eyed son Johnny, who hadn't lived until spring. And she found a quiet repository for her old nightmares and new insights.

Frank brought her home ten days later to an empty house and an almost frantic Magnum. That Molly could almost deal with. It was the sorrowing Sam she couldn't handle.

"I should rip my shirt," he insisted, as he eased her into a chair at her kitchen table.

Molly smiled. "Don't disown anybody for me, Sam. It's been good for me, actually."

"Good for you?" he demanded, his eyebrows bristling so hard they almost took flight. "*Gottenyu, taibeleh,* how could this be good for you? You're slumped like an old man at the table, and your name is always linked with that monster."

That monster she still, oddly, felt sorry for. Molly reached out to Sam, tears in her eyes. "It taught me all those maudlin old lessons, like what's important and what's not. And how high on the important list my friends are."

Now Sam was wiping tears off his papier-mâché face. "I'll never forgive him," he said, and Molly knew he wasn't talking about Kenny.

Molly could only sigh. "Never forgive his parents, Sam," she said. "Pray for him. Maybe there's still a chance."

If there was a chance, Patrick was going to get it. The Protector of the Rice Tariffs had finally shown up to collect his son inches ahead of notoriety and hustle him off to a private, posh, protected psychiatric hospital in D.C. Molly's only regret was that she hadn't been conscious at the time so she could fully apprise her brother of his culpability in the matter.

"Now, go on home, you two," she said. "I think what I'd really like after two weeks in a hospital is peace and quiet."

Sam bristled again. "But, *taibeleh*—"

Frank was right there, a hand on the old man's shoulder. "We'll wait till she falls on the floor and can't reach the phone, and then we'll show up and make fun of her."

Sam didn't think he was funny. Molly was holding her chest again. "Thanks for the moral support, Frank."

"Moral support, hell, St. Molly. Be thankful I didn't bring the kids to hug you good-bye."

Sam gave Molly a kiss that made her think he was afraid the top of her head would break. Considering the fact that it still hurt only a little less than her left lung, he probably wasn't that far off the mark.

And then Frank took his turn. He didn't kiss the top of her

head. "Ya know," he said, his eyes twinkling. "I've seen you naked too, now."

She should have shoved him out the door. She laughed and kissed him back. "Wanna compare scars, big boy?"

His eyebrows lifted. "Now?"

"We compare scars now," she assured him, "that's all we're gonna do."

He kissed her one final time. "If there's one thing I do well, it's wait."

For a long time after they left, Molly just sat at the table, enjoying the emptiness. No staff, no grand rounds with every doctor on the planet staring at the railroad tracks up her sternum, no surprise visits from friends and police.

Silence. Blessed, sweet silence.

Damn, she thought, with a new grin. I do like the house.

There was just one more thing she had to do to get her life back again. She had to get off her overused butt and clean out Patrick's room.

She didn't want to. She wanted to leave him in that amorphous place where her lost friends from Nam still lived. Half real, as if she'd imagined them, so that losing them didn't hurt quite so badly.

She'd lost Patrick. Maybe she'd never had him; she didn't know. She just knew that whatever snakes lived in that handsome head, he was one of The Game's losers. Confused, frustrated, frightened, enraged. Destined to destruction.

Maybe if Kenny hadn't come along, he wouldn't have been so seduced by such violence. Maybe if he could get far enough away, he might stand a chance. Baitshop had been furious that Patrick hadn't stood trial as an accomplice. Molly didn't have a clue if she was right. She didn't know whether prison would help Patrick or this fancy-ass teen town he was heading for. She just knew that she ached for those flashes of brilliance, of vulnerability, of light. And she knew without a doubt that no matter what happened, Patrick was beyond her ability to help.

Oh well, she thought, lurching unsteadily to her feet. No use putting it off. Magnum, curiously subdued, followed her

upstairs as if making sure she didn't fulfill Frank's promise.
Molly got to the top of the steps and opened Patrick's door,
her poor sore heart tripping unsteadily, her hands even
shakier.

God, she didn't want to do this. It was like throwing him
away for good.

But she couldn't keep him here.

She got his athletic bag and began stuffing in his clothes,
his scent, his magazines. A boy's room, nothing more. Molly
wanted him back. She wanted another try. She knew it
wouldn't do her or him any good.

She was stripping his bed when she pulled a magazine
from beneath the mattress.

Penthouse.

Big deal. After clearing out all the *Hustler*s, Molly
couldn't figure out why Patrick would hide a lousy *Penthouse*. She reached in beneath the mattress and discovered a
nest of them and gave a yank.

Paper fluttered, glossy and explicit and uninspired. Molly
bent to pick it up and then caught sight of one of the pages.

She froze where she was, her hand inches from the photo,
her head suddenly spinning.

She should throw it away without looking. She should get
the hell out of this room.

She couldn't.

Slowly, carefully, she sat down. She flipped through the
first *Penthouse* and then checked one more. Then another.

The pictures weren't that bad. It was what Patrick had
done to them that was threatening to bring up Molly's lunch.
The pictures had been slashed, heads missing, eyes gouged,
weapons drawn with the same heavy hand that had written
her notes. Violent, obscene, terrifying. So classic, Molly simply couldn't breathe.

So she'd been wrong again. It hadn't been Kenny who had
brought Patrick to that last stage. Patrick had been practicing
for a long time.

Sobbing with the effort, Molly got to her feet. She called
Washington, D.C., information and got the number for that

hospital they'd sent Patrick to. She'd left the magazines on the floor, but she couldn't look at them. She couldn't face what Patrick had been practicing in the privacy of his room.

"This is Ms. Armbruster," a quiet, comfortable voice introduced herself when Molly finally got the extension she requested. "I'm working with Patrick. Is there something I can do for you?"

Yes, Molly wanted to say. I want you to face him. I want you to look deep and find what I failed to find.

"I'm sending you something," she said instead. "Something I found in his room."

Molly sucked in a breath, another. She couldn't quite get the words out, because what those magazines betrayed was the fact that they hadn't killed the worst monster.

They'd let him loose.

Aunt   Molly   talked   to
Armbruster today.
It   probably   means   she
found my stash.
I wonder what she'd think
if I sent her my diary.
I should
just to pay her back

now I'm going to have to
wait for my first kill

Read on for an excerpt from
Eileen Dreyer's next book

SINNERS AND SAINTS

Coming soon in hardcover from St. Martin's Press

NEW ORLEANS NEIGHBORHOOD BIWEEKLY
Bobby's Byline

June 2—Eddie Dupre had an uninvited guest at his
hurricane party last night. As you all know, Eddie always puts on the finest celebration to kick off the beginning of hurricane season. There was a parade down
Bourbon over to Royal—where Eddie lives in the Fau-
bourg Marigny—with music, dancing, and appropriate
costumes (Eddie was luminous as Dorothy Lamour).

Unfortunately, the party mood was soured when it
was discovered that a nun lying passed out in the alley
behind Eddie's yard not only wasn't a party-goer, she
wasn't passed out. She was dead, with her face obliter-
ated, possibly by a shotgun blast. Too, too gruesome.

Now she might not even have been a nun, but we'll
never know, will we? It seems that by the time Eddie
got back to the site with the police, the holy woman had
vanished...along with any evidence she'd ever been
there.

Here's the best part, though, babies. It seems that
when she went to her last reward, our good sister was
wearing a near-flawless seven-carat emerald and dia-
mond ring. Sure redefines those vows of poverty, chastity, and obedience. Don't you just want to know what
kind of obedience earns you sparklies like that?

ONE

Omens come in all sizes. Hair standing up at the back of the neck. Crows on a telephone wire. Shapes in a cloud or a chill in the wind. A hundred innocuous things designated by tradition or superstition, and a thousand more kept in a personal lexicon.

Chastity Byrnes carried around quite a full lexicon of her own. Not just the regular omens handed down from generation to generation of Irishwomen, like birds in the house meaning death, or uncovered mirrors at a funeral meaning death, or any of the other myriad Irish omens meaning death. Chastity embraced a plethora of personal portents inexplicable to anyone but her.

Chastity was a trauma nurse, and only ballplayers and actors were more superstitious. So in addition to the usual signs of doom, Charity dreaded quiet shifts, the words "I think something's wrong," and holidays.

And the number three. Chastity absolutely loathed the number three. Everything happened in threes, from births to deaths to every disaster in between.

Like the omens Chastity received that hot June day in St. Louis. She should never have ignored them. After all, Chastity paid more attention to her omens than to her bank balance. She lived by Murphy's Law as if it were the first

commandment. But that hot, sultry summer day, even though
she knew better, she blew off those three omens as if they
were parking tickets.

To be fair, they weren't easy omens to recognize, like a
black cat or the hoot of an owl. They were more like odd
things that made a person want to look over her shoulder.

The chaos theory.

A phone call from a brother-in-law she didn't know she
had.

Lake Pontchartrain.

Innocuous in themselves, but each of them sent a skitter-
ing of unease down Chastity's back that should have had her
keeping a wary eye out for trouble where there seemed to be
none.

Three omens.

Well, maybe four. But the fourth could have just been
Chastity's bad luck. On the way in to work that day, Chastity
lost her driver's license. She didn't consider it an omen at the
time. More a "shit happens" kind of thing. But if it hadn't
happened, she never would have heard about the chaos theory, and Chastity would always believe that if she'd missed
that, nothing else would have followed.

The cop who stopped her was a buddy. All cops in town
were buddies of trauma nurses. But he wasn't smiling when
he strolled up to the window of her hot red Mini Cooper.

"Not that I'm not impressed, Chaz," he said, an eyebrow
raised at the speeds she managed. "But this is your third
warning. In three weeks." There was that number again.
"And there are all those unpaid parking violations. . . ."

Chastity ended up locking her car at the side of the highway and riding into work in a police cruiser, thirty minutes
late for her shift. Which put her smack in the middle of a
trauma code just in time to hear the chaos theory.

She'd been scheduled to work triage that day. She got
bumped instead to Trauma Team One. Not that she minded.
Chastity had joined the staff at St. Michael's especially for
the trauma. Particularly the kind of trauma they saw at St.
Michael's.

Chastity wasn't just a trauma nurse anymore. She was one of two new forensic nurse liaisons at St. Michael's. It was her job to not only save patients, but preserve any viable forensic evidence that might prove a possible criminal or civil case. She made sure abuse victims didn't fall through the cracks, rape victims got better treatment from the hospital than they did from their attackers, and unknown patients were identified. She helped police and hospital personnel work more efficiently together.

So she wasn't surprised that she didn't even get a chance to reach her locker before she got yanked into Trauma Room One to help resuscitate a sixteen-year-old gunshot wound victim.

"About time you showed up," one of the nurses said from where she was pumping in fluids.

The room was already in turmoil, half a dozen staff members spinning and colliding around the room like random ions. Blood oozed over the side of the table, and paper and sterile wrappings littered the floor. The patient had been shot in the upper abdomen. He'd already been paralyzed and intubated, x-rayed, ultrasounded, and evaluated. A forest of lines snaked from chest, arms, throat, and penis, and blood was being recycled from his chest. The staff had probably been working on him for about five minutes.

"You're lucky to have me at all," Chastity assured them all, slipping booties over her brand-new magenta tennis shoes. "I was supposed to be on crowd control out front today."

"Are those uniform?" Moshika Williams asked from her position by the boy's left chest. Moshika Williams was the trauma doc in charge. A seriously brilliant trauma fellow, she stood square and solid, and ran a code like a traffic cop on speed.

Chastity lifted a foot free of the sticky mess on the floor and spread her magenta-clad arms. "They match my new scrubs."

"Which are very . . . bright."

"Bright," Chastity agreed with a nod as she finished

gowning up. "Exactly. It all reflects my new attitude."

"Your forensic attitude?"

"My happy attitude. My life is in harmony . . . well, except for the need to find a ride to work tomorrow. But otherwise, I am now in balance. Harmony, Moshika. It's the word of the day."

"Not for Willy here. His clothes are on the counter, by the way. We didn't even cut 'em through the bullet hole this time."

"I'm very proud of you all. You've saved the crime lab untold grief. Now, if you just haven't sneezed on everything. . . ."

Gowned, gloved, and shielded, Chastity pulled out her camera and her swabs, her rulers and her paper bags to save the evidence that hadn't already been washed away in the attempt to save Willy's life.

Moshika bent back to the chest tube she was preparing to insert. "And you're in time to hear what I just learned."

Chastity wasn't the only one in the room who groaned. The only disadvantage to working with Moshika was the method she used to keep herself calm in a crisis. Some people whistled. Some cracked knuckles or told jokes. Moshika lectured. She shared all the tidbits of random scientific information she'd been stuffing into her overheated brain, as if anybody hip deep in blood and vomit really wanted to know the latest guess about what the hell a quark was.

This time what she wanted to share with the class was the chaos theory. Bent over her patient, she waved a scalpel in Chastity's direction. "You missed the first part of this, Chaz."

"I'll get the notes later. Everybody smile."

Everybody smiled. Chastity snapped shots of the slightly elliptical bullet hole just below the kid's sternum, and especially the soot ring and powder stippling that surrounded it. Willy had been capped at very close range.

"Well, it's interesting," Moshika assured her, bending back to her work. "The chaos theory says that no experimental result can be perfectly replicated. There is always a variable that can't be duplicated."

Chastity nodded as if she understood and hummed

Brigadoon as she measured and swabbed and sealed. It was easier that way. Chastity hummed show tunes to keep herself focused. The fact that they drowned out Moshika's lectures was just a fringe benefit.

But then Moshika went and ruined it all. Her fingers probing the patient's chest for the tube placement, she looked straight at Chastity with those huge, bright black eyes of hers and said, "Now here's the part that you should find most interesting. Especially considering your new attitude. It seems that according to chaos theory, just at the moment when a system attains its most perfect harmony, that's when it's really just about to spin out of control."

The hair literally stood up on the back of Chastity's neck. Right in the middle of a trauma code, she stumbled to a dead halt. "What the hell did you have to say that for?" she demanded.

Moshika, too busy with intercostal spaces, didn't hear. But the damage had already been done. She'd said it, hadn't she? She'd said it to Chastity, who had told Moshika no more than three minutes ago that life had finally found a certain harmony.

An odd thing to contemplate during a trauma code, certainly, but the truth was that Chastity was at her happiest during trauma codes. She loved action, she loved the rush of adrenaline, she loved the challenge of forensics. She loved living on the edge, and she could safely do that within the oddly precise ritual of a trauma code. Chastity was practicing at the forefront of twenty-first–century nursing, and she loved it.

Even knowing that she was to be separated from her lovely little car for a bit, until Moshika had opened her interfering mouth Chastity had been happy.

Instinctively she reached a free hand into her lab coat pocket, where along with pens and penlights and laminated trauma scale cards, she always kept a small velvet drawstring bag. She wrapped her fingers around it for a minute, just for the feel of it. Just to make sure it was still there.

"Chastity?"

She could have used a better name, of course. Chastity was, after all, such a cosmic joke. Her mother had named her daughters Faith, Hope, and Chastity.

Not Charity.

Chastity.

As if Mary Rose Byrnes had either had an odd sense of prescience or a catastrophic need for denial.

"Chastity, there's a call for you."

Chastity looked up to see the new secretary leaning in the doorway, her focus more on the disaster in the room than on the recipient of her message. No big surprise. The secretary was new, and it took a while to get used to the ambience of the place. The patient lay naked and alien-looking in the midst of bedlam. The air was rank with the smell of blood and bowels. Machines crouched at each corner of the cart, and staffers shuffled around like bumper cars in an attempt to get Willie safely to surgery before his heart gave out along with his liver and left lung.

Chastity was now helping the team do that very thing. She'd collected all the evidence she could. She'd taped the boy's hands inside brown paper bags to protect defensive or blowback evidence, and she'd collected photos and personal effects. While everybody else ran Willie Anderson to OR CT-Scan, Chastity would instead pass her information and her specially taped bags to the police.

"There's a *call* for you," the secretary repeated, her lips pursed into a moue of distaste at the wreckage in the room.

"I'll call them back later, Kim," Chastity answered as she dropped an empty IV bag onto the littered floor and stretched across two techs and the patient to change EKG leads.

"Call her Chaz," Moshika told the secretary as she finished sewing in the chest tube. "Gives her stature."

"Makes her sound like a made man," a paramedic snorted.

Moshika laughed, her big horn-rimmed glasses glinting in the fluorescence. "Considering the fact that she looks like Peter Pan, it couldn't hurt."

So she still shopped for her jeans in the boys' department, Chastity thought. Big deal. So she wore her hair in one of those cheesy pixie cuts, and it happened to be blonde. It was easier that way. She was in harmony, damn it.

She had a boxer puppy named Lilly and a flat in south St. Louis painted like a Mexican cantina. She had friends she socialized with regularly, enough money to support her habits, and a fast little car to give her the illusion of control. No surprises, no problems, no new traumas that woke her up any more than the old traumas did. She had some peace within herself, as long as she kept to her comfortable rituals and safety zones.

She was in harmony.

She was happy.

Which, as any Irishwoman knew, spelled disaster. The chaos theory was just the scientific spin on that old, unimpeachable Irish truth that good things never lasted.

"I'll still call 'em back," Chastity said.

"It's long distance," Kim insisted. "From New Orleans. He said it's a matter of life and death?"

For a second everyone in the room stopped and looked at her.

"Yeah, okay," the secretary said, blushing because she was still that new. "But he says he's your brother-in-law."

Chastity only hesitated for a second before pulling up a new Lactated Ringer's IV bag to hang. "Really? I didn't know I had a brother-in-law."

"And that your sister's missing?"

Another lurch nobody saw. "As opposed to the last ten years she's been missing?"

Again there was a brief silence. But then, Chastity wasn't going to explain that, either. Especially when her heart was suddenly pounding and her hands had gone sweaty.

Balance. Harmony.

Shit.

Chastity made another grab for the bag in her pocket. Soft velvet wrapped around tumbled hard edges. Reassurance. Comfort.

"You have a sister?" Moshika asked, sounding a bit affronted.

Chastity didn't face her friend. "I never said I didn't."

"She seems to have found a husband."

"I heard."

"Well, he's lost her," Kim reminded them all.

Chastity should have done more than recognize that omen. She should have run from it. Bought a plane ticket for parts unknown and blown this pop stand before anybody knew she was gone.

Before that brother-in-law chased her down.

She could feel whispery feet tiptoe right across her grave. She could feel her life lurch imperceptibly out of balance. And no more than hours after she'd acknowledged it had existed at all.

A brother-in-law.

She checked her pocket again, just to make sure. She usually didn't need to check it more than twice a week. This had been, what, four times in an hour? Not a good sign. Not good at all.

"I'll still call him back," she said. "Get his number."

"This something you want to talk about?" Moshika asked quietly as she sidled over to where Chastity was crouched by the cart doing a final check on chest tube output.

Chastity looked up at St. M's best new surgical turk. Moshika had managed to get a lot of information out of Chastity since they'd been friends, but nothing this pertinent.

Chastity smiled. "And give you the satisfaction of knowing that my family's more screwed up than yours? Thanks, no."

Moshika chuckled. "Honey, nobody's family's more screwed up than mine. We're listed in the *Guinness Book of World Records* for most screwed-up family in existence. There are even pictures."

Chastity bet not. Chastity bet Moshika's family was just run-of-the-mill screwed up. Not operatically fucked like Chastity's.

But that wasn't something Chastity was going to think about right now. Right now she was going to do the same thing she'd done for the ten years since she'd last seen her sister

Faith. She was going to pretend she was all alone in the world, so she'd be safe, and she was going to get on with her life. Which was why she smiled again and climbed back to her feet.

"It's time to take your boy down to CT," she said and popped the brakes on the cart.

Moshika flashed a mighty scowl, but in the end she gave in to the inevitable. Grabbing hold of IV poles and monitor, she took her place on the team and helped maneuver Willie out the door for his run down to CT. Gathering the bulging evidence bags from the counter, Chastity headed in the opposite direction to meet with the police.

For the rest of the shift, she did her best to avoid Kim, the secretary. If Kim didn't find her, she couldn't hand off that damn phone number of the brother-in-law Chastity hadn't known she had. And if Chastity had no phone number, she couldn't call to have him tell her that her sister was missing and he wanted Chastity to help him find her.

Kim found her anyway. Right before end of shift, Kim ran Chastity down in the nurse's lounge and handed off that phone number like the nuclear codes. And Chastity, fool that she was, took it. She took it in front of witnesses, so that later there would be no way to deny culpability.

She walked out into a purpling dusk and thought that she had a few things to say to Moshika. Because maybe if Moshika hadn't mentioned that damned chaos theory, she wouldn't have recognized the moment her harmony slipped the tracks.

Willow Amber Tolliver had shown up at Jackson Square sometime between Mardi Gras and Easter. A thin, anxious girl with stringy blonde hair and a pierced eyebrow, she wore flowing skirts and a tank top that exposed the I LOVE BRUCE tattoo on her right shoulder. Her wrists jingled with cheap beaded bracelets, and her backpack was stuffed with fantasy novels.

It took only a week or so for her to join the psychics and

tarot card readers who controlled the Chartres Street side of
the square. At first too shy to mingle, she simply staked out a
corner with a battered little card table covered in an old purple scarf. On it she lay her oversized tarot cards, an assortment of crystals, and a candle she'd bought at the Wal-Mart
in Biloxi, which was where she said she was from. With a
hand-painted sign that said, "Let Madame Nola see a better
life for you," she set up her own little corner of business.

Willow didn't have much of a gift, but she was earnest.
She told her customers only the good things she thought she
saw in their cards and crystals. She played with any baby
who came by, and petted the dogs the other street kids
brought around. She struck up a relationship with another of
the tarot readers, an irascible seventy-year-old ex–Black Pan-
ther by the name of Tante Edie, who couldn't tolerate most
people and made it a point to frighten the customers who displeased her.

But she liked Willow. They kept an eye on each other's tables, traded food and stories, and shared the late night when
the cathedral church bells chimed into darkness and their
candles flickered in the desultory breeze.

When Willow didn't show up for six days in a row, it was
Tante Edie who notified the police. She cornered one of the
uniformed officers who regularly watched the square from
the unit he pulled right up to the edge of Chartres and St.
Ann.

"I ain't seen the girl for a good few days," Tante Edie said,
leaning in his car window. "You see or hear anything?"

"Nah. You know where she lives?"

"Algiers Point, I think."

It was where most of the homeless street hustlers huddled
at night. Tante Edie preferred a real house, which she'd been
squatting in over to Bywater way for the last year. The last
week or so she'd been thinking of letting Willow share it with
her, but she'd never gotten around to asking.

"Was she in a warehouse, do you know?" the policeman
asked, jotting notes on the paper his muffuletta had come
wrapped in. "There was a fire in one the other night."

Tante frowned. "I don't know. Anybody killed?"

"Not that I heard."

"Can you ask around?" she asked, because this was one of the cops who would help a street performer.

"Yeah, sure. Do you think Willow's her real name?"

Tante Edie could only shrug. Who knew in New Orleans?

The officer never did hear anything. The next day a new girl took over Willow's corner with a henna tattooing stand, and Tante Edie went back to sitting alone. Willow Amber Tolliver, it seemed, was meant to fade into the lore of the Quarter, just like most ghosts before her.

It was inevitable, really.

Once Chastity got that phone number in her hands, there was no way of holding off the rest. She tried, she really did. For four days she hid in her house, where she painted her bedroom neon yellow. She took Lilly out for walks in the park down the street. She worked extra shifts, and she tested her limits in the clubs on Washington Avenue, where she went to be pummeled by thumping rock 'n' roll and drink herself into a quiet stupor.

Finally, though, she gave up and called her brother-in-law.

"You were the last person I wanted to call," he said, sounding thin and harried.

"Not the way to entice me down there, Mr. Stanton."

"*Doctor* Stanton."

"Ah. Doctor, then."

"I'm just not sure Faith wants anything do to with you."

"Well, I'm sure. She doesn't."

"But I can't *find* her," Dr. Stanton insisted. "And I don't know where else to go."

Chastity fought a shiver of prescience. "Why me?"

"Because you're a forensic nurse."

Another short pause for disquiet. "How'd you know that?"

"Your mother. One of her friends from home sent her an article in the *St. Louis Post-Dispatch* about how you helped solve some big murder case. She showed it to me."

"I see."

"The article said that you knew people all over the country. Police and coroners and such. It said you found missing people."

"Identify unidentified people. There's a difference."

"Nobody will listen to me," he said, as if not hearing. "I was hoping you'd know somebody down here who'd listen to you."

As a matter of fact, she did. She didn't tell him, though.

"What about my mother? Doesn't she know where Faith is?"

After all, it had been her mother who'd disappeared with Faith the first time. Who'd decided that Chastity had no right to know where either of them were. Well, evidently while Chastity had been tied to St. Louis like a sacrificial goat, the two of them had been in New Orleans enjoying gumbo and jazz.

How nice for them both.

Suddenly Chastity realized she was hearing a very awkward silence on the other end of the line. "You didn't know," Dr. Stanton was saying. "Of course."

Well, that sent her stomach sinking. "No, I guess I didn't. What?"

"Um, your mother passed a few months ago."

It was Chastity's turn for the uncomfortable silence. Tears. How ridiculous, after all this time. She looked down, to find her hand clenched around her drawstring bag. She fought the need for details, fought the urge to apologize, when it couldn't have been her fault. At least not this time. So she emptied the contents of the bag and spread them across the table she'd bought from a bankrupt Mexican restaurant.

"I have no desire to ever see New Orleans," she said.

Her brother-in-law never said a word. Chastity could hear his need in the rasp of his breath, though. In the weight of the silence that stretched taut across the miles. She listened and she fingered her cache, the garnets and citrines and clear water aquamarines that tumbled across her table like pirates' treasure.

Her treasure. Amethysts and tourmalines and one small

emerald the color of spring. The treasure she'd accrued from the late night shopping channels she watched when she couldn't sleep.

Glittery, colorful, solid.

Hers.

She kept staring at it all, touching it, watching it glitter in the kitchen lights, as if it could tell her something.

It told her something, all right. It told her she was an idiot if she thought she was going to avoid this.

"All right, Dr. Stanton," she said, rolling a garnet beneath her fingers. "I'll come help you look for my sister."

Which was how, four days later, she found herself confronted with her third omen. The omen that finally frightened her beyond escape.

Lake Pontchartrain.

Chastity didn't really know what it was when she saw it. She only knew that as the plane circled New Orleans for a landing, she looked out her window and saw water.

Everywhere, nothing but water.

And only one, endless bridge.

Chastity hated water. She hated it worse than she hated late night phone calls. Worse than she hated the words "It can't get worse, can it?" Worse than she hated her own history.

No, not hated.

Feared.

Chastity was paralyzed by water. She couldn't so much as take a bath. She couldn't sleep some nights because she woke to the sounds of lapping water and laughter, and it made her cry out into her empty bedroom. She couldn't bear to look at that much water in one place.

She did, though. She sat in that claustrophobic little seat looking down on an endless expanse of metallic, shifting water, and suddenly she knew for a fact that she'd made a mistake. She should never go to New Orleans, no matter what was at stake.

It was too late, though. She was already there.